Phoenix Rising: Initiation

The Trybrid Chronicles, Volume 1

Rebecca A. Nagy

Published by Rebecca Nagy, 2023.

Disclaimer

This novel is a work of science fiction, metaphysics, and fantasy, blending both imaginary and real elements with a body of teaching known as the Ageless Wisdom. While certain scenarios, spiritual teachers, historical figures, prophecies, and organizations depicted in the story may be based on or inspired by actual people, events, or entities, the narrative should be considered as part of the artistic license of the genre.

The views and interpretations are the author's alone and may not align with those of any mentioned person or organization.

Readers are encouraged to engage with the material as a fictional exploration of broader themes, recognizing the blend of truth and fantasy that shapes the narrative. The author encourages those interested in the subjects explored to seek authoritative sources and engage in personal reflection or study – many of which are available on the author's website.

For more information and to download meditations from the book, please visit: https://www.rebeccanagyauthor.com/

Published in the United States by The Golden Quest

Initiation

Acknowledgements

This book's journey began with an "otherworldly" visitation that occurred when I was young and still playing with Barbie dolls. At that time, I believed an angel visited me, sparking a lifelong quest to explore the unseen realms of angels and fairies and to uncover the hidden truths they held.

I owe a deep debt of gratitude to my father, Richard Nagy, whose profound faith, and unending quest for spiritual understanding constantly spurred me to question and explore beyond the surface of our world. And to my mother, Rita Nagy who nurtured a creative child who lived in a fantasy world and spoke to the entities that inhabited it.

To Anya Seton, the author of *Green Darkness*. Although I never knew her personally, the discovery of her novel during college led me into the rich fields of metaphysics and esoteric philosophy. Her influence on my journey has been significant, and I am forever thankful.

I would also like to recognize my spiritual mentors and teachers: Reverend Ellen Resch, Reverend Dr. Joseph Vaughn, Reverend Dr. Carol Parrish-Harra, and my advisors at Sancta Sophia Seminary, Reverend Katie Anne Yarborough, Reverend Marjorie Stuth, and Reverend Sarah Brown. They taught me that true spiritual growth demands tough love, and their guidance helped shape my path.

I owe a special acknowledgment to Steve Nelson, the gentle "wizard" and brilliant mythic astrologer, who shared with me a prophecy about Charlotte, North Carolina. I felt his spiritual presence when the idea for this series first dawned on me. Shine on, Bright Being.

My editor, Art Fogartie, deserves praise for his crucial guidance in navigating the pitfalls of a first-time author, and teaching me valuable principles like "show, don't tell." Through his insights, I discovered my writer's voice. And – he affirmed I didn't "suck."

My sincere appreciation to Brad Swift, a fellow visionary fiction author, mentor, and writing coach, whose support and encouragement have deepened my purpose as an author.

A warm thanks to my spiritual "tribe" and Alpha readers, who helped me birth this first novel: Karmic Astrologer Susan Reynolds, Reverend Constance Baldwin, Diana Mahaffey, Uni Smith, Heather Scovel, and Lisa Soria. Their steadfast encouragement was instrumental in convincing me to soldier on, even when I felt I couldn't possibly be good enough.

Gratitude is also extended to my Beta readers, Diana Mahaffey, Ann Swift, Jane Lavigne, Charlie Williams, author Kate Ashbrook, and those who preferred to remain anonymous. "Good catch" on those places that needed clarification and/or improvement!

Lastly, I extend my heartfelt thanks to my long-time spiritual sister, Glenda Bradshaw. Our shared spiritual quest, which began years ago in New York City, has led us on many adventures. From exploring the crystal mines of Arkansas and experiencing "first contact," to visiting the sacred caves of Boynton Canyon, and frequenting every metaphysical bookstore we could find both in the states and abroad, where books seemed to leap from shelves and Native American Shamans mysteriously crossed our paths—the journey has been extraordinary. And still, it continues. Thank you, my dear friend, for sharing this remarkable journey with me!

Cover Design by BetiBup33, MidJourney and Rebecca A. Nagy
First Edition

Part One: Karma's a Bitch

We are not brought into existence by chance nor thrown up into earth-life like wreckage cast along the shore but are here for infinitely noble purposes.
— Katherine Tingley

Prologue

She stared in horror at the killing fields. Her right hand trembled as she held the blood-stained sword.

Crumbled stone and shattered columns lay strewn, remnants of a once-majestic temple and palace. Wisps of smoke curled skyward, a haunting eulogy. Among the ruins, priests, and priestesses, their faces streaked with ash, gathered. Eyes dimmed by fatigue met as fingers, calloused from prayer and battle, tended to each other's wounds.

Misshapen creatures surged from fiery cracks in the earth, monstrous demons reanimated by a pervasive evil. Holy defenders reeled, realizing the betrayal from within. Exhausted and devastated, they steeled themselves for battle.

The buildings were not the only things shattered; the Covenant of Non-Interference with humans, once the lofty pinnacle of Celestial cooperation, was now in ruins. It had become the empty promise of an unrepentant liar, the hope of the shamelessly gullible. Shockwaves pulsed along the telepathic bond, pinging from one Celestial to the next.

Head for the ships.

They knew they had to lift off before the continent dissolved in the face of the gale force winds and thrashing rain created by the deliberate over-charging of the master energy crystals.

She watched the priests, priestesses, and many of their acolytes leading the surviving humans toward the inter-dimensional flying craft. Some clutched the sacred tomes of the ancient wisdom to their breasts. Others carried seed pods from the storehouses, food, clothing, tools, and the few remaining weapons.

No one – no one! – had suspected the treachery. One of their own, a high priest, had forsaken his vows and turned to the Dark Brotherhood. The betrayal seemed beyond comprehension. She had felt the imbalance –

something out of sorts with the renegade's energy. She'd known it for some time but had chosen to ignore her intuition.

Now it was too late.

She heard a sound ... a deep, primal scream. It sounded like the Earth was keening the loss of its innocence and vitality. The wail grew louder with every passing second. Only when her throat began to ache did she realize the shriek of remorse was her own – the misery of her soul shouting its shame and grief. She was a high priestess of Sirius. To her belonged the responsibility of balancing the energies of Cause and Effect – karma – not just of her actions, but those of all in her sphere of influence who had followed her into battle.

First and foremost, she was a teacher. She knew whatever thoughts or acts she or her students committed against the Codex settled on her – and no one else. Her screech gave way to hoarse sobs, tears cascading from her eyes – a river of remorse for things done...and left undone.

"Mistress, please come, the ships are preparing to depart. We must hurry!"

A handmaiden reached for her arm and tugged her toward the landing platforms at the far side of the plateau. Silver disks were already elevating into the clouds of dust. High above the carnage, she could see flashing, multi-colored lights disappearing into interdimensional portals. The Celestials would lead the human crafts and help to establish new bases, build new homes, start anew.

She pushed to her feet. "Go," she said. "I am right behind you."

She moved as fast as she could – little better than a trudge. The pain in her body was nothing compared to the agony of her spirit. Just before she stepped onto the gangway, she looked around again at the chaos.

Manu stood behind her, a look of horror on his smudged face.

"We need to depart, my love," she said.

She reached for him. He stepped back. No, he recoiled.

"We cannot," he said.

"We must," she said. She swept her extended palm over the blighted landscape. "There is nothing else we can do."

Again, she reached, but this time only with her hand. Again, Manu slipped out of her grasp, his own palm held up like someone trying to stop a child from running into a busy street. His eyes were wide and full of disbelief. He pointed to her.

"Ayesha, is that yours?" he asked.

The High Priestess looked down at her robes, once white, now dyed in crimson from the blood of her victims.

"No," she said. "I am unhurt. This is the blood of those who followed the Dark Priest."

"But human blood, no?"

"Yes," she said. "Those who betrayed us and turned to evil. I had no choice."

"I know," he said, "but surely you have not forgotten the Codex of the Masters of Wisdom."

A look of dismay spread across her face – the dawning of an irreparable mistake.

"The Hierarchy of the Human Kingdom," she said.

"Yes," Manu said. "You have shed human blood. Even now, it stains your sword. It is forbidden for you to come with us."

She stared at the weapon she had forgotten. "I sacrificed my immortality."

He slid past her as one would sidestep a viper. He could not touch her – he could not be tarnished by the stain of her sin.

"My love—"

She could not finish. Once again, she felt tears on her cheeks.

The gangway retracted. She stepped onto the ground – onto the planet she had once defended – the planet now destined to be her prison.

Manu's face was all she could see. He touched two fingers to his lips and said, "I will come back for you. I will find you in the next life."

And the door to the ship – and to eternity – closed.

Chapter 1: Somewhere Out There

The emerald-green grass caressed her back like cool fingers and the day's heat wandered into the dusk. Darkness came in hues of gray until the sky was a canopy of black interspersed with the flickering lights of a host of celestial bodies. Cassie Oberon always felt most at home when looking at the night sky. She used Venus as a starting point and branched out in search of constellations. She knew the number of stars didn't change – at least not in a discernable way – but tonight the sky looked a little crowded.

Cassie inhaled deeply the crisp aroma of newly mown grass, the cloying perfume of gardenia trees, and the sticky sap of Virginia pines that lined the outer edges of the backyard. Drowsiness cajoled her to close her eyes. Half asleep, she did what she'd done since childhood. She stretched both arms toward the heavens and imagined she could fly – soar amongst Creation's nightlights until she became one with them. Long ago, she had learned about meditation from her mother, how to breathe in different colors, depending on her mood. She breathed in green when a little under the weather, sky blue if a little scattered mentally or unable to focus on her schoolwork, and indigo when she was working out a problem and needed insights from her angels. She had experimented with other colors over the years and always used her mother's collection of crystals as focal points.

Tonight, she picked her beloved rose quartz, large and weighty. Setting it on the ground above her head, she connected the crystal with the special breathing exercise her mother had learned at the Monroe Institute called Resonant Tuning. She inhaled to the count of ten, held for one beat, then exhaled while humming through slightly parted lips.

She achieved a state of mental equilibrium, where her body was asleep, but her mind was fully alert. She breathed in the vivid hue emanating from the crystal, letting its rose-colored light permeate every cell of her being. A deep diaphragmatic breath...a pause...a release to "aum." A slight tremor tickled her spine. She surrendered to the tuning fork sensation, feeling lighter and lighter until she felt as though she was floating up and out into the night sky. "Lift off" always filled her with joy and her consciousness shot into the stars.

She willed herself to go higher and higher, looking down over her neighborhood. She could see a nearby lake and then the entire city below. Still, she climbed. The exhilaration of complete freedom erased every thought and care from her conscious awareness – she was light!

A jolt of energy shot through her, unpleasant and distracting. She thudded back into her body like a bird that had run into a plate glass window. She bolted upright and clutched her head between shaking hands. Wave after wave crashed over her, ripples of energy jolted through her, like someone sticking a finger in an electrical socket.

Images of veiled faces imprinted themselves on the inside of her eyes, and she blinked repeatedly much like a blind woman attempting to regain sight. She gulped in air, desperate to regain some semblance of balance. Thoughts bombarded her subconscious – they were not her thoughts. The veiled figures were whispering to her, clawing at her, trying to pull her somewhere. She planted the palms of her hands and soles of her feet into the ground, flesh-and-blood tent pegs. The images and voices crept away. She opened her eyes and took in the darkness, then rose to her feet, cautious and unsure.

Her beloved cat Gabriel charged out from the house, his furry gray and white body wrapping protectively around her legs. When she acceded to his will and picked him up, he nestled around her neck and began to purr.

"There, there, my darling," she said. "I'm okay."

She looked back up at the stars.

Did I contact something out there, she thought. *Or someone?*

GLENDA PACED. WHAT could Master Elena possibly want with me? She wondered. No one is granted access to Master E unless it's a really big deal.

Glenda knew Master Elena as her acolyte but being called to the inner sanctum was rare. The command came from behind the ornately carved wooden door. "Enter."

Glenda turned the filigreed brass knob and inched open the door. She stepped into the office. The warm glow of firelight pulsed from an ancient fireplace on the left-hand side of the cavernous room. Glenda breathed in the familiar scents of rosewater and patchouli from the ever-lit golden incense burner dangling from the center chandelier. The office was paneled in dark oak and engraved with runes and magic symbols, as protective wards designed to hide this sacred place from dark forces – and from the uninitiated.

Glenda's eyes widened. The Master was there with two others – one in corporeal form and the other a projected hologram through the spirit screen, a communication device that crosses dimensions.

"Don't dawdle, girl, come in, come in!" Master Elena said.

Master Elena, as usual, was draped in a deep purple sari edged with a gold border. Her abundant mass of white hair was piled in a topknot. Cascading tendrils framed her unlined face. No one knew exactly how old Master E was, but she had been head of the network of Mystery Schools since the Battle of Atlantis. She only appeared garbed in her Master robes when she was with members of the Order. To the outer world she glamoured herself as a middle-aged teacher. Glenda lowered herself into the indicated chair. The door closed with a slight thud and the hologram spoke.

"We have a situation, and we have all agreed you are the best person to handle it."

"M...m....me?" Glenda's voice was froggish. Her brown eyes spread wide, and she was rigid in the carved-back chair.

"Yes." Elena said. "You are uniquely qualified to head up this mission. There is a young woman who is a candidate for training in the Mystery School. She may well be the missing Seventh Avatar. Her name is Cassandra Oberon."

The hologram took over. "As you know, seventeen years ago the astrological configurations indicated that the Aquarian Avatars had begun entering the Earth plane and were being born into human bodies. We had prepared for this. In this shift of the ages, we knew there would be more than one Avatar."

"In past Ages," Elena said, "there was only one messiah or avatar—and always a male as dictated by the norms and mores of the current state of consciousness upon the planet. Now, with the group energy of Aquarius, we know there will be seven. We also know that The Seven will be Hybrids. They will have DNA from both the Human Kingdom and one of the other kingdoms currently inhabiting earth; either Celestial or Devic." Elena smiled at Glenda, "Like yourself, Dear One—you are both Human and Devic."

The Sirian Oracle continued. "Once the Avatars complete their mission of awakening Humanity, the Prophecy given to the Master of the White Circlestates that there will be a thousand years of peace and prosperity on the planet. A new Golden Age. Earth will shift into a higher dimension and take its Sacred Initiation, a move with ramifications throughout the entire cosmos. There will be a more direct connection to the Radiant One. All living creatures will reach their true potential: 'Ye are gods' as our sacred scriptures have taught."

They waited for Glenda to assimilate the information. Glenda knew she looked dazed. She felt a little giddy.

"Humanity is going through a birthing of sorts," said Master Elena. "They are feeling the pull toward the New Age of Aquarius but lack the necessary mental tools to make the shift. Many are opening to their extra senses, but do not know what to do with them. Some have found spiritual teachers, but many are lost in a miasma of pain and fear. They need teachers—and The Seven Avatars will fulfill that role."

The Holo picked up the conversation. "Six of the Avatars have already been identified, taken to the Mystery Schools, and matched with their teachers and trainers. We continue to search for the Seventh. Based on the locations of the other six, we believe the last one must be in North America. I placed a Mother ship into orbit in the Etheric Plane around Terra and we are prepared to contact them so we can bring them to The Institute for training before the time of The Quickening at the full moon of Aquarius. That time is fast approaching, and the Council has stepped up its efforts to identify their location. It is imperative to find the Seventh and to train him...or her."

Glenda stared at the Holo.

"I am sorry, Ms. Glenda," he said. "Please excuse my lack of manners. You do not know me. I am Commander Mon-ka, Head of the Intergalactic Forces assigned to Terra, Earth as it is now known. No doubt you know of the Ashtar Command through your studies. I am part of that Command."

"Yes, of course. They are Celestial beings from various star systems living in a parallel kingdom with the Human and Devic Kingdoms that currently inhabit Earth."

The robed figure next to Master Elena's chair stepped forward. Glenda recognized the Oracle of the Sirian Council. She wore the traditional shimmering violet-white robes and was veiled according to custom. Members of the Oracle seldom spoke because they preferred telepathic communication with those whose minds had been trained as an amanuensis, one able to receive dictations from holy ones and convey them to the outer world. But Glenda did not possess the gift – at least not yet, so The Oracle used the spoken word.

"During a recent conclave, we were all in deep meditative communion and reached out to the minds of the known Hybrids on Earth. One of the acolytes felt an energy surge, heretofore unknown – almost like a seismic wave of both electric and magnetic frequencies. It shot through the energy fields of the entire conclave and brought us all back into full waking consciousness."

Glenda's mind was swimming. So much information. She strained to focus.

"The acolyte who received the impression was in a fugue state for days before she could articulate the vision she received," The Oracle said. "She is convinced she tapped into the mind of the last of the Avatars in the vicinity of the southeastern United States in Charlotte, North Carolina to be exact. She had the distinct impression the energy emanated from the body of a female human and holds the energy of not two, but three evolutions: Celestial, Devic, and Human. She is a Trybrid."

Glenda felt like someone had hit her with a mallet.

The Oracle continued. "The Avatar of every age had always been in the body of a human male. But we have reached the time of a great awakening of the Goddess Energy, the Divine Feminine. The swing from Piscean patriarchal rule to full-on matriarchal rule requires the balance of energy."

"Okay," Glenda said, "let me see if I follow. We want to find the missing North American Avatar and bring her into the Temple Institute to be trained. We think it may be Cassandra Oberon, a young woman who lives in Charlotte, North Carolina."

"Correct," Master Elena said. "The issue is to aid her in maintaining her spiritual center. She cannot be lured by ego or anger. She cannot walk the left-hand path with the Dark Brotherhood. Factions of the Dark Brotherhood are also looking for the Seventh Avatar. They want to tap into her powers and turn her to their side before she understands her Soul Purpose and Mission. Once harnessed, her powers and those of the other Six, would allow the Dark Brotherhood to call in reinforcements from the Dark Planets throughout the galaxy. This could lead to a battle resulting in the extinction of humanity!"

The Oracle's voice was steady but insistent. "Master Elena has used the façade of sorority and fraternity lodges throughout the world since the founding of Phi Beta Kappa in 1776. Before then she used secret student societies at the major centers of learning dating all the way back to the time of Hermes and Ancient Egypt. Mon-ka smiled. "I know you are fully aware of all this, but I want to affirm how important you are to this endeavor. You are a highly trained acolyte. I understand you are getting ready to take your next initiation?"

Master Elena nodded. "Yes, indeed she is. It is also why we need to mount a major operation in Charlotte to ascertain if Cassandra Oberon is the Seventh Avatar and, if so, bring her to the Institute for training.

"I understand," Glenda said.

"There is one other piece," Master Elena said. "Many years ago, I had a rising acolyte, Rebekah St. Claire, who gave birth to a daughter. She and two of her best friends left the New York Institute when the toddler approached her second birthday. We were never able to find them. I need to confirm whether Cassandra is her daughter."

Master Elena handed Glenda a flash drive. "Here is everything you need to know about organizing a Rush event on the Queens University campus. We will establish a sorority there and you can use magic to incorporate it into the established Greek culture at Queens. Pick two dozen of your fellow acolytes, especially those skilled in the use of glamours. That should help you keep to the deadline. The fall Sorority Rush events are scheduled to begin in two weeks."

Chapter 2 The Dreams That Come

The neighborhood hugged a winding road and overlooked the valley below. The top of the mountain was shrouded in iridescent mists of pinks and gold, blues, greens, and silver. Cassie could see the outlines of mansions and small castles, building otherworldly – out of time and place. She drove closer to the top of the mountain.

She was totally lost.

She was on her way to meet her mother for their annual fall trip in the Blue Ridge Mountains. Somewhere, she had zigged when she should have zagged and was climbing into the clouds with no way to turn around. In this fog, an approaching car would be on her in a second. So, she continued the white-knuckled drive up the mountain, the switchbacks becoming more and more treacherous. She would stop at the first opportunity and ask for help.

The mist cleared enough to make out the front gate of a monolithic structure straight out of Harry Potter – or Dracula...stone façade, countless gables, and at least two turrets.

She could not see a drawbridge but would not have been surprised to discover one.

This should be interesting. But how am I supposed to get through those gates?

As if by telepathic cue, the gates swung open, and she steered up the drive. The house was more beautiful up close, reminiscent of the castles along the Rhine. The sun had knifed its way through the cloudy shroud and the building shimmered as if made of gold. She mounted the stairs – all ten of them – and approached the front door. Her stomach began to flutter. Anticipation? Excitement? Fear?

A large knocker inscribed with vaguely familiar symbols (like something she might have seen in a class on Ancient Egypt) dominated the center of the door. She traced the etchings with her index finger, then hoisted the heavy metal ring and knocked. Once...twice...again.

Footsteps approached, heavy and hurried. The door swung open.

A striking gentleman, perhaps mid-thirties, looked at her with a mixture of curiosity and annoyance. His blue-black hair contained enough hair gel for a production of *Grease*. Piercing green eyes stood above cheekbones that could have been sculpted by Rodin. Power radiated from every inch of his body.

"Who are you and how in the hell did you get through the gate?"

Her first thought was to respond with a fusillade of profanity, but she suddenly found it hard to speak. "H...hi," she said. "I...uh...sorry to bother you. I'm lost. Ended up outside your house and the gate was..."

She trailed off when an elegant woman appeared as if out of thin air. "Really, Xander, don't terrify the girl – let her in."

Xander's entire demeanor changed. His eyes widened and something akin to recognition spread across his face. A wave of warm, fresh air washed over Cassie, and she felt – well – she felt loved, the kind of affection one feels when nestled in the arms of a grandparent. The woman smiled; her turquoise eyes flecked with gold. She was dressed in a gold-edged, violet sari. Her snow-white hair was twisted into a braid pinned over the top of her head almost like a crown. She radiated a visceral inner light. Cassie fought the urge to reach out for a hug.

But the woman swung wide her arms. She embraced Cassie and said, "We've been expecting you, Cassandra St. Claire. It's time for you to awaken, dear one, and to remember who you are."

CASSIE'S EYES FLEW open, the dream had been more real this time than all the others. In one form or another, she'd had the recurrent dream since childhood. But since her mother's disappearance two years ago, the nocturnal images had come more frequently. She clasped the crystal pendant her mother had given her on her tenth birthday and swam through drowsiness toward the light of full wakefulness.

She could smell the mountain air and the rosewater the old woman had been wearing. A hint of patchouli hovered in the room.

What the hell?

She reviewed the dream, then thought about the old woman's face.

She's not old; she's ageless.

An insistent purring began next to her. Gabriel kitty snuggled between her neck and left shoulder.

"My little familiar." She smiled and nuzzled him. She recalled how her mother had referred to him when he had appeared out of nowhere one day on their front porch, walking in like he owned the place. It was the morning of her thirteenth birthday and his little gray and white body barely fit into the palm of her mother's hand. She had scooped him up and gently handed him to Cassie.

"Looks like you have an early birthday present." Mother never considered turning the kitten away. She cocked her head, "He says his name is Gabriel; do you remember what that name means from your angel book?"

Cassie nodded since angels and fairies were two of her favorite subjects. "Yes, it means 'strength of God and messenger.'"

Taryn smiled. "It looks like you have been sent a protector of sorts."

Over the next few months her mother had taught her how to tune into the animal, and she learned about the astral plane and how thoughts, coupled with positive emotions like love and compassion, would allow her to communicate with him. Taryn taught her to build pictures in her mind and to hold Gabriel in her arms, look into his eyes, and "send" the pictures. It did not take long until communication became as easy as speaking.

"It's like magic," she whispered to her mother one day. "He really understands me, and he sends me pictures too!"

"He will always be your most intimate friend. Remember he is not just an animal; he is now intricately interwoven with you. We, as humans, are responsible for the Animal Kingdom and their own soul evolution. That's why it is no longer appropriate for us to consume animal flesh without blessing the soul that sacrificed its body to nourish ours. It's a process called 'sacrificial service' and we honor them as we do any living being that relinquishes its physical form to aid or nourish others."

Cassie took a long, wavering breath and let the memory fade into present time. *Wow, what a dream!*

She hugged Gabriel. "So, oh wise one, what are these dreams all about?"

The cat yawned and stretched, kneaded her shoulder, and sent her a picture of his dish sitting empty in the kitchen. Cassie absently patted the top of his head.

St. Claire? The ageless woman called me "St. Claire." But that isn't my name.

Still, it felt familiar as though she should own it. Oh, how she wished her mother were here; she would have been able to take her back into the dream and help her gain understanding.

"Mommy, where are you?" she asked. The alarm clock buzzed, and Cassie crawled out of bed behind Gabriel, who was expecting immediate attention and his breakfast. Her aunt's head popped through the door.

"Cassandra, are you up yet? I know you have your morning routine, but I need to leave right on time this morning. I have an important meeting, and if you want me to drop you off at Queens you need to get a move on."

"I'll be down in a jiff," she said. "Can you put out Gabe's food, please?"

She scooped Gabriel up. "I'm running late, boy. Go to Auntie Isla."

She gave him a quick peck on the top of his head, scooted him toward the bedroom door, and sprinted toward her bathroom. Gabriel swatted at her legs indignantly, turned up his fluffy gray tail and stomped out, practically tripping her aunt as he changed his morning allegiance.

Cassie grimaced at the mirror. Her eyes were sunken with dark smudges like she hadn't slept at all. "Well," she said, "under-eye concealer today for sure."

She scowled and started going over the next two weeks. There were several events on the Queens campus she wanted to attend, many of them pertaining to sorority Rush. But now she had very mixed feelings about it. She didn't really care about being a part of a group of girls who were probably silly and more focused on finding a husband than they were about school. She shrugged her shoulders in resignation. She still had plenty of time to say no, and Rush was important to her aunt.

"At least give it a try, honey, college helps you find your tribe – your group. You have become isolated since your mother...left...and have gotten too emotionally involved with Paxton."

Isla was her father's sister. Cassie had never even heard of her when her mother was still around. It was a massive surprise when her aunt appeared at the front door of her home a few months ago. Cassie did not know much of anything about her father, who had been killed in a train wreck in Europe right after her parents had gotten married. A little bit after the tragedy, her mother discovered she was pregnant. Cassie had always wondered what he looked like, but there were no pictures of him anywhere. Only after meeting her aunt did she see how her coloring was from her father's side of the family. Isla had alabaster skin and silver-blonde hair that she kept in a low bun, ideally suited to her status as one of the East Coast's most prominent litigation attorneys with offices everywhere. Cassie on the other hand preferred her wavy long white blonde kept loose and free, but this morning she swept it back into a ponytail. She was a little hurried.

Cassie's thoughts returned to the recent sorority events she had attended. Due to her high GPA, attractiveness, and her family's affluence, many of Queens campus' top sororities had pursued her. Her legacy status with Alpha Omega, passed down from her mother, was a detail Garnet St. Jacques had inadvertently revealed when Cassie began receiving Rush event invitations. Although Cassie had been sociable and well-liked in the past, her mother's sudden absence made her retreat to her books and tech hobbies. The few sorority gatherings she'd been to had made her uneasy.

After her mother's disappearance, Garnet and another of her mother's business associates, Haley O'Brien, had taken care of her. Both, former sorority sisters of her mother, shuttled between their own homes in New York and London, respectively. They worked diligently to ensure the success of her mother's business, intending to safeguard Cassie's financial wellbeing. As a result, Cassie's world shrunk. She occasionally felt isolated, but she found solace in her academic success and her love for technology.

The lavender scent of her shower gel filled her nostrils. Cassie let her thoughts drift back to the dream. It had been so real. She and her mother loved hiking in the Blue Ridge Mountains during their annual fall trips. They delighted in looking for fairy rings in the woods. When they walked, they imagined stepping back in time to the primordial forests that their Celtic ancestors had cherished when they had first settled on the continent. Her mother always had encouraged her imagination, claimed Cassie had "the sight," which would become stronger as she got older. Cassie closed her eyes and began to recall the last trip they had taken just before her mother left on the fateful trip to England from which she never returned. Her mother's beloved face came into sharp focus and seemed to be right in front of her. She gasped, stepped back, and banged her head on the soap dispenser. She swore and rubbed a small knot.

Geez, I'm such a klutz.

She rinsed her hair – and heard a faint whisper, "Cassie."

The voice echoed. It sounded like her mother's. "Cassie, it's time."

She stepped from the shower. Her crystal pendant thrummed and felt warm against her chest. She reached for her purple towel but was careful not to move too quickly. She knew the voice was from the unseen world, a world that she had not been able to tap into since her mother disappeared.

Wrapped in her terry cloth robe, she crept into her room to her meditation corner, picked up her spirit crystal. It was humming in unison with her pendant. She sat in half-lotus on her Zabuton meditation pillow. Touching her left hand to the pendant, the twin to one her mother wore, she focused again on the soft whisper and visualized her mother's face. She breathed deeply, in through her nose and out through slightly parted lips – just like her mother and her yoga teacher had taught her – and moved into the inner place of peace once more. She focused on her mother's violet eyes, remembering how filled with love they could be.

Mommy? she reached out in her mind, *is that you?*

She heard faint whisperings, like the wind blowing through the trees right before a spring storm. She continued to reach up and out with her mind, allowing sensations of becoming bigger and bigger to overtake her. Up and out, she reached through the top of her head, through the top of the house, over the city, and up into the clouds. The whisperings swirled around her, a vortex of voices, soft but unintelligible and undefined. She kept focusing on her mother's eyes, repeating her query across the void, "Mommy, is that you?"

One voice became clear, and she turned her attention toward it, pulling herself in the direction of the familiar energy signature of Taryn.

"Cassie. Find me. Meet me in your dreams."

Cassie mentally reached out toward the voice, but it was already gone, dissipated when her eagerness broke the fragile link between her physical reality and the astral plane. She focused once more on her body, lifted her arms over her head in a side-to-side stretch, and gradually came back to full consciousness. She opened her eyes and allowed herself to wallow in disappointment for just a second. She rose from her cushion and into downward dog, finishing her stretching with five sun-salutations. That was better. She looked at the clock.

Jeez, Auntie Isla is gonna have a fit!

She shifted into high gear and finished getting ready for her day and thought about the directive, "Meet me in your dreams."

She was sure the message was from her mother. Making her aunt late wasn't an option, so she threw her dream journal into her backpack. She would write down both the message and the prior night's dream as soon as she was able.

The journals had become her lifeline over the past four years of high school. She had written volumes. The past time kept her sane during the turbulent years since her mother had disappeared without a note, without a call, without a trace.

Abducted by aliens maybe?

Cassie shook her head and laughed.

"Yeah, right!"

Chapter 3: Dark Brother

Sirkan's citrine eyes, like those of a cat, followed the girl bounding out from her aunt's car and hurrying toward the cafeteria. He had been careful to glamour himself to fit into a university campus with torn jeans, a hoodie drawn up over his head, and aviator sunglasses. He ran his fingers over the large ruby ring on his left index finger and felt its power reverberate throughout his body. He knew his destiny was about to be fulfilled; he *would* come into his rightful power.

Oh, he had plans! His acolytes were entrenched into the mystery schools around the world. They fed him information in a constant stream of telepathic waves. A tiny implant in his frontal lobe served as his interface with the digital world, bypassing the need for screens or keyboards. His face, a rugged landscape of scars and sharp angles, carried the weight of countless intergalactic skirmishes. Those deep-set eyes, windows to a soul far older than any Earth-bound human, held untold tales of cosmic warfare. A Lyran by origin, his ships had touched down on Earth millennia before any recorded history. Power wasn't handed to him; he crafted it, meticulously shaping an aura of masculine magnetism and authority. He had been thoroughly ensconced in the priesthood of Atlantis – a position of prestige and authority. A shadow puppeteer, he had orchestrated the downfall of that very institution, replacing it with his own shadowy brotherhoods strategically located around Earth's energy vortices.

He indulged in a mental moment of self-congratulation. His network had spread like dark tendrils beneath the very feet of the naive priestesses and priests who thought they were guiding humanity toward enlightenment. As Atlantis sank, they scattered, establishing their temples worldwide in a misguided attempt to decentralize their wisdom. Little did they know, this played perfectly into his hands.

Information, once flowing like a slow stream, was now a roaring river feeding into his mind, always keeping him one step ahead of those who would claim to be the true Masters of Wisdom.

His covens had thrived the most. Humans were so taken with magics. Once he engaged their innate lust for money and power, they were easily turned to the left-hand path. They even created religions where followers relinquished personal power to the leaders of the covens. Those leaders, the witches and warlocks, had built reservoirs of dark energy with their castings and spells from which he could draw.

A smirk curled at the corners of his mouth as he thought of Isla, his present consort, busily directing the coven's activities. She wore her sense of authority like a cloak, but it was a thin one. Her notion that overseeing a few covens granted her some measure of control was amusing. If she only knew the vast reservoirs of influence he drew upon, her understanding of "power" would shatter like fragile glass.

His grin widened. Isla, like all the beings of these lesser realms—be they Human or Fae—were so easily swayed, so simply manipulated. They were mere threads in the vast tapestry he wove, and Isla, despite her endearing confidence, was no exception.

His blood-born clans had sunk their roots in every major city in the world. From New York to Tokyo, they were everywhere. Humans had coined a name for them: "vampires." Folk tales and pop culture had done the work for him, romanticizing these creatures into mysterious, alluring figures. The promise of eternal youth and beauty seemed to overshadow any whispered rumors about the darker aspects of immortality.

His lips twitched in amusement at the thought of goth-clad teenagers sporting faux fangs, unwittingly pledging allegiance to his shadow empire. These humans were signing up in droves, tantalized by the allure of eternity, completely oblivious to the strings attached.

The real beauty of it? They believed they were merely joining a trend, a subculture. In reality, they were enlisting in an army they didn't even know existed—yet. And when the call came, they'd find out just how steep the price of eternal life truly was.

Natesh Nandwani led the charge in the Western Hemisphere. He had aspired to be the leader of a major clan since the time he had been sired during the turbulent days of the French Revolution. His desire for ascendancy wasn't merely an ambition; it was an all-consuming fire that left no room for hesitation or morals. With each maneuver, every subterfuge, he clawed his way closer to becoming the uncontested clan lord of this half of the world.

Not that his desires were limited to power alone. Natesh was a man of dark appetites, his love for violence and sex intermingling like poisonous flowers in a twisted garden. His cunning had borne fruit a century ago when he forged a pact with Morgandrian, High Priestess of the East Coast's most formidable coven. That alliance had not only solidified his political standing but also granted him dark resources that others could only dream of. And so, he continued his relentless climb, leaving none to question the depths he would go to satisfy his insatiable appetites.

While their alliance had initially been a boon, it was becoming increasingly clear that both had begun to nurture their own visions for the project—visions that didn't necessarily align with his own grand design.

His eyes narrowed at the thought. It wasn't just a question of their autonomy; it was the audacity to think they could steer the course without his say-so. This was a game of cosmic chess, not a sandbox for underlings with outsized ambitions.

He smiled as he considered what devious schemes his consort, Isla, might be concocting. And Natesh and Morgandrian? If they persisted in this reckless independence, a reckoning would be unavoidable. He wouldn't let years of intricately woven plans unravel at the whims of two or three individuals, however powerful they might consider themselves. If Isla was entertaining the idea of aligning with Morgandrian and Natesh in some gambit for power, she would find herself stepping into a snare of her own making. Their individual ambitions could never eclipse his overarching plan. And so, he mentally drafted the terms of their forthcoming confrontation—a reminder that in this complex web, he was still very much the spider at its center.

The smile deepened, almost a growl. Ah, the surprises he had in store for them—they wouldn't even see it coming.

He had reached a pivotal point; he required only one more piece to coalesce his plan. He needed to break the energy of The Aquarian Avatars by ensuring they would not acquire the final link in completing their circle of power. That link was the girl, Cassandra Oberon.

Chapter 4: It's All in the Fingertips

Cassie ran across the parking lot to the cafeteria. She didn't like summer school, but she wanted to get her core freshman courses out of the way, so she could jump into her major in the fall. Her scholarship in AI design would also help her skip the basic computer classes. Computers had always fascinated her. There was something magical about connecting with the waves of energy that flowed from her mind, through her fingers to the keyboard. She had won her scholarship for designing a program that transformed thoughts from her brainwaves into code. She had been inspired by her mother's use of healing energy.

"Over the years of practicing Reiki," Taryn Oberon had told her, "I began to feel that the tips of my fingers had little minds of their own. When I surrendered my control over the healing session, they automatically went to the part of the body most in need of healing. My hands felt like heating pads when the energy began to transfer into the body of the person on my healing table. The clients told me they could feel the heat when the connection was made. They relaxed into a light sleep. After the body absorbed all the energy it needed, my hands 'turned off' and felt cool. I knew it was time to move to another part of the body, or to wrap up the session."

Cassie remembered those magical years with her mother, the way she explained the wonders of the unseen world. The memory ignited warmth in her own hands; her Reiki energy flared for a moment. Her mother had initiated her at thirteen into the ancient healing technique which was seeing a worldwide resurgence. Reiki had even been included into the Holistic Nurses practicum at Charlotte's Presbyterian Hospital. Cassie had volunteered to be a part of the program so she could practice various healing techniques with her mother's Reiki Circle.

"There is an electro-magnetic energy that connects the human kingdom with all the other living beings on the planet," Taryn had said. "Soften your eyes a little and allow them to go out of focus. Then begin your yoga breathing as I taught you and focus about six inches above your point of concentration, you will start to see the light that emanates from all living forms. It's called an aura."

There was something else about vibrations and vibratory frequencies, but Cassie had since forgotten the specifics. It was strange how her memory had become so foggy over the past two years.

Since her mother's disappearance Cassie had focused on her schoolwork. Her fervor both delighted and concerned her teachers. She was determined to make her mark in the world of computer science and Artificial Intelligence design and was relentless in her search for unexplored areas of the web and its uses. She was especially interested in how to educate the children all over the world to lift them from the dire poverty and starvation sweeping across the globe like a plague. The news channels were full of it. Oftentimes her own dreams picked up on the agony and fear of thousands of souls screaming out in terror. Nighttime scenes of blood and death bombarded her. She awakened with the feeling of being on those killing fields and bolted upright, her eyes filling with tears. She knew emotion would not solve anything, but sometimes the sense of urgency to do whatever she could to save the innocents threatened to overwhelm her. She knew her mother had tapped into similar scenarios during meditation or in dreams and had kept journals about her insights, but they too had vanished.

Shaking herself back to the present moment yet again, Cassie thought about the days ahead as she prepared to enjoy her last summer before entering her first full year of university.

Two strong arms scooped her up and swung her around. Paxton's laughing green eyes gave her the once over as he leaned in to kiss her.

"You look good enough to eat," he whispered into her ear. He put her down, hooked her arm through his, and walked her up the stairs into the cafeteria. He brushed two fingers along her brow as though to smooth away the worried furrow.

"You are thinking hard about something, Darlin'. Wanna share?"

"The mixer. I don't know if I want the whole 'sisterhood' thing. The sorority deal is outdated...you know, objectification, marginalization."

"Yada, yada," he said. "I am woman...geez!"

She punched his arm and steered him toward the breakfast bar. She picked up a bagel, put it back, and reached for a nonfat yogurt and a dish of cut-up fruit.

"If it matters, I love my frat." Paxton said. "The upper classmen helped me navigate my classes and some of them are steering me through the campus political climate. In my not-so-humble opinion, I would go for it." Paxton piled eggs, bacon, and hashbrowns on his plate, took the rejected bagel and added a generous heap of grits to the pile.

"Uh huh."

"Earth to Cassie. Where'd you go?" Paxton touched her hand across the table.

"Sorry, I was remembering what my mom told me about the importance of her sorority in her early years in New York City. She changed her mind later – felt like the sisters were too intrusive when she began to establish her fashion business. She had cut off all ties to them, except, of course, with Aunties Garnet and Haley."

Paxton nodded. Neither spoke. He had been talking about her mother's disappearance with his father the night before. Taryn had disappeared during a trip to a board meeting in London. She stepped into a limo and never arrived at her suite at the Dorchester Hotel. There was no trace of the car. Taryn Oberon had vanished.

They both jumped when the alarm on Cassie's smart watch sounded.

"I'll take your tray," Paxton said. He kissed her on the cheek. "Pick you up after your yoga class. And do not forget—we have a date tonight!"

And they were off and running in different directions.

Chapter 5: Dark Sisters

Morgandrian ground her teeth and circled the throne of the High Priestess. The coven was about to convene, and Morgandrian was not in a good mood. Word had reached her. The Oracle sect of the Sirian Council had possibly identified the last of the seven Expected Ones.

Damn it to hell. I wanted the identity hidden until I could get my hands on her.

Morgandrian was prepared to do everything she could to turn Number Seven to the left-hand path before the Initiation at the full moon of Aquarius the next year. She had even accepted the help of the devilishly handsome vampire Natesh. He was supposed to seduce the silly chit. Now, thanks to Adrianna's report, another problem had been identified. There was a boyfriend. He seemed to be a mundane human, someone who was dragging the target along in a dewy-eyed teenage crush.

Or is he part of another rival coven or vamp clan and glamoured to appear human?

Morgandrian had surmised Taryn Oberon's disappearance represented the last obstacle to procuring the girl. By the Crone, she would soon find out! And where was Natesh? He was to have contacted the girl long before now and started the seduction to the Left-hand path.

Has he even started? Or does he think this will be so easy that he can swoop in at the last moment? Arrogant bastard!

She twisted the ruby ring on her left forefinger unconsciously. She was growing quite weary of depending on others to adhere to their promises. It was time to act.

A timid voice chirped from behind. "Mistress, the sisters await in the vestibule."

Morgandrian pivoted and bellowed. "Enter!"

The coven sisters glided into the Throne Room and formed a half circle around the dais. Morgandrian swirled her red velvet cape around her and sat on her throne with a theatrical flair.

"Sisters, we are at a turning point in our work. It's time we put our combined powers together to take charge of bringing the last of the Chosen Ones into our sisterhood. For too long we have waited for her to come to us on her own or assumed others would bring her to us. *No more!*"

Natesh smirked. He was some distance away, but Morgandrian's shields were no match for his advanced hearing and magical talents. Morgandrian had never been good at strategic waiting. Impatience was her fatal flaw. How she had ever risen to the office of High Priestess of the most powerful coven in North America was simply beyond him. Ever since they had fallen in lust during the French Revolution, he still could not fathom how the covens operated on such high emotional energy and got anything done. Of course, the high emotion propelled their magic...emotion coupled with rage. But still he was perplexed. The Blood Born were more in control of their emotions, which granted them the mesmerizing powers their prey could not resist. If they engaged their emotions, the Blood Born would be totally powerless – and extinct.

Perhaps I should accelerate the timetable, he thought.

His spies kept him informed. "Cassandra" – the suspected Seventh Avatar was attending summer school before starting her advanced studies in the fall. Seemed she was some sort of whiz kid when it came to computer science. He could use those abilities in his ongoing project of subliminal programming through popular social media platforms.

There were two hurdles to overcome. One was the boyfriend, and the other was the Sirian Council. He had to get to Charlotte, take care of the boyfriend situation, and get her under his control. It would be a simple matter to use her as a bargaining chip with Morgandrian, or any other lieutenant of the Dark Brotherhood. Natesh would not give over his prize to anyone. Well, apart from his Master. Natesh shook his head. Cassandra Oberon would be *his* ace in the hole—no matter what.

He had a plan in mind. But let's see what Her Bitchness has up her sleeve before I determine my next step.

Natesh returned his focus to the drama unfolding in Morgandrian's throne room.

"And so, my sisters, I have determined that we will set up a special Rush event in Charlotte to recruit her into our sisterhood under the guise of a sorority. Pull out your best coercion spells, glamour up, and get to work. Adrianna, as my second, you will be in charge. Pick your strongest sisters and head to Charlotte." She glared at the assembled. "You have two weeks. "

An audible groan rolled through the room. The witches looked at each other in dismay. They had been asked to do some impossible things in the past, but this ...

"And I will not tolerate failure," Morgandrian said in an icy tone. "Heads will roll if we do not get this girl under our control. And you know I keep my promises."

Ah ha, she is indeed on a rampage. Cassandra Oberon will be my crowning achievement, and leverage with "The Boss." This will vault me to the position of Clan Leader of North America.

With that, Natesh buzzed off into the night sky on his little black wings and returned to his lair.

Chapter 6: Things Remembered; Things Forgot

Cassie was just putting the finishing touches on her makeup. "Keep it tasteful and subtle," her mother often told her even though she was a makeup maven of the first order, her eyes lined in black kohl with plenty of blush and deep rose lipstick. Only Taryn Oberon could pull it off with her exotic Mediterranean coloring, her face accented with high, sculpted cheekbones and walnut brown eyes. Her dark hair was always styled in her signature chin-brushing bob. It was so perfectly coiffed that one reporter, during an interview for *The New York Times*, had asked her if she wore a wig, to which she threw back her head, laughed, and invited the woman to pull on it. Cassie was lucky to have inherited her mother's hair genes, although her coloring was evidently from her father. Her abundant white-blonde hair hung down her back in waves, her heart-shaped face fringed with wispy bangs.

Cassie shivered when she recalled how Paxton liked running his fingers through her long tresses.

The former captain of the high school football team, Paxton, well-muscled and athletic, stood at 6'4". He made 5'6" Cassie feel diminutive and dainty when they were together. His hazel eyes always seemed to be laughing in amusement. He pulled his dirty-blonde hair back in a stylish, half ponytail to keep it out of his face, but allowed the rest of his straight hair to fall to his shoulders. His "man bun" gave him a rakish look when combined with the carefully groomed five o'clock shadow on his perpetually tanned face. They had become closer since her mother's disappearance. He was a calming influence. He had slipped into the role first of big brother and protector, and more recently into something more.

THE DOORBELL RANG. She ran down the staircase and yelled to Isla. "Going out with Paxton. I'll be back by curfew."

Thirty minutes later they were walking toward their favorite bar in uptown Charlotte with a group of their friends.

"Oh, I just love this Irish pub!" Cassie said. The little band of revelers headed toward the Rí Rá Irish Pub on North Tryon Street. "It feels like we have stepped back in time. I love, love the cave-like atmosphere with those stone walls!" She reached for Paxton's hand.

He took her hand into his and gallantly lifted it to his lips for a kiss, "That's why this is our place. Do you remember when we first met?"

It was good to see her smiling for a change. She seemed so serious these days.

Their eyes locked as she remembered the night when they had been in the upstairs room of the pub for a rehearsal dinner for her friend, Kaitlin's older sister. Cassie had been laughing with several of the younger set of various branches of their family who were attempting to help themselves to mugs of beer, under-aged as they were. Her mother's financial advisor and close friend, Tristan, had been keeping an eye on them but winked when Cassie sidled up to the bar and snagged one for herself. Smiling back in return, Cassie was raising the mug to her lips when suddenly she felt a little warm tickle down her spine. Turning, she met the gaze of an amazingly beautiful boy. Her eyes widened when she realized it was her childhood friend – a child no more!

Tristan's son, Paxton, two years older, had been her best bud since the two were toddlers. He had been away for most of the summer in Scotland, an annual trip he had been taking since he turned thirteen. The young Adonis was like someone out of one of the romance novels her mother loved so much. He had let his hair grow longer over the summer. His face was sculpted, his cheekbones more defined, and his sensuous lips curved up in a lop-sided grin. She allowed her gaze to move down. His white silk shirt was opened at the neck and stretched a bit over his broad shoulders and toned chest. It was like he had grown from a boy into a man overnight, or, at least, over the summer.

He had been watching with amusement as the not-yet-legal-to-drink set had been attempting to abscond with their ill-gotten libations. She smiled, remembering how after each trip his vocabulary contained more and more Scottish slang words, especially when he became irritated and angry. She was suddenly brought back to the present when she tripped over a crack in the sidewalk in front of the bastion of Charlotte's finance, the Bank of America building. Paxton grabbed her around the waist before she landed on her backside.

"Whoa there, Missy," he said. "We don't want any broken bones before you are introduced to the world of college life."

Cassie looked up at his laughing green eyes. She was a little embarrassed.

"Yeah, I know," she said. "A body cast won't exactly go with my new collegiate outfits!"

Something felt off. A slight dizziness hit her as they crossed the intersection of Trade and Tryon Street. Her ears buzzed with the sound of a thousand hornets. The feeling gradually subsided and soon she was back to normal.

Low blood sugar. She took a deep breath and focused on the enjoyable sensation of Paxton's arm around her waist. The headiness of his spicy cologne filled her nostrils, and a tightness in her core began to pulsate. Over the past year their friendship had deepened into something more and it was getting more and more difficult to keep the feelings at bay. She yearned to explore the forbidden parts of him – and for him to do the same to her. But innately she knew it wasn't time yet. They needed a firm commitment before intimacy entered their relationship. Paxton had never suggested taking their relationship to the next level, something she felt needed to be addressed soon, especially since she was poised to make some major decisions about the next steps in her education – and in her life.

PAXTON BENT DOWN TO brush his lips across her forehead. "Earth to Cassie – yet again. Where did you go?"

"Oh," she said, "just thinking about freshman year, turning 18, who am I, and where am I going – you know, small stuff."

"That is much too serious for a night like this," he said. He pulled her through the front door of the pub. "Race you to the bar!"

She laughed while he tugged her along to the front of the bar. He stationed himself behind her so he could encircle her waist. She snuggled into his muscular arms, relishing their feeling of strength and security, and smiled up at him. He ordered two ginger beers. He was faithful not only to his own training schedule, but also to the strict rules of both her mother and her aunt – no underage drinking allowed unless under the supervision of an adult – and at home. There was no way he would give in to her cajoling as she motioned at some of the schooners in front of their friends.

"Seriously?" he asked. "No way I'm gonna get you or me in trouble for a pint." He grinned and he motioned to the bartender.

The bartender plopped down a pair of bottles. "Two Guinness stouts."

Paxton looked at him. "Nope, not ours. We ordered ginger beer. Like to run a tab—"

Paxton zeroed in on the bartender. The hair on the back of his neck stood. Something wasn't right.

"Max" (according to his nametag) smiled. "Name on the tab, buddy?"

"Ah...never mind," Paxton said. He slid a twenty across the bar. Max corrected the order and handed over the change.

After a few sips, Paxton reached for the nut bowl. Empty. He looked for Max. Nowhere to be seen.

Something's not square with that guy, Paxton thought.

He held Cassie a little closer and vowed to stay alert.

NATESH CURSED AND STALKED along the alley behind Rí Rá. His shapeshifting had been flawless, but somehow the boy Paxton had been alerted.

Not as mundane as I suspected, Natesh thought. I need to know more about him. And the girl, Cassandra. There is something familiar about her, her energy. It's more than her being one of The Seven. I have to figure this out."

Natesh shook his head, ducked behind a dumpster, and opened a portal back to his lair.

Chapter 7: Master of the White Circle

The white-robed figure continued pacing across the parapet of the Citadel, his amber eyes staring off into the distance, chiseled jaw clenched. His Soul Essence was still adjusting to his physical body settling into the third dimensional vibration, one much heavier than his native sixth dimension. But his well-honed warrior's body was gradually beginning to feel like his own once more. Rolling his shoulders, he breathed in the crisp mountain air. It was good to be back on the Earth plane once more. He looked out at the mountains shrouded by the clouds below. He had grown to love this retreat during his journeys between dimensions; it gave him a sense of peace and tranquility, a welcome respite from the duties of his office. Since arising this morning, however, every fiber in his being had been tingling with nervous energy. Something was brewing, and it wasn't good.

For ages untold, the Brotherhood had stood vigil, their eyes on the cosmic clock, awaiting the moment when the Age of Aquarius would dawn. The planet could become a celestial battleground where the Forces of Light would clash with the Dark Brotherhood over the destiny of an awakening Earth. One group wanted to aid and support; the other wanted to control and manipulate while Earth was preparing to take its sacred initiation. The Radiant One had crafted a grand design yet had left room for human free will. Now that very gift was backfiring. Cities burgeoned with skyscrapers while spirits withered; stock markets boomed as souls went bankrupt.

And then there were the seekers, or so they believed themselves to be—humans entranced by the shadows of forbidden magics, unknowingly dancing to the Dark Brotherhood's tune. They rallied behind a man who had appeared as if from the ether, preaching populism while occupying the most powerful office on Earth—the American presidency. To them, he was a messiah. They didn't realize they were pawns in a much older, darker game.

Conroe Soter had sown discord and divisiveness across the globe and caused people from all walks of life to turn on their friends, families, and anyone else who did not agree with their truth. Civil wars, kidnappings, assaults, and murder of anyone who was "different" ran rampant on every continent, even in countries hitherto relatively stable. There were also other forces at work, things controlling the masses of humanity. They no longer thought rationally; they accepted blatant lies as truth. There had to be some sort of manipulation going on having to do with the world wide web.

A deep tremor passed through him. Memories of that malevolent force during the epoch of the Second World War surged back - a dark energy that had threatened to obliterate an entire race of humanity. Although celestial beings and his valiant Warriors of Light had joined forces with humans to conquer much of this darkness, the untimely harnessing of atomic power had torn asunder the etheric veil protecting the Earth, unleashing torrents of ultraviolet energies far sooner than the world was prepared to absorb.

The subsequent decades bore witness to disturbances that threatened to unmake the Earth. Alterations within the planet necessitated a transformation, a resonance at a higher frequency. This shift was paramount, not only for Earth's healing but also to elevate its inhabitants to an ascended state of consciousness - the Fifth Dimension: the realm of the Mind. It was within this expanse that true restoration could unfold.

Artemus gazed toward the sea and squinted into the rising sun. His thoughts turned once more to the visions he had been having of late and wondered, "Is she the one?" He had seen glimpses over the past few weeks, visions of a beautiful young girl with long, white-blonde hair and flashing violet eyes. The signs in the heavens confirmed it was time for the Avatars of the New Age of Aquarius to come forward. They would lead Humanity into their next step in evolution. But one was still missing. The seventh Avatar. The Avatar from North America.

Time was running out. The Avatars were due to be initiated during the full moon of Aquarius in February next year. He knew he needed to descend onto the Earth plane to search for them and resume his command post.

He had received the Scroll of Prophecy, a legacy handed down to him by his Master in the moment before death's embrace. The words inscribed upon it had traveled across the stars from Sirius, millennia old yet still as vivid as the day they were penned. Coordinates and cosmic alignments danced across the parchment, pinpointing the exact moments and locales for the rebirth of the Seven Avatars who would herald the Age of Aquarius on what was now known as Earth.

His mind drifted back to Atlantis, to that fateful era when some of his kind had shattered the sacred Codex of the First Order and spilled human blood. Those actions had ensnared many of them to the wheel of rebirth, a karmic debt that had cycled through ages. He felt a tingling sense of finality, like a chord reaching its resolving note. The time to balance the scales was at hand.

"A penny..." a soft voice interrupted his musings from the arched entrance behind him.

Artemus swung around, a look of pleasure upon his face. "Master Elena, how wonderful to see you! I didn't know you were coming today." Then he noticed the expression on her face.

"Something is amiss?"

Elena sighed with her palms together in a traditional Eastern greeting. She bowed.

"Namaste."

Artemus mirrored the greeting.

"You are correct," Elena said. "I am here to discuss a situation. The Oracles brought it to the attention of the Intergalactic Council. We need your expertise as the Master of the White Circle."

"Ah," he said, "I haven't heard that title in many years – not since I worked with Rebekah St. Claire and your other two rising stars, Isabeau Renault and Elyse Weiks. They were instrumental in bringing forth teachings from Master St. Germain. Rebekah dubbed them "The Transmissions." They were of great service to him while he attempted to finish the work he had begun in his lifetime as Nikola Tesla."

Elena nodded with a bit of excitement. "I believe there is a young girl who may very well be the Seventh Avatar. And I believe she may be Rebekah St. Claire's daughter."

She recounted the prior morning's meeting at the New York Institute, and her decision to send one of her acolytes to Charlotte to get a handle on the situation and check out the girl.

I was right, he thought. She is the one.

Energy surged up his spine. His solar plexus pulsed.

"I have been pacing this balustrade for days now, sensing something along the same lines. I was just mulling over the idea of the missing Avatar being a female, and you appear. This is not a coincidence. Admittedly, I have allowed myself to become a bit frustrated of late about the disappearance of Rebekah and what had happened to the daughter she birthed seventeen years ago. I thought the child would be a strong candidate for the missing North American Avatar. However, I have sensed neither Rebekah nor her daughter in the current timeline."

Elena rubbed her chin. "Commander Mon-Ka cannot find Rebekah either. You are correct. We all have been focusing too much on old paradigms when the great Avatars were in male form. Of course, that is no longer the case."

"Do we have this girl's birth chart?"

Elena shook her head, her eyes narrowing with a mixture of regret and resignation. "Rebekah was in my inner circle when the child was born. The astrological chart we had was comprehensive, but it vanished along with her. I do remember that there was a great deal of potential for the girl. She was born in the sign of Aquarius and had Scorpio rising."

She paused, tapping her fingers on the table as if trying to summon a forgotten memory or a lost spell. "You know Rebekah—always the esoteric astrologer. If she took the chart, it was intentional. She'd think, 'If they can't see the chart, they can't know her destiny.'"

Elena leaned back, her eyes taking on a distant look. "Rebekah must have gleaned an understanding of her daughter's celestial potential, the monumental destiny that could be hers. But," she sighed, "as esoteric wisdom goes, 'the stars impel, they do not compel.' Free will is still the Creator's greatest gift to us."

Elena went on to apprise him of the directives she had given to Glenda.

"How can I be of service to you?" he asked.

She took a deep breath and smiled. "You, my dear friend, can help me keep the Dark Brotherhood at bay as we determine who Cassandra is, and if she needs to be brought into the Circle. I would also ask you to put one of your initiates from the White Circle in charge of finding Rebekah, so we can not only ensure her safety, but also so she can have a hand in opening her daughter to her soon-to-be awakened powers."

Artemus raised an eyebrow. "Oh, is that all? I thought you would ask me something difficult."

They grasped one another's forearms in a farewell salute. Elena opened a portal to the New York Institute and was gone as quickly as she had appeared.

Chapter 8: Time and Time Again

Running breathless into the cafeteria three mornings later, Cassie bumped into a tall brunette. Coffee, fruit, eggs, and pastries flew everywhere.

"Oh my gosh, I'm such a klutz," the girl said. "Did anything get on you?"

Cassie examined her crisp linen blouse, khaki shorts, and white tennis shoes. "Nothing," she said. "Like magic!"

"Oh, thank goodness," the girl said.

Cafeteria workers glared on their way past, mops and dish towels in hand.

The girl reached out. "Hi, I'm Glenda."

"I'm Cassie."

"Nice to...ah...run into you." The girl let out a nervous titter. "Why don't we give breakfast another try? Maybe this was a sign to get something a little less carb loaded."

Paxton came up from behind and put an arm around Cassie. He surveyed the carnage. "I know that wasn't yours, Sweetie," he said. "Never seen you touch a pastry this close to beach season."

He laughed and hugged her. Cassie threw back her head and giggled. "Nope, but I gotta admit, I am tempted." She gestured to Glenda. "Meet my new friend Glenda. Glenda, this is Paxton...my...ah...conscience."

Paxton reached out his hand. "Hey, Glenda, shall we go back and replenish your ruined breakfast?"

"Oh, I don't want to intrude," Glenda said. She made to turn away.

"No, no, please join us," Cassie said. She pointed to Glenda's Alpha Omega polo shirt. "I could use a heads up on the Greek life here. I firmly believe there are no accidents. I'm a legacy through my mother to AO."

And there it is – total confirmation that this girl is indeed Rebekah St. Claire's daughter!

"Wow, go figure!" Glenda said. "I am Chair of the Rush Committee this year. We've got a big mixer right here in the cafeteria at seven tomorrow night."

"I was planning on going," Cassie said. "Co-ed, right?"

"Every party should be," Glenda said.

"Good," Cassie said. "Paxton said he'd come and bring some of his frat brothers."

Glenda grinned.

"Method to my madness," Paxton said. He flashed his patented smile. "I want them to find *their own* girls. They love to swoop in on sorority pledges. No way I'm leaving you at their mercy."

ADRIANNA WATCHED THE exchange from across the cafeteria. She knew Glenda had just used magic to orchestrate the whole breakfast tray caper.

Wonder who she is, Adrianna thought. The spell wasn't on the Coven's frequency. It reeks of white magic. This "Glenda" must be using a glamouring spell to cover her true identity.

Adriana's eyes narrowed. Then there's the boyfriend. I need to find out if he is aligned with the White Brotherhood or if he is just a Mundane.

She stared at Glenda a little longer. Long brown hair...blue eyes...attractive. She pinched herself. None of that, my girl. There are more important things afoot.

She looked around to be sure no one would notice, then blinked out with a bit of portal magic.

AFTER DINNER, CASSIE was ensconced on her window seat. She was reading *Green Darkness* by Anya Seaton. It was one of her mother's favorite books, a gothic romance, a genre both she and her mother liked. She had been eager to dive into the tome to take her mind off her activities. The copy was well worn with underlined text and notes scribbled in margins. Perusing the preface written by the author, the words, "Karma" and "reincarnation" jumped off the pages. Both had been highlighted. The more she read, the faster her heartbeat.

"That's it! That's the missing link between science and religion." She shot up off the window seat and grabbed her laptop. She connected to the New York library's card catalogue and did a search on both topics.

"Thanks, Mom," she whispered. Her mother had multiple addresses. Consequently, she enjoyed privileges at some of the largest libraries in the world.

An abundance of books populated the screen. When she scanned the list, one title jumped out at her: *What is Theosophy* by Helena Blavatsky. She downloaded it onto her e-reader and began to devour it. She took notes. Hours later she woke with a start, having fallen asleep at her desk. She slipped into her night shirt, crawled into bed, and fell back to sleep almost before her head hit the pillow.

Tonight, the dream was different.

SHE STARED UP INTO a seemingly endless spiral staircase. Each turn branched off into a landing. Each landing opened onto numerous closed doors. Glyphs in various geometric patterns abounded.

The elderly woman, clothed in a flowing sari of violet tinged with golden trim, extended her hand toward her. "Come," she beckoned, her eyes locking onto hers as they stood before an enigmatic entrance, framed with ancient inscriptions.

As they stepped closer, doorways materialized along the corridor, each pulsing with an ethereal light, as if hiding worlds behind them. "These," the old woman breathed, "are the portals to your past lives. The Akashic Records are beyond. It's not just about remembering who you were, but about reclaiming your gifts—skills long dormant yet never forgotten."

Eyes wide, Cassie put her hand into the woman's. She felt safe, secure, and surrounded by love. Her curiosity far outweighed any doubts or fear. They followed the first turn of the spiral and began to walk to the left down the first hallway.

"The doorways on the left side are from your most immediate past lives. As you continue up the spiral, they go further and further back into the centuries. The very top tier links to your first incarnation when your soul was breathed into existence by The Radiant One on your home planet. Choose where you want to go; there is no wrong choice. All are you."

"Wait – what? Home planet?"

The woman turned her around, both hands on her shoulders. "Your Soul did not originate on the planet on which you currently reside. To know more, you must do the discovering. It is not mine to tell."

Cassie looked around, uncertain where to go. "Close your eyes and do the yoga breathing you know so well," the woman said. "Reach out and ask, 'What is mine to know at this time? What do I need to bring forward to begin my mission?'"

Sighing, Cassie did as she had been told. She centered her breathing, reached out, up and around with her conscious mind. The fingers of her right hand began to tingle, a sure sign that her intuition was beginning to ignite. Her attention was drawn to a landing two turns up the spiral. She felt herself lift off the floor and float up to the landing. An intricately carved door to the left drew her attention. It was glowing. She went to it. She recognized the Rococo style that was popular in the reign of Louise XVI and Marie Antoinette. Serpentine lines were etched into the thick wooden door; gold and pastel colors glowed in the trompe l'oeil window painted on its surface. She reached for the ornate gold doorknob, opened the door, and stepped into a candle-lit room.

A man in a powdered wig stood in front of a white marble fireplace resplendent with carved scrolls and acanthus leaves. He clasped his hands behind his back. He was staring into the fire deep in thought but turned around at the sound of the opening door. When he saw her, his eyes lit up.

"Ah, mon coeur, come in, come in. I was hoping you would find some time to resume our lessons today."

Her feet felt like they were bolted to the floor. He frowned.

"Please, come in and sit."

He motioned to the book-strewn table across the room with six chairs pulled around it, an astrolabe the dominant centerpiece. She finally made her legs move enough to step forward. She clapped her hands together when she saw a particular volume – leather bound with gilded lettering on the spine.

"Mon Dieu, this is the book you were searching for!"

The Compte de St. Germain put his arm around her shoulders, helped with her chair, then leaned over her to open to a page halfway through the tome.

"Yes, my agent in Athens finally found this rare copy of the teachings of Hermes Trismegistus, *The Emerald Tablets of Thoth*. It just arrived this morning."

He slid a blank journal over to her along with quill and ink. "I want you to begin to translate from this page. Continue until you reach the feather. Then we will discuss it." She started to ask a question, but he put his finger to his lips. "No questions, Giselle. Let the words flow through you as you transcribe them, even if you don't know what they mean. Remember, words are simply symbols for a concept beyond them. Your tutors have taught you enough Greek. You should be able to grasp most of the lesson."

Hmmm, looks like my name is Giselle in this life.

The Compte took another book from the table and crossed back over to the fireplace. He settled into one of the two throne-like chairs and picked up a crystal wine glass. They sat in companiable silence for over an hour when a loud crash sounded outside in the courtyard. Looking up in alarm, they saw a mob of people breaking through the front gates. Unintelligible shouts rose in a crescendo as the rabble came closer and closer to the house.

The Compte de St. Germain cursed. He grabbed a small rucksack from next to the table and shoveled in books and papers.

"Quickly!" he shouted, "put the book and your notes in here, and follow me." He sent a telepathic message to his fellow Masters as he went to one of the bookcases to the right of the fireplace. He pulled out one of the books and pressed a hidden knob. The bookcase swung out. He took her arm, grabbed a torch, and entered the passageway. The wall shut behind them. Giselle's eyes were round as saucers; her breath came in gasps. "Who are those people, why are they storming the house?"

He shushed her, his voice barely above a whisper. "I will tell you when we get to safety. For now, watch your step. This passage is very old, and the footing is uncertain. The last thing you need is a turned ankle."

She had not been surprised by the hidden passageway. They were a prerequisite for the huge estates of the aristocracy. What she could not understand was why anyone, let alone a mob, would be attacking the Compte's domicile. He was much beloved by commoners. His teachings had inspired their thirst for freedom from the royal yoke.

Following him, she heard a whooshing sound and then other footsteps just ahead. The Compte motioned her to stop as he cocked his head to listen. Two figures approached. He sighed with relief.

"Ah, Elena and Artemus, I am glad you received my message!"

He handed the man the rucksack. The woman took a hooded cloak from over her arm and wrapped it around the girl. Giselle had seen these two at the Compte's Salons over the past few years, but she did not know them well. Everyone treated them as royalty and equals to the Compte de St. Germain. He often left with them but always returned to close out the Salon and take Giselle back to her apartments in the Palace.

"I believe we are now at the crossroads we have been anticipating, my friend." Artemus said. "Is she prepared for what may lie ahead?"

The Compte glanced at him. "As prepared as possible without putting her into danger with too many details."

Giselle began to understand. For years she had been trained as an Intuitive who could see beyond the physical world and into the future – a future with endless possibilities created by choice. The mob outside had made their selection and put one of those futures into motion. She did not have time to finish her train of thought. They emerged into a clearing just at the edge of the walls of the estate.

A tall, cloaked figure awaited them – hooded and mysterious. Artemus placed Giselle's hand into the stranger's "Guard her well, my friend. Your passage to England has been arranged when you can get her on the ship at Calais. May the Radiant One ever protect you."

He turned to Giselle, "Dear One, you are loved. All will be made known to you as soon as you are safely away."

A thick fog surrounded them. Artemus, Elena and the Compte disappeared from her sight. Giselle opened her mouth to say thank you, but a cloth reeking of some potent substance enveloped her face and she fell into oblivion.

HEART POUNDING, CASSIE'S eyes shot open, the faces of the three people still clear in her mind's eye. She knew beyond a doubt that she had just experienced a past life as a young French woman named Giselle. She also knew it was no accident she had been drawn to pick up her mother's copy of *Green Darkness*. She was being guided by the unseen worlds of Dream Walking that her mother had introduced to her. Cassie glanced at the clock: 2:00 AM. Further confirmation. Her mother called it "the hour of contact" when the astral plane was clearest and messages from one's guides and teachers could be imprinted into the dream world. Her mother had always made extra time to listen to her dreams from the week before and helped her differentiate between garbage and guidance.

Cassie grabbed her journal from the nightstand and began to record the dream in as much detail as she could remember. She took a purple Post-it note and wrote in big letters, "Who were Compte St. Germain and Hermes Trismegistus?" and slapped it onto the inside cover of the journal. Another research project for tomorrow. With that she snuggled up with Gabriel and slipped back into a restless sleep.

SHE AROSE EXTRA EARLY the next morning eager to begin her research. She texted Paxton and her aunt that she would be taking an Uber to school since she was leaving ahead of schedule. She gulped down a cold Frappuccino and bounded out the front door to wait for the car.

She loved doing research in the quiet of the campus library, which was open round-the-clock. The cool darkness and the smell of the old, leather-bound books, the paper and ink of the new ones, and even the low hum of the computers ignited her creativity like nothing else. She opened her laptop to connect to the college's intranet and began to search for books and papers on the Compte de St. Germain. She pulled up the file she had begun the day before to start transcribing her notes from Blavatsky.

She was in a whole new world. Link upon link began to populate her screen about the Ageless Wisdom Teachings all the way back to earliest Egypt. There were even links to ancient aliens visiting during the time of Atlantis. These made her fingers stop mid-stroke as she stared at the face of a supposed visitor from distant star systems. Her heart began to beat faster. She clicked...clicked...and clicked again until the alarm went off on her wrist.

Time to get to class.

She was tempted to skip this morning, but sighed when she remembered the reason for summer school was to get some of the basic required courses out of the way so that she could jump right into her computer science major. She hustled out of the main entrance of the library. To her delight, she saw Paxton grinning at her. He was holding a paper cup of coffee and a pastry bag from the local bakery just up the street from the campus.

"Paxton! Oh my god – my hero!"

He handed her the coffee, took her backpack, and then opened the bag so she could reach in and explore it. "Your favorite, my lady. An almond bear claw."

She pulled back her hand as if the bag contained a copperhead. "What about beach season?" she asked.

"I won't tell if you don't," he said.

She took a gulp of the coffee and a bite from the flaky pastry. "You are the best boyfriend ever!"

"Yeah," he said. "I know". They hurried along the walkway. "What is the big project that got you out so early this morning?"

"I was reading one of my Mom's gothic novels, and it opened up an ah ha moment about a couple of topics: the Ageless Wisdom and Theosophy. Then I had one of my dreams. Turns out it was about a real person – the Compte de St. Germain. I wanted to do some research on him and the two topics. I needed to know more."

Paxton was uncharacteristically quiet.

"What?' she asked.

He did not meet her eyes. "That sounds really out there. You said you had a dream about some dude who turned out to be a real person. This guy, he wasn't in the novel?"

She shook her head. "No, but the topic of past lives and Theosophy were. I started researching them a few days ago. But there was no mention of the Compte guy. I've been looking into someone named Blavatsky, the founder of the Theosophical movement. Everything aligns with what Mom told me – to look beyond organized religion to the deeper meanings that connect all spiritual practices. She believed there is a bigger understanding of what we call god. She always said, "God is too big to fit into one religion."

"Sounds pretty interesting," he said, "especially when it comes to that dream. What do you think it all means?"

"I really don't know, to be honest. But I sense it has something to do with Mommy and her disappearance. It's just a feeling, but you know I follow my gut, my intuition, and it never has let me down."

"Well, you are a bull terrier when it comes to researching something that snags your interest."

"Are you calling me a dog?"

"Woof, woof," he said, and planted a quick kiss on her cheek. Dodging her playful jab, he tossed a casual, "See you at the Mixer!" over his shoulder and made his exit.

What she didn't see was the tension etching lines on his forehead as he left.

What's going on here? What am I missing? Why is she dreaming about such deep, esoteric stuff? I need to check with my teacher ASAP.

He turned the corner of the Administration Building and felt a sharp sting in the back of his neck. Through gradually dimming eyes, he saw two boys wearing baseball caps with his fraternity insignia on either side.

One of them peered into his face. "Yo dude, time to go."

Then nothing.

Chapter 9: Sisterhoods

Cassie's eyes darted around the cafeteria. It was packed with chattering groups of girls scattered like clusters of exotic birds. The room echoed with unintelligible chirps and squawks. To her left was a group of patrician-looking girls clad in uber-sophisticated, soft pastel dresses with the appropriate family status jewels of pearls and diamonds wrapped around swan-like necks and "Oh, you did not" wrists.

She, on the other hand, was wearing her favorite Boho ensemble in brightly colored florals with big puff sleeves and a high-low hemline. Her feet sparkled with her favorite heels featuring a smattering of rhinestones. Layers of semi-precious beads encircled her neck, complemented by an amethyst pendant—a cherished gift from her mother. An array of bangles jingled on her left wrist, and her long tresses were held back with a Chanel headband, her only bow to tradition.

She scanned the room for Glenda and saw the Alpha Omega banner in the middle of the cafeteria. A gaggle of partiers milled around, laughing, and drinking out of turquoise plastic cups.

I'll head over in a minute, she thought. She looked for Paxton and his frat brothers. Where the heck is he? It's not like him to be late, let alone a no show. She checked her texts for the umpteenth time.

A magnolia-infused accent floated in from her side. "Oh hey." A vivacious raven-haired girl stood to her right. "Love, love, *love* your outfit! So artsy. Neiman's?" She looked Cassie up and down.

Cassie backed up a step. "No, actually," she said, "mostly from little boutiques in No Da."

"Oooo, even betta!" Ms. Congeniality said. "I wish my mum would let me shop down there. I hear it's really outstanding. Kinda like Soho in New York City. She loves to wander the art galleries when she's in The Big Apple."

Unsure how to answer, Cassie smiled, her self-consciousness growing by the minute. Something wasn't right.

An upper classman, radiating confidence, extended her hand. She stood tall and slender at 5'7", with artfully curled black locks cascading to her shoulders.

"Aren't you Cassandra Oberon?" she asked. "I have been so looking forward to meeting you. We can certainly use a Sister with your impressive creds."

Ya, lots of money, but not much on glamour, Cassie thought, reading between the lines. Cassie shook the proffered palm.

"Y...yes...most...ah...everyone calls me Cassie."

Cassie felt butterflies in her stomach. She decided to put it off to nerves and her own innate sense of insecurity when it came to being around the perfect model of upper- class sophistication and pushed the feeling in her solar plexus aside.

Adrianna assessed Cassie's outfit. "Adorbs," she said. "Literally adorbs. Cassie it is then! It looks like you can teach us a thing or two about fashion! I just don't know if I could even *begin* to put such a creative ensemble like that together."

Adorbs? What century is this girl from?

She slipped her arm through Cassie's and guided her into the throng of smiling Lambda Chi sorority sisters and eager Rush candidates.

Cassie's head was swimming. Girls she'd never seen began telling her how much she would "totally fit in" and how valuable being a member of their sorority would be as they kept shoving punch into her hands.

ISLA OBSERVED THE DELIGHTFUL charade through the Spirit Screen cleverly disguised as a mirror on the cafeteria wall. Her devotees were doing well. Cassandra appeared swayed by all the attention. The drugs in the "punch" were doing their job.

GLENDA WATCHED THE unfolding farce in consternation as she observed the Dark Sisters make their bold move. She discreetly clutched the small glass vial of antidote she always kept on hand. Silently channeling green healing energy into the potion, she affirmed right action. A reassuring warmth spread through her palm, confirming the potion's readiness.

She made her way to the jumble around Cassie.

"Cassie is that *you!*" The pitch of her voice made her wince a little. She hoped she had not oversold. "I just knew you would be here. Isn't this a super mixer?"

Glenda threw her arms around Cassie and steered her away from the pasted-on smiles and faux camaraderie. Grabbing two glasses of sweet tea from the Alpha Omega table, Glenda surreptitiously dumped the entire contents of the vial into one and handed it to Cassie.

"Here you go," Glenda said. "Our House Mother made this. Drink up!" She faced the rest of the gathered acolytes. "Cassie, meet my sisters from Alpha Omega. They've been excited to meet you since I told them about your legacy."

She shot a quick glance at the Lambda Chi's and barely held back a smirk. They were glaring at her – most likely plotting a revenge move. Not to worry, she thought. There's no way they could know who we are.

Cassie's mind started to clear almost immediately as she sipped the tea down. "Have you seen Paxton?" she asked.

Glenda's internal warning system kicked in. She pushed her energy field beyond the cafeteria but couldn't detect him anywhere. She would need to call in more power to reach out over campus but didn't dare now for fear of alerting The Coven.

"Oh, I'm sure he'll be along," she said. "There's a lot going on all over campus. He might have been stopped by one of his upperclassmen and given some tasks to complete for the pledges. That's a common tactic of fraternities. They want first dibs on the up-and-coming sorority pledges."

Cassie looked skeptical, but the band began to play and there was a mad rush to the dance floor. Couples paired up and threw themselves into a series of gyrations a novice could easily mistake for a seizure.

With a sense of accomplishment, Glenda surveyed the scene before her. Things seemed on target and on schedule. The weight of overseeing such a crucial task had always cast a shadow of doubt over her abilities. Yet, the memory of Master Elena's gaze from their last encounter filled her with an urgency. She needed to relay the developments. Now.

Chapter 10: No Doubt

When Natesh Nandwani strode into the cafeteria, he was pleased to see that the Clan Vamps he had planted in Paxton's fraternity were keeping an eye on Cassandra. One had even approached her and was doing his best to pull her away from one of the protective sisters. Natesh looked at the embroidered logos on their class sweaters, "Alpha Omega" and inwardly shrugged.

Not Isla's group then.

He sauntered over just in time to hear Cassandra say, "Have you seen Paxton? He was supposed to meet me here before the mixer, and I haven't seen him anywhere."

"I am afraid I'm at fault for that. You must be his girlfriend – Cassie? I am Natesh Nandwani, an alum from our New York headquarters."

Natesh insinuated himself into the group. He was about to reach for Cassandra's hand when his nostrils flared, and he stumbled back a step. His cellular memory recognized her on a different level – or did it? He shook it off and refocused on the task at hand. He released his most dazzling smile.

"I assigned Paxton and three other brothers to run an errand that took them to Banner Elk. They should have been back by now. I wouldn't worry – I'm sure he will send you a text as soon as they are back into an area that has cell phone service." His voice was buttery.

"Oh," Cassie said, "thank you so much, Mr. Nandwani. I was getting worried."

Natesh steered Cassie away from the agitated brunette and led her toward Isla's group again. He was still feeling a bit off-center. He kept trying and failing to ascertain what was bothering him about the girl.

"Please, call me Natesh," he replied with his upper-crust British accent, maintaining his disarming grin.

Cassie looked into his intense, dark, almost black eyes. His raven-black hair, framing a chiseled face, gleamed with aromatic pomade. He was easily the most beautiful man she had seen this side of a movie screen.

"Su...sure" was all she managed.

When she shook his hand, something like an electric shock zipped up her arm. His gaze sliced into her as if he was reaching for her soul with his eyes. She felt a little paralyzed... until Adrianna sauntered up and looped her arm through Cassie's. She hit Natesh with an ingratiating grin and a drawl, "Oh hey, so nice to see you, Mr. Nandwani. Haven't laid eyes on you since last year's celebrations in the Hamptons!"

Natesh narrowed his eyes in displeasure at the interruption. Cassie continued to gape with unconcealed admiration at his remarkable visage almost as though she were hypnotized, which she was. At Adrianna's touch, however, the thrall was broken. Cassie took a few moments before she recognized Adrianna.

"H...hi there," she said. "Mr. Nandwani was just telling me that he sent my boyfriend Paxton on a frat errand to the mountains. I was hoping to introduce him to you all."

"Oh, no worries," Adrianna said. "There will be plenty of time to get to know him—"

Natesh interrupted. "Yes, there will be plenty of time for all of us to get to know them both. I'm sure your alumna representative *Morgan* will arrange it – and more. She always takes such a personal interest in all the important relationships of your ... sisters."

Adrianna paled and took a confused step back. Was she unintentionally interfering with a plan Morgandrian had approved, or was she holding the line? She attempted to communicate with Morgandrian through the telepathic bond they shared, but her message was blocked by what felt like a mental wall. She was certain Natesh was behind the obstruction.

Then she heard a voice she knew all too well.

"Well, if it isn't my old friend Mr. Nandwani," Morgan said.

She looked like a queen in a tailored red silk dress. It clung to her curvaceous form like body paint. Her voice dripped with honey. She extended her hand to Natesh with a flirtatious smile. "It's so very nice to see you; it's been *too* long!"

Natesh hid a smirk and executed an exaggerated bow while he raised her hand to his lips. "Why Miss Morgan, you look good enough to eat."

He turned her palm up and pantomimed a little nibble.

Bastard! Her snarling retort blasted into his mind. It was all she could do to refrain from slapping his chiseled countenance.

He smiled deferentially and lifted his lips from her hand. "Always ravishing," he said aloud. "Red is definitely your color." Then, telepathically, he crooned, *And that glamour! My dear, you should definitely use that dark-haired siren look more often!*

"Always the gallant, Natesh," she said. She hoped the youngsters who were gaping from the circle around them were unaware of her contempt. "Would you care to join me at the refreshment table?"

She wanted to grab him by the scruff of his starched collar and drag him outside for a thrashing, but she resisted the temptation.

A reckoning will come, she thought.

They sauntered away together. Morgandrian discharged another glamour to hide the animosity vibrating between them like waves of heat. She hissed through her smile. "Where the *hell* have you been? The situation is way off schedule, and now I see that Master Elena's merry band of acolytes is here. Since we have both shown up, I'm sure one of them has alerted her. This is exactly why I had asked you to intervene months ago!"

"Now, what would be the fun in that?' he asked. "I am in need of a good old-fashioned Immortal smack down."

Morgandrian's hands curled into fists, even as she continued to smile up at him with a flirtatious flutter of her lashes. He made her blood boil, and not just in anger. However, she knew she had to keep her centuries-old attraction to him at bay. Their very existence was at stake. The timeline was starting to unravel, and their continued future hinged on the actions of a single human adolescent across the room. This young woman had no idea who she was or where she was headed, but as she approached her eighteenth year of life, she would cross the threshold into her destiny.

Chapter 11: Let the Games Begin

Elena sat back in her chair, closed her eyes, and sighed. She remembered the first time Rebekah had come to her in NYC a young woman grappling with her burgeoning abilities.

In those days, before channeling became "hip" and the term "New Age" had reached common usage status, Elena had led weekly meetings at Steinway Hall on West 57th Street a stone's throw from Carnegie Hall. The iconic structure, pulsating with artists rehearsing their crafts, infused their meetings with an eclectic zeal, lifting not just their spirits but also the aura of the locale. Creatives, after all, had a knack for elevating energy.

Outside a spacious room on the second floor, Elena welcomed both devoted attendees and fresh faces. On the night Rebekah St. Claire stepped in, Elena felt a stir in her gut, a premonition of Rebekah's significance. Astrological portents had hinted that Elena would soon mentor someone special, a conduit for one of the prophesied seven Avatars, ushering in the dawning Aquarian Age.

Elena, a Keeper of Wisdom, had spent millennia working alongside Earth's Hierarchy as humanity stumbled and soared through its cosmic adolescence. With an eye fixed on the celestial clock, she had long awaited the dawning Age of Aquarius.

Meanwhile, Yeshua ben Joseph—the Piscean Avatar—was gradually stepping back from his earthly mission. His task had been to channel the Radiant One's message of unconditional love, a message that had found root in receptive hearts. Now, it seemed, his work was nearing completion.

Elena was among the original twelve Celestials who had journeyed from the star system of Sirius, entrusted with the Wisdom Teachings of the Radiant One. Once on Earth, they established temples, enclaves of higher learning, where humans could be taught by Elena's group of acolytes. Through their instruction, humans began to grasp the complex, interdependent relationship they had with Gaia. They learned that as they evolved, so did the planet, and vice versa. In those early epochs, humanity was like a sponge, absorbing the teachings about the Great Sun God—known to the Celestials as the Radiant One—with an eagerness that suggested a bright future.

That night, Elena stood outside the meeting room and waited. Rebekah walked up accompanied by a long-time devotee, Ilya.

"She is a potential student," Ilya said.

Rebekah's dark brown eyes shimmered beneath a cascading mane of chestnut hair, styled with the voluminous flair of the '70's. Her makeup was generously applied, and when she spoke, the drawl in her voice echoed tales of the South.

Holding out her hand, she said, "Thank you sooo much for allowing me to come tonight. I have been looking for a place where I could learn more about ancient wisdom and astrology stuff."

Elena smiled and waved her in. She did not want to fawn over someone who obviously wanted special treatment. Elena would soon disabuse her of any such notion.

The Tuesday night gatherings were intended to give people an introduction to the Wisdom Teachings and karmic astrology. The vibratory frequencies of New York City and London were the same as those of the drowned Atlantis. Elena had devised her meetings to attract the reincarnated forms of her former students of the lost city. She had no trouble identifying acolytes. They were invited to participate in ongoing classes and Sunday meditation services. A chosen few were given weekly one-on-one instruction. Rebekah would be important, but she needed to get beyond the tinsel of New York and the thrill of being a rising star in the fashion business.

ELENA SNAPPED BACK to the present when a signal came through the Spirit Screen from the Sirian Mothership. Waving her right hand over the surface of the screen, she saw a familiar visage.

"You were somewhere else," The Celestial said.

"Greetings in the name of The Radiant One, my brother Manu," Elena said. She placed her palms together.

"Adonai, my sister Elena." Manu responded.

"Yes," she said, "I was lost in thought. I was remembering when I first met Rebekah St. Claire. Incredible, isn't it? Cassandra, the Seventh Avatar, is her daughter. One of our oracles picked up on an energy signal a few weeks ago from Charlotte, North Carolina. But we have not been able to discover her mother's location. I take it you have spoken with The Master of the White Circle?"

"Yes, and scanned through the planet's etheric level for any energy readings that might be Rebekah, but to no avail. I have instructed my team to continue to look for her as best they can, but I am focusing on the daughter. Now that we know the girl is in Charlotte, we need to pick up the pace. It is nearing the Summer Equinox and the energy from the Central Sun causes time to speed up by a few minutes." He paused.

"What else are you picking up?" asked Elena.

Manu hesitated. "I'm not sure. But there is something about the energy signature of this girl that feels deeply familiar...". He shook himself and sighed, "wishful thinking...we need to focus on securing The Seven."

"Indeed," Elena said. "I am concerned. The whole timetable is off. Toxic emotions on the planet may cause more and more cataclysms. Every negative thought is like the sting of a red ant. I would not blame Gaia a bit if she tried to shake those insects off her precious body. I am not sure we can calm her enough to prevent thousands of lives being lost. The Dark Brotherhood is alive, well, and active."

Manu grunted. "I am afraid the entire world will be suffering with PTSD soon, especially considering the Earth's meteorological changes. I'm sure the Dark Forces are rubbing their hands in glee with the chaos and divisiveness across the globe. It is so like the time in Palestine when the Piscean Avatar Yeshua ushered in the last New Age. I cannot believe intelligent human beings are falling for so many lies."

"But Manu," Elena spoke, her eyes focused intently, "this overlapping of Ages is meant to be a crucible, a proving ground. Discernment is a prerequisite on the path of initiation that each Age brings. You can't hand the powers of White Magic to an unthinking mob."

She paused, choosing her words carefully. "Think of it as a refining process. The ancient teachings tell us to separate the wheat from the chaff. Emotionally driven individuals may step up, but their abilities won't fully awaken. We need rational minds, people who recognize truth when it confronts them."

Leaning forward, she added, "We need those capable of higher intuition, who won't be ensnared by lower psychism's illusions. Could you imagine the chaos, even planetary destruction, if individuals, unable to master their baser emotions, could manifest their darkest desires just by thinking about them? The cosmic fallout would be unthinkable."

Manu huffed. "Yes, I know, my dear," he said. His voice had an edge. "I was present for the last two ages shifts, remember? But this one is just so nonsensical. The lies are so blatant, and the people are being led by their noses—"

"No," Elena said. "Pardon the interruption but they are being led by fear. They are a small group compared to those who *have* awakened, but they are so very loud. They control much of the media, so it *seems* like there are many. However, there might also be some subliminal manipulation being used on the conspiracy networks and websites, things geared toward those prone toward violence. I see the same message a lot: 'I am the only one who is right; those who are wrong need to be annihilated.' The premise is rampant. Now that we have found the last of The Seven, we can train them all as a group so they can combine their abilities in tipping the scales toward the Light. I suspect, knowing her Soul Mission, Cassandra might be the most powerful of them all."

"We need to link the awakened humans and train the next generation of leaders as well," Manu said. "They will usher in the new Golden Age." He paused. "The three evolutions that are a part of The Plan – Human, Celestial, and Devic – are all on track. Once the Humans are awakened and trained, they will be able to move in sync with the Earth in taking its sacred initiation and rise to the mental plane of the Fifth Dimension."

Suddenly he froze. "Ayesha!" he said.

Their eyes met through the Spirit Screen. They had worked together for countless years. They needed no more words...they understood.

Manu nodded...and his image vanished.

Chapter 12: Mischief and Mayhem

Paxton tried to open his eyes. He groaned. He felt as if he had fallen down a thousand stairs. He tried to sit. He could not move. He shot a glance to his right. Seven boys clad in all black gathered around a table with tall glasses containing a red liquid. One of them heard his groan. His chair scraped against the stone floor, and he wandered over with a smug look Paxton wanted to smash from his face.

"Looks like the college boy is coming back around." Samuel said. "How are you doing, dude? Head a little cranky?"

Paxton tried to speak, but his throat was raw and sore. He glared and imagined the plethora of pain he wanted to inflict. He flinched when a hand touched his brow.

"Gently, my boy." The voice was raspy but carried a perfect British accent. "Take a few breaths and don't panic. We're not here to hurt you; just need to delay you a bit. Drink this. It will help with the pain and let you sleep."

The others in the room had rocketed to attention. The hand moved and the dark clad figure rose from the side of the cot. He turned to address the others rooted in place.

His voice hissed. "I told you not to hurt him, you imbeciles. Totally unacceptable!"

Natesh flicked his right hand toward the closest minion. A blast of energy threw the boy to the floor. "Just be grateful that I don't stake you on the spot. Now get back to your posts. This is your final chance to prove that you don't belong in the ground!"

Natesh motioned to Samuel to walk with him out into the tunnel and away from the others. "You are just now finding out that Paxton has been glamouring himself?" Natesh asked. "That means he is either a member of the Seely Court or the White Circle. Either way, he has some power."

Samuel began to speak, but Natesh raised his hand to stop him. "No excuses. We can use this to our advantage. Don't harm him! Let him escape on my signal. Then assign someone you trust to tail him. We need to track his every move. And I want to know his allies." Natesh shoved Samuel against the wall, poking a finger into the young man's chest. "We cannot afford any mistakes!"

Natesh swept out of the cave, shimmered through a portal, and reappeared at the Queens University mixer.

"I need to address the Cassandra situation," he thought. He felt a deep connection with the girl, as if they had shared a past life together. "I'm starting to grasp Morgandrian's perspective more," he reflected. "It's as if I have to handle everything on my own, and I'm growing sick of it. This generation is just so *unbelievably* fucking lazy!" He straightened his spine, rolled his shoulders, and shifted his focus into battle mode.

Time to cause a little mayhem.

Chapter 13: Callin' in the Big Guns

Artemus whirled around when he heard the alarm from his Spirit Screen. Elena's pale face appeared. Artemus imagined he could taste his own heart.

"We have a situation in Charlotte," she said. "Morgandrian and Natesh have upped the game and gotten personally involved. Glenda just sent a message via rune stone; I'm preparing to port there. Paxton is missing. Care to join me?"

"Well, Natesh is the most likely suspect. I am on my way." He thought for a moment. "I think we need to bring along one of the Fae -Siobhan from the Sinclair Clan? She has ties to the St. Claire bloodline. She can use the portal in uptown Charlotte – not too far from the campus."

Elena nodded. "I will reach out to her while you prepare. I know it's been a while since you have been in this dimension and will want to gear up."

"Yes," Artemus said. "I'll meet you outside of the cafeteria. No more need for subterfuge. And please tell Glenda to pull out all stops. I am sure Natesh and Morgandrian did not show up because they didn't have anything better to do. They are obviously on to the fact that Cassandra is the missing Avatar. Glenda needs to keep her protected until we get there." He hurried along the gallery to the armory in the training rooms of the Citadel.

SIOBHAN'S INNER ALARMS had been going off all afternoon. Something was afoot in the human realm. She continued her ride through the copse of sessile oaks around her little compound, but her intuition turned her bay mare back toward her small stone cottage. She walked through the red oak door and felt the vibration of the Spirit Screen from her library.

Master Elena, the head of the Terran-based Mystery Schools, appeared when Siobhan touched the screen.

"Greetings in the name of the Radiant One." Elena said. "We have urgent need of you in Charlotte, North Carolina on the Queens University campus. It concerns the North American Avatar, who is being compromised by the Dark Brotherhood. Artemus is preparing to meet me outside of the cafeteria there, and we are hoping you can join us. Natesh Nandwani's clan is involved, along with Morgandrian's coven. We could use your Earth Magic's defensive abilities."

"Send the coordinates and I will port through as soon as I fetch my tools," Siobhan said. She stopped. "Wait, where is Paxton? He is highly trained in the Earth magics and—"

"Missing, I will fill you in later. Hurry!"

Siobhan flew to her still room and grabbed her satchel full of an array of athames, wands, and potions. She was always prepared; it felt good to swing into action.

She put her long auburn hair into a battle-ready braid, pulled out her portal rune stone, and headed for the front yard. A ginger-haired man galloped up on a large black stallion, his green eyes flashing, his rugged face taut.

"I felt the alarm from the Terran Realm," he said in a soft Scottish accent. "Do ya need me?"

"Nay, Mac" Siobhan said. She appreciated her cousin's offer. Ian MacGregor was more like a brother. "I would rather you keep watch here. Both Master Elena and The Master of the White Circle are already enroute. Make sure you are here as a counterbalance of energy. The three of us should be more than enough to block whatever mischief the Dark Brothers are up to. Remain on high alert. This is about Rebekah's daughter, Cassandra...and Paxton is missing!"

Ian's eye darkened. "Damn it! Well, it looks as if the games have begun. Is Cassandra the missing Avatar then? And does she know it?"

"Unknown," Siobhan said, "but for the moment we need to join forces with our Celestial brothers and get her to the safety of the Institute with Master Elena. However," she turned to him over her shoulder as she strode toward the portal to Charlotte, "be prepared for anything!"

Chapter 14: Where's the Mixer?

The air in the cafeteria courtyard sizzled with electricity as the Triumvirate of Light Masters strode together toward the building, each of them glamoured to appear as a normal mortal to Mundane eyes. Elena took on her housemother persona, her gold-edged sari replaced by a flowing navy skirt paired with a pale blue sweater set. Her white hair was close-cropped in a modern wedge. Siobhan's veneer was one of the university administrators in a crisp linen pantsuit, her auburn hair in a knot at the nape of her neck, which lent some weight to the authority that would help infiltrate the gathering and keep curious Mundane onlookers at bay. Artemus, dressed in a dark blue, looked every bit the business executive.

The only ones who would know who they truly were would be their own acolytes and, of course, the Dark Brotherhood.

Two faces greeted the trio with fury in their eyes. Natesh's jaw tightened; Morgandrian snarled in frustration.

"I *told* you they would be alerted. Well, at least we are all out in the open and can confirm the importance of the girl."

"Indeed," Natesh said through gritted teeth. He began to move forward.

From the doorway, Siobhan stepped forward, every inch the embodiment of authority. She approached the cluster around Cassandra and declared, "I've heard rumors of alcohol here, a clear violation of University rules." While human eyes darted away and bodies retreated to avoid association, the Vamps and Isla's acolytes defiantly remained, unyielding. They knew Siobhan could not do anything to them in the presence of the Mundanes. But the atmosphere grew heavy as earth magic began to ooze through the cafeteria.

Master Elena began subtly drawing sigils into the palms of her hands and throwing them around the room to establish a field of protection. She did not want to have a magical cleanup if this thing got out of hand.

Siobhan continued toward the refreshment table of the Lambda Chi's, gesturing to one of the girls manning the punch bowl, "Please pour me a cup of the punch." She took a sip then slammed the cup down.

"This mixer is officially over!" she said and shooed all the Mundanes and their chaperones out of the cafeteria.

As the humans began to scatter, Elena and Artemus stood in front of Morgandrian and Natesh. Each of them was ready for battle; sparks snapped at Morgandrian's fingers.

Natesh looking at his opponents. "I was wondering when you would finally figure this out. It took you long enough."

Elena's soft voice was barely a whisper. "We don't go charging into situations that are still under the jurisdiction of the Human Kingdom and thus The Hierarchy. We continue to honor the Codex of the Radiant One of non-interference with free will unless we are *asked*!"

Natesh rolled his eyes. "Oh, come now, isn't that exactly what you are doing now? Interfering?"

Artemus took a step forward. "We are merely protecting one of ours, as you well know."

"I don't believe she's made that choice as of yet," Morgandrian said. "She is still at the crossroads."

"Perhaps," Artemus said, "but drugging her into submission won't be allowed nor tolerated."

Siobhan offered a cup of the punch from Morgandrian's table. "Care for a sip?" She smiled sweetly.

Looking around at the room now empty of any human presence, Morgandrian sneered. "I don't answer to any of you, nor your ...rules. ... your Bitchness." She shot a derisive glance at Siobhan. "What the hell are you doing here, out of your fairy tale dimension? Grew tired of concocting potions with your bore of a cousin, Ian?"

Siobhan's pasted-on smile never wavered. "You've never been able to turn him," she said. You were slipping even 500 years ago, and you haven't gotten any better. Really, dear, it's quite a yawn."

A tipping point. The sparks began to fly in earnest.

Shields went up around the periphery of the cafeteria like scales on a dragon. The forcefields of magic interlocked. Mortal eyes could not see the battle.

Artemus fired electro-magnetic blue energy from his fingertips. Natesh staggered, unsheathed his rapier, and used his lightning-fast vampire speed to circle behind his attacker.

Artemus pirouetted and drew two broadswords from the sheaths on his back.

"Do your worst," he said. They began slashing at one another. Natesh had the speed advantage, but Artemus had been fighting for thousands of years on the fields of battle in multiple dimensions. There was no greater swordsman in existence and they both knew it. Keeping his emotions under control, Artemus' eyes gleamed in anticipation. There was nothing he enjoyed more than this dance of steel with a well-matched opponent.

He also knew Natesh could choose to morph into one of his various winged forms and flash away at any time, but Artemus was counting on his foe's pride. Their enmity stretched across the far reaches of time and neither was willing to concede...not until the other was dead.

Artemus touched the end of the silver tipped stake hidden in the breast pocket of his gray wool Armani suit. He would not hesitate to use it tonight.

Natesh jerked his head up. Something was different about Artemus. Natesh realized he was fighting for his life. The Master of the White Circle was fully prepared to end Natesh once and for all.

Master Elena unleashed white light to repel the red lightning emitting from Morgandrian's fingertips. The two streams met with a thunderous clap. The combatants extended their arms, willing their forces toward one another.

Rage welled up in Morgandrian's eyes. They deepened into onyx. "That all you got?"

Elena kept her anger at bay. If she erupted, she knew her rage would make her weaker and susceptible to Morgandrian's energy. Her mouth twitched into a grim smile, and she redoubled her efforts to increase the potency of her stream of white light. Through the power of the Radiant One, she began pushing back on Morgandrian. The upper hand flickered like a faulty fluorescent bulb.

Elena attempted to breach Morgan's mental shield, but it remained unyielding. Shifting strategies, she adopted a confident grin that said, "You're going down." Morgan's momentary blink gave Elena the opening she needed. She transformed her white light energy into ice, rapidly cooling the blazing flames. The fire solidified almost instantly, resembling a volcanic flow that had abruptly halted, and crystallized into an unbreakable igneous stone. Morgandrian let out a shrill cry and recoiled.

Elena continued her assault and fashioned the rock into a cage. Just before she finished, an agonizing pain shot up her spine, an arrow quivering between her shoulder blades. She looked back and saw one of Morgandrian's handmaids who was standing with three others reloading crossbows. One of Elena's acolytes ran to her to dislodge the arrow and send healing green light into the wound. The rest of the Alpha Omega's shot energy bolts toward the crossbow girls and obliterated their bows into splinters. Razor sharp fragments hurtled through the room like predatory mosquitoes. Elena ducked and heard the shards spit past her head. Elena's concentration broken, Morgandrian burst from her prison with a scream of triumph. She directed a blast at Elena's acolytes. Four of them dissipated into a fine red mist.

Artemus nipped Natesh across the arm. Natesh feinted, flipped backwards, and slashed Artemus' left shoulder. Blood spurted onto the floor.

Siobhan shifted her attention to the Vamps. They would become uncontrollable if the blood flow continued, especially if it came from someone as powerful as Artemus. They screamed and snarled in a frustrated frenzy as they clawed to get out of the barrier she had created.

An unwitting and perpetually late Mundane wandered into the room. He looked around in bewilderment. "Hey, where's the mixer?"

Artemus pointed. "How the hell did he get through the warded barriers?"

Siobhan cursed and motioned to Master Elena's acolytes to go to his aid. She was using all her power to hold the force field in place.

The Vamps clawed at the barrier. They bared their elongated canines and slathered. The young man blanched, stammered, and tried to back away. Too late.

One of the older, wilier Vamps escaped. He buried his fangs in the young man's neck. The boy fell unconscious to the floor. Sated, the Vamp rushed to the cage holding his compatriots. Unable to release them, the Vamp inserted himself into Natesh's battle with Artemus.

Without missing a beat, Natesh hissed. "I don't need you. Get the rest of the clan out of here and back to the lair."

The fresh blood was still dripping from the Vamp's chin. It had instilled near-herculean strength – a freshened aggression. The vamp threw himself at Siobhan. Her momentary lapse of concentration reduced the forcefield. As if on a signal, the Vamps transformed into bats and swarmed toward the glass-walled cafeteria. Panes shattered into a million pieces and the winged colony screeched out into the night sky.

Chapter 15: Taken

The warm summer night was full of the clicking of cicadas and the scent of magnolias. Glenda hustled Cassie away from the confrontation in the cafeteria following a telepathic command from Master Elena. Glenda had done her duty. She wanted to make sure Cassie was safe and sound. She had the girl by the hand, but Cassie kept holding back.

"What the hell is going on?" she asked. "Glenda, I don't understand! Who were those people that came into the cafeteria? They looked like something out of *Lord of the Rings.*"

Glenda stared at her. "What did you see?"

Cassie opened her mouth to speak, but the words were stolen by a deafening boom, and the acrid stench of ozone and sulfur filled the air. The ground quivered beneath them. As Glenda began to weave a shield of protection, she caught a shimmer of light, delicate threads of energy dancing from Cassie's fingertips.

A dormant power within Cassie had stirred to life, answering the call of danger. Cassie's gaze fell on her glowing hands, eyes widening first in awe, then shadowed by fear. Her bewilderment was interrupted by a husky voice that sliced through the night.

"Leaving so soon? Why, I haven't had a chance to introduce you to my new friend."

Adrianna stepped out of the shadows followed by a hooded figure; the southern belle persona gone. Everything became very still – the eye of a hurricane – an island of calm in the middle of a whirlwind of destruction. The glow from Cassie's fingers disappeared. Glenda tried to access her own energy to no avail.

Something, or someone, was already beginning to siphon off her powers. *Damn, I let my guard down. I thought the real danger was back in the cafeteria.*

She stepped in front of Cassie. More figures emerged from the shadows. She recognized the stench of rotten meat.

The hooded figure stepped in front of Adrianna. "You can go now. I no longer need your services."

The figure flicked its wrist and Adrianna disappeared into the darkness. A low chuckle emerged from the figure's throat; amusement mixed with disgust.

"Pathetic. What in the world was Morgandrian thinking to put such a sorry specimen of a witch in charge of such an illustrious prize?"

The figure turned its attention to Glenda. Cassie was mute. Her mind was trying to process what she was seeing and hearing. *Witch? Prize? A robed figure in the middle of the campus? Sparks coming out of my hands? Am I losing my mind?*

"And you, Glenda – seriously? Your own demons betray you into the very inadequacy that you fear. You let your fragile ego get in the way of protecting your charge. You should have known better than to let your guard down just because you had called in the troops. Disappointing."

Three robbed figures appeared and began to encircle Glenda. They were joined by hideous black shapes with drooling maws crawling out of fissures in the ground. They formed a stygian barrier and separated her from her charge.

Cassie, unable to do anything else, stood frozen in shock and fear. Her head swiveled from Glenda to the hooded marauders and back.

"Glenda!"

The dark robed figure grabbed Cassie. In one fluid motion, he swept her off her feet, and they rose into the inky sky. Cassie's screams began, sharp and terrified, but were quickly silenced as he pressed a cloth, damp with a potent substance, against her face. Her struggles waned, and the world around her blurred into darkness.

The minions and demons howled with glee as their master released them to do what they would. Attempting to freeze Glenda with fear, the three that had stopped her projected horrific scenes of demons ripping her apart with their drooling claws and fangs. She mentally rolled her eyes at the futile attempt at mind control.

She reached for the magic dagger she always kept strapped to her thigh. When one of the demon's lunged, she gutted it. It crumpled in a pool of black blood. The circle of attackers was no match for her years of warrior training. Plunge, slash, rip...her whirling blade danced with a deadly mind of its own. The stench rose – more unbearable by the moment, but Glenda was operating on muscle memory.

A pulsing surge hit her in the stomach. A demon twice her size thundered toward her. He'd come out of nowhere. Just as suddenly, Adrianna appeared, daggers flashing.

Adrianna chanted in an ancient language Glenda did not know. Black strands emanated from her knives. The demon turned its full attention to her...and his back to Glenda. Adrianna's magic ringed the demon; the spell began to burn its flesh. Its howl rose in a deafening roar.

Glenda sunk her dagger into its neck. Greenish-black blood spurted toward her. It barely missed her eyes. When it splattered on her arm, it blistered.

Poison!

But she didn't stop stabbing at the demon's neck until it sagged and melted into a puddle of steaming green goo. She leapt back to avoid falling into the slime and then slid to her knees.

The pain in Glenda's body was spreading like wildfire. She groaned. Adrianna, panting, faced the trio of remaining demons. She yelled at Glenda.

"Can you get up? I don't know if I can take all of them."

Glenda rose on unsteady feet and pitched herself toward the demon to her right, dagger meeting target as she sliced through its leathery neck. The pain of the spreading poison made her knees buckle yet again. She watched with relief as Adrianna severed both demons' heads with a whirling attack.

Then there was silence. The remaining demonic energy simply vanished, as if summoned back to their master.

Sweating and gasping for air, Adrianna ran to Glenda's side. Her energy turned green: healing. She put two hands to Glenda's chest and attempted to siphon the poison from her blood. When she could pull no more, Adrianna shook her head, "I'm sorry that's all I can do. Hurry inside so your kind can help." Then she flashed out.

Glenda rose shakily to her feet, her entire body covered in revolting substances. She stumbled, panting, up the stairs into the cafeteria. She tried not to retch as she fell into the room. Stomach heaving and her mind whirling in confusion, fear, and humiliation, she prepared to announce the unspeakable news.

The combatants took one look at her and stopped. Glenda's body was mapped with gore and welts.

"Cassandra has been taken!" she cried out.

Master Elena rushed to her. Ignoring the vile and viscous secretions dripping from the girl's body, Elena asked, "Who took her?"

"I...I don't know. They wore a hooded cloak and had enormous iridescent black wings.

Five voices spoke in unison, "Azazel!"

Natesh clenched his jaw. His plans were in shambles. How had he not foreseen this? But he knew it was time to leave. He shifted into black smoke and vanished.

"Damn it!" Artemus watched the Clan Leader disappear. "How the hell did Azazel get involved in this – and one of our sources of information just evaporated."

SIOBHAN BRANDISHED her dagger. "Don't even think about it," she snarled at Morgandrian. "I'm not done with you yet. You have interfered with The Circle's business one time too many."

She whipped out her athame and began to trace sigils in the air. The signs formed an electro-magnetic barrier.

Morgandrian sneered. "Seriously Siobhan, you don't think your tired old sigils will stand up to my magic, do you?"

Siobhan laughed. "I've added a few more things to my bag o' tricks since the last time we met." She took the athame and sliced the palm of her left hand. Drops of blood began to fill the sigils, giving them form.

Morgan's eyes widened. "Blood magic? What the hell, Siobhan? You can't wield that kind of power and not step onto the left-hand path – unless you already have."

"That is how much you know, Morgan," Siobhan said. "This athame has been forged out of metal from the stars. It changes the chemical makeup of blood. It becomes the life force that originally came to this planet from

Sirius. My blood is transformed into something over which you have no power at all. Welcome to twenty-first century White Magic!"

The blood red sigils coalesced into a vortex of violet flame. The High Priestess of the Witches screamed in agony as the Violet Flame of Transmutation began to burn the black magic away from her. She shouted obscenities at Siobhan and flailed away with her hands, attempting to draw her own magic signs – but to no avail.

With one final shriek, she exploded in a flash of light.

"You killed her?" Glenda asked.

"Oh no," Siobhan said. "I just transported her to a dimension where she can be held for a bit. She will be there long enough for the Master of the White Circle to do a little exploratory session with her."

Glenda looked around. "Where's Artemus?"

Everyone shrugged.

Siobhan ran toward Glenda "What else happened?" She touched her face. "What is the poison I can still feel in your bloodstream? What is the source of the filth that covers you?"

Glenda filled her in on what had happened, including the perplexing actions of Adrianna. Master Elena shook her head. "I shudder to think what would have happened if you had not stopped those demons. And I don't quite know what to make of Adrianna's behavior but let us give thanks to the Radiant One that she had some sort of change of heart to come to your aid in the end."

Glenda nodded, but in her heart, she felt she knew why the witch had come back for her.

"Come now," Elena said, "let's clean up this mess. We need to ensure this young man's memory is wiped before we revive him. We cannot let any Mundanes get suspicious about what went on here tonight. I know there are numerous protection wards around Charlotte. The Masonic Lodge will know we were here, and it may draw unwanted attention to this debacle."

"Why don't we elicit the Mason's help?" Siobhan asked. "They know as much as we do about the Shift. After all, Charlotte was built in accordance with Masonic principles. Maybe now is the time to bring them into the fold."

Elena eyed her for a moment. "You may be right, Siobhan. Do you know who to contact?"

"I do indeed," Siobhan replied. I will port to him at once."

Chapter 16: Blade Brothers

Paxton clawed his way to consciousness, but feigned sleep while he assessed his situation.

What the hell is going on?

He had just left Cassie when someone jumped him from behind. *Should have been more alert. Stupid, stupid, stupid.*

He should have known one of the Dark Factions would make a move sooner rather than later. He had grown complacent, comfortable with the assumption he had kept his word to Cassie's mother to protect her. Cassie leaned on him – hard – when Taryn had gone missing. His teacher had warned him not to allow emotion into the relationship – it would cloud his intuition and pull down his vibrational frequencies. Cassie's continual proximity had turned into something far more than he intended. Now he knew full well that his feelings for her could jeopardize his taking the next initiation.

He needed to get his wits about him. He reached out into his weakened auric field and tried to figure out his captors' position. He focused his thoughts in the middle of his forehead, the third eye chakra, and visualized breathing in fresh, vibrant, white light energy so it would build, balance and heal. The drugs in his system had already begun to dissipate; his abilities began to awaken; his mind grew ever clearer.

One of the Vamps closest to him felt the shift in the energy of the room and started to his feet.

"Shi—"

He never finished. Paxton, in full power, threw off the glamour of being a "mere" mortal and shot a burst of energy at his captor, who disintegrated into a fine, red mist.

The room erupted in movement. The other three in the room leapt to their feet, pulled daggers, and rushed him. The reek of their blood-soaked breath made him gag, but he persevered. His Krav Maga training kicked in and he lunged toward them. Even their super Vamp speed was no match to his angelic velocity.

"I would be running in the other direction if I were you!" Paxton thrust out his hands, palms open, and summoned his innate firepower. Streams of flames spit at his adversaries. Before Paxton could blink, they were a pile of ashes.

Samuel watched from the entrance to the tunnel. His phone vibrated: a message from Natesh.

Perfect timing!

But before he had a chance to respond, a fireball hit him square in the chest. He disintegrated into ash.

Paxton shook his hands as though to extinguish the fiery energy still swirling around the fallen vampires. He took a moment to center himself, then reached out with his mind to search for others nearby.

Finding no one, he looked at the place of his captivity. He was in a chamber carved from rock. Torches flickered on the sides of the cave. He knew he had been taken by the minions of the Clan Leader Natesh Nandwani, but the simplicity of the surroundings did not fit the opulence he knew Nandwani preferred. This had to be one of the hundreds of base camps Natesh's minor lieutenants used.

Insulting, he thought.

Then he remembered the dolts probably had not seen through his glamour and had no idea who he really was.

He moved to the far side of the room to the only opening he could see. On his way though, his nose twitched with the distinct odor of blood and rotten flesh. He saw piles of mutilated humans littering the floor.

He vomited.

He spit once...twice...then made his way through the carnage. Heads thrown back in silent screams, large fang marks gouged into throats, chests smashed open to reveal heartless rib cages. These poor souls had been tortured in unimaginable ways and their bodies drained of blood.

He drew blessing sigils in the dirt floor, said a brief prayer, then vowed to return to burn the bodies. The searchlight of his mind's eye swept for the nearest route to the outer world. He had to get out into the open to use his portal rune stone to return to Charlotte.

Paxton stopped...there! To the right he could "see" an opening. He rewrapped his glamour to appear human. No need to give away his true identity to any chance encounters.

He got to the entrance without mishap. At the opening, he swore. There were wards all around the perimeter. He heard dogs growling. He sighed in resignation and dropped the glamour to completely access his powers.

They were on him in a flash, fangs bared, snarling maws, drooling foul-smelling green slime.

Poison.

One bite and he would be paralyzed, or worse...breakfast. He raised an energy shield and summoned his battle sword out of the Etheric Plane. The first hound fell quickly – then the second. By the time the third one had stilled, the remainder of the pack was wary. The canines circled him like sharks waiting for a sailor to dip a foot in the water.

Eight more. He switched to offense. He assumed battle stance, knees bent, sword in his right hand. He shifted his energy to manifest bursts of fire from his left hand. Three of the dogs were incinerated.

Five left. No, more were charging from the forest. *Shit*.

Not fully recovered from the drugs, his breathing was shallow. He could feel the shield buckling. A claw ripped through the barrier to his left. Four of the beasts leapt through.

I do not want to die this way.

"Need some help brother?"

Paxton grinned when he saw a magnificent white-winged being hit the ground behind the hounds. Shock waves shook the ground.

"About time, Brother," Paxton said.

Khamuel whirled his sword. Decapitated heads flew through the air.

"These are the very Hounds of Hell," he said. "I can't wait to hear how you managed to attract them." Paxton dropped his sword. He extended his palms. A wall of flame erupted around them. The smell of burning fur and flesh accompanied the howls of agony as the hounds turned to cinders. Then, it was over.

Khamuel turned to Paxton. Both were covered in indescribable viscera. Paxton bent, hands on his knees. When he stood, he locked forearms with his rescuer.

"May the Radiant One be ever with you, brother," Khamuel said.

"And also with you," Paxton responded. "You certainly took your time."

"Pretty hard to track down my Blade Brother when he is unconscious, glamoured, *and* in a warded cave." Khamuel cocked his head. "And where are your wings?"

"Drugs," Paxton said. "I can't summon them at the moment."

"Well, do you have your portal stone?" Khamuel asked. "I don't think there are any ley lines close."

"Gimme a second," Paxton murmured. He dug into his pocket. "Anything happen since I've been gone?"

Khamuel rubbed his neck, his ebony face filled with chagrin. "More than a little," he said. "Cassie was miffed when you were a no-show. She told one of Master Elena's acolytes, Glenda. Moments later, poof – Natesh Nandwani himself appears in the guise of one of your frat's alumni liaisons and tries to cover your abduction. Says he sent you off to the mountains on some second-year frat errand. That was three days ago."

"Three days? What the hell!" Paxton processed for a moment. "Wait... you said Nandwani showed up. Why would the most powerful vampire lord in the Western Hemisphere concern himself with a college mixer? And Cassie's friend Glenda knows Master Elena? Something doesn't track here. What the crap is going on?"

"Well, that's not mine to know at this point," Khamuel said. "I got a message about your being taken and was instructed to hightail it to the mountains to find you. I couldn't pick up anything for a long time – I was getting a little panicked. Then, wham, I got blasted. You pack a powerful punch on the etheric when you get going, my brother."

Khamuel filled him in on everything, including the battle at Queens. He left off the part about Cassie being taken.

Paxton was still trying to wrap his head around how Glenda, the girl who had so recently befriended Cassie, had brought in three masters of the White Circle. There were a lot of missing puzzle pieces.

"Okay," he said, "I must still be feeling the effects of the drugs, because I don't understand how five of the most powerful beings on this planet just had a battle in the middle of a university campus in Charlotte, NC."

His Blade Brother blinked. "Again, don't know. Hopefully, all will be filled in when we meet with Master Artemus. I have been instructed to take you to the Citadel."

Paxton's eyes widened, "The Citadel!"

He looked back at the cave entrance, "Before we leave, I have two things I need to do. First, there are bodies of innocents in the cave. They need to be sent to the Light in a proper fashion. Second, would you like to join me in blowing this place to smithereens and back to hell, so there's one less lair for the Vamps to gather?"

"After you," Khamuel said.

Chapter 17: The New Jerusalem

The nondescript house stood in the Cotswold section of Charlotte, an older part of town but safe and clean. Nothing on the outside indicated it was the bastion of the Masonic Order. The door was opened by an equally unremarkable middle-aged gentleman dressed in a three-piece suit with a watch fob draped across his spreading middle. With slicked back, thinning hair, he looked every bit the bank president that he was.

"Siobhan Sinclair!" he said. "It's been a long time since one of The White Circle visited here. Please come in."

The Grand Master of the Lodge stepped aside to wave Siobhan into the great room just off the entry. Siobhan's heart leapt when she saw the handsome Greek standing in the room. He offered a cup of steaming tea.

"Your favorite, my dear, Scottish breakfast with a dash of milk – and another dash of something for fortitude!" She took a long sip. Cloves, cinnamon, and the welcomed nutty sweetness of Amaretto. *Perfection!*

"Mateus Nephus you never fail to amaze!" she said. "What in the name of the Radiant One are you doing here."

He hadn't changed a lick in all these centuries. *He certainly epitomizes his name, Gift from God indeed.* His laughing brown eyes still radiated the same warmth she'd seen when she met him during her first trip to the Athens branch of the Institute almost 500 years ago.

"Under the heading of "no coincidences" I felt a strong urge to come here last week," he said. "A lot of earth magic activity going on here lately. When I heard about the Sirian Oracle's message, I knew I would be needed here. And now – here *you* are!"

Siobhan narrowed her eyes. She trusted him – sort of. He always seemed to be in the right place at the wrong time. She wondered if misdirection was the order of the day, but she realized her own emotional attachment to him might compromise her intuition. Her weight shifted from one foot to the other and she hoped no one noticed her discomfort.

"I always know something significant is afoot when Mateus contacts me," the Grand Master said. "Just a few hours ago, to borrow from a famous movie, there was 'a disturbance in the Force.' He grinned, very proud of himself for the popular reference even though it was more than forty years old.

"An understatement," Siobhan said. "After I fill you in, perhaps you will help us ferret out exactly why Charlotte is being used as a focal point."

She went through everything. The Grand Master and Mateus exchanged a knowing look. Mateus deferred to the Grand Master. "Perhaps it is time to share with Siobhan the prophecy about Charlotte?"

"There's a prophecy about Charlotte?" She almost spewed her gulp of tea all over his impeccably starched linen shirt.

"Oh yes," Mateus said, "the Founding Fathers of both our nation and of Charlotte were Masons of the highest degree. I'm sure you have heard about the secret destiny of America. What most people don't know is that Charlotte was built on a ley line that intersects at the corner of Trade and Tryon uptown. The line is directly connected to the Capitol building of the United States in Washington, D.C. It all relates to the Ageless Wisdom teachings that Master Elena has guarded since the sinking of Atlantis *and* to this time of The Shift."

Siobhan was well schooled in the Codex prophecies. Artemus had received them millennia ago. Now it seemed a great many rivers of knowledge were beginning to converge into an expansive sea of truth.

He motioned to the twin couches across the room in front of a wide screen TV, which also doubled as the Lodge's Spirit Screen.

"The Capitol Building was inaugurated under the sign of Libra, as were most of the main buildings in Washington," the Grandmaster said, "The symbol for Libra is the scales, balance. Most people think of the United States only as its sun sign of Cancer. But the *destiny* of the country is contained in the ruler of its astrological chart – and that ruler is Scorpio."

Mateus told Siobhan about the prophecy and how The Shift was of great importance to the secret destiny of the U.S. Charlotte was built purposefully on a matrix of energy and its strongest point was the intersection of Trade and Tryon Streets. Ley lines often appeared at such crossroads where the major portals between the dimensions and the worlds existed. This specific ley line also creates an interdimensional portal, accessible only to those with Fae or Devic energy in their DNA.

"According to the prophecy, once Charlotte, North Carolina is opened to its spirituality and transformative powers she will rise like the phoenix from the ashes," he said. "The craving for material wealth will be incinerated. Transformational energy will travel the ley line from Charlotte to the Capitol of the United States. Once the connection is made, Washington will also be reborn, and America will realize her divine destiny and lead the world into a thousand years of peace. The Earth will finally take its next initiation and become a sacred planet."

Siobhan's voice was a whisper. "Charlotte has the ability to change the world."

"Yes," Mateus said. "However, the Dark Forces are aware of this too and will exert every ounce of their influence to ensure Charlotte and Washington remain ensnared in the pursuit of power and wealth. While D.C. stands as the epicenter of political authority, Charlotte's prominence as a banking hub signifies affluence. This craving for material wealth and dominance needs to transform into the elevated virtues of the Godman, the Spirit-man, embodying a soul-infused persona."

He waited. There were no questions. He continued.

"Current events have been foretold since *before* the United States was officially established. This country was referred to as *The New Atlantis* by Roger Bacon, who encoded the ancient wisdom teachings into the King James version of the Bible. He was a Master Mason, as were the signers of the Declaration of Independence. There is a lot more, but suffice it to say, that ancient prophecies about the founding of this nation have been anticipated since the fall of Atlantis."

He picked up a well-worn book from his desk. "This is *The Secret Destiny of America*, by Manly P. Hall. The author was one of the great mystics of the last century. He says, 'When the mob governs, man is ruled by ignorance; when the church governs, he is ruled by superstition; and when the state governs, he is ruled by fear. Before men can live together in harmony and understanding, ignorance must be transmuted into wisdom, superstition into an illumined faith, and fear into love.' This is the mission we face today. America must once more focus on her Divine Destiny and fight with everything they have, everything they are, to bring about the next step in Human evolution. This is bigger than all of us but will not succeed unless and until we can come together as one."

Siobhan blinked and tried to absorb everything.

"I would also venture to say that Cassandra's chart will have a great deal of Scorpio energy in it if she is to be a pivotal point in this prophecy being fulfilled. When was she born?" Mateus asked.

"She is an Aquarian with Scorpio rising. That's all we know. Rebekah took her chart with her when she left with the child."

Mateus rose from his seat and began to pace the room. "I am concerned she might be easily turned to the left-hand path by the Dark Brothers – now, when she is at her most vulnerable. Her powers will begin to activate soon, and she has no idea who she is." His eyes met Siobhan's. "I am at your service and that of both councils. You know I was part of the original forces from Sirius who chose to stay behind after the battle of Atlantis."

Siobhan nodded. "I will relay all of this to Artemus and Elena. There is another Celestial who needs to be brought into this conversation. I believe he is still on the Mothership."

"Yes." Mateus said. "Manu."

Chapter 18: Dark Rescue

Morgandrian pushed against the electro-magnetic energy field. Sparks flew. She shook her hand and cursed.

"It's no use," Elena said. "Master St. Germain spent thousands of years perfecting the violet flame of transmutation. It will burn away the dross of the Piscean Age and you are definitely in that category!"

"I will kill you, Bitch," Morgandrian said. "This will not hold me forever, and I, too, have powerful forces at my command. It is only a matter of time before reinforcements arrive. They will destroy you and your Lady of the Glen, Siobhan Sinclair!"

As if summoned, Siobhan strode into the chamber. She was wearing battle gear made of Sirian leathers. Their iridescent metallic overlay gleamed in the glow of the purplish fire. She flicked away an imaginary speck of dust from her shoulder and stood in front of Morgandrian.

"Taking my name in vain?" she asked. "You know better. It is the most basic of conjuring spells – speak it and it manifests...*poof.*" She touched her first two fingers to her thumb then opened them as if releasing a handful of dust. "Seriously Morgan, I am shocked at your lack of control. No wonder your acolytes fail so abysmally."

Morgandrian hissed. Her hands curled into claws. She wanted to reach through the vortex of sizzling energy and wring Siobhan's neck.

"You have been defeated," Siobhan said. "Beaten by your own inability to lead." She stepped back and looked at Elena. "She's all yours."

Elena put on her gauntlets. The energy in her fingers increased. In her armor, she had been transformed into a Celestial Warrior, her very nature.

"I am not into torture," she said. "Cooperate and we can end this very quickly. Tell me how you knew about Cassandra and her destiny as one of The Seven. I simply want your source. Is that too much to ask?"

"If I cooperate with you, I will indeed be ended, and not by you," Morgandrian said. "Do you think me a fool? My so-called source would atomize me into oblivion without a moment's hesitation. Even if I wanted to, as soon as I said the name, I would cease to exist and then where would you be?"

"I would be all the wiser and counterstrike," Elena said. "What if I told you we can protect you from any fallout. What if I said—"

A massive explosion rocked the room. Shards of rock and crystal spit across the room. Elena and Siobhan shielded their heads and hit the ground. The force field protecting them shattered. Cosmic electricity shot pulsing pain through their bodies.

A hulking figure of dark energy stalked into the room. Morgandrian began to laugh. The dark-robed specter kept Elena and Siobhan pinned with his extended hand while he disintegrated the violet flame with the other. Smoke billowed from Morgandrian's former prison. The room filled with poisonous vapor.

This is not possible, Elena thought. The violet flame is one of the most powerful energies on the planet.

Still, the flame sputtered and died. The figure reached out its hand to Morgandrian, then turned toward Elena and Siobhan. All they could see was a black vortex of energy beneath the hood. Thought waves pounded their brains.

The girl is mine! You will not be able to bend her to the service of the One. We have been with her since the fall of Atlantis, and she will soon be one with us.

High-pitched screeches filled the air. They covered their ears but could do nothing to block the searing pain in their heads.

Elena and Siobhan slipped into twin pits of darkness.

Chapter 19: Opening Salvo

The Institute was in chaos. Black-winged figures swarmed through the building. Windows exploded and doors shattered. Hundreds of demonic beings attacked with fangs, claws, and talons. Acolytes and initiates, trained for years on combat, held their own but every time a demon or hellhound was demolished, another materialized from its remains and renewed the assault. Overwhelmed by sheer numbers, members of the Institute began to fall. Demons of every kind battled the acolytes.

Amidst the chaos, Xander's voice thundered, "Protect the younglings! Take them to safety!" He recognized that the fledglings wouldn't endure the siege for long; their survival was crucial for future battles.

Acolytes hustled the younger ones to safety, while veteran warriors formed impenetrable phalanxes, standing shoulder to shoulder in groups of six or eight. Their unified defense aimed to halt the demoniac onslaught. Xander, wielding dual blades, became a whirlwind of destruction. With every swing, adversaries lost limbs and heads. Though eons had passed since his last engagement of such magnitude, millennia of rigorous mental discipline empowered his every move, rendering him an indomitable force.

Soon, reinforcements appeared: trainers and their respective proteges from distant Institutes. The infernal hounds responded with ear-splitting howls, their forms expanding with every echo. Yet, the newly arrived warriors remained resolute. Taking their battle positions, they thrust swords, daggers, and spears into the looming beasts. However, the ceaseless tide of hounds persisted.

One of the trainers from the Milan Institute fought her way to Xander's side. Cecelia Brighenti lunged at a huge demon with a gaping mouth large enough to swallow a horse, its fangs oozing with green, poisoned saliva. Xander dodged a swiping claw of another beast, then sent the attacker's head flying across the room. Xander's enchanted blades kept slashing, whirling so fast they seemed to disappear. Blood, gore and heads flew across the room.

Then...they were gone. All that was left were the gradually vanishing bodies smeared across the floor and smoldering piles of ash.

"What the bloody hell was that?" Xander bellowed. He looked at the group of trainers, acolytes, and initiates. "How did they get past our wards?"

Baffled faces stared at him. Marcus from the Milan Institute (the first of the new Avatars to be identified) stepped forward. "I believe we have just been given an opening salvo from the Dark Brotherhood. I have been feeling something was about to happen, which is why we were already on high alert. Since many of us are about to reach the Quickening of our eighteenth year, we are particularly vulnerable. I believe this is just a taste of what awaits us when the stars align for us to come into our full powers."

A resonant voice sounded from the opening arch. "You are correct." Master Artemus strode into the hall.

Xander grasped forearms in the Celestial greeting. "Adonai, Master Artemus. We are honored by your presence."

A murmur flitted around the room. This was the infamous warrior priest and Master of the White Circle. He had not been upon the Earth plane in centuries. Surely, the next steps in the Shift were beginning. The years of preparation and training were about to be put to good use.

Chapter 20: A Traitor in Their Midst

Elena swam back into consciousness, her head thrumming with pain. She looked around. She was lying on a bed in the Institute's infirmary. Her ears might as well have been filled with honey. She saw the face of one of the healers hovering over her but could not hear a thing. She tried to talk but found it was beyond her capabilities. The healer ran her hands over Elena and sent energetic waves down to the cellular level. Everything in Elena's body relaxed; her muscles surrendered to the restorative light emanating from those healing hands. She allowed herself to sink back into oblivion with a sigh of relief as the pain receded.

Artemus stood at the foot of her bed studying his old friend with equal measures of anger and guilt. How could this have happened in the very center of the Institute? What had happened to the wards, the sentries, and all the other safeguards? There was only one answer.

A traitor.

An implausible idea, to be sure, but...

No one from the outside possessed the requisite power to overwhelm all the security. They had to have had inside help.

He motioned to the Sister attending Elena to follow him into the hallway. "Sister Ninian, is Lady Siobhan able to have visitors?"

She nodded and led him to the room where Siobhan was sitting up in bed. She sipped purplish liquid from a crystal goblet. Every time she swallowed her scrunching nose registered her distaste.

"Hello," she said. She put aside the goblet with obvious relief and scowled at the Sister who put it back into her hand. "Bah, why do healing elixirs always taste so bloody foul?"

Artemus laughed. "Because otherwise we would not think them effective. What is that modern saying? 'No pain, no gain.' Just hold your nose and gulp it down?"

Siobhan made a rude gesture and continued to sip.

Artemus waved the Sister outside and closed the door. "I was just with Elena. She is resting, albeit fitfully. She seems to have taken the brunt of the attack."

"Yes, I could feel the entity behind it focusing more on her than on me. It seemed personal. I should check on her myself." She tried to step out of the bed but fell back with a grunt. "Or not."

"She is being attended to by the best we have in the Order, and you, my dear, need to get your own strength back as soon as possible," Artemus said. "I do not believe we have much time before you will be needed again. This opening attack is a clear indication that the Dark Forces are gearing up. The attack was both a test and a demonstration of their power."

Siobhan nodded.

"What about your meeting with the Head of the Masonic Lodge in Charlotte?" Artemus asked. "Does he understand the situation?"

"Oh yes. And more," Siobhan said. "Do you know about the secret prophecy about Charlotte being The New Jerusalem?"

Artemus raised his eyebrows. "No. Fill me in."

Once she shared what the Grand Master had told her, and the need for Cassie's entire astrological chart, Artemus went in search of Glenda to send her on an urgent quest.

Chapter 21: His Maker

Natesh wasted no time. He knew about Paxton's escape and the destruction of one of his most prized mountain hideaways."

Dolts...morons...imbeciles. And they cost me one of my prime lairs.

He had spent centuries perfecting the wards and intricately carved tunnels to connect a network of safe places for his clan throughout the Blue Ridge Mountains. Now, much of his work was rubble. Since he first arrived to explore this new world after meeting Benjamin Franklin in Paris, he had carefully planned his ascension to the position of Grand Master of the North American Clans. He had learned about the secret destiny of the up-and-coming America while a member of the inner circle of the Compte de St. Germain. Many believed the Compte had been walking the earth since the time of the pharaohs and was a member of the group known to Mystics as the Masters of Wisdom. The idea of the New World as the next great empire of power intrigued Natesh. He wanted to know more about the "mystery teachings" that St. Germain espoused.

In the dazzling court of Marie Antoinette, Natesh first glimpsed Giselle, the talented protégé of Rosalie, the renowned couturier to the Queen. From the instant Natesh glimpsed Giselle at a lavish court ball, she captivated him. Instead of donning the elaborate costumes typical of those of noble descent, Giselle had confidently appeared unmasked and with her natural hair, setting her apart from the powdered wigs that adorned most heads. Her eyes, a brilliant shade of chestnut, danced with playful intent as he swept her into the rhythm of a waltz, the new scandalous dance embraced by the royals. His maharaja costume did nothing to disguise his identity. Natesh was the eldest son of one of the most powerful families of the Indian Kshatriyas Caste and was in Paris to learn the ways of the West. Beyond his opulent costume lay Natesh's true identity: the foremost heir of a prominent Kshatriya family in India. Having come to Paris to absorb Western nuances, he was poised to inherit his father's vast realm, armed with the artful diplomacy learned in European courts.

Their love affair began that night, and he was determined to present her to his father as his bride. But the plans crashed when Cagliostro betrayed him to the most powerful Vampire Queens of the time, Philinnion.

It was 1794. Natesh was leaving one of the Compte's salons when he was ambushed and overpowered by the minions of Philinnion and taken to her lair deep beneath the streets of Paris. Whispers of Philinnion's reign of terror circulated through every European court. Rumors painted her as an immortal from the times of Pericles in Athens. Now, she sat at the epicenter of vampire aristocracy, her name whispered with a mix of reverence and dread.

She had seen Natesh from afar a few weeks earlier and had fancied him for her consort. But he was in love with Giselle and rejected Philinnion's advances. Knowing she had an eternity to change his mind, Philinnion turned him and guided him through his rebirthing process. She fed him his first blood from her own neck and took him into the streets of Paris for his first kills.

Emerging from the haze of his transformation, Natesh was met with a Paris consumed by the Reign of Terror, its grip on the nation unyielding for almost a year. He had foreseen the impending revolution and had laid out a meticulous plan to ensure Giselle and Rosalie would escape from its looming shadow. But his unforeseen descent into bloodlust had thrown his plans into disarray. The streets buzzed with grim news: Marie Antoinette and her inner circle were now prisoners of the Bastille, their fate to be sealed by the cold blade of Madame de Guillotine.

Natesh buried his face in his hands. The end of Giselle's life flashed through his brain...her walk up the stairs with hands bound... forced face down onto the block... the roar of the crowd when the blade fell, and her head hoisted high for all to see.

The only relief from his agony was his unwavering belief that Giselle still lived...a reincarnated soul in the body of a college freshman...Cassandra Oberon.

Chapter 22: Contingencies

The Triumvirate and Glenda were ensconced in the Great Room of the New York Institute. Master Elena sipped her tea and watched Glenda with concern. "You are not responsible for this, Glenda. None of us saw this coming."

Glenda took a deep breath and nodded but did not reply. She was still feeling the effects of the poison and had not regained all her strength.

Siobhan touched Glenda's arm. "You need to let this go and focus on the next steps. Our little plan of having Cassandra pledge Alpha Omega to get her to her training has encountered a little hitch, that's all. Plans always need to be adjusted. Remember, free will and outside influences are usually the rule, instead of the exception. If things went perfectly all the time, everyone would be an Ascended Master."

"That is cold comfort, I know," Artemus interjected, "but it is truth. Now we must devise contingencies to rectify the situation. We have identified the Seventh Avatar, and *you* are responsible for that vital piece of information. The other six made a fine showing yesterday during the attack on the New York Institute. We need to move the timeline up a bit – a small adjustment considering we have been preparing for two thousand years."

He turned to Xander. "I want all trainers and teachers to do more battle training. Alert the institutes to prepare their arsenals, especially those who are connected to cyberspace. We are readying for a whole new type of war. We must ensure that every kingdom is on high alert and ready to muster at a moment's notice."

Siobhan stepped forward. "I believe now is the time to bring the Masonic Lodges into the circle as well. May I go to them and ask them to arrange a conclave of the human leadership?"

Elena and Artemus both nodded.

"Yes, of course." Artemus said. "Meanwhile, reach out to the Seely Court and inform the King that I want to meet with him. If it *was* Azazel who took

Cassandra, the king would be the instigator." He took a deep breath, "Last but not least, we have a rescue mission to plan!"

He turned to Elena. "We should move to the Citadel. It will grant us more protection and shield the Institutes from being targeted if we remove ourselves from the Terran plane for the time being. I will tell the Guardians to assign additional protection to the Six while you oversee the move."

Chapter 23: The Citadel

The deafening silence of the Citadel's grand chamber, nestled atop the Himalayas, was shattered as Paxton and Khamuel materialized, landing with a crash. Their arrival startled two white robbed figures.

Paxton, wide-eyed, rushed toward one of them.

"Master Artemus," Paxton said. His voice squeaked a little "What is happening?"

Artemus, a look of relief evident on his face, stepped forward and embraced Paxton. "Ah, Paxton. The Radiant One be praised! And Khamuel," he nodded in acknowledgment, "I see you've located my pupil. Our situation is dire, and we require the expertise only our combined efforts can bring. Is he aware of the unfolding events?"

Khamuel, straightening from his landing posture, responded, "I gave him a cursory explanation, but thought it best to bring him straight to you, sidestepping any disruptions at the Institute."

Elena stepped toward Paxton and grasped him by his forearms. "There is no easy way to tell you this. It has been confirmed by the Sirian Oracles and The Masters of Wisdom – Cassandra is the Seventh Avatar."

Paxton backed up a bit. "One of The Seven!" was all he managed.

"There's more," Artemus said. He motioned to someone sitting by the fire. Glenda approached. She recounted the events at the university and how Cassie had been taken. Paxton felt a sudden chill, then rising anger. The palms of his hands began to glow.

"Breathe," Master Artemus said. "This is no time to allow your emotions to rule."

It took a while, but Paxton calmed. He nodded to Artemus. "I'm good."

Master Elena said, "We all agree it was most likely the Watcher, Azazel who took Cassandra. Other than Master Artemus and myself, The Watchers can only intervene in human affairs at the direction of either a ranking member of the Dark Circle or one of the Fae royals. We are preparing to send an envoy to the Seely Court. Azazel works with the King of the Fae."

"I want to go," Paxton said. "I have known Cassie practically our whole lives, and she has been my responsibility since her mother vanished. I *need* to go."

Artemus met Elena's eyes and gave a slight nod of agreement.

"Alright, you can go," Artemus said, "but since this is a diplomatic situation, I am putting Khamuel in charge. He is one of the Watchers of the White Circle. You will keep silent, observe, and let him take the lead. *Do nothing.* Is that understood? This is an emotionally charged situation for you and I will not have you compromising the mission. You are still a year away from completing your training."

Paxton took a deep breath and bowed his head in assent.

Artemus filled him in on the events surrounding the mixer and the confrontation with Morgandrian and Natesh.

Paxton interrupted. "I thought Natesh was behind my abduction." He recounted his recent trials.

Master Elena motioned to another white-robed figure who had kept in the background. A slim white hand pushed the hood back and an amused Siobhan smiled.

"Hello Youngling," she said. "Seems you have been doing some growing since you last visited Ian and me."

Paxton swooped her up into his arms and swung her around.

"Why if it isn't the Lady of the Glen herself!"

"Put me down, you big lummox. A little respect please."

Paxton stopped mid-pirouette and put her down. He cringed a little and apologized.

"No need for that," Siobhan said. "Let's get down to brass tacks and lay out some scenarios for the visit to the Fae royals. We need to understand protocols and customs. They are not like we are in the Devic Kingdom, and we need to ensure they remain our allies. I understand that the old king passed about three years ago, and his son has ascended to the throne. He is unknown to me, but I am aware that he spent some time in the Human Kingdom when he was about your age. That could be to our advantage."

Siobhan looked Khamuel and Paxton up and down. "But first, a shower and change of clothes. I will not have that blood and gore in this sacred place. Then, we'll eat." When Paxton did not move, she shoved him playfully, "Get on now. You both stink."

Khamuel led Paxton to the upper floor. "You have never been here, have you? Let me fill you in."

Paxton took in his surroundings and gaped at the circular stairway. It wound up and up into infinity like a nautilus shell.

"It's built like Fibonacci's spiral," Khamuel said. "The fortress has been here as a way station since the dawn of time. Many of the Masters call this their home when they are on the Earth plane. It has also been referred to as Mt. Olympus, and Shamballa, as it moves around the globe from age to age. I know you studied this in your first years of training, *Youngling*," He poked Paxton in the ribs and laughed.

"Oh great," Paxton said. "Something else for you to taunt me with. I will make Siobhan pay."

They stepped onto a landing. Khamuel headed down a marbled hallway. Countless doors opened onto the gallery below.

"Here is my apartment," he said. "Two bedrooms." He pointed to the left. "You can use the one through there. A full bath and a closet chock full of clothes. I'm sure you will find something that will fit you, although I don't keep jeans and tee shirts around. We are a bit more formal here. There's lots of Sirian battle gear!"

He laughed and went into his room.

Paxton closed the bedroom door and stripped off his bloodstained clothes. The gravity of this situation swept over him in an icy deluge. He needed to come to terms with what he had just learned – the girl he loved had a great destiny...a terrible responsibility.

Chapter 24: Revelations and Recriminations

Tristan was waiting in the hallway when Paxton and Khamuel emerged, clean and dressed. When Paxton saw his father, he grabbed his arm.

"Why the hell didn't you tell me about Cassie and her mother? You had to have an inkling, a sense they were a vital piece in the Shift." The last sentence was riddled with sarcasm. "Bugger it, Dad, this is a goddamn nightmare!"

"Watch yourself Pax, this is not the time or the place—"

"It's bloody well the *exact* time and place!" Paxton voice continued to rise along with his Scottish slang. "You watched us grow into adulthood. We are much closer than brother and sister. You never once suggested I back off. What were you doing, projecting what you couldn't have with Taryn onto me and Cassie?"

Artemus walked toward them with purpose.

"Alright, Paxton, enough," he said. "We're not deities; our knowledge has bounds, especially within Earth's third dimension. Stand down!"

Khamuel tried to restrain Paxton by placing his hands on his shoulders. Paxton shrugged him off, rushing to the upper levels toward the roof. "I need a breather," he exclaimed. Before anyone could react, Paxton jumped off the nearest balcony, unfurling his wings in flight. "He won't stay out long," Khamuel remarked. "The cold will drive him back inside soon." He began to descend the spiral staircase, making his way to the dining room.

Tristan and Artemus trailed behind.

"Thank you for alerting me about this latest turn of events," Tristan said. "The Grand Master of the Charlotte Masonic Lodge also contacted me. Have you apprised Manu of the latest developments?"

Artemus paused in his descent. "No, but Elena has. They have a long history. He is already beginning the descent process from the Mothership. He may very well be here in full corporeal form in a matter of days. I haven't seen him since we all were with Master St. Germain during the American independence days. What a time that was, eh?"

"Indeed."

Chapter 25: Manu Returns

Two days later, Manu arrived in the breakfast room, resplendent in his Sirian Commander's raiment that was both battle-ready and ceremonial. The armor, in shades of cobalt blue and gold, was adorned with elaborate patterns and symbols, many of which resonated with the teachings of the stars. A large sapphire, the central gem on his chest plate, glowed with an ethereal light, a beacon that signified his heart-mind connection. Gold epaulets held his blue cape that marked his status as a leader of the Intergalactic Forces. His eyes swept over the assemblage, the energy of his presence moving over them with cosmic electricity.

Tristan knew about the Soul level relationship Manu had with Cassandra and was grateful Paxton had not yet appeared. The father was not looking forward to his next conversation with his son.

Elena rose from her place at the head of the table with arms outstretched. "Adonai, Dear Friend, it is so good to see you amongst us once more."

Manu greeted her formally and turned to the rest of the company and said hello to old friends and comrades. His nostrils flared as the aroma of the food on the sideboard reached him. He walked to the sideboard and picked up a plate.

"Ah yes, Terran *food* – a wonderful benefit of being back in a third dimensional body."

They all laughed as he stacked his plate to the tipping point. Artemus waved him into an adjacent seat.

"I take it you are up to speed," Artemus said.

"That's why I am here. Now the question is..."

Paxton came into the room with Khamuel and slid to a halt when he saw Manu. The young man looked bewildered.

The Celestial's eyes reflected warmth and compassion. He knew the next few moments would be crucial in the life of the young Angelic.

Elena stepped over to the Blade Brothers and guided them toward Manu.

"Paxton and Khamuel, I would like to introduce our dear brother, currently with the Intergalactic Fleet on one of the Sirian Motherships and a former High Priest of Atlantis, Commander Manu Abulafia.

Manu bowed, then grabbed each by the shoulder.

"Adonai, my brothers in service to the Radiant One." Manu began. "It is an honor to be back on Earth and to finally meet you all. Your commendable efforts during these trying times haven't gone unnoticed." He flashed a warm smile. "No need for formalities with me. Just call me Manu."

Paxton stared intently at the Commander. Memories of whispered stories from his history lessons about the Celestials from Sirius, known as the Originals, flooded his thoughts. But meeting Manu in person dispelled all his prior beliefs.

Instead of appearing as a venerable ancient, Manu looked remarkably youthful, seeming to be around 25. Paxton pondered internally, considering how the unique vibrational frequency of the Mother Ship could slow down the aging process, making one day feel like centuries on Earth. In many ways, Manu resembled Artemus. Both exuded the aura of warriors—strong and authoritative. They had the same rich honey-hued skin and shared chiseled features. Both were athletically built and carried themselves with unbridled authority. Manu's ebony hair, wavy and untamed, cascaded down to his shoulders, whereas Artemus' honey brown mane was more conservative, curling just at the jawline.

But it was the eyes that set them apart. While Artemus' lapis eyes had an intense gaze, Manu's cerulean eyes seemed almost otherworldly, like laser beams scanning everything, missing nothing. Paxton felt those eyes pierce through him, sensing the Celestial's acute observational prowess.

Manu ignored the stare. "Paxton, I hear there is a bit of a ruckus in North Carolina."

Paxton's eyes flickered for a moment; his head full of a million questions.

Better to get this over with quickly, Manu thought. It will not be easy.

"After your morning repast, perhaps you can walk with me for a while along the balustrade," Manu said in an accented voice Paxton could not quite pinpoint. Somewhere between British and Middle Eastern.

Twenty minutes later, they were finished. Paxton noticed the tense glances flashing between Artemus, Elena, and Tristan, but he said nothing. He followed Manu out of the hall.

The two walked in silence for a while. Each of them measuring the energy strain between them. Paxton was on high alert even though he attempted to act normal in the presence of this great general. It was difficult for Paxton to get a read on Manu as the Celestial was still settling into his third dimensional body, and his energy signature continued to vibrate at a very high level.

"How long has it been since you were on the Earth?" Paxton asked.

"The last time I walked in a third dimensional form was during the birth of the United States, when I was privileged to be a part of Master St. Germain's inner circle," Manu said. "After the American Revolution it was decided that I would return to the etheric plane and monitor events from the Mothership until such time as I was needed. He paused. "It seems that time has come."

Before Paxton could continue with his barrage of questions, Manu put his hand on his arm. "That time has to do with my relationship with Cassandra."

Paxton stopped dead in his tracks. Fear and anger rose from his gut like liquid fire, but he remained silent.

Manu continued. "You know I was part of the original landing team from Sirius; I fought in the third and final Battle of Atlantis just before the continent sank. Those of us who had not taken human life did not break the First Order of non-interference from the Codex. We were able to leave the planet to continue our missions. Unfortunately, many did not or could not adhere to the directive. They were thrown onto the karmic wheel of Earth's evolution until such time their karmic debt was balanced. Such a one was my Soul Mate, the High Priestess Ayesha."

"Cassie." It was not a question. It was a resignation.

"Yes," Manu said. "Whoever took her knows of her significance in The Shift but only Master Elena and Master Artemus know about our Soul connection. We have all been together throughout history during great Earth challenges, but Ayesha is the only one whose Soul had to weave through various bodies across the millennia. When Elena made the connection that Cassandra is Ayesha's current incarnation, she reached out to me."

He locked his eyes on Paxton. "Cassandra cannot be told; she must uncover the truth by herself. But *you* need to know because of the bond you have formed. I cannot interfere and will withdraw for now. Since this is one of the few places on the Terran...Earth...plane that acts as a waystation, I will remain in corporeal form here at the Citadel so I can move freely between dimensions.

Paxton bowed his head and blinked back the moisture in his eyes. "Cassie had some dreams early on," he said. "They seemed to be recollections of past lives...something about being left behind. I thought they were about being abandoned by her mother, but some of the details didn't track. She talked about spaceships, fires, and temples. Nothing made much sense and after a while she quit telling me about them..."

He looked off into the distance. "When her aunt appeared on the scene, I figured the dreams stopped."

"Her aunt?" Manu's face was a map of puzzlement. "What aunt? Rebekah doesn't have a sister."

"Isla is her father's sister," he said. "I am foggy on the details on how she found Cassie; she just appeared one day and took charge. And I have always known Cassie's mother as Taryn, sooo..."

Manu searched his memory and could not find any recollection of Cassandra's father, let alone his family. "I ask that you discuss this further with Elena and Artemus. They may be able to shed some light on it."

Chapter 26: Lost Vows and Hidden Paths

The next morning after breakfast, Elena listened to Paxton's story, thinking back to the days in New York City when Rebekah had returned from the London Institute and her summer training with the powerful white witch Tatiana. A few months later, Rebekah discovered she was with child. She was not forthcoming with information about the father at first, but as the pregnancy progressed, she turned to Elena. She explained that the couple had exchanged vows in a handfasting ceremony officiated by a Druid Priest. Her husband was of Fae lineage, but Rebekah never revealed his name. Soon after the handfasting Rebekah awakened to a note from her Fae mate. He had been called away on a family matter and would return as soon as possible. After waiting six weeks for him, Rebekah decided to return to New York. Then she discovered she was pregnant. After her baby was born, she wove a story about the baby's father being killed in a train crash. Only Elena knew the truth.

One day just before the baby's second birthday, Rebekah took the toddler and disappeared along with two of her fellow Acolytes, Elyse Weiks and Isabeau Renault. Numerous tracking spells were implemented but they had vanished. After a year, Elena called off the search. Rebekah had been one of Elena's most promising students and she knew her glamouring abilities were immense.

Rebekah must have realized her daughter's potential once she cast the requisite astrological chart. And so, she chose to disappear in order to safeguard her child.

"The stars impel, they do not compel." Elena had told Rebekah when she had cast her baby's chart, "Every Soul has free will." She remembered how Rebekah had clung onto the concept as a life preserver, using it almost like a mantra. Now it was clear why.

"If only she had trusted me more," Elena pondered, "We would not be in this situation. The girl would be prepared to protect herself as she approaches her Quickening and the advent of her powers."

As Paxton spoke, Elena moved to the window on the distant side of the library, her hands clasped behind her. There were numerous gaps in the timeline leading up to the present day, and countless unanswered questions that could only be addressed once Rebekah was located.

Elena turned back to Paxton; her eyes full of determination.

"Thank you, Paxton, for sharing. I understand how difficult this must be for you, especially given your feelings for Cassandra. However, our larger mission and the vows we've taken must take precedence. Manu understands this all too well; he sacrificed his profound love millennia ago for the greater good. Now, we stand at a pivotal point and must prioritize serving humanity and our planet."

She put her hands on Paxton's shoulders. "Master Artemus and I will meditate on this matter. I ask you to do the same. Manu has determined not to take any immediate action regarding Cassandra, an appropriate stance regardless of its difficulty. We will reconvene tomorrow after the midday meal and determine our next steps." She bowed. "Namaste."

Chapter 27: Defiance and Destiny

After his meditation, Paxton felt the urge to distance himself from Cassie by seeking an assignment far away. Despite drawing upon years of discipline and training, he couldn't shake off the sensation of an unbearable pain in his chest. It felt as though his heart was shattering. He was reminded of the heart-wrenching tale of Ayesha, the High Priestess, and Manu, the High Priest. While Manu remained immortal, Ayesha faced mortality after breaking the Codex by spilling Human blood and journeyed to balance her karma over many lifetimes. Their story, a poignant example of unconditional love, had been etched in history. Paxton wondered, could he show the same strength and release Cassie for a higher purpose?

Khamuel tapped on Paxton's door. When he saw Paxton, Khamuel's ebony face went ashen. His walnut-hued eyes observed the roiling emotions in his Blade Brother's countenance.

"Do you want to talk about it?"

Paxton rose from his meditation bench, suddenly filled with anger. It emanated from him like the wind before a storm. Khamuel prepared to throw up a force field, he said, "Paxton stop – get a grip! This display of high emotion will lead to nothing good."

"Nothing good? Are you serious?"

Paxton noted Khamuel's defensive posture and stepped back. "Sorry brother. I am working to get a handle on this, but it's an impossible situation. I just can't wrap my head around the idea that Cassie – *my* Cassie – is the reincarnation of some great High Priestess and one of the Originals."

Khamuel chuckled and said, "Looks like the Universe thinks you are badass enough to handle it."

Paxton snorted. "Yeah, right," he said. "It's a shit show. How can the Universe hint at the promise of love only to snatch it away at the last moment? Where's the justice in that?"

"I know it's hard, but you need to let her go, my brother," Khamuel said. "Leave for a time. Let's get her back and then, as Manu said, she will make her own decisions."

Paxton swore and stomped out of the suite; the floorboards protesting each pounding step.

This is not going to end well, Khamuel thought. He rushed out of the room after his Blade Brother.

The others were already assembled in the dining room when Paxton burst through the door. Artemus started toward him. Manu's voice cut through the commotion.

"Let the boy speak."

Though loud enough to bring everyone to a halt, the Priest's voice carried a wave of compassion. He knew Paxton's heart was a cauldron of conflict. This was a critical moment in the young Initiate's path.

"I'm done," Paxton said. "This is not what I signed up for, and I will *not* give her up. We can have more than one Soul Mate, and she is mine in this life walk. You let her go long ago." He pointed to Manu. "As far as I'm concerned, you do not deserve her."

He turned on his heels, walked onto the veranda, and opened a portal before anyone could say a word.

Khamuel started after him, but Master Artemus held him back.

"No, he needs some time to sort this out. You know as well as I that we all have both a Soul purpose and free will. Paxton must find his own way."

Chapter 28: Two Worlds Collide

This time the doors to the castle keep were wide open as she ran up the stairs, hundreds of candles illuminating the marble hallway. A dark robed figure stood at the top of a circular stairway – arms opened wide.

"Welcome home my daughter. Your mother is here and has been waiting impatiently to see you."

Sobbing with relief, Cassandra bolted toward the stairs, but the marble floor beneath her feet started to buckle. It opened into a chasm, and she was falling and falling and falling.

The dream continued, and Sirkan smiled in satisfaction. He enjoyed watching the Dream Weaver work. Cassandra should be unconscious long enough for Isla to arrive and put her into a stasis chamber. Cassie's human form could not handle interdimensional travel and Isla still had to decide if they would be going back to his Mothership or to her Faery Realm. He was leaning toward recommending the Land of the Fae, since Cassandra's father, Isla's twin, was now king of the Fae and sat on the throne of the Seely Court. Cassie's aunt needed to help her embrace her unknown heritage so that her powers could be fully realized once her Quickening occurred. They would need Cassandra's power to solidify their dominance of both the Fae Kingdom and the Celestial Realm. Isla's newly formed Non-Seely Court was still coalescing as a vital resource for the Dark Brotherhood and would need to be stronger if his plans were to come to fruition. Sirkan had waited millennia for this time and nothing – nor no one – would get in his way.

In the meantime, Sirkan would focus on getting the ship ready for a shift out of the Earth's heavy third dimensional energy. He had already been here too long, and his mental focus was fading. The heaviness of the Earth dimension always drained him. He waved his hands over a group of black crystals to activate the ship and merged his mind with the craft. The vessel seemed to sigh in relief. Vibrations increased...higher and higher in anticipation. Then the inner circle of the ship signaled Isla was aboard. Sirkan scanned the command center door and awaited her appearance.

Her figure stood silhouetted on the third ring of the deck, backlit from the landing dock. She descended onto the first tier of the command center and threw back her black velvet hood. Silver eyes studied his face. Queen Isla approached and drew his face to hers. Her lips devoured his. It had been months since they had been able to steal away. The lust was almost overwhelming.

She sighed and pushed away. "Three years I've been waiting for this moment and there is nothing I would rather do than..." She let her voice trail away but noticed her suggestion had its desired effect. "We will have plenty of time, but first things first. How is my little niece?"

Sirkan smirked. "Cassandra is resting, albeit fitfully thanks to the Dream Weaver. The nocturnal visions make influencing Cassandra much easier since you discovered the child is a Dream Walker."

She smiled and bowed her head, accepting the compliment. "Credit where it is due my dear. You were brilliant in glamouring yourself as Azazel. That should keep Artemus and Elena busy for days while they attempt to figure out why the King of the Fae would send his Watcher."

Sirkan bowed with a flourish. "I thought you would appreciate my creativity. One of my favorite pastimes is misdirection."

"Oh yes. It has been quite helpful in sowing doubt and fear into Cassandra's subconscious over the years," Isla said. "And it was a welcome gift when Rebekah encouraged her to learn about dreams. We need to continue to focus on bringing all those abilities from her past lives to the fore soon. Her eighteenth birthday is a little over eight months from now. I want her on the left-hand path by then. We need to awaken her Fae lineage first, I think. So, I have decided we will take her into my kingdom. From there I will present my brother with his long-lost daughter. I think it would be great fun to make my dear twin a dupe in the whole business, once he finds out he sired a daughter. I still remember his agony over not being able to bring Rebekah to the Seely Court as his wife after our father's death threats. The poor bastard has been carrying the torch all these years. Once we get her to our court, we can easily transfer her to my brother's Seely Court, and let the fun begin!"

They kissed again, this time with Sirkan being more demanding.

"Enough, darling," the Queen said. "You will have us up all night if we keep this up. Back to business."

Sirkan acquiesced without enthusiasm.

"The second issue is the royal torc, a necklet given to the first daughter of the king upon her thirteenth birthday. It vanished from my neck when I made the decision to leave the Seely Court to establish my own court. It is now Cassandra's birthright, and she needs it to be bestowed by her father since he is king. Once she puts it on, cellular memory of her Fae lineage will be awakened and with it the attendant talents and abilities. She must have the torc before we can turn her to the left-hand path. Once turned, it won't matter if it disappears again; the mission will have been accomplished."

Sirkan looked at her dispassionately, knowing that her feeble efforts would be no match for his well-laid plans.

Chapter 29: A Battle in Dreamtime

Cassie continued to plummet through the endless abyss. *I am a Dream Walker*, she thought. *Enough is enough.* She stopped falling and sprouted a set of iridescent wings. She looked at the jagged crack in the marble floor above and lifted through it into the hallway. She turned and waved her hand over the chasm. It sealed over perfectly.

Better.

She looked back to the top of the stairs. The dark robbed figure was still there. She sensed his consternation.

Oh yes, that is a man.

She charged toward the landing where he stood.

"Where is my mother?"

The Dream Weaver flinched. He had lost control of Cassandra's dream. She was the strongest person he had ever worked with in Dreamtime. He signaled through the ruby ring on his finger that synced with the one on Sirkan's. The message was simple. "Need help."

Instantly, the Queen appeared with Sirkan fast on her heels.

The Dream Weaver bowed. "Your Majesty." He was careful not to break his energetic connection with Cassandra. "The princess is proving a bit more challenging than anticipated. She knows she is dreaming and has taken control of the dream. I can no longer influence her."

"Can you see what she is dreaming?" the Queen asked. "Are you in there with her?"

He shook his head. *No, but I can go back inside, even though I'll be an observer, not the creator.* She is rejecting the idea of her father being alive and has superimposed the story her mother told her about the train crash. She simply will not accept that her father still lives." He hesitated. "She has also grown fairy wings."

Isla threw back her head and laughed. "Well, it seems the little darling's DNA is awakening." She paced, reviewing her options. "Alright then, record the dream for me so I can get a better handle on her emotional state and send it to me through the Spirit Screen when she has slipped into Delta."

Beckoning Sirkan to follow, she went back to the command center. "Let us proceed into the Fae slip stream and to my palace. I need you to help me figure out how we will present Ayden with his daughter."

Chapter 30: A Test of Will

Cassie felt a shadowy presence like someone was watching her. Then she felt another presence – her mother! A vague memory emerged of Rebekah teaching shielding techniques long ago. She felt other memories but bypassed them. Right now, she needed to deny access to her thoughts and feelings from anyone on the outside. It felt like it was a matter of life and death, so she built an energy shield in her third eye until it was an impenetrable wall. Someone's thoughts reached toward her like smoky tendrils of evil, but she pushed them away with the power of her mind. No one was going to reach her in the dream dimension.

The competing wills battled. Pain flashed through her head. She continued to push back against the pulsing intrusion.

"No way, buddy!"

She kept building, stacking layer upon layer. Another bolt shot through her head. She screamed in her mind, but her drugged body remained immobile while struggling to escape the vision. She took slow, deep breaths through her nose, and breathed out through slightly parted lips. One breath at a time, she pushed back the pain. She felt the dark energy dissolving.

Suddenly a vision of her mother, hanging in chains from the ceiling of a cave deep within the Earth, broke through. Demonic forms tortured Taryn. They flailed her with strips of leather studded with shards of glass. Each downward stroke cut deeper into her flesh and muscle. Blood ran down her alabaster skin and pooled at her feet.

"Help me," her mother said. She could barely hold her head up.

Instinctively, Cassie reached out, then recognized the trick.

No!

The vision disappeared.

She saw a faint blue light. It inched forward. She caught a flash of what looked like opalescent wings, but it left as quickly as it had appeared. The dark tendrils swirled around her once more, but she wrapped herself in her own energy, like a cocoon of light and fell into a deep, and dreamless sleep.

Chapter 31: Between Dreams and Reality

It was good to be home. Isla sighed, walked into her expansive bedroom, and dropped her cloak onto the settee by the fireplace. Sirkan put his arms around her. When he kissed her, he reached for her zipper.

"Want to get out of those Mundane clothes?"

"I thought you would never ask," she said.

She melted into his embrace.

"Please, no niece drama tonight," she said. She drew him into her curtained, four-poster bed. "Just. One. Night."

The next morning, Sirkan unleashed a wolfish grin. "Wish granted." Isla smiled and stretched. She then ran her lips up his neck and nipped him on the sensitive spot behind his right ear. He shivered and was instantly awake against her thigh. "It only gets better," he said. "Truly amazing after all these years. I cannot get enough of you."

She threw her head back and laughed. "That's because we go on sexual starvation diets waiting for our plans to coalesce. When we finally get to sit down to...ah... 'Thanksgiving dinner,' we are always interrupted and must leave before we get our fill. Then we must wait another year."

In the middle of their "fourth helping," the ruby ring on Sirkan's finger began to thrum. He closed his eyes with a sigh. "Well, at least we did, indeed, get your one night."

He rolled off, put on his silk dressing gown, and tossed hers across the bed to her outstretched hands.

He waved his hand to activate the Spirit Screen on the wall, voice only. "Update?"

"Master Sirkan, I am sorry to bother you, but the Princess has come fully awake and is...quite...agitated. I believe you both should come immediately."

Isla rolled her eyes and began to dress in her Fae Queen garb.

"No more Mundane premise," she said. "Cassandra needs to start getting used to the fact that I may be her aunt, but I am in no way a Human."

She stalked into the stasis area and heard the curses emanating from Cassie's chamber. She walked to the pod.

"Calm down darling, Auntie Isla is here."

The transparent dome opened without a sound. Sirkan reached for Cassie's shoulders. "Easy, easy," he said. "Don't try to sit up too suddenly. You have been in a stasis chamber and need to get accustomed to the gravity here."

Cassie's violet eyes flashed. Fury emanated from her like solar flares. Sirkan glanced at Isla, who took Cassie's hands.

"Please listen to Sirkan, my dear," the Queen said. You woke up earlier than anticipated and we must ensure your safety. All will be explained. But first I need you to do your yoga breathing and calm yourself."

She lifted her chin to Sirkan, who let go of Cassie's shoulders as she attempted to do as her aunt had instructed. He walked to the medical cabinet and returned with a vial and a syringe. He filled the syringe and jabbed it into Cassie's neck. Her eyes glazed. She sagged and drifted into unconsciousness once more.

"Well, that was interesting," Isla said. "Her abilities are stronger than I thought. Put her on a drip to keep her out for a while longer. I need to review the visuals from the Dream Maker."

Sirkan tapped the ruby ring to signal the Dream Maker, then prepared the IV. Isla found the aging Dream Weaver standing by a window and gazing at the palace gardens. It had been almost three years since he had been off the ship. When he heard her come in, he waved his hand toward the Spirit Screen to begin the playback.

Isla watched intently. She chewed on her lip when Cassie sprouted the fairy wings and scowled when she heard the girl's protest about her father.

"She's stronger than I anticipated, especially in an altered state of consciousness

"Well, she has more spine than I gave her credit for – at least in an altered state of consciousness," Isla said. "I thought she'd become more malleable after losing her mother and support. I'm curious to see if her resolve remains once she's fully conscious."

Chapter 32: Ancestral Shadows

Isla fell into an uneasy silence while the Dream Maker recounted Cassandra's resistance and the wall she built. Sirkan stepped into the room.

"Rebekah must have taught Cassandra many things as a child – things she could recall in crisis mode. That is the only explanation as to how the brat has these abilities."

Sirkan knew Rebekah was here, in the Fae Realm. He had created a special stasis chamber for her in the depths of the subterranean maze of caves beneath the palace. No one could access the locking mechanism but him. Only he could open it using the hidden key he had created, which was made of Lyran metal with a shard from an Atlantean crystal.

The lack of information angered Isla, but he found solace in the fact that his path would eventually diverge from the Queen's and he would bid her adieux, permanently. A pity. He had never had such an...engaging consort.

No big loss, he thought. She is not the one I've been waiting for.

He turned his attention back to Cassandra. He would need all his finesse and patience in the coming months to achieve his goals.

He had fallen in love with her when he and his acolytes first landed from his home planet, Lyra. His mission was to conquer Terra and create a race of slaves in partnership with the Anunnaki, who had seeded the planet millennia before. Construction of the Sirian temples was well under way, so he took on the persona of a High Priest and infiltrated their ranks. From there it was easy to put his plan for conquering the planet into motion.

Over the centuries, their paths intertwined again and again. She had always been strong in spirit and breathtakingly beautiful. When it became clear her heart and her soul belonged to Manu, Sirkan's jealousy knew no bounds.

"I detest that smug bastard," Sirkan mused. "I loathe his mission from the Radiant One, the way they assist developing planets whose inhabitants were awakening to consciousness. Who gave them the authority to 'educate' these nascent beings transitioning from primordial existence into tangible forms?"

He had witnessed the scene ad nauseam. Star system after star system, planet after planet. They with their sanctimonious non-interference Codex. Why shouldn't the slugs be interfered with? Lesser beings were meant for breeding slaves and servants for the more powerful intergalactic races. Evolution be damned.

He returned to his inner sanctum on the far end of the palace grounds, a small temple he had constructed when he first solidified his liaison with Isla. The building was heavily warded; only he could enter. Not even Isla dared to attempt entrée. The one constant in their relationship was the mutual respect they held for the other's sacred space. He granted no one access to his sanctum sanctorum.

Several had tried and paid the ultimate price. Isla was no fool; he was confident she would abide by his restriction. Besides, she had her own agenda. Her energy was focused on conquering the Devic Kingdom, a conquest he was happy to grant – for now. Once the planet was under his control, he already knew who would rule by his side for eternity.

And it was *not* Isla.

PART TWO: Dream Walker

"There is no use trying," said Alice; "One can't believe impossible things."
"I dare say you haven't had much practice," said the Queen. "When I was your age, I always did it for half an hour a day. Why, Sometimes I believed as many as six impossible things before breakfast."

- Lewis Carroll.

Chapter 33: Reunions and Revelations

Ayden gazed down into her sleeping face. "God, she is breathtaking," he whispered, his silver eyes roaming over her like a starving man presented with an unending feast of every delicacy imaginable. His eyes filled; how much he had missed. *But those clothes. Her mother would have had a conniption.*

Thinking about Rebekah, he looked for the resemblance of the face he had known so well and saw it in Cassandra's straight nose, rose-pink sculpted lips, and the shape of her body – long and slender, with a hint of the roundness in all the right places. He smiled and remembered Rebekah all those years ago before duty had torn them apart. The memory of the wild summer in Europe when the first blush of true love had made them forget everything and everyone as they tasted life and one another. He thought he would go mad with his desire for her, lose every bit of who he was. All he wanted was to be with her, in her, surrounded by her.

That had been almost eighteen years ago, and here was the result. He reached out to stroke Cassandra's hair in awe of what he and Rebekah had made. Anger flashed when he remembered he had been denied any knowledge of her until now. He had been denied the love of a husband and a father - a life. Pushing the roiling rage down, he focused on who he was now. He knew how easily he could turn down a different path if he allowed his temper free rein. It was a path his twin, Isla, had chosen years ago when their father had named him heir apparent over her.

He looked up at Isla. "Thank you for bringing her to me, sister. I know we have had our differences over the years, but this gift is beyond measure."

Isla inclined her head. "There are certain things that are sacred, brother. When I found Cassandra adrift after Rebekah disappeared, I knew watching over her was the right thing to do. We may not see eye to eye on many things, but blood ties are paramount."

"How did you find her?"

"You know about the connection between the Mystery Schools Rebekah attended and the Intergalactic Council. I have monitored their missives for many years. I learned that Rebekah disappeared a little over two and a half years after you returned home. My network checked out every lead. We finally struck pay dirt when we followed a thread about a designer named Taryn Oberon. Press photographs of her did not look like the girl you had shown me. But then I thought – magic. You said she had been studying at a Mystery School. And it was too much of a coincidence with her having our last name. Unfortunately, by the time I tracked her, she had disappeared once again. This time, she'd left both her business and her daughter behind. I knew in my gut that her disappearance was involuntary. I went to Charlotte, North Carolina, and presented myself as Cassandra's aunt. Then, I assumed guardianship."

Ayden's head shot up. "And you didn't tell me?"

"How could I? Father was still alive. I'm sure the death threat against Rebekah would have then transferred to her daughter. There's no way that Father would have permitted what he termed 'an abomination' to survive."

"Then father died."

Isla nodded. "Yes. A few months ago, there was scuttlebutt about one of the Sirian Oracles getting a jolt from a girl in the Charlotte area of North Carolina in the United States. The Oracle determined she was a Hybrid – and something more. They also had sent in one of Master Elena's acolytes to learn if the girl was Rebekah St. Claire's daughter. It wasn't much of a leap to figure out they had picked up on Cassandra."

Isla recounted the whole scenario at Queens.

"I sent in my own consort to rescue her, since I didn't have enough confidence in anyone less to keep her safe. The Celestials and the Hierarchy are incredibly territorial when it comes to who is going to influence the Human Kingdom while it attempts to take its sacred initiation."

Cassandra moaned, stirring restlessly. Sirkan's drugs were wearing off. Ayden ran his hand through his long silver-blonde hair. Cassandra's eyes fluttered.

Isla sent Ayden a telepathic message. *I will check in with you in a few days.* She held his eyes, then backed away.

He nodded in gratitude and turned his attention back to his daughter.

Isla gloated.

Gullible as ever, she thought. He's smitten by his little girl. The jackass deserves whatever comes.

Chapter 34: I Am Your Father

Cassie's temples throbbed, each pulse echoing the sensation of her skull smacking hard ground. Her nostrils flared, inhaling the unfamiliarity of her surroundings—a mix of foreign spices and something sterile. Her eyelids felt heavy, but with effort, they parted. To her right, a figure emerged: a man with flowing pale hair restrained by an intricate silver band. As her focus sharpened, she noticed the delicate wing-like patterns that gracefully arched above his eyebrows. She squinted, half-expecting him to be an illusion. He bore a striking resemblance to the Elven lords from her beloved films.

"Where am I?"

She skittered back into the cocoon of pillows and blankets, but her body would not move with the speed she wanted.

"Easy my dear, you are safe. You have nothing to fear from me." The deep voice carried something distinctly *not* American...Irish or Scottish, perhaps.

The man extended a goblet toward her. "Drink, it'll soothe you." Gently, he cradled her head, pressing the rim of the cup against her sealed lips. A palpable tension filled the air, the weight of her unease tangible. With as much strength as she could muster, she tried to fend off his hand. Her efforts in vain, she murmured through barely parted lips. "What's in it?" The sensation of fire clawed at her throat, but she remained wary of sipping an unknown concoction, especially from a man resembling a misplaced Lord of the Rings actor. He replied, "Merely an invigorating tonic; it'll sharpen your senses and alleviate your throat's discomfort."

She took a tentative sip. Cherry... delicious. She sat up, took the goblet between her hands, and drank deeply. She didn't take her eyes off him. Her fear gave way to anger.

Who the hell is this guy and where am I?

"Easy," he said, "don't drink it down so fast. It is meant to be sipped. I have some lemon water here as well, which will quench your thirst and rehydrate you. You can have anything you like; all you need do is ask. Are you hungry?"

Her anger barely allowed her to nod her head. Relinquishing the goblet, she fell back down onto the pillow, but her gaze never wavered.

"Who are you?" she asked. "And where am I?"

"All in good time, my dear," he replied. "I know you have a lot of questions, but for now let me just say that you are safe. This is my home. Now it is yours. I was never able to bring your mother here, but I knew her tastes well, so I designed these apartments for her in the hopes she might join me one day."

Cassie's eyes widened in disbelief. "You know my mother? How?"

His smile conveyed affection and warmth. "I will tell you everything soon. For now, let's just get you up and feeling more like yourself."

He put his hand behind her head to help her sit.

"I can do it myself – don't touch me!"

She swung her legs around to the side of the bed, took three deep breaths, and staggered to her feet. A wave of nausea forced her back down.

He backed away a few feet. She was looking around at the room. She took in the heavy curtains on the massive fourposter bed, the rich tapestries on the walls, the Rococo furniture, and the muraled ceiling, all in shades of powder blue and cream and edged with gold.

Yep, that's Mom, she thought. *One more try. Easy girl, you got this.* She swung her feet to the floor and leaned against the bed for support.

Enough of this shit. "Tell me who you are."

"What do you know of your father?"

"My father? I never knew him. My mother said he was killed in a train accident in England before she even knew she was pregnant with me."

Ayden closed his eyes.

"Your mother and I met when we were on holiday in England. It was like being struck by lightning. I was walking into the Standing Stones at Stonehenge just before dawn to do a ritual. She was sitting in meditation, illuminated like some kind of goddess. The rays of the sun seemed to emanate from her. I was dumbstruck. Then she opened her eyes – those incredible violet eyes. I was lost. I knew I had met my life partner, the love of my life."

Cassie opened her mouth, but nothing came out.

He paused for a moment. Emotions he had long suppressed washed over him.

"We were married with a Handfasting Ceremony by a Druid Priest on the Summer Solstice a month later. That's when you must have been conceived."

Conflicting emotions battled for control in Cassie's head and heart. She wanted to hold the man sitting next to her – she wanted to squeeze him until he fought for breath. She also wanted to strangle him...this odd figure...her progenitor...the figure about whom she'd dreamed...whom she'd imagined. She'd never seen a picture – never heard a description. And now he perched on the edge of her bed as if he'd been there all her life.

Her father. She stared at him, mouth agape.

Ayden soldiered on, unaware of Cassie's growing agitation as he lost himself in the memories of that fateful summer. "We thought we could change destiny. We imagined our love would supersede our Soul Missions. But the Universe had other plans. I was young and stupid. I thought I could convince my father to allow me to go back for her and bring her into the Fae Kingdom as my consort. So, I snuck off like a thief in the night. I left a note telling her I would come back. The note ended up being a lie."

Cassandra's hand shot out with a life of its own. She struck Ayden across the chin.

"Bastard!"

Chapter 35: Royal Blood and Bitter Truths

She had been crying for ten minutes or so. Whenever he tried to touch her, she recoiled. Ayden waited until she lifted her tear-streaked face.

"Why didn't you come back?" she asked.

"My father had very rigid ideas about the intermixing of races," Ayden said. "I am of royal blood, and the bloodline must remain pure. An antiquated concept, I know, but it has been the norm for thousands of years. My father's Angelic Watcher, Azazel, came to bring me home. I was the High Prince of the Fae. I asked to bring Rebekah with me."

Cassie's eyes narrowed, her lip twisting in disdain. "So, you let Daddy dictate terms?" Her voice dripped with sarcasm. Then a shadow of confusion crossed her face. "Wait – Rebekah? Mommy's name is Taryn."

"Your mother changed her name, along with her appearance, when she left New York with you. Her birth name is Rebekah St. Claire. And no, that's not it," Ayden said. "I was forbidden to bring her here under penalty of death."

"You really think your father would have killed you?' Cassie's eyebrow rose. "I doubt it."

"You are right," Ayden said. "Not me - your mother. She was nothing to him. He would have crushed her like an annoying insect. My father put your mother under a death warrant. If she set foot in the Fae Kingdom, she was dead."

Cassie waited for a moment. "What about now?"

Ayden smiled without warmth. "I am king now," he said. "I want to bring the Seely Court out of the dark ages. There are no longer rules governing inter-species marriage. Love is love."

He told her that Rebekah had then returned to her training in the Mystery School in London. The White Witch Tatiana deemed it necessary to send her back to America to finish up her training with Master Elena in New York. It was then that Rebekah learned that she was part Celestial and part Human. Rebekah must have found out once their child had been born that she was a unique being. What better way to protect her than by using her considerable glamouring abilities to "hide in plain sight" and take the child away and to safety back to London and Tatiana? He had gleaned this by piecing together what little Isla had told him, along with the intel that Azazel had gathered over the years.

Ayden took a deep breath and stopped his narrative. He understood why Rebekah had hidden Cassandra. He did not want such a dangerous future for his daughter, either. Duty, karma and being a servant leader was a philosophy of life he shared with his comrades in the Celestial and Human Kingdoms. This was a crucial moment in history, one they had all known was coming. The best he could do was prepare and train his daughter for her role in it, which meant he had to relinquish her to her destiny, no matter how difficult it would be. But that exposition could wait.

The door opened.

"Come in, Brigida," Ayden said. He pointed at the stocky woman. "Cassie, this is my long-time nurse and governess. Now she rules my domestic domain with an iron fist in an iron glove. She looks benign, but she brooks no foolishness."

The apple-cheeked woman grinned. "Majesty," she said, "let the poor girl alone. Your multiple stories can wait until she is feeling better."

While there was warmth in the smile, Cassie detected steel in the eyes. Something told her to cooperate.

Ayden bowed his head. "As always, you are the voice of reason." He looked at Cassie. "I have burdened you with a lot of information. Rest a while. I will leave you in Brigida's very capable hands."

When the door shut, Brigida put a tray on the small table next to the bed. She helped Cassie to her feet. Cassie looked into the woman's startling emerald eyes and felt safe for the first time in days. She inched toward the table and sat in a chair. Brigida shook out a napkin and tucked it around Cassie's chin.

"I made you an assortment of dishes, as I don't yet know your tastes," Brigida said. She motioned to the covered dishes. "There is a vegetable omelet and apple cinnamon pancakes with honey. There are also scones and a special granola I make. And tea, of course. I know that coffee is a popular drink in your realm but I'm afraid we don't have any here. I can always send one of the kitchen elves to find some if you like."

"Tea is fine. Thank you so much."

Brigida nodded and folded her hands across her ample stomach. She watched in satisfaction as Cassie dug into the omelet.

"Oh, my god, this is the best omelet I've ever tasted."

Brigida smiled. "Our food here in the Seely Court is the best on this planet. Of course, your human senses are heightened here, so perhaps you are giving me too much credit. Still, we use select spices and herbs, many of which are not found anywhere else." She patted Cassie on the shoulder. "I will leave you to your meal. There is a bathing room off to the left and a wardrobe full of clothes. Make yourself at home, since this *is* your home, at least in this realm. If you need anything at all, either press that button on the desk," she motioned to a delicate French provincial piece of furniture, "or simply ask the house."

Cassie raised her eyebrows.

"Oh yes, a very important detail," Brigida said. "The house is enchanted. Speak your request out loud, and it will be so. Only the members of the royal family can use that ability here. Well, the royals...and me."

Cassie shook her head, then stuffed another bite into her mouth.

Curiouser and curiouser, Alice, she thought.

Chapter 36: Turning Point

Paxton was standing in front of the Oberon house when a small furry body flew at him with a wail. Gabriel slipped across Paxton's chest, clawed at his leg on the way down, then settled at his feet and scowled.

"Oh my god, Gabriel – did they leave you here all alone? I know the feeling." He scooped up the cat and tucked him into the crook of his arm.

Paxton glanced towards the row of flowerpots beside the front door, reaching instinctively under the second one to the right. His fingers brushed against the familiar cold metal of the "secret key." Slipping it into the lock, he stepped inside. The echoing stillness of the rooms and the untouched air immediately spoke of absence.

"Cassie's aunt has to know she's gone. It's been two days," he murmured to himself, the weight of worry evident in his voice.

With a sigh, he made his way down the hallway towards the kitchen. He filled Gabriel's water bowl then rummaged through the cupboard for a can of food.

What the hell am I going to do with this cat?

Gabriel weaved between Paxton's ankles. The cat's low grumbles sounded like an engine in need of a tune-up.

"Don't waste your time," Paxton said. "I know when I'm being manipulated. You will be fine with your little door and dry food after this. If you want snacks, act like a cat, and find a mouse – got to be plenty in this old place."

Gabriel swatted at Paxton's ankle, a less than endearing habit.

"Damn cat understands every word," Paxton said.

Paxton trudged up the winding staircase to the second floor. His heart twisted when he opened Cassie's bedroom door. Every inch conveyed...her – from the soft mauve walls to the art nouveau posters of Mucha and Klimt. He inhaled the lingering scent of her favorite patchouli incense intermingled with the light floral scents of gardenia and rosewater, Cassie's signature scent ever since her mother had brought it back for her from Paris. He went over to the alcove window seat. *Green Darkness* lay open on the plum velvet cushions as if someone had put it down after reading for a while. He imagined Cassie taking a break and looked to the door as if expecting her to return.

"She really got into this," he said. He flipped through the pages. Rebekah's name was scrawled on the frontispiece. "Why didn't she teach Cassie anything about magical self-defense?"

He sank down onto the window seat and rifled through the pages. There were notes and highlighted passages, but he was too lost in memories of Cassie to pay attention to them. They'd been separated before. Every summer he went for training in the Devic Realm. But this absence was different.

"I don't know where she is. I don't know if I will ever see her aga—"

He stopped, afraid voicing his fears might bring them to life. He stomped his foot on the floor. His foot caught the edge of another book.

Cassie's journal.

He picked it up and read the purple Post-it note on the cover.

"Who are Compte St. Germain and Hermes Trismegistus?"

Who are they to you, my dear Cassie?

He dropped the journal and leaned his head back on the pillows.

Holy Shit.

He bolted upright with an intuitive flash. He ran out of the room and up the winding stairway toward the walk-in attic on the fourth floor. What better place to hide the truth? The locked door could not stop a white magician, but it took a few tries. Rebekah had been a powerful spellcaster. He used an ancient incantation he had learned from Khamuel, and the door swung open.

Gotcha sucker.

Paxton stood on the threshold, disappointed. A lot of boxes, a ratty artificial Christmas tree turned over on its side, and dusty bookcases filled with knickknacks and tattered looking tomes.

There's more here. There must be.

He stepped in and felt for a switch. Taking tentative steps through the gloom, he fanned his arms in front of him until he brushed against a cord hanging from the ceiling. He pulled the string. shadows splayed across the room.

Must be a 20-watt bulb.

He squinted.

There.

A variation in the wall on his left caught his attention. He went to the bookshelf and inched it away from the wall. Dust rained from the upper shelves...a cascade of wheeze-inducing motes. He wiped his nose and pulled the case about three feet into the attic. Still nothing.

He ran his fingers along the wall. It's here...I know it's here...take your time...you'll – ah!

The wall felt spongy. He pushed.

Click.

A hidden door swung open. He stepped through and into an altar room resplendent with sacred icons of East and West painted across the middle of the walls. A table covered with candles of varying shapes, sizes, and colors dominated the small space. An array of essential oils stood on shelves that were mounted to every wall – except the far one – where there was another small door.

Paxton ducked a little – the ceiling was about ten feet, but he felt cramped – and opened the door. He saw a caldron, dried herbs hanging from the ceiling, books on the Kabbalah, the writings of Alice Bailey, Helena Blavatsky, Manly P. Hall, and other mystical and metaphysical authors. Astrological diagrams and charts were pinned up on one side of the room. He went over to examine them. In the middle was a birth chart. And at the top of the chart, a name: Cassandra Oberon.

Next to the chart was another one. Rebekah St. Claire, not Taryn Oberon. So, the scuttlebutt was true. Cassie is Rebekah St. Claire's daughter.

A photo was tacked between the two charts, a laughing girl and young man to whom Cassie bore a resemblance. White-blonde hair to his shoulders, pale skin. Fae. The girl was not familiar in any way. *Of course. Glamoured.*

Cassie's mother was, indeed, a White Witch.

Paxton was trained in esoteric astrology, a required class for all neophytes during their first three years of training in the mystery schools. It was an essential tool in understanding the Soul Purpose of anyone's current incarnation.

His hands shook as he unpinned Cassie's chart. He studied it. The first thing he looked at was her rising sign, a major indicator of the Soul Purpose. Her potentiality hit him like a rock to the middle of his chest.

Scorpio. One of the most powerful signs of change and transformation. He scanned the other indicators in her chart like her moon, which indicated what she brought forth from past lives – Aries, the passionate warrior.

Her sun sign was in Aquarius. She possessed the power, passion, and purpose of a very, very old soul. His heart skipped a beat.

Doubt gnawed at him. "Does she deserve more than what I can offer?" His heart tightened at the thought. He shuddered, not allowing himself to fully form the name of the great High Priestess that Manu had revealed.

He pinned the chart back in place with icy hands and lurched through the door and down the stairs. Gabriel sprinted behind him. The glass in the back door spider webbed when he slammed it against the wall. He stumbled into the garden and fell to his knees.

Damn them. Father must have known. And Taryn – Rebekah – kept everything hidden. Damn them all.

He wanted to scream - wanted to kill someone - turn back time and be somewhere else, anywhere else but here. But more than anything, he wanted to hold his precious Cassandra. Protect her, serve her, be her champion.

He fisted his hair in his hands and yanked his head back and forth. He tried to make sense of the past twenty-four hours. Gulping in air, he dropped onto the manicured backyard lawn.

The grass cushioned his back when he lay down. He took a deep breath, let his mind go blank, and stared at the fading light of the late afternoon sky. Years of mental training were not helping. The techniques of stepping outside of emotional responses crumbled. Emotions could overpower him and lead to the left-hand path and black magic. He knew he needed to get a grip.

One deep breath...then another...the ancient pre-battle technique of a warrior preparing for battle. Centering took longer than usual. He wanted his mind awake and his body at rest, so he could dig into the deep levels of knowing and connect with his inner guides. But the high emotions of the past day overwhelmed him. He surrendered to his exhaustion and fell into a deep sleep.

When Gabriel awakened him by licking his cheek, it was well past midnight. Paxton buried his face in the cat's fur hoping he might catch a whiff of Cassie. Her scent barely clung to the cat's fur, but it was there.

He reluctantly got up and went back into the kitchen, Gabriel fast on his heels.

There was canned soup in the pantry along with some crackers. Paxton found cheese in the fridge and took his simple meal onto the porch.

He looked at Gabriel. "I can't stay forever," he said. "Someone will find me. But I can use portal magic to go wherever I wish. I don't need to maintain this Mundane cover anymore." He paused. "Why am I talking to a cat?"

A puff of wind blew out of the open doorway. It seemed to originate from the front hall. Paxton stood, turned, and stepped inside. A vortex materialized and a familiar figure emerged.

"Aunt Isla!"

She smiled, the circlet of a Fae Queen upon her brow, flowing crimson robes encasing her willowy form.

"My dear Paxton, how delightful. Looking for someone?"

Paxton swallowed hard; his eyes swept up and down her regal form. He did a double take when he noticed slightly pointed ears peeking through her long tresses. She offered him a lop-sided grin.

"Cass...Cassie?" was all he managed to get out of his suddenly dry mouth.

"Yes, my dear," Isla said. "I know all about it. I even know where she is. The question is, do you want to know where she is – and – how much would you give to have her?"

He spoke with no thought. "I would give anything to have her back."

"Be careful what you ask for," she said. "A bargain with the Fae is not easily broken."

Paxton shook his head. It throbbed from information overload. "Are you really Cassie's aunt?"

"Cassandra is indeed my niece, dear boy, make no mistake." Isla smiled when she mentioned Cassie. "When her mother went missing, I stepped into the Human Realm to care for her."

Recognition inched across Paxton's face. "You are the Fae Queen."

"Yes and no," Isla said. "Yes, I am from the Fae Kingdom. But my twin brother was given the throne over me, even though I am first born. I have established my own realm outside of the Seely court and become its queen."

"And so, your brother is Cassie's father."

She threw back her head and snorted. "Biologically, yes. But his position as the King of the Fae took precedence over his relationship with Cassandra's mother. But now..." She trailed off.

Paxton continued the thought. "Now he knows who she is, and he wants her to secure her power and importance."

"Yes," Isla said. *Very good. He is headed in the right direction.* "Well, I cannot speak for him, of course, since we haven't exactly been close for many years. But I am sure his ascendence to power is quite an enticing reason to make his presence known to her. And of course, there's his ever-loyal Watcher, Azazel."

She let the last piece of information settle. She was pleased to note the boy's rising ire.

"I want her back!" he said. "Tell me what to do to make that happen."

"W...ell," she said. "You have a connection with Devic Kingdom. It would be an easy task to slip from there into the Seely Court. It's not really a spell, just a shift in focus."

Paxton's eyes brightened. "Yes, of course. No big deal at all."

He stood like a man ready to begin a race. She put her hand on his arm. "Not so fast," she said. "Let's not run off without a plan. Come with me to my court, and we will put together a solid strategy."

She opened the portal again and stepped into the vortex. Paxton never hesitated – and Gabriel leaped in after him.

Chapter 37: A Step Back

Manu came out of his meditation. He kept his eyes closed while he reviewed what he had been shown from the inner plane experience – a glimmer of the energetic sense of Ayesha's Soul essence, albeit a faint one.

Paxton had not returned. And so, he needed to take the situation in hand and meet with the Fae King and accompany Artemus to the meeting. He had no recent interaction with the Devic Kingdom, only with the Angelics, and he was a bit rusty on Fae protocol. The added support of Artemus would be a necessity. Manu's no nonsense, direct approach clashed with the archaic style of the Fae – past dealings had not gone well. They spoke in circles and used hyperbole to the point of annoyance.

He went back to reviewing the impressions he had received about Ayesha, a flashback to their time on Sirius before they had accepted the mission to come to the newly awakened world called Terra. The sentient beings on the young planet had reached a point in their individuation where some were ready to be taught the most basic mysteries concerning the sacredness of their bodies as a vehicle for their Souls. They needed to be made aware of The Radiant One and taught both physical and mental techniques that would allow them to begin the evolutionary journey toward realizing their divine potentials.

Ayesha had not been convinced that she was ready for such an important mission. She had always been hesitant about accepting her power since her third initiation, which granted her the mental abilities to manifest "from thought to hand." She was concerned her ego in her abilities would hinder her Soul Mission. No amount of reassurance could put those fears in abeyance. Manu saw the volunteer mission to the burgeoning planet as the solution. He approached the Council to see if he and Ayesha could head the expedition. At first, Ayesha was furious for going behind her back. But as the days went by, she began to see the wisdom in this act of service to an infant race and leapt into the organization of the expedition.

Manu swept the memory from his head and walked to the decompression chamber; it would allow him to begin to descend into the lower vibratory frequency of the third dimension of Terra.

It was time.

Chapter 38: Lineage

Cassie paced and clutched at the dress she had chosen from the proffered wardrobe, the least ridiculous one available. It was like something out of the time of Napoleon and Josephine, high waisted with puff sleeves and a long columnar skirt reaching to her ankles. She caught a glimpse of herself in the full-length gilded mirror on one wall. Hysterical laughter bubbled from her throat.

Oh my god, I look idiotic – like something from one of Mother's art history books.

But there was something vaguely comforting about the style. A scene from her dream about the Compte de St. Germain flashed across her vision.

She had never had a chance to research the Compte fully. She knew what little she had learned about the Theosophical Society and the Compte were important. But how and why?

Someone knocked on the door.

It's Ayden. She screamed at the slab of solid oak. "Go away! Leave me the fuck alone."

Her hands flew to her mouth. She had never spoken in that way before. A moment passed.

"Screw it," she said. "I'm entitled."

The door opened. Ayden walked in with a load of leather-bound books under his arm. He walked to the desk and laid them down. When he turned, concern etched his face.

"Is that the type of language young ladies are being taught these days in the Human Kingdom?" he asked.

"It's really none of your business, *Father,*" she spat.

He sighed and put a hand on her shoulder – more authoritative than affectionate. "It *is* my business," he said. "I am your father whether you like it or not. And your misplaced anger must stop. We are both the victims of other people's decisions, and I will no longer tolerate infantile behavior from you. It is getting us nowhere."

She knew he was right, but she pulled away, sullen and slit-eyed. Ayden motioned toward the books, each of them almost three inches thick.

"These are some of the histories of our family, and the Land of the Fae. You need to learn more about who you are and where you come from. There is a blank journal in the stack for your notes. The more you know, the better you will be able to make some decisions regarding your next steps. You are not a prisoner, but as long as you are here, I recommend you learn as much as you can about your roots and your innate abilities. As the saying goes, the more you know about history, the less likely you will repeat the mistakes that were made – or something like that." He shrugged and went out the door, closing it gently behind him.

Cassie glared after him through the closed door. Why am I acting like this? Rationally I kinda understand, but I'm just sooo angry.

She went to the desk and picked up the top book: *A History of the Seely Court.*

Not interested. She put it aside. The next was *The Path of the White Magician.*

OK, more appealing.

She vaguely remembered her mother's Reiki group discussing magic and the proper uses of the powers and abilities that came along with opening to the healing energies of "the Universe." She certainly understood the untapped capabilities of the human body – but magic? The third book looked ancient, the worn leather of the embossed binding showing regular handling.

The Emerald Tablet of Thoth.

It looked like the same book she had seen in her dream about the Compte de St. Germain. She went to one of the winged backed chairs and opened the book with trembling hands. Cassie took a deep breath, then she opened the book. The language was foreign. About to put it aside in frustration, she saw the words begin to dissolve and morph into English as her fingers ran over the pages.

"Okaaayy", she said, "this is interesting. I wonder if it will work in the real world when I take advanced French."

She began to read, then reached for the notebook and began taking notes. Thoth was an Atlantean who later was deified as a god. In the Greek Pantheon he was Hermes, messenger of the gods. He was considered the god of wisdom by both the Greeks and the Romans and was also the author of the "seven universal laws." She read that the seven universal laws included the Laws of Mentalism, Correspondence, Vibration, Polarity, Rhythm, Cause & Effect and Gender. The Universe exists in perfect harmony and order by virtue of these Laws. Continuing to page through the book, she felt her body begin to vibrate and she closed her eyes to become centered. She did *not* want to lose any control here, of all places.

She pulled her thoughts back to how she had ended up here and the wild synchronicities that had occurred between her visions, dreams and now this. Cassie also realized she did not feel like herself, once again the frustration was fast approaching anger. She pulled up – what had gotten into her? She really *did* understand that her father was just as hurt as she was in finding out about her and her mother. Still, she just couldn't seem to find any empathy for him or the situation. She felt like she wanted to scream and slap someone – very "un-Cassie-like" as her mother would have chided her.

After about an hour, she put the heavy tome aside. She pulled herself to her feet, stretched, and rubbed her eyes. Noticing that one of the floor-to-ceiling glass doors to the stone terrace encircling the palace was open, she stepped outside. The cool spring breeze caressed her burning cheeks as tears streamed down her face once more.

Ayden was her father! A book she had dreamed about was in his library. She was his heir -a princess. She had Fae blood and magical abilities...

This is one of the best dreams I have ever had. But it was time to wake up, find Paxton, and get back to school. She dug her nails into her palms. With a start, Cassie realized she felt pain shoot up her arms. She blinked...then blinked again. "Well, damn I'm awake." The icy shower of reality washed over her.

"My life, my entire life, has been one...big...*fucking* lie!

Chapter 39: Royal Legacy

Ayden came back to Cassie's sitting room a little later. He entered without knocking and walked with intent to the painting of a fairy circle over the marble fireplace. With a wave of his hand, it swung open to reveal a safe. He twirled the dial until the door popped open. When he turned around, he was holding a large blue velvet box.

"Please don't tell me that's a crown," Cassie said.

"No, my dear, something far more valuable, and useful," he said. When he lifted the lid, Cassie saw a bejeweled, silver choker. He tilted the box until the choker caught the sun. A brilliant white light engulfed the room. Swirls of engravings in the metal and prismatic gemstones cast rainbow-colored reflections off every wall.

"This was your aunt's. But when she decided to leave my court and establish her own, it remained here." he said. "We have passed it on to first daughters for thousands of years. It is your inheritance; it will help you to awaken your Fae magic when you put it on." He lifted it to her. "See, it is engraved with magical sigils that represent the latent talents and abilities woven into our ancestral cellular memory. I am not certain how it will respond to your combined Human, Celestial, and Fae DNA, but what happened between your mother and me was no accident – it was ordained. We thought our love would conquer all. Duties and prophecies didn't enter into it. But my father knew exactly how to bend me to his will and to my obligations by threatening your mother's life."

Cassie shook her head and stepped back from the glowing necklace.

"No way am I going to put that vile piece of jewelry around my neck. It looks like a slave collar."

Ayden smiled ruefully. "No, it's just a very ancient design called a torc. The High-Born Fae have been wearing them for millennia instead of a crown. When the Royals wear anything on their heads, it's a simple woven circlet of silver or gold worn across the brow with the jewel of our houses in the middle." He pointed to his forehead. "It is bestowed during our coming-of-age ceremony on what you would call your eighteenth birthday. Yours is only months away."

Cassie stared at the sparkling choker. Ayden kept speaking.

"The Torc, on the other hand, is usually given to the Younglings at their thirteenth year coming of age ceremony. Once it is given, the Youngling goes to the training temples so the High Mage can determine their innate abilities and assign them the proper trainer. You were denied such an opportunity because your mother did not have the chance to tell me of your existence, nor did she know who I really was."

Cassie turned her back and growled over her shoulder. "Only because you were too much of a coward to tell her the truth."

Ayden did not respond. There was nothing he could say.

"Get out." Cassie said. Her voice rose with each repetition. "Get out, get out, *get out*!"

He closed the jewel case, laid it on the desk, and left.

How do I reach her?

Chapter 40: Turn to the Left

Paxton landed on all fours as he fought to keep the sudden vertigo in check. He had never experienced this reaction to portal travel, but he realized the Fae Court emitted a different energy signature to limit accessibility. He stood, swallowing constantly to keep from vomiting. He swatted at a disturbance at his right leg. He heard a yowl of protest.

"Shit, Gabriel. What the hell are you doing here?"

The cat glared, then reconsidered his options, and jumped up on Paxton's shoulder where he clung like a living fur collar.

"Maybe it's good he followed us," the Queen said. "When Cassandra sees him, she will feel safer by his presence, I'm sure."

Gabriel hissed at her.

"Let me show you to a suite of rooms where you can be comfortable."

The marble hallway appeared endless. Richly appointed rooms branched off on either side. They passed a winding staircase where Paxton could not see the top.

Isla mounted the first stair and motioned to be followed. They stopped on the third floor where there was a magnificent courtyard with tinkling fountains, verdant green topiaries sculpted like woodland animals, and small peach, cherry, and apple trees. Ivy-framed, steel-studded wooden doors guarded the perimeter. She led him to the largest door at the far end. Past it was a luxurious suite of rooms, richly appointed with brocaded furniture and damask curtains in deep jewel tones of emerald and sapphire, reminiscent of the Human courts of old. Each room offered a sumptuous feast for the eyes.

She looked over her shoulder at him. "The palace is enchanted, of course. If you wish for anything to be changed, for food, for anything, simply ask out loud and it will be provided."

"Should I start off by saying, 'Hey Siri?'"

Isla did not laugh.

"I will leave you for now to rest and get your bearings. We will convene in the dining hall for the morning meal at seven in the morning. Sleep well."

She melted away. Paxton let out his breath, not realizing he had been holding it, and explored. He touched fabrics, opened closets, and searched through armoires. There were enough clothes to dress an army of men.

He wandered out into the courtyard, surprised to see stars twinkling overhead. He had assumed they were somewhere deep in the Earth. But no – this was another dimension. He had been hiding behind a human façade for a long time; limited to third-dimensional thinking. It was a relief to abandon his subterfuge.

He explored the other suites and found the one directly opposite his. It was obviously decorated for Cassie, right down to the window seat and her favorite perfumes and soaps. He smiled wistfully, imagining her here, and felt a sense of excitement well from deep inside.

He went back to his suite and into the spa-like bathing room and turned on the ornate golden faucets at the alabaster tub.

He poured himself a glass of wine and lowered himself into a steaming bath.

"This is living."

The heat felt good. His muscles began to relax, and he thought back over recent events.

It's only been a week!

The enormity of what he had done began to seep into his consciousness. He had left behind his sense of duty and honor because of his love for a girl. He had betrayed the trust of his father, and the mission he had been granted as one of the Guardians of the Radiant One. Did no one really know of Cassie's importance until now? How could that be possible? Weren't the Masters of Wisdom – the Hierarchy of the Human kingdom – all-knowing? Then he stopped himself. Of course not.

Master Artemus had reminded him that, yes, they were Masters, but still Human, and were not privy to every Soul's mission. And then there was the free will thing. No one except the Radiant One could know what was in the heart of any living being. The great Yogi Berra was credited with the saying went, "It ain't over 'til it's over." Paxton shuddered and realized once again that every action had its consequences, the Law of Cause and Effect.

After he toweled off, he pulled on a pair of comfortable black pants and a loose white cotton shirt, throwing a navy cabled sweater over his shoulders. Turning to the veranda, he went out into the cool fall night and smiled to himself. Guess the seasons weren't the same here as in the Mundane World, which made sense. After all, this world was woven of desire and magic. Desire. This was why he was here. He had turned his back on years of training, history, and purpose, and allowed raw emotion to rule his mind. A sense of dread began to grow in the pit of his stomach as the enormity of what he may have started by his impulsive actions began to dawn on him. Well, he would have to stay the course for now. The important thing was Cassie.

SIRKAN MET ISLA IN their apartment. It was evening, and the luxuriousness of it was inviting. The scent of burning wood and pine filled the air, and the only sounds were the crackling of the fire and the gentle ticking of a clock on the wall.

"It went better than I could have hoped," Isla said, "The boy is full of anger and longing for Cassandra. It will be no time before we can welcome him into our court. He will be a wonderful addition with all his abilities. And the intel – why, this could be the biggest advantage we have had in centuries."

Sirkan narrowed his eyes, trying not to be annoyed at her exuberance. "I'm glad that you are pleased with this outcome, my love. However, how do you plan on getting him into the Seely Court? I can feel his negativity from here, and the court will notice the change in his energy signature before he ever appears in the physical."

Isla waved a hand as if swatting away a gnat. "We will be able to add our energy to his through the sheer power of his will to weave an impenetrable glamour. It should hold for as long as we need to get her out and back here. I really don't anticipate any issues."

Don't stir the pot, Sirkan thought.

"I need to get back into the Human Kingdom to check in with Natesh," he said. "I take it you have been keeping your reins on The High Priestess of Darkness?"

Isla raised an eyebrow. "Morgandrian is well in hand. She has her uses – for now. One of my handmaidens in her court reports to me. Just like you, my love, I have my spies embedded just about everywhere."

"I have no doubt," he said.

Chapter 41: Watchers and Secrets

Artemus waited impatiently as Azazel was escorted into the Citadel's opulent library. The Citadel was protected by some of the most powerful and magical Devic and Celestial warriors in the Terran Realm. Both Manu and Khamuel were standing at the ready.

Azazel tucked his wings under the black hooded cloak he always wore and swept into a deep bow before The Master of the White Circle.

Artemus nodded his head in acknowledgement. "Thank you for coming so promptly, Azazel. You have spoken with the king of the Fae concerning the disappearance of Cassandra St. Claire?"

Throwing back his hood, Azazel met Artemus' steely gaze. "Yes, Master Artemus. And he wants to meet you in person at the Winter Palace to discuss the status. There is a situation. I am not at liberty to speak about it since it is of a personal nature, but he will only disclose it to you face to face. But I will confirm this – I did not take Cassandra. His Majesty will have to tell you the rest."

Artemus signaled Manu and Khamuel to enter. "I believe you all are acquainted?"

Manu held Khamuel back by the shoulder. Before either could speak, Artemus said, "Based on the description of the entity that took Cassandra, we assumed it was the High King of the Seely Court's Watcher, Azazel. He, however, has assured me that he was not complicit. Neither was the High King. It is important for us to get the full story before jumping to any conclusions or taking any action. Khamuel, inform Master Elena that the three of us will journey to the Seely Court. We cannot have any more misunderstandings."

Khamuel bowed his head and backed out of the room, never taking his eyes off Azazel.

Artemus turned to Azazel. "We will leave in the morning. Inform his majesty we will be three."

Azazel bowed and ported back to Ayden's castle to inform him of the next steps.

Artemus motioned to Manu, "I must have a brief discussion with Master Elena before we depart. See if you or Khamuel can get a lead on where Paxton is. I have an uneasy feeling about leaving for the Seely Court when he is still persona non grata."

ELENA WAS SITTING AT her desk at the New York Institute. When Artemus tapped gently on the open door, she opened her eyes. "Please come in. I am neither meditating nor sleeping, although I could use a healthy dose of both."

Artemus sank into one of the comfortable, high-back, cushioned chairs in front of her desk. "I need to meet with the King of the Fae at the Seely Winter Palace. Azazel claims Ayden has information about the disappearance of Cassandra even though he was not involved."

"I understand the new king is quite revolutionary in his approach to governing," Elena said. "He wants to do away with the caste system and the divisiveness between our two realms."

"Yes, I have heard the same," Artemus said. "That's why I decided to take Manu and Khamuel." He waited for a response. When none came, he asked, "Have we gleaned anything about Paxton and his whereabouts?"

Elena pursed her lips. "Regretfully no. After his revelation about his feelings for Cassandra, his continued absence concerns me. He has left himself in a vulnerable position."

Artemus drummed his fingers on the arm of his chair as he considered the implications of Elena's statement.

Elena continued. "It's not the first time an angelic has fallen in love with a human. But Paxton is neither an El nor a Watcher. It was the fallen Els who mated with human females and thus created the horrors called the Nephilim. However, this particular human is not exactly normal. But I digress. We need to focus on finding Cassandra and get her training started. The rest will sort out in time. And we have the matter of Natesh."

Artemus could not repress his scowl. "Yes. I would like to handle that myself once I return from the Winter Court. Perhaps I will bring Manu with me. He has a vested interest from what I remember from the French Revolution. I believe the time has come to balance the scales between him and Natesh."

Rising, the two Celestials grasped forearms in a formal salute "May the Radiant One be ever with you."

"And also, with you."

Chapter 42: Winter Court

The Winter Court of the Fae was located in the etheric layer of Earth, juxtaposed to the high alps of Switzerland and invisible to third-dimensional sight. The bright white of the court momentarily blinded the three members of The White Circle who ported into the throne room. Two hundred and seventy degrees of curved glass walls afforded a panoramic view of the snow-capped mountains. Braziers of blue fairy fire warmed the space. A throne built into the sole solid wall of blue-veined marble sat under a bas relief carving of the royal stag surrounded by intricate vines, the family crest of the House of Oberon.

Ayden came forward dressed in the royal purple of his rank. His ermine trimmed velvet cape was secured at the shoulder with a jewel-encrusted golden stag clasp. He put out his hands to Artemus who grasped the King's forearms in greeting.

"It seems that both condolences and congratulations are in order, your Majesty."

Ayden nodded. "I accept your condolences, but please, we have known one another far too long for such formality. We now have an opportunity to deepen our friendship. Let's not spoil it by being overly formal."

Artemus dipped his head in acquiescence. Ayden waved toward an ornate oval table. "Shall we?"

The table, marble but not as intricately carved as the throne, was laden with food and drink. A blend of appetizing aromas wafted through the room.

"Please let's share a meal as we discuss the current situation," Ayden said. "The wine here is extraordinary, if I do say so myself."

He took a seat in the middle of the table and indicated the space opposite him to Artemus.

Manu and Khamuel flanked Artemus. Azazel sat to the King's right, indicating his stature as a trusted companion.

The repast was typical of the realm, the Fae abstaining from animal flesh. There were assorted breads, crusty and still warm, rich-colored wedges of cheeses, platters of steaming vegetable redolent with butter and herbs, and flaky pies and pastries. The requisite cornucopia of succulent fruits nestled between candles and flowers crowned the middle of the table. Amber-colored wine, decanted into crystal and silver pitchers, stood at each place setting.

Ayden picked up the decanter closest to him, poured Artemus a glass, and then filled his own goblet. He looked at the group. "Please, help yourselves. We will not stand on ceremony here today."

Ayden sipped, then helped himself to a piece of the crusty bread and a wedge of what looked like cheddar cheese. He glanced at Khamuel.

"I don't believe we have met," he said.

"This is one of my trusted Watchers," Artemus said. "His name is Khamuel. His Blade Brother has a personal connection to the young lady in question."

"I see," Ayden said. He studied Khamuel for a moment.

Khamuel inclined his head before returning to his assault on his heaping plate of food.

"As pleasant as it would be to while away the afternoon with you, Majesty, I believe there is a rather serious discussion to be had," Artemus said.

"Indeed, there is," Ayden said. "But first I must know about your interest in the girl. Why were you at her university and in apparent battle with two of the Dark Brotherhood?"

"Sorry, your Majesty, but the ball is in your court. You instigated this meeting, and I need to know what your interest is in this whole affair."

Ayden put down his wineglass and cleared his throat. *Why, he seems nervous*, thought Artemus in shock.

"Cassandra is my daughter."

Khamuel choked on his wine.

"Easy boy, relax," Manu said. He patted Khamuel's arm.

Ayden recounted the summer trip to Europe, where he fell in love with Rebekah. "My father felt it was important for me to understand the Human kingdom since it is so intricately intertwined with ours. He never dreamed I would fall in love with one of them. Unfortunately, he called me back to court before I was able to tell her who I was and my destiny as a royal. She knew I was Fae. How could she not?" He waved a hand over his pale visage and pointed ears. "I asked her to marry me without hesitation. It was the time of the Summer Solstice, and we found a Druid priest to perform a handfasting ritual at the Standing Stones. A week later, Azazel came to take me back home. The biggest mistake of my life was not being forthcoming with Rebekah. Coward that I was, I left her a letter and said I had to return home for a brief period. I promised to return and swore all would be well. It wasn't. My father was furious. He forbade me to continue the relationship. I wasn't even allowed to contact her, on pain of death – hers, not mine. I knew he would kill her if I disclosed who I was. My father thought my marriage to a human-celestial hybrid was beyond detestable. I never contacted her again. I did not know she was with child. Cassandra must have been conceived in the energy of the Solstice." He paused to take another gulp of wine, his eyes glistening.

"I had heard Rebekah had gone back to London to finish her studies with Tatiana, the White Witch in charge of the London Institute, and then on to New York City, where she continued training with Master Elena. I attempted to keep track of her, but was not able to, even though my father had spies everywhere. But I never gave up hope. Once my father passed from life to light three years ago, the threat to Rebekah's life no longer held, so I reached out through my angelic connections to see if I could locate her, but to no avail."

Artemus tented his hands to his chin.

Truth, he thought. *No artifice...no subterfuge. But there's something he's not saying.*

Ayden paused and looked Artemus squarely in the eyes. "Now, it seems, we have a bit of a situation."

"*Oh, you have no idea,*" Artemus thought. Out loud, he said, "There is even more to this story than you know."

"There's more to mine as well," the King said. "My twin Isla found Cassandra before I knew about Rebekah – glamoured as Taryn Oberon – disappeared." He recounted Isla's story. "She embraced her role of aunt and took up residence in the house in Charlotte. She and her consort were the ones responsible for taking Cassandra. Isla considered it a "rescue". She brought the girl to me three days ago. Until then, I did not know I had a daughter. Cassandra now knows of her Fae lineage, as well as the Celestial heritage she has through her mother."

"How did your sister learn of her?" Manu asked.

He had been watching the exchange with growing unease. He did not want to tell Ayden about his Soul connection with Cassandra just yet, but there was something else pulling at him.

Who was this consort?

Ayden turned to him. "When our father was on his deathbed, he named me the heir, even though Isla is first born. She was not ... pleased and left the court in a rage. She aligned herself with a dark lord and created a court of her own. I understand they now have a large army that includes every level of the Devic Realm, from Watchers to Fae, elves, and elementals. It's also widely known that she is aligned with a dark coven of Witches from the Human Kingdom. I only recently learned she has a consort, but the specifics are still well hidden. I don't know if he is Fae or Celestial, although from what I know of my sister, she wouldn't choose another Fae as her consort. She would look for someone powerful in other ways. I did glean, however, that he can shape shift."

Artemus had been quiet for as long as he could. "Which is why we all jumped to the conclusion that a Watcher took Cassandra," he said, "and why I turned to you, since only the Fae, the Dark Brothers, and I have Watchers in attendance."

Ayden continued. "Isla told me she found out about Cassandra through her consort. He has a large network loyal to him in the Human and Celestial Realms and they have been searching for this missing Seventh Avatar as well. Cassandra drew their interest a few months ago. Apparently, some of her powers ignited and were sensed by the Sirian Oracles. It drew his interest, and he shared it with my sister. She knew of my love for Rebekah and how I had tried to find her. I never kept my love a secret. Isla, being Isla, decided to search on her own. She traced the fashion connection, looking for a Rebekah St. Claire. But once she found Taryn Oberon, she made the connection, since she knew we had been joined in a Handfasting and Oberon is our family name. By the time she got to Charlotte, she discovered that Taryn-Rebekah-had gone missing, and Cassandra was living with two of Rebekah's friends and business partners. Isla went to check out the situation. The moment she saw Cassandra, Isla knew she was my daughter. The resemblance to the Oberon line is unmistakable. She then concocted the plan to step in as Cassandra's aunt and take care of her. Isla told me that she knew Cassandra had her mother's latent gifts of healing and Dream Walking. She monitored the girl to discover the depth of her understanding. Cassandra was relatively unaware of her powers."

Artemus interrupted. "And the whole university debacle?"

"That was somewhat vague. I was so overwhelmed with having my daughter with me, I did not ask for much more detail. Isla told me she was feeling uneasy about the whole sorority issue and had sent one of her handmaids to the mixer to keep an eye on Cassandra. When the emissary signaled Isla that Cassandra was in danger, her consort went to rescue her."

Artemus kept silent for a few minutes and processed. "There are still pieces of the puzzle that need to be clarified. But suffice it to say, you and Rebekah created a being who could very well be pivotal in changing the world as we know it. Perhaps even saving it."

Ayden's eyes narrowed. "I have been getting visions of Cassandra wielding a sword of flames and light on fields of battle. I hoped they were glimpses of her past lives, and not premonitions for this one."

"Oh, you are correct on both counts," Artemus said. "Your daughter is a critical player in the evolution of both humanity and this planet. However, she still has free will, and we cannot burden her with the prophecies yet. She must come to her Soul Destiny through her own efforts and convictions. In the meantime, we need to consult with the others regarding the best way to apprise her about her destiny." He turned to Khamuel, "To use your vernacular, we don't want to 'freak her out.'"

No one had noticed the figure who had slipped into the room while they were talking. They all jumped a little when interrupted by a female voice.

"Your Majesty, may I speak?"

Ayden looked to the back of the room and smiled. "Of course, my dear Brigida, please come in. You may speak freely." Turning to his guests, he introduced her. "May I present to you my trusted friend and confidant. She was my nursemaid, then my governess, and now basically runs my entire life." He chuckled with affection.

Brigida curtsied to the king and then to Master Artemus. She nodded to the others. "I have been with the princess these past few days," she said, "and I believe she is beginning to come to terms with her Fae lineage. However, she is very vulnerable at the moment. She has a lot to process and may not be able to take much more. I'd like to propose an idea."

Ayden nodded. Brigida continued. "Cassandra is a Dream Walker. She is beginning to have dreams about her past lives. She may very well be under a spell of forgetfulness. Some of her dreams may be flashbacks from her childhood that have been unlocked since she has been in the Devic Realm. I believe we can counteract that spell. If we can convince her to accept the Royal Torc, she will receive the memories of her Fae ancestors. Along with those memories she may very well be able to unlock memories of this lifetime as well. I believe this process will be less...ah...jarring for her."

"Interesting," Artemus said. "Brigida, are you trained in the arts of White Magic?"

"I did the basics as all Fae children do, and then was fully trained with the great, great grandame of the current Lady of the Glen once I hit my own maturity."

"It seems that we are in the midst of the circle of destiny indeed," Artemus said. "Brigida, would you feel comfortable teaching the rudiments of White Magic to Cassandra?"

"Aye, I would indeed," Brigida said. "His Majesty is also a master of magics. I would say I can start her off with the basics, but he should teach her some of the more advanced techniques."

"King Ayden, what are your thoughts?" Artemus asked.

Ayden had stood. He was pacing in front of his throne with his hands clasped behind his back, head bowed in deep thought. He threw it back with a laugh. "My friends, we keep interfering with the natural order of something that was ordained long before we were born. Don't you think it is time to allow destiny to take its course? We need to get out of our own way, and out of the way of The Divine Plan. Let us pull back a bit and look at the situation. We have a very advanced Soul who has spent lifetime after lifetime honing talents and abilities from the three realms dwelling on the planet. We are acting like Cassandra is some delicate flower who will fall apart when she is confronted with who she is at the core level. Oh yes, she may get angry and will show a bit of emotion – I have certainly been privy to that part of her personality lately. However, I believe she will be able to bring herself back to center and step into her Soul Mission. Of this, I have no doubt."

"You are right, of course," Artemus said. "We are acting like Cassandra is just a normal teenager and she is not."

Manu was quiet – and disturbed. His Soul Mate, his Twin Soul, his love, had committed to a Soul Mission that was beyond his comprehension. Her Soul was powerful, yes, but she was still a teenaged human girl. No one had prepared her for any of this. He did not want to speak, but he was feeling compelled. *It's time to complete this story,* Manu thought. He got up from his chair and cleared his throat.

"King Ayden, I believe I need to share with you why I am here and to tell you why I should be the one to bring Cassandra back to the Terran Realm."

Chapter 43: Soul Mates

Ayden swiveled his head to the High Priest, his eyebrows raised.

"Since you know who I am, you also know about my original mission," Manu said. "I was here during the dawn of Humanity's coming of age when we established the Mystery School in Atlantis." He paused for a few heartbeats, "Cassandra is the reincarnation of my Soul Mate, the High Priestess Ayesha. Her soul mission is also mine. Once she sets her mind to something, nothing will keep her from manifesting the desired outcomes. I have seen no one as focused as she when it comes to the power of the mind. I have seen her manifest crystals out of thin air just by visualizing them. Her talent enabled us to create the crystal fuel chambers of Atlantis. From what I have learned of her in this current incarnation, Cassandra has brought forth those abilities to manifest from thought to hand through tapping into the Divine Matrix. We know she has used her abilities to develop a thorough understanding of the World Wide Web. Her university scholarship honors her ability to create a computer program capable of transforming thoughts to code virtually instantaneously. Her skill will be invaluable in the coming battles between the Dark Brotherhood and the Light Workers. The Internet is the new battlefield, and it will take a master soul to lead the charge. I have every confidence that she will overcome any hesitation and realize her fullest potential as one of The Seven."

Everyone remained silent as they attempted to process what they had just heard. Manu certainly had unique insights into Cassandra's essence.

"I concur," Ayden said, "we know there are other forces at work here. We need to be on high alert, especially since she has not met you in this lifetime and may balk at going with you." He paused and looked at Manu. "Despite your Soul Connection, she is a seventeen-year-old and you are …. not. Hopefully, she will recognize you on a Soul level and trust you enough to get her to the Institute and under the protection of The White Circle."

He let out a long breath. "I will return to my palace and start laying the groundwork for you to take her back."

Manu thought about Ayden's comment regarding the age difference. At the time of the fall of Atlantis, they had inhabited physical bodies and looked to be in their mid-twenties in human years. Since he had spent most of the ensuing years on the Mother Ship, he had not aged physically, but had certainly matured with millennia of experience. Elena was the only one that had aged since much of her time had been spent in the heavy vibration of the Earth.

Artemus said, "Insofar as getting Cassandra under the tutelage of Master Elena, Brigida has come upon a good plan." He looked at his former caregiver, then back at the King. "But once Cassandra has been taught the rudiments of White Magic and apprised of her abilities, I have another request. With your permission, your Majesty, I would like Brigida to come into the Human Kingdom and continue to care for Cassandra. She will act as a bridge between the Fae Kingdom and the Human. I will assign Angelics from the Guardians to protect them both."

Brigida's jade eyes glowed in anticipation. The idea of assisting Cassandra was both a challenge and a labor of love. She was eager to help Cassandra develop her powers and to see what she could accomplish.

Ayden turned the matter over in his mind. "It is a good plan," he said after a while. "When I feel she is ready, I will send Azazel to you, Artemus."

"I have an additional thought," Artemus said. "I would like to elicit the aid of the Sirian Oracles to see if they can help us find Rebekah," Artemus said. "My senses tell me she is being held against her will to keep Cassandra off balance. This all seems like something the Dark Brotherhood would orchestrate at the highest of levels. Those lower on the pole like Morgandrian are oblivious. That's why they were trying to recruit Cassandra into their little sorority."

Ayden nodded and motioned to Brigida, who left the room to return to the Seely Court.

Manu spoke again. "Ayesha...I mean Cassandra... can handle the truth of who she is," Manu said. "But Isla has not made her last move. She is up to something."

Ayden's face was grim. "My sister has a fatal flaw," he said. "She always assumes she is the smartest person in the room. Consequently, she likes to believe everyone else is stupid. We are not."

Chapter 44: The Stars Don't Lie

Elena sat across the desk from Artemus the following morning. They bowed their heads in the intense study of an astrological chart.

"I am glad that we sent Glenda to do more digging at the house." Elena said. Finding Cassandra's chart in Rebekah's hidden attic altar room was a stroke of luck.

"Her chart is certainly interesting. I see why Rebekah wanted to keep her safe and shielded. With Scorpio rising, Cassandra's life will be a constant series of obstacles or crises," Artemus said.

"Well, we've witnessed her struggles in the little time we have known her," Elena said. Her power and potential in this lifetime are limitless. She will be like a phoenix rising out of the ashes of her trials. Her Soul Purpose is about a total transformation from the mundane to the magnificent." Eyes sparkled with a glimmer of something ancient and knowing. "The opportunity to regain her immortality is now before her."

Their eyes met. "And leading the charge to the thousand years of peace," Elena said. "Once The Quickening occurs on her eighteenth birthday, her Aquarian sun and aptitude for group dynamics will strengthen. I agree with Brigida. There may very well be a spell of forgetfulness preventing her from accessing her innate powers. Surely, they would have manifested early on otherwise. The other six Avatars started awakening on their thirteenth birthdays."

Artemus reached for a large metal box adorned with an array of gemstones and engraved protection sigils. He lifted the lid and extracted a black leather-bound book. Book markers of thin strips of vellum dripped from the pages. "We have this book on loan from the Charlotte Masonic Lodge," he said. "I am under threat of extinction should anything happen to it."

Elena smiled when she saw a twinkle of amusement in his eyes.

"Charlotte remains a city deeply influenced by Scorpio." Artemus began. "Its devotion to materiality is causing it to self-destruct. Since banking and its subsequent focus on money, power, and status are such a primary focus of its banking community, the city has not yet entered the second phase of its spiritual purpose. The ley line at the corner of Trade Street and Tryon Streets is of the greatest interest to our mission. It connects with Washington D.C. at the U.S. Capitol. Once Cassandra begins her own journey of transformation within the Charlotte city limits, her energy will ignite a shift of the city's energy. Once the transformation begins, The Seven will be able to shift the entire city to the next level. Then we can prepare to ignite the ley line into the Capitol. It will cause a massive shift in consciousness and reverberate throughout the country and the world."

"How do you envision that?" asked Elena.

Artemus replied, "Do you believe there is a worldwide subliminal manipulation that controls the weak-minded?"

Elena nodded.

Artemus continued, "The strongest weapon against mind control is a meditator's mind. We need to redouble our efforts to get as much of humanity meditating as possible."

"I agree," Elena said. "The first thing will be to establish meditation training centers and magnetize like-minded people. We can reach out to colleges, universities, spiritual groups, yoga centers and such in and around Charlotte and Washington to teach meditation. Once the groups are trained, we can gather them at the apex of the ley lines in both cities and hold regular Full Moon celebrations with drumming and chanting. The ritual will raise the vibratory frequency and spread throughout the cities—and, of course, down the ley line."

"Excellent suggestion." Artemus said. "Then we will work toward having the acolytes from the Institutes head up similar groups throughout the world."

"Exactly." Elena jumped to her feet without realizing it. Embarrassed, she sat. "We must establish a network of meditation groups. Building the energy grid will be right up Cassandra's alley. With her innate understanding of the World Wide Web, she will be the keystone to shifting the energy into the next upward spiral of human evolution. We need to bring her back from the

Seely Court as soon as possible. Her training is long past due, and I do not want to risk the Dark Brotherhood getting its hands on her."

Her face furrowed with concern. "But we still have the aunt business. Why would she take Cassandra only to return her to her father? Isla has obviously embraced the left-hand path by establishing her own dark court and crowning herself queen. If she wants Cassandra's power, why give her back? This doesn't track."

Artemus shrugged. "Who knows how a mind works? Especially one warped by anger, vengeance, and a lust for power. There is also this consort of hers. Who is he? I agree with the King—whoever he is, he is powerful. Otherwise, Isla wouldn't have anything to do with him."

A knock resounded at the door. "Enter," they said in unison.

Paxton stood at the threshold.

Chapter 45: Reconciliation

Ayden found Cassie at the Dream Temple again, curled up in a deep blue velvet chaise longue with intricate gold embroidery along the edges. She held a book in her lap, engrossed in the words. Startled, she looked up when he entered the pavilion, and released a tentative smile.

"Hello Father, we missed you at lunch."

He grinned, overwhelmed with emotion. She'd addressed him as "Father" with genuine warmth. "I've come back from an enlightening meeting and wanted to share it with you," he said. Nodding toward the book, he asked, "What's caught your attention?"

She showed him the spine, revealing the title: *Psychic Self Defense* by Dion Fortune.

"Ah, Dion Fortune, a remarkable spiritual teacher from the nineteenth century. She collaborated with your grandmother in the realm of White Magic. Dion was adept at interdimensional travel and frequented our realm. I imagine you'd have enjoyed meeting her, given your interest in her teachings."

"That would be epic!" Cassie exclaimed. "She also seems to have a good understanding of psychology. It adds credibility to her insights. Without that, some parts of this book might come off as delusional."

He sighed. "Many individuals with extraordinary abilities were unjustly locked up by society, labeling them as lunatics, or of the devil.'"

Cassie put down the book. "Speaking of ESP, you have something to discuss with me?"

He arched an eyebrow. "I do indeed. After considerable thought, I would like for you to work with Brigida on Fae magic. She is a well-trained White Witch, and I feel it is time to begin to deepen your understanding of your abilities. Brigida is enthusiastic about helping you. Your abilities will reveal themselves quickly since we completed the torc ritual. I'm intrigued by your choice of a book on psychic self-defense, something you'll need to become proficient in. What do you think?"

She searched his eyes and saw only love and concern. Cassie nodded. She paused a moment and then jumped up. "It's time for afternoon tea. I'm suddenly famished."

She scooped up the book and beckoned her father back toward the house.

Ayden stared after her open-mouthed and a bit dumbfounded. Who was this person she was becoming? She was undeniably different from the young girl he met only a few days earlier. With a shrug, he followed her into the kitchen.

The torc must have other powers other than remembrance, he thought.

Entering the kitchen, they found Brigida icing a honey and walnut cake with what looked like butter frosting,

"Ah! My favorite!" Before she could stop him, Ayden swiped a finger across the side and Brigida slapped at him with a spoon.

"Have you regressed to childhood then? Ruin my masterpiece again and I'll pop your behind with this." She brandished the spoon while he licked his finger and backed away. "Now, get...we'll have tea on the terrace since it's such a beautiful afternoon."

Ayden feinted at the cake again. The spoon stung him on the back of the hand. He whimpered in exaggerated fashion and chuckled on the way outside.

"The old girl has not lost her spunk," he said.

Cassie laughed. Father and daughter sat in the afternoon sun and waited for their tea. They were so lost in their conversation that they never saw the shadowed figure watching them from a position camouflaged in the hedges at the far end of the garden.

Brigida rolled out a tea cart. It was laden with tea cakes and other pastries still warm from the oven; the newly iced cake dominated the center position. Cassie's mouth watered when Brigida began to put the plates of delectables in the middle of a lazy Susan. Brigida sat down after confirming that the treats were exactly what she wanted. A tiny kitchen elf decked out in a white apron came out to pour cups of steaming rosehips tea. Another followed closely behind, a jar of honey at the ready.

Brigida took a sip of tea and began. "I apologize for barging in on your private time with your father, however, he and I have discussed what he has learned about why the situation at your university occurred. We agreed that I would be included in apprising you of the facts."

Brigida let out a breath. "Cassie, you are a very special soul. There are three kingdoms inhabiting the Earth currently: the Human, the Celestial, and the Devic. The Devic Kingdom, as you have seen, includes angels, fairies, elves, elementals and more. Your mother is the daughter of a Human mother and a Celestial father. We call her a Hybrid. Your father, of course, is Fae. The unique mixture of your bloodlines makes you distinctive. You're the only one we know of who inherited talents and abilities from all three kingdoms. The first Trybrid."

Brigida paused for a moment to allow Cassie to absorb the idea.

Cassie looked from her to Ayden. "Mom is an alien?"

Her father winced a little. "No, no. Your mother has DNA from two compatible evolutions, both humanoid. One is native to this planet, and the other originates in another star system. Visitors from other planets have been coming to Earth for millions of years. Some of them are of the Light and some of the Dark. A male who came from the Pleiades sired your mother. Whether he is alive is unknown. Your mother told me your grandmother was human and passed away long before you were born. What she vividly remembered of her father, your grandfather, was that he was frequently away on 'business trips.'

"While in college, your mother joined a sorority called Alpha Omega, which you know. Alpha Omega is not just a training school, but a profound Mystery School that imparts ageless wisdom teachings to extraordinary humans and hybrids, encompassing the foundations of religions and cultures. Materialistic and rational thinking conceals these teachings, making them accessible only to those who have achieved a certain level of intuition. Your mother was such a one. And so are you."

Cassie shook her head. "My brain is exploding. Why didn't Mommy tell me any of this?"

Ayden took a deep breath. "She wanted to shield you from your potentiality for as long as she could. I sense she imbued the necklace she gave you with some kind of binding spell designed to keep you under the radar of anyone who was searching for a special group of highly advanced hybrids that were prophesied to incarnate around the time you were born. Somehow the spell deactivated a few weeks ago and—"

"Wait! "A few weeks ago?" She described her meditation in the Charlotte garden, where she had felt she had contacted someone "out there."

Her father and Brigida exchanged knowing glances. "Well, that explains a lot! Your latent abilities, dare I say your powers, are due to be activated fully on your eighteenth birthday. They are straining at the leash, so to speak. Your inherent ability to connect with Celestials was most likely tapped into during your deep meditation because of the use of rose-colored light. That is the frequency of the Mother Ship."

Ayden explained how different light frequencies can raise the vibrations of a being from one dimension to another.

"Curious," Cassie said. "I thought when Mommy gave me those stones to meditate with, it was because they connected them with my chakra system."

"Yes, they are," Brigida said. "Yet, they also act as portals to heightened levels of awareness, especially given that your energy system is a fusion of three kingdoms. It's fortunate that your mother possessed the wisdom and foresight to protect you."

"Do you think that is why she has gone missing?"

"I don't know, my dear," Ayden said. "But I suspect there is a connection. Either she was taken to make you vulnerable, or she left to protect you. Regardless, we must find her – and soon." He paused. "Your mother had been training with the White Witch Tatiana at the Mystery School in London. What I have since discovered is that when I didn't return, Tatiana deemed it necessary to send Rebekah back to America to finish up her training with Master Elena in New York. It was then that she learned she was part Celestial and part Human. Rebekah must have found out once you were born that you are a unique being. I cannot think of a better way to protect you than by using her considerable glamouring abilities to "hide in plain sight" and take you back to the safety of London and Tatiana."

Cassie nodded. *This is making sense for the first time.*

"Here's something interesting," Cassandra said. She told them about the books she'd found on her mother's bookshelf, *Green Darkness*, and the book from his library on Hermes. She recounted her dreams, especially the one about the Compte de St. Germain.

Ayden rubbed his chin. "The Universe has a way of confirming when we are on the right path. You are exactly where you are meant to be." He stood, walked over to Cassie, and put his hands on her shoulders. "You are wise beyond your years, my dearest daughter. I am proud beyond measure to be a part of your journey and thrilled to see how you are moving along with the ordained directions of The Radiant One."

He sank to his knees and locked his eyes on hers. "Never forget, though – you have free will. You are under no obligation to do anything or go anywhere unless you want to."

Cassie never looked away. "I won't," she said. "I am gaining a better understanding of my abilities and the potentials. There's so much I don't know. I am going to need a lot more training."

Ayden hoisted himself to his feet. "That we can do. Come, we will go to the Dream Temple, and Brigida and I will begin your new lessons."

Chapter 46: A Matter of Time

Isla circled Morgandrian in a fury. "You must be the most incompetent witch I have ever known! How in the hell did you fall into Elena's clutches? You stupid, *stupid* bitch! All these years of preparation gone in an instant. I should incinerate you where you stand!"

Morgandrian straightened her spine and threw back her shoulders; her gaze did not waver.

"There is equal blame here, Isla. While you were playing the doting auntie to Cassandra, you were tasked with influencing her with the limited help of Natesh Nandwani. If you will recall that little piece was orchestrated by your, um, *consort*."

Isla narrowed her eyes; sparks beginning to fly out of her fingers. Morgandrian didn't flinch. She knew her worth to the Dark Brotherhood. Isla held a top position within the group, but she lacked the authority to decide on eliminating Morgandrian or any other clan or coven leader. Her jurisdiction ended at the boundaries of the Fae. Sirkan's influence ended with the Dark Celestials. Both wanted total control of the planet. But Morgandrian sensed that Sirkan and Isla were not the only ones in charge. There was someone else above them, someone who pulled the strings. She didn't know who it was, but she was determined to find out.

"Be very careful, Morgandrian. You forget who you are dealing with."

True, Morgandrian thought, but you can't do anything about it, your Bitchness.

A flash and Isla disappeared

SIRKAN STOOD SILHOUETTED against the backdrop of his temple's altar room. His gold-embroidered black robe glimmered in the flickering light of the fireplace. His slicked-back hair made his handsome face appear like something carved in stone. He was a man of power and authority, and it showed in every movement he made. His eyes, a profound and penetrating citrine hue, appeared to possess the capacity to gaze directly into one's very essence. He was used to getting what he wanted, and he would stop at nothing to achieve his goals. He watched the vampire pace.

"How could you not know the boy Paxton was a Guardian?" Natesh bellowed like an enraged bull. "What happened to your network of spies?"

"I advise you to moderate your tone and recall to whom you address," the Dark Priest uttered with a venomous hiss. "I understand your anger, but it pales in the face of what I am experiencing at this moment. I ended your sire for less and, believe me, there are quite a few in line waiting for you to screw up enough for me to end you as well. Fortunately for you, none of them has your level of expertise when it comes to influencing the weak-minded with their proclivity for subliminal programing. Your work along those lines and your grasp of cyber warfare are indispensable – at least for now."

Natesh realized he had been holding his breath. *Well, that's a relief.* "I am gratified to hear you appreciate my special talents in that area, my lord. My team has demonstrated exceptional skill in integrating messages of violence across various conspiracy websites, television news channels, and social media platforms. I find it delightful when liberal groups express disbelief in obvious falsehoods. I want to shout - you imbeciles! It's subliminal messaging!

Sirkan grimaced at the show of pride. Natesh would have to go. But for now, his twenty-first century talents were invaluable. For years, the Dark Brotherhood had successfully spread messages of hate and divisiveness. *Hashtag: controltheignorantmasses!* Their manipulation was about to reach the desired crescendo in causing civil wars and genocide across the globe. And the one proclaimed as the Messiah was doing a masterful job. Oh yes, President Soter was performing just as they had created him. Messiah indeed!

Sirkan knew that gaining access to Cassandra's abilities in manipulating the World Wide Web would push the balance of control to his side of the chessboard. He was champing at the bit to get her under his control. He knew she was a long-time meditator, especially given her ability to resist subliminal messages.

"Paxton, being brought into the Queen's court is the only reason I am not ending you. You can thank her later. I plan on his securing Cassandra for us once and for all."

Natesh stilled. "Paxton has joined you?"

A crooked and insincere smile adorned Sirkan's face. "Indeed. Isla is indoctrinating him as we speak. He will prove an invaluable asset when he is back in the middle of the White Circle."

Natesh hid his consternation. He did not want to tip his own hand regarding Cassandra, especially since he knew beyond a doubt that she was his long-lost love, Giselle. *These damnable past lives are becoming a real pain in the ass.*

SIRKAN FURROWED HIS brow as he watched Natesh leave. He sensed the bastard was not telling him everything. With Cassandra so close, thoughts of her consumed him. He had pursued her for millennia. Longing. Lusting. And yes, loving her.

He wanted her in every aspect of her being. He wanted her by his side and within his power. His thoughts drifted back to the years after the sinking of Atlantis. He remembered his lips crushing hers, her legs spread open to him while he filled her with his very essence. Their countless couplings had produced powerful children, offspring who had become some of the most formidable rulers and demigods of the ancient world.

His breath shallowed; he felt the throbbing between his thighs. Having to watch her mortal body wither and die had been unbearable. The anguish he felt when he had first lost her to mortality was a deep-seated scar upon his soul. He knew she had not loved him, not in the way he loved her. Instead, he had been content with possessing her. *But she had loved their children.*

And now – finally – the long wait was over. The Quickening was upon her, and then they would rule side by side into eternity. He clenched his fists and took several deep breaths until his body and emotions quieted.

Patience. It was simply a matter of time.

Chapter 47: House of Oberon

Ayden, Cassandra, and Brigida were in the opulent library surrounded by the ancient tomes of wisdom and memorabilia from eons of Fae rule. Cassandra sat in a royal purple tufted high-back chair, with the blue velvet box opened on her lap, her father standing before her.

I'm thankful and relieved that you've embraced your heritage, my daughter. Ayden's throat constricted. "This torc will help you embrace your lineage as a member of the Fae royals." He raised her chin to look into his eyes. They were full of love for her. "Now, please take the torc out of its case and hand it to me. This will signify your permission for me to give it to you."

Taking the intricate band of silver and jewels in both hands, she held it out to her father, and then rose. The amethyst pendant around her neck warmed, and she grasped it with her left hand. "Mother told me never to take this off. Will the torc interfere with its energy in any way?"

"Highly doubtful," Ayden said. "I cannot imagine anything that your mother gave you would have any effect other than strengthen the love imbued into this torc."

His hands trembled with emotion. He stood behind her and clasped the torc around her neck. She ran her hands over it, feeling the delicate necklet tingle against her skin. She felt a brief wave of dizziness. Images flashed across her inner eye.

Brigida gently guided her to sit back into the chair and whispered. "Close your eyes. Let the images come as they will."

Cassie saw her father's eyes. Tears began to stream down her face. A beautiful woman with silver eyes replaced the image. *Grandmother!* A series of scenes unfolded that could only have been memories from her ancestors as seen through the eyes of those who had worn the torc before her. Her body pulsated. It was a pleasant – no – wonderful feeling. She felt like the Scarecrow in *The Wizard of Oz*. Her mind expanded with ancient wisdom that spanned millennia. Her father's voice came from far away. "Take long, deep breaths Cassandra. They will slow down the visions a bit more and allow the energies to settle."

She did as he bade and immediately felt more balanced. The pendant her mother had given her began to thrum in unison with the torc. Suddenly, she felt a hand interlacing with hers. She gasped, her eyes flying open. "Mommy!"

Ayden knelt before her and took her hands into his. "What is it?"

"It's Mommy. I can *feel* her!"

Chapter 48: Well-Laid Plans

Paxton was pacing the floor inside Master Elena's office yet again, awaiting the signal from Ayden through the Spirit Screen. Elena watched his escalating anxiety with growing concern.

"Paxton, stop. You need to get your emotions under control. I will not allow you to continue with this mission while you show so much agitation. You will only intensify a highly volatile situation with your anxiety."

He stopped in front of her desk, shaking out his hands and taking a deep breath. "You are right, of course, Master Elena. Until this whole situation developed, I hadn't realized just how much I had cared for her. I know it's against the First Order of my mission, but I can't help myself. I truly feel that she is my soul mate."

"Soul mate or not, this high level of emotion simply cannot continue. Go to the meditation garden and get a handle on yourself. I will send for you when King Ayden contacts me."

Watching him go, Elena took a deep breath. They were all experiencing tension. The attack from parties unknown during Morgandrian's interrogation had shaken her to the core. Even though she was fully recovered, the idea of a spy in their midst dripped away in her mind like a leaky faucet. She was also concerned about the time Paxton had gone missing. He seemed to have changed somehow. He had always been exuberant about life, but now he had become secretive and withdrawn. Elena didn't know what to make of it. She knew she needed to watch him.

Master Artemus had devised new security protocols – a lie detector of sorts. An arch at every entrance and portal into the Institutes could pick up the slightest rise in temperature caused by either mental or emotional aberrations, even those of low frequency. Nonetheless, they were on high alert, and additional Guardians had been called in to monitor activity. Their trainers and personal Guardians accompanied every avatar.

Elena was not as concerned with their safety since most of the Avatars had been trained with battle and defensive skills. They had honed their mental abilities over lifetimes; most were telepathic and highly intuitive. Still, Cassandra's abduction paired with the demonic attack had put everyone on edge.

Again, her thoughts shifted to Paxton and his return. Artemus felt Paxton's training would hold him in good stead, but she felt a nagging concern at his low-level energy signature. They had agreed with Manu that Paxton would be the one to retrieve Cassandra from the Seely Court.

Paxton came back into her office just as the Spirit Screen vibrated with an incoming request. Waving her right hand over the screen, Ayden's image came through, his eyes bright with unshed tears, a sad smile on his face. Elena could sense his reluctance to proceed further.

"Greetings King Ayden," Elena said. "I know this is difficult for you. You can be confident that we're doing everything possible to keep Cassandra safe during this transfer. She stepped aside and motioned Paxton forward. "Allow me to introduce you to a member of the White Circle, and one of Master Artemus' acolytes, Paxton."

Ayden's eyebrows shot up over widened eyes. "Well, the infamous boyfriend! Cassandra has regaled me with tales of your role in her life since you were children. It is nice to put a face to the image on the pedestal."

Paxton gave him a lopsided smile and bowed deeply. "Your Majesty."

"Yes, well..." Ayden trailed off. Elena felt his reluctance to take this next step in letting go of his daughter across the distance.

"So, we have had a bit of a change in the cast of characters," Elena said. "Since Cassandra knows Paxton so well in this lifetime, we decided he will come to you and ease her back into this dimension and her newly discovered status. The other details will not change, just the players. Are you still fine with Brigida coming here?"

Brigida's round figure came into view as Ayden pulled her to his side and draped an arm around her shoulders. "Are you still game, my Brigida?"

She looked at her king with adoring eyes. "Aye, majesty. I must admit, I love her just as much as I have loved you. I would give up my life willingly for her."

Ayden's jaw clenched. "I pray that will never be a choice, dear one." He tightened his arm around her shoulder and addressed Elena. "I have instructed Brigida to proceed to Charlotte and prepare for Cassandra's return." He smiled. "I have a few more past life regressions with Cassandra, so let us say that we will meet in three days' time. Come to me first, Paxton, and I will take you to Cassandra."

Paxton's head inclined, his eyes shining. "I am at your command, Majesty."

Ayden gave him the portal coordinates and set the time for their meeting.

Chapter 49: Contingency Plans

Ayden sat in the Dream Temple with Cassie in half-lotus position, watching as she began breathing and relaxation exercises. The past two days had been incredibly fruitful. Cassie's ability to focus and concentrate exceeded anything he had ever seen in one so young. The regressions had helped bring her mental acuity forward from former lives, and he was frankly in awe of her abilities. Now they needed to increase her power so she could handle the tricky and dangerous days ahead. He was loath to let her go, fearing for her safety above everything else. But the courage of youth prevailed, and she was eager to take the next steps.

"Cassandra," he said, "I want you to put the psychic self-defense techniques I have taught you in place and build an adamant wall in your mind's eye now."

Her breathing became shallow as she went deeper and deeper into the place she called "the cave." It was rather like an inter-dimensional way station she had pulled from a past life as an Indian Shaman. Ayden felt her click into it and then did his best to go in after her. His own psychic abilities were considerable. He had always been able to gain access into another's mind – but not Cassandra's. Her shield did not even bend.

An hour later, having pulled every trick and technique he could muster from his mental toolbox, he withdrew and waited. Watching her face, he knew the exact moment when her concentration relaxed.

She took a series of deep breaths and opened her eyes. "I could feel you trying to get in." She grinned. "And boy could I feel your frustration."

"Well, Miss Cocky, you certainly did a good job. I don't have any more tricks up my sleeves." He paused and looked into her eyes - questioning.

She nodded. "I'm ready."

"Good." He got up and took her hand. "There is something I want to show you. Then we will explore your past life with the Compte." Ayden walked Cassie over to a large carved wooden box. "I wanted you to see these pictures of your mother I took that special summer. You have known her in her glamoured state. You need to see her before the transformation." He opened the box and took out a bundle of photos wrapped in a blue silk scarf. Cassie grabbed them eagerly.

The treasured photos showed Rebekah St. Claire with long, layered auburn hair, not the fringed black bob she "wore" as Taryn Oberon. She was curvy and looked to be about 5'4'. Cassie burst out laughing.

"What?"

"Mommy glamoured herself to look like a starving European model with black Cleopatra hair. I always kinda resented the fact that she didn't have the same problem I had with carbs. And here is proof that she actually did!"

"Women and their obsession with weight. I've never understood it."

Cassie looked up at him and smiled. "Neither does Pax. I can't wait for you to meet him." She continued to shuffle through the pictures, smiling, and then exclaimed, "This one must have been the day you got married." She held up a picture of a dewy-eyed couple, grinning from ear to ear. They were draped in gauzy white tunics and matching, loose-fitting pants. Her mother's head was adorned with a garland of white flowers. They were holding up their hands with silver wedding bands, mugging for the camera.

Ayden nodded. "One of my happiest days. She is the love of my life." Their eyes met. "We *will* find her." He coughed to cover his emotions, then said, "Now let's explore that past life."

Chapter 50: Shattered Trust

Paxton ported to the Seely Court at the agreed upon time, his face full of determination. Once he was off, Elena put out a Spirit Screen request to Artemus. Several minutes later, the plasma-type surface shimmered, and his face materialized.

"Adonai, my sister. All is well?"

"Well is a relative term," she said. "Paxton is off to the Seely Court to bring Cassandra back to Charlotte. But my gut is sending out alarm bells. Can you pull Manu into this conversation?"

Instantaneously, Manu's face came into focus. "Adonai…" He noticed the pinched look on Elena's face. "Something is amiss."

A statement, not a query.

"I just sent Paxton to the Seely Court, but something feels off. I am concerned. Do you still have access to the King?"

No sooner were the words out of her mouth, than Manu vanished.

"It appears so." Artemus said. He gestured to the figure beside him. Khamuel stepped forward.

"On it, Master," he said – and he vanished.

Artemus met Elena's eyes. "Shall we?"

THE GROUND GROANED when Khamuel landed onto the marble floor of the throne room, his huge iridescent wings extended. Ayden was nowhere to be found, but Khamuel sensed the energy of his Blade Brother. Retracting his wings, he bolted from the room, sprinted toward the main hallway of the palace, and ran into the throne room. He slid to a stop. Cassandra was weeping and wrapped in Paxton's arms.

"It's okay, my love," the boy said. "I've got you."

Paxton's head shot up. "Back off, Kam."

Khamuel looked at him in confusion. Then he noticed the prone body of the King of the Fae on the floor.

"Shit, Pax, what have you done?" *And where the hell was Azazel?*

"I am protecting the girl I love," Paxton said with the growl of an angry bear, his emerald eyes flashing with defiance. Cassie had not looked up. *Thank God for intuition.*

Three portals flashed open. Manu, Elena, and Artemus catapulted into the room. Cassandra's head whipped around, her sobs catching in her throat. Her eyes locked with Manu's, and she felt an electric shock shoot up her spine. His eyes were the color of the deepest depth of the ocean, and she felt herself drowning in them. She felt an irresistible pull toward him, and she strained to free herself from Paxton's arms. She heard her mother's voice telling her, "The eyes are the windows to the soul," and she knew that Manu's soul was calling to hers.

Another portal erupted at the far end of the room, spewing forth Azazel. With a bloodcurdling roar, his emblazoned battle sword drawn, he flew toward Paxton, only to be thrown back by a well-built force field.

Paxton tightened his arm around Cassie's waist.

"Too late," he said. Another flash of light opened a portal – and the young couple was gone.

The echoing boom of Manu's roar filled every corner of the palace. As the whirlwind faded, he charged its last wisp, every muscle taut with fury. He halted, his chest heaving, his mind racing to find its center. Artemus, attempting a comforting touch, found his hand pushed away.

"Artemus, now's not the time," Manu's voice held a warning. "Give me space until my storm subsides."

Respect and caution in his eyes, the Master of the White Circle retreated a step. A silent, urgent thought flickered from Artemus to the other side of the room: Elena, *be prepared. His storm is yet to pass.*

Elena's chest tightened as she nodded, watching the powerful Warrior Priest of Sirius wrestle with his inner tempest.

Azazel ran to Ayden's side, kneeled, and cradled the King's head in his hands. "He's alive, thank The Radiant One."

Ayden groaned as Azazel helped him to his feet. "Cassandra's intuition was spot on. She sensed something was wrong as soon as Paxton came through the portal. She warned me telepathically, and I just barely had time to put up my shields." Ayden rubbed his jaw. "Paxton packs a punch, but you should know that Cassandra and I expected this. She felt something was off, and she was right. We didn't think it would be Paxton, though. We thought Isla would double-cross us and intercept Cassandra on her way back to Charlotte. So, I gave her some new spells and techniques to help her mask her emotions and thoughts. So now, it seems that she's going to act as a double agent. I especially want her to find out more about Isla's consort."

Manu whipped around. "You suspected this would happen?"

Artemus cleared his throat, but it was Elena who answered. "I was not quick enough on the draw, I am afraid. I ignored my intuition in favor of trusting Paxton, taking him at his word. He told us he had come to terms with Cassandra's destiny. He said he would ease away from her once he brought her home. I wanted so desperately to believe him. I am so sorry Manu."

"You have a big heart, my dear," Artemus said. "How could you conceive of one of our own betraying us – and the mission – so despicably. Paxton has chosen the left-hand path, thereby relinquishing his position as an Acolyte of The White Circle. He no longer has my protection."

Manu's voice hissed from behind. "Nor mine."

Part Three: The Past is Present

One aspect of power is to bring our past-life awareness into this lifetime. The second aspect of power is to go into new fields of awareness that we have never experienced.

- Frederick Lenz

Chapter 51: Misdirection

Emerging from the portal, Cassie's grip tightened around Paxton, the vibrant hues of Isla's palace courtyard enveloping them. A woman adorned in intricate royal attire, jewels reflecting the sunlight, strode toward them with a mix of grace and urgency.

"Cassie!" Isla's voice, filled with genuine concern, echoed in the space. She enveloped Cassie in a hug, the weight of her royal robes pressing against Cassie's frame.

As they separated, Cassie's eyes, glistening with a mix of fear and relief, met Isla's gaze. She swallowed, feigning relief. "Auntie Isla, it was so terrifying."

Extending her hand to Paxton, Isla's expression softened. "You've done us a great service, young man."

With a respectful bow, Paxton replied, "Only what's right, especially when it concerns someone I cherish. Those claiming to be Light Workers? Deceivers, every one of them."

Isla sighed deeply, her eyes clouded with a mix of sorrow and understanding. "Even my brother fell for their ruse. Fooled into thinking he was an ally."

Drawing Cassie closer, Isla brushed her lips against Cassie's forehead, then pulled back to take in her niece's full face. "Now, Cassie, here you will find truth, love, and your destiny awaiting you."

Inwardly Cassie shuddered. *Such a Bitch!*

The torc had been going crazy since leaving her father's kingdom. Thank the Radiant One the Merkabah pendant from her mother had melded with it. The energies of this dark place must have set off the protective shield programed into the necklace.

Cassandra looked at her aunt and said, "I don't understand any of this. Father kept talking about my 'mission' and my 'power.' He said I was special because of some predestined thing between him and Mom. It didn't make any sense to me. There were so many holes in the story." She trailed off and turned to Paxton's embrace once more. *Careful, don't let your emotions get the better of you.*

"C'mon," he said, "I am going to take you up to your apartments. They are right next to mine and heavily warded. No one is going to harm you ever again; I won't let them."

Isla watched them ascend the winding stairway. She turned when she sensed Sirkan's shadowed presence. He was leaning in the doorway leading from the Great Room, arms crossed.

"Well, that seems to have gone according to plan. I understand from my spy at the Seely Court that Manu and company burst in just in time to see Paxton's exit. Manu's roar of anger shook the very mountains for miles around the Winter Court."

Isla threw her head back and laughed. "Oh, I would have loved to see that. His High and Mightiness screaming in frustration at seeing his long-lost love snatched away by an acolyte right under his nose. He must be planning all sorts of torture for the poor boy."

Sirkan went to the heart of the matter. "Well, we need to up her training schedule. Enough time has been wasted with all this back and forth, and we only have months when we should have had years. It's a pity you didn't know her full significance when you had her under your control – before this shit show began. No matter. I will start with past life regressions. She needs to bring all the abilities she has gained over the millennia forward to present time. Mornings should be focused on warrior training. I will go over what I want Paxton to teach her."

"She also needs to learn spell casting," Isla said. "You work with her directly after our midday meal and I will have her to myself after tea each day." She paused. "And I need to get my hands on that torc."

Sirkan bowed his head so she could not see his wooden face. "Your wish is my command."

She did not seem to notice he had dropped "my love."

Chapter 52: Beyond Time

Manu gazed out onto the mountain vistas, eyes unfocused, and relived the surge of electricity that had jolted through him when he looked into Cassandra's eyes. The flash of recognition had been immediate.

My God, how I love her!

Intense physical desire pulsed through his body; desire not felt since he'd last been with Ayesha in her lifetime in Victorian England. She had been born into a noble house and he had taken on the persona of a peer of the realm. He drew in a breath and closed his eyes. He could sense her in their bed, remember taking her firm breasts into his hands, then into his mouth as she gasped in pleasure and release. They had perfected their lovemaking over the centuries. He groaned, feeling the pain of longing he had buried deep within his heart.

He vibrated with longing. Cassandra's current physical form was almost identical to the body she had inhabited when she was Ayesha. It was quite remarkable. But the longer he considered the coincidence, the less surprised he was. The doppelgänger nature of the situation signaled the closing of the Karmic cycle that had begun at the Fall of Atlantis. The long wait was over. Their destinies could finally intertwine. He threw back his head and let out a long, agonized breath.

Cassandra must remember who she was – who she is. She must remember before the Quickening on her eighteenth birthday. She must remember, so we can walk together once more.

He had found her throughout the millennia in most of her incarnations, both female and male. And not always as a lover. Those lifetimes where they had other relationships, sometimes as friends, sometimes with him as teacher or mentor, were oftentimes more meaningful. He had gotten to know her in different ways. There was a time in Ancient Greece when she had incarnated into a male body as the young soldier named Kleitos. The Lords of Karma had granted Manu permission to co-inhabit the mind of the philosopher

Aristotle. Manu had acted as an "inner voice" in ethics, metaphysics, and critical thinking, which were basic axioms of Sirian spiritual science. Aristotle was a star pupil of the great philosopher Plato. The years of telepathically partnering with Aristotle had given rise to the Peripatetic School, and the inception of the underpinning of modern science.

The young man, Kleitos, would mature into one of Alexander of Macedonia's greatest generals. But when Manu first met him, Kleitos was full of the passion of inquiry and the desire to find The Truth. Manu had instantly recognized the Soul of his beloved. Kleitos followed Aristotle around like an eager puppy, constantly questioning, offering unsolicited opinions, and generally making a nuisance of himself.

As the months progressed, Manu, through the mind of Aristotle, came to understand how romantic love could transform into something deeper. He learned to love the *mind* of his Soul Mate. Aristotle would sit with the young man for long hours in the lush gardens of the Lyceum where the Athenian youth gathered to be taught by some of the most brilliant minds of the time. They would talk, theorize, and argue. Manu's consciousness merged with Aristotle's. Sometimes he would merely be an observer; other times Manu would send Aristotle thoughts meant to ignite exploration of esoteric concepts. The debates subsequently attracted other students and teachers, most notably the great Plato himself. Plato enjoyed the opportunity to take Aristotle down a notch or three. There were times when Manu almost forgot he was merely a "guest" in Aristotle's mind and would have to withdraw for a time, lest he take full possession, a violation of the Codex.

The gift of that life experience was a turning point in the Soul relationship between Manu and Ayesha. Their relationship moved to a different level – one of Unconditional Love.

Shaking himself out of his reverie, Manu decided it was time to check in with Elena on the current conundrum. He also wanted to discuss with her the wisdom of withdrawing once more to the Mother Ship until Cassandra gained more maturity. He was beginning to feel like Ayden had a point about the age difference. When Atlantis fell, the Celestials all appeared to be in their mid-twenties by human standards, even though their actual ages were hundreds of years old. Since the sinking of Atlantis, Artemus, Elena, and Manu had all rotated between the Mother Ship and Earth to maintain their

Immortality. Elena had physically aged the most since she insisted on leading the Mystery Schools personally and had spent little time on the Mother Ship. Manu only descended to the Earth plane when Elena sensed it was necessary for Manu to be with Ayesha. Artemus descended when he was needed to lead the Light Warriors during times of great wars and upheavals. It was rare for all three to be on the Earth plane at the same time. But then again, this was a time like no other. The Shift of the Ages was about to begin.

Chapter 53: Connecting the Dots

Cassie eased into the infinity pool, allowing the water's warmth to envelop her. The black marble, streaked with blue, gave it the feel of a bottomless lagoon. She inhaled the soothing scent of lavender, letting her thoughts drift to the Seely Court's events.

Her fingers absentmindedly danced on the water's surface as she replayed each moment. With all the unknown variables at play, including her aunt's capabilities and the palace's inhabitants, she needed clarity.

She recalled the chilling mention of her father and the tight rein she kept on her emotions. Playing the naïve pawn to Isla's machinations was vital. Yet, it was the haunting gaze of the stranger with ice-blue eyes that left an indelible mark. Their brief connection sent tremors of familiarity coursing through her, an enigma she couldn't shake off.

Who was he?

She knew that the other man and the woman had been at the debacle at Queens. She had mentioned them to her father, but he had not fully explained who they were, only that they were beings of great power and were on her side.

After enjoying the warm caress of the water for a while, she had a renewed sense of calm. With a sigh, she convinced herself to step out of the bath. Towel-drying her hair, she went into the bedroom and saw the knapsack of her things on the foot of her bed. Paxton had grabbed it before porting them here. She checked the hidden compartments that her father had thought to have sewn into the linings; the precious objects were still well-hidden. She sighed with relief. Then a small furry body wound between her legs. She shouted with glee.

"Angel Gabriel! Oh, how I have missed you, my sweet kitty."

She scooped him up. His tiny freight train purrs rumbled through his body. She laughed, fell on the bed, and cuddled him until...

She shot up.

That man and woman from Queens! They were in my dream about the Compte de St. Germain!

She might have panicked a little, but Paxton tapped on the door and cautiously swung it open. He was beaming. He told her about his adventure at her house but left out what he found in the attic and chuckled when he told her how Gabriel had jumped after him into the portal that Isla had opened between her house and the Non Seely Court. Cassie tried to concentrate on what he was saying.

Something was off. She picked up an energy signature that did not feel like Paxton. She watched his eyes intently.

He hasn't met my eyes once!

She unconsciously touched the torc, seeing in her mind's eye the embedded amethyst Merkabah. According to her father, the Merkabah was a sacred geometric symbol with the ability to weave an energetic field of protection around her. Ayden had also told her about her mother being trained by the White Witch, Tatiana, while she was in England. He was sure the necklace possessed powerful, protective magic. Her fingers tingled.

When she focused about six inches above Paxton's head, she saw his aura. It was tinged with gray.

He's not being totally honest, she thought.

Paxton had not quit talking. "And so, I wanted to teach you some self-defense techniques." He was grinning with pride as he reached for her hand. "You know all those summers I went on trips to visit family in Scotland? Well, they were actually warrior training."

"Warrior training?"

"Yes!" He started spewing all the techniques he knew. "You won't always have a weapon. You might get disarmed or even get caught unaware. So, one of the first things you need to learn is marital arts. Then I will teach you the rudiments of handling weapons."

"Could have used that a little while ago", she thought. Has it only been a week?

"I would love to learn martial arts," she said. "They are an extension of my yoga practice, yes? But weapons...I don't know Pax. That scares me."

"Well, like you said, you already have a lot of the basics from yoga. I will layer on some of the more powerful stances to build muscle and we'll progress to the basic moves with some tai chi." For that moment, he was more like the old, enthusiastic Paxton. "The weapon training is pretty important because the enemy will have armaments of all kinds. You need to learn about them and how to use them. You also want to know how to disarm an adversary."

She suddenly realized she was still in a bathrobe and scurried over to the large armoire on the other side of the room. She began to rummage and found four tunics with matching leggings in her favorite shades of plum. Dressing quickly, she said, "I need shoes."

Instantaneously a pair of purple flats appeared onto the floor in front of her. She started a little, then bent down to put them on. "Okaaayy. That was interesting."

Paxton turned back around and laughed. Paxton said, "I forgot to tell you - this place is enchanted. All you have to say is what it is you want, and it will materialize."

Just like in the Seely Court, she thought.

Someone lightly knocked on the door. One of the serving elves bowed and entered. The elves were much smaller than the fairies in her father's court, and were androgenous looking, their gender only apparent by the clothing they wore. This one was dressed in a bright lime green tunic layered under a yellow vest over baggy, navy blue pants.

Male, she guessed.

His eyes hooded in deference as he chirped in the distinctive sing-song voice shared by all elves. "Princess, the Queen has sent me to take you to the evening meal. Will you please follow me?"

Gabriel jumped into her arms. She could tell he was trying to send her a vision, but Paxton took her hand.

"Sorry, Boy," she said. "I'll get back to you later."

He swatted at her as he always did when he was displeased by her humanness, put his tail in the air, and plopped down in disgust.

Paxton cocked an eyebrow at her. "Wow," he said. "Talk about 'tude. That cat is almost human. I don't think I've ever seen an animal so communicative."

"Yep." Cassie smiled. "Mommy used to call him my 'little familiar.'"

The mention of her mother melted the joviality for a moment and pushed forward a sensation of longing and separation. Sobered, she continued down the staircase toward the main floor of the palace. She oriented herself, wanting to memorize the path they were taking. No telling when she might need to make a run for it. The staircase ended at a large horseshoe-shaped black marble foyer with a mother-of-pearl shell mosaic pattern around the edges. Hallways branched out in three directions. They headed for the middle one, which was lit by a myriad of flaming sconces with green-tinged incandescent lights.

"Fairy lights," Paxton said. "They function as both illumination and heaters."

She nodded and recalled the blue lights in her father's home. Since it was perpetually spring there, artificial warmth was not required.

The hallway ended at a large arched mahogany doorway. It shimmered like a dark mirror. Upon entering the room, the smells wafting from the heavily laden dining table made her mouth water, and she realized how hungry she was.

Her aunt rose regally from her throne-like chair at the head of the table to come forward and embrace her, then led her to the seat to the right of her. She motioned Paxton to the seat on her left. The place at the end of the table was vacant.

"That is where my consort sits," the Queen said. "He will be here momentarily. He had some pressing matters to deal with. Let us make ourselves comfortable in the meantime and begin our first course."

With that, a troupe of elves appeared by each chair and offered steaming dishes of meats and vegetables along with generous slices of bread. Cassie stared at the platter of meats; no animal flesh had been allowed in her father's court. Her aunt caught her surprised look.

"We do not ascribe to the vegetarian dietary rules your father's court holds. Such self-effacing nonsense. Here we understand the importance of high-quality protein!" She speared a slice of roast beef the size of a catcher's mitt, the spicey smell of cloves and cardamom assailing Cassie's nostrils. Paxton took what smelled like rosemary chicken off a proffered platter, followed by crispy garlic-roasted potatoes and greens of some kind.

Cassie waved the meat away but took a little of the white-fleshed fish smelling of tarragon and lime. She had never eaten much beef; her mother preferred seafood and poultry. The same crispy potatoes and greens that Paxton had chosen also made it to her plate. She inhaled deeply as the spices hit her tongue and almost groaned in ecstasy. The food here was just as delicious as in her father's court, although seasoned with a little too much enthusiasm. Everything was excessive – the spices, the opulence, the sweetness, and light.

Isla must think I am insipid or stupid, to think I'm taken in by her "I love you so much" act, Cassie thought. She must have forgotten I earned a scholarship to university. I'm not a dummy.

Clearing her throat, she let out a low sigh.

"Is there something wrong, Cassandra?" Isla asked.

"N...no, Auntie Isla. I was thinking about how sad I am about my father."

Isla narrowed her eyes for a moment, then slapped on a too-wide smile. The rest of her face did not match her pseudo concern. "Yes, well, we are all a bit disappointed in him, I must say. Never mind, girl. You are safe here and we will never allow you to be in danger again."

The energy in the room shifted – something like a small tremor. Cassie turned to see a large, well-muscled male stride into the room, his gaze fixed on her.

Paxton jumped to attention, but the male waved him aside. "Sit, Boy. No need for formality at family dinner." The man sat in the empty seat and looked at Cassie. "Cassandra, welcome home."

He emanated power and authority. A jagged scar ran from his left temple, through his eyebrow, and down to his chiseled cheekbone, but nothing could hide the handsomeness of his square-jawed face. Cassie stared for a moment at his voluptuous lips. His citrine eyes raked her up and down as if she were unclothed. She flushed in embarrassment. Isla was glaring; Paxton's countenance had gone wooden.

Isla broke the strained silence. "This is my consort, Lord Sirkan. He has been very instrumental in bringing you back to us."

Lord Sirkan bowed his head in acknowledgment. "Yes," he said. "I am thankful we all could combine our efforts to get you here safely." His eyes flickered while he stared at her, and she thought she saw a tremor in his hand as he gestured to the elves to serve him. Raising a golden goblet full of red liquid, he took a long drink.

His attention felt odd – like he knew her, which, of course, was ridiculous. She side-eyed him through lowered lids. *There's something.* She gasped as a vision of him holding a rowan staff with a crystal atop it emanated bolts of lightning toward fiery fissures in the Earth flashed before her eyes. All heads swung toward her.

She looked up, embarrassed, and thought it was best to stay as close to the truth as she could. "I am so sorry. I had this weird feeling that we had met before, Lord Sirkan. Silly, I know." She smiled wanly.

Her aunt responded immediately. "Lord Sirkan was on the ship that brought you to safety from your ordeal in Charlotte. I'm sure you glimpsed him once or twice and his face was buried in your subconscious mind until meeting him just now."

"Oh, yes, of course, that must be it," Cassie said, but she knew that was not the case. There was a deeper memory here, one she needed to explore.

Sirkan did not speak. He kept drinking what she assumed was red wine. He helped himself to great slices of lamb generously flavored with rosemary and thyme. He waved away the garlic potatoes in favor of herbed rice with toasted almonds. Crispy seeded rolls, kept warm in a covered basket, were slathered with creamy butter, which dripped from his fingers. He ate his food almost ritualistically, taking the three-pronged fork in his left hand, and knife in his right, continental style. He ate slowly and savored each bite before taking another.

He looked at Paxton. "Tomorrow morning, I want you to begin Cassandra's martial arts training. You were correct when you suggested she needs to learn a variety of self-defense techniques, so she can use her body as a weapon. I have directed a training ring to be readied in the armory."

He shifted his attention once more to Cassie. "Cassandra, I will work with you after the midday meal to teach you advanced mind control techniques. The first level of any magical being's education should always consist of the power of the mind."

Lastly, he addressed Isla. "My dear, I know you are eager to impart your wisdom in magics to your niece. What are your plans?"

Isla looked regal in her seat. "I would like to have Cassandra to myself for three or four hours after tea each day," she said. "It is important for mind and body disciplines to precede magics so that all energies will be in balance."

Sirkan nodded in agreement. Cassie felt a glimmer of anticipation and a little excitement as she contemplated all the training coming her way. But she also knew they would all be training her more in the dark arts than the light. *I'm really going to have to keep my emotions in check.*

Thinking back to her mother's Reiki training, she surreptitiously traced the protection symbol into the palm of her right hand. She did not want to touch the torc. No need to call undue attention to it. If her aunt discovered its importance, Cassie might have to surrender it.

And there was no way this side of hell that is going to happen!

AFTER DINNER, PAXTON suggested they stroll through the gardens. She was eager to be outside the palace and get the lay of the land. Gabriel shadowed her every step. Paxton looped her arm through his and pulled her to his side. For a moment she allowed herself to lean her head on his shoulder, savoring the familiar scent of his masculinity, the spicey musk so dearly familiar. *I wish we could go back in time."*

"Pax, this is so confusing to me," she said. "If only we could go back to the way things were. I'd like to wake up and realize all this was just one of my funky dreams."

He expelled his breath in a big sigh. "Me too," he said. "Life certainly was simpler when all we had to worry about were carbs and which sorority you were going to pledge."

She choked back a sob. "Wouldn't that be awesome? I have so many questions. How could you keep what you were from me? I mean, we grew up together. There was never any indication that you were an *angel."*

"I couldn't," he said. "When I started to come into my angelic abilities, Dad sent me away to Scotland to be trained. They taught me how to hone my skills and how to conceal them from the Mundane world. Humans have believed in angels since the dawn of time but believing is different from meeting a real one. And neither Dad nor I knew the extent of your mother's glamouring capabilities. We saw her as the world saw her, not as she really was. So, to reveal ourselves to her wasn't even an option."

"Her glamouring capabilities? What do you mean?"

He stopped and faced her. "Your mother was trained by a very powerful White Witch during a summer trip to London."

I know.

"That's why she was in Europe and how she met your father. At least, that's what I gleaned from listening to discussions between Artemus and Elena. I don't believe you have officially met them. Master Elena instructed Glenda to get you away from that shit show of a mixer at Queens, but they were very much at the center of all this, long before your father was."

Cassie closed her eyes and took a deep breath. She remembered the sparks from her fingertips, along with the horrifying being that had abducted her. She could still feel the claw-like fingers grasping her by the waist and hauling her into the air before she lost consciousness.

Paxton saw her eyes darken and face pale. "What's wrong Cass?"

Careful. She shuddered and shook off the memory as best she could. "I was just remembering the horrible – thing – that took me away. There was a black hole under the hood where its face should have been. Then I blacked out. The next thing I knew I was in an enclosed chamber and my aunt was looking down on me. I was so scared...and helpless ...and angry."

Cassie buried her face in her hands. She remembered the powerlessness and the confusion. She hated small spaces, always had.

Paxton tried to embrace her, but she shoved him away. "No, Pax. I don't need to be comforted. I need to be in charge of my life again. I am done feeling like a prisoner. I want to get started with my warrior training."

Paxton grinned. "Well," he said, "like Lord Sirkan instructed us, we begin tomorrow morning. You need to be well rested, so let's kick back a little and enjoy this amazing place. There are incredible gardens with waterfalls and pools. How about a moonlight swim?"

She looked toward the glowing orb in the night sky. It bathed the grounds in a silvery light, casting shimmering shadows on the ground from the lush trees lining the periphery of the gardens.

"You know, that sounds awesome," she said. "I could use a good swim to work out the kinks." She stretched her neck and rubbed her shoulders. "I'll go get a suit."

"There won't be any in the armoire," Paxton said. The Fae Kingdom is not ashamed of the body."

"A pretty cheesy way to get my clothes off," she said.

"A bonus of being here," he grinned.

He grabbed her hand and steered her toward the faint echo of splashing water. They stepped out of the trees and onto a beach of black sand. The surface of the lagoon rippled with concentric waves stemming from the base of a waterfall at the far end of the water. It was unlike anything she'd ever seen before.

Speechless, Cassie slipped off her sandals and took a tentative step toward the water. The beach looked hard; instead, it felt soft and pleasant – cool against her sensitive bare feet. She stepped forward with more confidence toward the waiting water, shucking her outer garments as she went.

Paxton stood transfixed as her slender form gradually revealed itself beneath the caressing moonbeams. He watched the girl of his childhood transform into the woman of his dreams before his very eyes. She moved into the water and looked back at him over her shoulder with an impish grin. She unhooked her bra, shimmied out of her panties, and dove into the water.

Paxton shed his clothes like they were on fire and followed. They had never been more intimate than making out and some over-the-clothes stuff, but tonight they seemed destined to take their intimacy to the next level.

She resurfaced just at the waterfall and treaded water. Paxton stared at the swell of her breasts visible above the waterline. Her face reflected the other-worldly essence of the place. She seemed to have transformed into a mermaid, a creature of myth luring him to his doom.

He swam for her. When he reached out his hand, she giggled and swam away. He sped through the water with masterful stokes, his muscular arms and practiced technique made the race almost unfair. She squealed in mock alarm when he caught her ankle and pulled. They embraced under the falls; the water sluiced over their bodies. Their mouths parted. Cassie was about to reach for him when a bellow erupted from the shore.

"Paxton! Let her go immediately!"

Sirkan stood with legs akimbo and hands fisted on his hips.

Startled out of the moment of their rising passion, Cassie, and Paxton pushed away from one another. Cassie made sure the water was covering her shoulders.

"Stay there, Cass," Paxton said. "I'll deal with this."

He thrashed at the water on the way to Sirkan. When he got to shore, he stalked out onto the sand, oblivious to his nudity.

"You have no righ—"

A shockwave from Sirkan's outstretched palm drove him to his knees.

"I have every right!" Sirkan said. "Cassandra is under my protection, and you will not defile her with your lust. Now put on your clothes, get back to your apartment, and stay there!"

With a wave, he pushed Paxton toward the pile of clothes on the shore. The boy had no choice. He had sworn to obey his new master, but he glared at Sirkan while he dressed. Cassie was still treading water, at a loss for what to do. She watched Paxton stalk across the beach and disappear into the foliage.

Sirkan watched him go, then called over his shoulder. His voice was calm and carried no hint of judgment. "Get out of that water and dress. I will escort you back to the house."

He folded his arms over his chest and waited with his back turned.

Cassie swam to the shore and dressed. "Okay, I'm ready."

Sirkan took her arm and guided her back along the path in silence. Though his touch was gentle, rage radiated from his every pore. He stopped in front of her apartment, pinning her to the wall.

"You are to stay in your rooms until Oleander comes for you in the morning. We will discuss this situation with your aunt then. But know this. You are not to be intimate with Paxton, nor any male before your Quickening. Period. Your body is a temple and not to be given to anyone other than your mate – and that boy is definitely *not* your mate!"

"My *mate*. What the hell does that mean?"

The veneer of deference evaporated. Sirkan backhanded her. She bounced off the wall. Shards of pain cascaded around her head and shoulders.

"Careful, girl," he said. "You *never* question my instructions – ever."

He pushed her through the door, locked it with a flick of his hand, and strode out into the hallway. She clutched at her face. It stung, but not as badly as her pride.

She screamed at the locked door, then beat it with her fists in humiliation and rage. She heard Paxton through the connecting door and ran to it twisting the knob. Locked.

"Cassie, are you okay? What happened?"

"He locked me in. What the actual fuck!"

She heard Paxton laugh.

"What's so funny?" she asked.

There was a pause, then Paxton's chortled response. "God, Cassie. I have never heard that word come out of your mouth."

She glared at the door, then doubled over with laughter.

"Well," she said. "You fuckin' better get used to it."

Chapter 54: Warrior Training

Paxton tapped on the door adjoining their suites. "Cassie, are you ready?"

Cassie looked with trepidation at the closed door. Butterflies played rugby in her stomach.

How am I going to pull this off? Father told me about my Soul Mission. He and Brigida gave me all the white magic tools they could. The torc is synced with Mommy's crystal. Am I ready?

Another thought hit her.

Ready for what? That Sirkan guy is dangerous, but are Paxton and Auntie Isla a threat?

She focused on Sirkan and gasped. She caught a vision – his rough hands pawing her body...his mouth pressing against hers...his tongue charging like an invading army.

Vertigo knocked her sideways. She steadied herself on the bedpost.

What the hell was that?

She heard a faint click at the hallway door as Oleander unlocked the door. Stepping aside, she allowed Paxton to come into the room, "are you decent?"

She turned around. One look was all he needed.

"Bloody hell, you look like you are going to faint!" He went to her side and took her hands in his, "and your hands are like ice. What's wrong?" His face swam before her eyes. Cassie tried to focus on the present. Her body, still in the grips of the vision she had, was reacting to sexual tension. She stepped back in fear Paxton would sense her arousal and act on it in the mistaken belief that he had ignited her passion.

"No, no I'm okay," she said. "A dizzy spell. I don't know what brought it on. I'll splash some water on my face and be fine. Hang on."

She stumbled into the bath and ran cold water from the tap, grabbed one of the washcloths stacked on a shelf beside the shell-shaped basin. She looked in the gilt-edged mirror and saw a feral animal, eyes wide and sweat beading on her upper lip. She put a trembling hand to her mouth. Her lips were fine, but they felt swollen by the violence of the etheric kiss. She wrung out the cloth and buried her face in it.

Get a grip, girl.

Cassie took a series of long breaths, then put the cloth on the back of her neck. She closed her eyes and pulled her attention back to the day at hand. The vision was still clear, so she kept rinsing her face until it dissipated. She pasted on a smile and returned to her room.

Paxton still looked concerned. "Are you sure you're up to doing your martial arts training this morning? We can always start tomorrow; one more day surely won't be a big deal."

She willed her hand to stop shaking. "No, I'm fine. I need some exercise. Let's go."

They walked through a series of catacombs in the lower level until they reached the training room. It looked like a typical human gym with the addition of weapons, targets, and a sparring ring. Cassie stared.

"My god, Paxton – swords, spears, axes, bows, and arrows. You weren't kidding about the weapons."

"Don't worry about those," Paxton said. "We'll get to them later." He ushered her toward the ring and showed her the series of padded mats arranged on the other side. "We're here to do martial arts. Hand-to-hand techniques first, okay?"

"Okay," she said. "But I'm not going to kill anyone."

His face registered a mixture of frustration and pique. "Let's worry about defending yourself first. They have identified you as one of The Seven Avatars of the Aquarian Age. There's a huge target on your back. Some people want you in power...some want you dead."

Cassie gulped. It was the first time anyone had been so blunt.

Paxton noticed her discomfort. "Good, I got your attention. We are living at a time when the world is about to implode. You are part of the solution – you must be. I know it's not the life you planned, but it's the life you have."

Without a word, Cassie walked to the wall and picked up a roll of Everlast hand wrap.

"Show me how," she said.

Paxton walked her through the process. "Around the wrist, around the thumb, through the fingers, across the palm."

She watched him and copied his every move. Once she was ready, she slipped off her shoes and stood on the mat.

"The first thing we are going to do is work on your balance. You need to strengthen your core muscles from the toes up. Watch."

He flexed his toes up and down and then gripped at the floor with them. "Five minutes," he said.

Can't be that hard, she thought.

Five minutes felt like five hours. Her calves and toes screamed for relief. Paxton watched in amusement as her opening pace slowed to an arthritic crawl. "Not so easy, huh?"

"Who knew?" she said. She tried to smile. Somehow, even that hurt.

"Okay," he said, "next five minutes, focus on your breathing as you lift on your toes. Lift up for a six count, then bring your foot down slowly and dig in your heels to another count of six. Ready? Go."

They progressed through body breathing, lifting, and stretching until Cassie held up her hands in a gesture of surrender thirty minutes later.

"I can't be that out of shape! This is embarrassing!"

Paxton nodded. "Five minutes can seem like an eternity when you engage muscles you have not used. Let's take a break." He pointed to a water cooler. "It is important to stay hydrated every step of the way, even with these seemingly easy movements. Next up is curls, pull ups and planks."

They stood in companionable silence as they sipped cups of the cool water.

Thirty minutes later, Paxton called another break. He reviewed the next part of the training and handed her a bottle.

"Gatorade?" she asked.

"More like Paxton-ade," he said. "It's my own blend of vitamins, herbs, essential oils, and other stuff. I worked with my trainer in Scotland to perfect it. They keep it down here and I'll have some delivered to your room. Don't drink too much and always follow it with twice as much water. It will help alleviate muscle soreness too."

She looked at it skeptically. "Mine's pink and yours is blue. Seriously?"

He shrugged. "Well, yours has some extra girl stuff too. Drink up."

They spent the next thirty minutes on various combat stances and how to position her elbows for what Paxton called "the best punchability."

"You made that up," Cassie said.

"Yep," he said, "but it's a great word, huh? Now, we're going to work on protection and self-defense."

Cassie jogged in place for a few seconds and rotated her head. "You don't let up, do you?'

"You need to quit?"

"Not on your life," she said.

"Okay," he said. "Close your eyes and turn away from me. I'm going to come at you. See if you can sense from what direction. Then use the defensive swing-kick and upper cut maneuver I showed you."

She closed her eyes and focused on feeling her body within its space. Pushing out her awareness inch by inch like she did when going into meditation. She couldn't hear anything, not even his breathing.

Oh, he's good. Then she smiled. *Gotcha!*

She bent her left knee as she swung her right leg around and up, fists following. She felt hard contact and heard a satisfying "Ooof."

When she opened her eyes, Paxton was flat on his back, holding his jaw. "Whoa, okay, I think you got it."

"What happened to all of your self-defense stuff?" she asked.

"I violated the first rule," he said. "I got overconfident. Never thought you'd see me coming."

Laughing, she offered her hand to pull him up. He stumbled into her. Their torsos touched. His eyes darkened. He could feel her racing heart. Desire shot through him with a jolt.

Her breath caught as her own body responded to him, this boy-man who had awakened her heart. She lifted her face to his, and he bent down to claim her lips, softly at first. Then when she yielded to him, they became more insistent, his tongue demanding entrance to her mouth. She opened her mouth. He wrapped his arms around her.

"I want you so bad," he said. "I need—"

"Shut up and show me."

She guided his hand to her left breast. His fingers brushed over her taut nipple. She gasped and pressed into him. He sank to the mat and pulled her on top of him. She felt his hardness through her flimsy workout clothes. He rolled over on top of her.

"What about Sirkan?" she asked.

"To hell with him," Paxton said.

"I have a better thought," she said.

She ached her back in anticipation.

"Ahem!"

Paxton sprang to his feet. His arousal obvious to anyone within fifty feet.

A young elf, red in the cheeks but resolute in her stance, looked at Cassie.

"So sorry to interrupt," she said, "but her majesty has instructed me to fetch you for the midday meal." Cassie stood. Embarrassment flushed her face.

"Thank you," she said. "And you are?"

"I am Oleander, mistress. Please follow me."

Paxton turned away, adjusted himself, and looked at the attendant.

"Oleander, we need to wash up before we come to lunch. Please inform her Majesty that we will be there as quickly as possible?"

Oleander bowed in acknowledgement. "She knows you have been…ah…strenuously engaged. Lunch will be served in twenty minutes. I have been assigned as Princess Cassandra's personal attendant."

Twenty minutes later, Cassie entered the informal dining room off the gardens. Isla frowned at the casual blouse and jeans.

"Cassandra, I expect you to dress for meals in the future. What you are wearing is not appropriate."

With a wave of her hand, Cassie's outfit changed into a long gown of blue flowing fabric embroidered with poppies at bodice and hem.

Cassie gazed down in wonder and then anger. "I will wear what I want, Aunt. This is the twenty-first century."

"True," Isla said, "but this is my court. I determine the dress and decorum of all members in it, especially those in the royal family. You will do as I say or suffer the consequences. I am not above punishing you for your disobedience."

Paxton raised his eyebrows at the last statement. He was about to speak when he caught Cassie's warning glance and stayed out of whatever clash of wills was going on between them. He took his seat in silence, bowing toward Isla in a show of the deference he knew she expected.

The serving elves began to set out platters of food when Sirkan entered and took his seat at the head of the table. "What's this now? I sense tension."

"It's nothing, my dear," Isla said. "My niece and I were discussing expectations of dress and decorum. She is a princess. She needs to act like one."

Sirkan took the judicious road – and said nothing.

THE ONLY SOUNDS CAME from silverware and the stealthy movement of elves. Cassie jumped when Sirkan broke the silence.

"Your training with me is up next," he said. "We will do your mental training in my temple at the far end of the garden after you change into something more comfortable. I suggest you choose only from those garments in your armoire. The clothes you brought from the Mundane world are totally inappropriate for a young woman of your status. On this, I am in one hundred percent agreement with your aunt." He rose from his chair; the meal was ended. "I will see you in thirty minutes. Oleander will show you the way."

Sirkan extended his arm to Isla and escorted her from the room while Cassie glared.

"Well, I guess the honeymoon is over," she said. She stalked from the room, leaving Paxton with a mouthful of food.

Chapter 55: Lost in Time

Oleander was waiting for her in her room, having laid out two outfits. They were perfect. One was a thigh-length blue cotton tunic embroidered with silver threads in a cloud and stars pattern. The other, similarly styled, was deep purple with green piping around a mandarin collar and cuffs. She picked up the purple tunic with matching loose pull-on pants and went into the bathing room to change. When she emerged, Oleander handed her a pair of eastern style flats with cranes embroidered on the toes. "I will escort you to Master Sirkan's temple."

I really, *really* don't want to be alone with that guy.

Oleander led her through the gardens to a well-hidden building, a cross between a Greek temple and a medieval chapel. Ivy trellised up its walls. Stained glass windows set into the dome filtered the light into cascading colors. Carvings of demons and griffins adorned the tops of the columns that framed the circular building.

The hair on the back of her neck stood at attention as they climbed the thirteen steps onto the porch. She hesitated on the threshold of the arched doorway.

Beautiful...and sinister.

"Don't just stand there, girl, come in." Sirkan looked at Oleander. "I will escort the princess back to the main house in time for tea," he said, and he dismissed her with a flick of his wrist.

Oleander bowed and backed away out of the entrance, her face impassive.

Cassie was still hesitant. "By the gods, girl, you are already trying my patience." He yanked her toward the middle of the circular room and pushed her down onto a purple tufted ottoman. He blew out his breath. "I apologize, but you have no idea how long I have waited for you." He suddenly switched to an instructional tone. "I know you are fully aware of the idea of reincarnation." It was not a question.

"Yes, yes, of course I am. The concept is as old as time. The fact that a truly loving god would only give you one short lifetime in which to become spiritually perfect..." she trailed off.

Sirkan was studying her. He kneeled and took her chin in his hand. "You are nearing the end of your karmic cycle," he said. "That is why you are experiencing some of the talents and abilities of countless lifetimes. I am an Immortal. I have had this same body since I first came to the earth from my home planet of Lyra. It was then that I first met you in Atlantis in the body of the High Priestess Ayesha. When the fighting broke out, you took a life, thereby losing your immortality. You had to enter the Human wheel of karma until you rectified the imbalance. Since then, you have manifested in both male and female bodies countless times. Many of those lifetimes I found you. I could always see through physical skins to the soul essence beneath them. We have been many things to one another, explored many relationships. Now we are going to explore those past lives together, so you can remember in totality who you are." He waited a beat. "Have you ever been hypnotized?"

She blinked at him. "No, and I don't want to be now."

He gave her a half smile. "There's nothing to fear. It is simply a form of deep meditation that will guide you beyond your current life walk and back in time to relive and remember who you are in your totality. I am an expert in taking others into those levels of consciousness. Your mind will be awake; your body will be asleep. You must bring forward your latent talents in magics and mind control to the present. You will need them in the future. There is a great war coming, a war in which you are a key player. You are destined to be by my side when we win."

Panic seized her, and she tried to stand. He put his forefinger on the middle of her forehead and spoke in a guttural language. Her third eye vibrated, and she was pulled into a vortex of swirling darkness as if she were falling down a deep well.

From far away, Cassie heard his voice. "You are traveling back through time to a place that is important to who you are now. It will reveal to your talents, abilities, and knowledge so you may bring them forward to use in your current life walk."

There were other words she did not understand, again in an odd dialect. She felt her feet land on solid ground. Cassie looked down. She was wearing leather sandals and a long white robe. A golden door was in front of her. She stepped toward it and pushed it open.

SHE WAS RUNNING TOWARD the Terran ships that were preparing to lift off from the sinking city. The earth rocked beneath her sandal-clad feet. Searing heat spewed from flaming fissures and burned her soles. She tossed away the bloody sword in revulsion. She ran as fast as she could.

I must reach the ship before it launches. My people are depending on me to lead them to a new world – to survival.

She was almost there when powerful arms grabbed her from behind. Someone lifted her off her feet and threw her over a burly shoulder.

"Not that way, my dear. Those ocean ships are not safe for such precious cargo. We will go to my Mother Ship and rise above this upheaval."

Her captor pointed his staff toward the far end of the plateau and opened a tunnel that sucked them in and instantaneously deposited them in an enormous spaceship. She struggled to get away, but he gripped her tighter and strode into the command center. They deposited her on the deck as the male began barking orders and directing the crew to prepare for liftoff. When he turned, she recognized him: the High Priest Sirkan.

"You bastard!" She spat on the floor. "How dare you abduct me like this? I am responsible for thousands of lives down there. I need to lead them to safety. Let me go!"

He ignored her and began to twist and press the multi-colored crystals on the ship's console. He yelled. Rough hands picked her up and shoved her into a large reclining chaise. She kicked and punched, but to no avail. The male was huge, a giant, a breeding experiment between the Celestials and the humans – the soldiers of the High Priest – the Nephilim.

"Easy my lady," he said. "Master Sirkan will take us to secure shores to an island we have been preparing just for this time. You are safe."

"Safe!" Her voice was shrill and strained. "How dare you touch me? You know the punishment for touching your High Priestess. You are a dead man!"

"Well," he said, "the punishment for not heeding my lord is far worse, I assure you. Please relax."

Struggle was futile. She closed her eyes and sent out mental commands to her handmaiden and generals, who were still on the Terran plane, but to no avail.

Sirkan put up a shield, of course.

Her stomach dropped when the craft lifted off. She looked down on the devastation of the planet and passionately prayed that her court and the humans entrusted to them could get away securely to the shelters she and Manu had prepared.

Thank the gods for the Oracles of the Sirian Council!

At least the human leadership had finally listened to her and taken steps to ensure their preservation. The sky ships were already in flight, along with a small armada of Terran sea ships. Hundreds of men, women, and children were racing for the docks when a gargantuan wave swept over the seawall.

When it receded, all evidence of Atlantis was gone.

She felt the momentary pulse of hundreds of souls crying out in fear – then, nothing. A primordial scream echoed through the control room. It took a moment before she realized it was coming from her own throat. Tears streamed down her face, and she shrieked at the horror of the senseless destruction of a race of people and the place she had called home for hundreds of years. She had known the uplifting sensation of a heart full of joy; now, she realized the sickening reality of a heart -ending in pain.

Cassie caught sight of the huge Sirian mother ship. She knew her mate was the captain and tried to reach him with her mind. The effort was wasted. All she could do was withdraw into herself and impose a deep state of calm to stave off the paralyzing fear.

She went deeper, searching for a way to contact her love, but she could not push through Sirkan's barriers. When she abandoned her attempts, she sank into a welcomed oblivion.

She awakened with a start. At first, confusion reigned, then reality slapped her with an icy hand. Sirkan was staring down at her.

"I cannot imagine what you think you are gaining by taking me, Sirkan," she said. "We have been at odds for years and now I know you and your dark faction are behind this destruction. You know I will not help you."

"Oh, My Dear, I don't need your aid," he said. He released her restraints and pulled her to his chest. "I just need you."

His mouth crushed hers.

CASSIE'S EYES SHOT open as she gasped with horror and came out of the trance. Vaulting up from the ottoman, she turned to run out of the pavilion.

Sirkan grabbed her arm. "What did you see?"

"You put that revolting vision into my mind, you, you...bastard!"

He took her by the arms and shook her. "What did you see?"

Rage flooded her being. "If you don't know, I thank god! If it was truly a past life remembrance, you have a lot to pay for. You are a monster." She spat in his face.

She ran out of the temple.

"Well, that went well," he said, and he slammed his fist into the nearest wall.

Chapter 56: Trapped

Paxton ran out of the training room and into the garden. *Cassie is in danger!* He could feel her fear. Running toward Sirkan's temple, he saw her racing toward the forest.

Holy Shit! Those woods are full of demonic forces.

Instinct activated his wings. He flew after her, ignoring the pain of the unused muscles in his shoulders.

"Cassie! Stop! Danger!"

She looked over her shoulder and skidded to a stop just shy of the thicket of trees. Black tendrils oozed from the forest and reached for her. Paxton whipped out his sword. He thanked the Radiant One that he had remembered to put it back into his scabbard at the middle of his back.

He wrapped his left arm around her and swung his sword at the tentacles. High pitched screams emanated from the trees; three wiggling arms of smoke disintegrated on the ground. Paxton continued to slash. A feline roar erupted from behind him. Before Paxton could turn, a huge black panther flashed past him and lunged at several demons emerging from the forest. He felt more than read the collar around the jungle cat's neck: Gabriel.

The panther slashed and mauled the demonic forms, synchronizing his attacks with Paxton's. A wave of hyena-like demons emerged and leaped toward them. Gabriel doubled in size and dispatched them with a swipe of his claws and a crunch of his fangs. Paxton backed away until he felt his right foot cross over the warded boundary well removed from the dark forest.

His fear turned to anger when he saw Cassie's pale face. "What the hell happened in there with Sirkan?" Paxton asked. "And even more WTF, *Gabriel?*"

By the time Cassie looked at her pet, the cat had shifted back into his familiar cuddly body. She picked him up. "Kitty got pissed off. Mommy always said he was magical, but I echo the question, Gabriel. What the—"

The cat licked her nose.

Cassie turned back to the dilemma at hand. "Sirkan is a monster, Paxton. Please, please get me away from here. We are in danger. I don't care why you thought you should bring me here. It is dark and dangerous. We need to get out!"

He stared at her. In a moment of blinding clarity, almost as though a spell had been broken, he realized, *What the hell! She's right. Isla is evil, and Sirkan is even worse. What have I done?*

He pulled her to him. "Okay," he said. "We'll get out, but we need to make careful preparations. This place is well-guarded, and the way out needs to be mapped."

"I'm done Damseling Pax. I am fully aware of what's going on here."

"Damseling?"

"Yeah," she said, "you can make up words, so can I. You know, a damsel in distress and all that shit. I'm not the innocent little girl I was just – what – three weeks ago? My father –"

Before she could continue, they felt a presence. Paxton spun; sword poised to strike.

A small Elvan form stepped out of the trees, hands up in surrender. "No need for violence, Master Paxton, it's only me, Oleander."

"What do you want?" His arm tightened around Cassie.

Oleander looked at him, her eyes pleading. "I would go with you. I have been trapped here for years, separated from my family in the Seely Court when the Queen built the barriers between the two kingdoms. This is an evil, *evil* place and I can't stand it here much longer. I know the safe paths through the dark woods, the hidden caves that will circumvent the wards. Please, take me with you, I beg of you!"

Cassie read the elf's aura. It was creamy white, tinged with green - compassion. There was also a glow of yellow, which indicated both fear and determination. She met Oleander's eyes and saw only sincerity.

"She's telling the truth, Paxton; I see it. We can trust her."

Paxton sheathed his sword. "Escort Cassandra back to the palace. We will need supplies and outer garments. There are at least four other realms between this one and the Seely Court. We won't be able to send out messages for a while. We need a fool-proof plan. I will work on that. In the meantime, how long do you think the journey will take?"

Oleander bit her lip. "Under a week if weather holds. Once we get past the first wards, there is a day's journey through a series of well-guarded caves. Still, after what I just witnessed, we will have a very good chance. There is a neutral region beyond the caves. We might be able to use your portal abilities to enter the outskirts of the Seely Court. It is well-warded as well, but since the Princess is wearing the royal torc, I don't think we will have too much resistance. Much will also depend on our pursuers and whether they have portal magic."

"Let me take Gabriel. You left him in the apartment, and we don't need to try and explain why he's suddenly out here. We can't tip our hand, so Isla and Sirkan cannot know what just happened."

"One of the other elves has been digging a tunnel from the kitchen for the last three years. He will want to come."

"What the hell," Cassie said. "The more, the merrier."

Paxton gave a thumbs up. "Solid," he said. Have him contact me if he can without being spotted. I'll work on the plan, and we will meet back here in two days."

OLEANDER LED CASSIE back to the house. Isla was waiting.

"What the hell is going on? Sirkan just came storming in looking for you."

Cassie opened her mouth to reply, but Oleander interjected. "I am at fault, your Majesty. I was late in getting the Princess and found her going the wrong way. She was on the path toward the dark woods. I was lucky to find her before she got lost."

Isla narrowed her eyes. "Cassandra, why were you wandering about by yourself? Lord Sirkan was to bring you back here himself. Why did you run out before your lesson was done?"

"I had a vision from a past life," Cassie said. "It upset me – frightened me. I ran out. I didn't know what else to do. Then I got turned around."

"And what vision could frighten you so much?"

Cassie hesitated. She knew her aunt would spot a lie. She tried a half-truth. "I saw the destruction of an entire continent with people dying all around me. I felt totally helpless. A huge tidal wave came, and that's when I came out of it."

Isla studied her for a while, then waved the back of her hand. "Well, go upstairs and gather yourself. Rest a bit, then we will have tea, after which we will have your lesson. I will send for you."

She watched Oleander lead Cassandra up the stairs.

There is more to this story, Isla thought. I'll get to the bottom of it.

She walked to Sirkan's study with determined steps.

"What in Hades is all this about?" Isla asked. "I am not pleased with how you look at the brat. She is not to be one of your playthings, Sirkan. I simply will not allow it!"

"You forget yourself, Isla," He warned.

"Don't try to scare me," she said. "Your appetites are infamous, but she is off limits. She must remain pure until the rite is performed. You know that."

When Sirkan slammed his fist onto his desk. Isla jumped. "I will not be chastised by you of all people. I will keep my own counsel on this, but rest assured, she is in no danger from me!"

Isla left the study, but she was not satisfied. *I know bullshit when I hear it,* she thought.

Chapter 57: Dark Magics

The afternoon session with Isla was conducted in a high tower of the palace. Two enormous trolls armed with axes guarded the door.

Geez Louise, Cassie thought, *they look like characters out of a freaking medieval fairytale.* The sight of their malevolent yellow eyes and drooling fangs caused bile to rise in Cassie's throat. She choked it back while one of them opened the heavy metal-studded wooden door and gestured for her to go inside.

The tower room was enormous. Floor-to-ceiling bookcases lined the left-hand wall. Shelves filled with vials and jars ran along the opposite wall. Around the arched windows directly across from the doorway were stone ledges filled with crystals and gemstones of every type and shape. In front of the ledges was a large trestle table. Four very large obelisks evenly placed down the center of the middle of the table drew Cassie's attention. She could feel the waves of energy emanating from them. She reached out a hand.

"Don't even think about touching anything," Isla said. She snatched Cassie's outstretched arm. "Sit."

I don't know why I don't just string her up in chains and bleed her powers out of her, Isla thought. All this cajoling and manipulation is growing wearisome.

The Queen pointed to a five-pointed star etched onto the floor in the middle of the room. "That pentagram is composed of blood from all of the kingdoms currently residing on this planet, Human, Celestial and Devic," Isla said.

Cassie shivered in revulsion. She pulled her eyes away from the symbol and focused on an ancient leather-bound tome in the center of the table. Isla waved her right hand over it. The pages fanned open and stopped on an illuminated page written in an elaborate script.

A Grimoire!

"This you can touch," Isla said.

She took Cassie's left palm and placed it on an intricately drawn diagram of complex geometric symbols and astrological glyphs.

"Your left hand receives energy, while your right hand sends it out," Isla said. "Close your eyes and focus on your left hand."

Cassie did as bidden. Her palm tingled and warmth started to travel up her fingers. *It's a lot like the Reiki energy,* she thought. Images came at her fast and furious, horrible scenes of disemboweled creatures, burning pyres, and bloody athames. She gasped and pulled her hand back.

Isla's eyes were slits. "Tell me."

Lips trembling, Cassie recounted as best she could the images that felt they were branded on the back of her eyelids. Some of the words would simply not come out of her mouth. She stopped and gasped for air.

Isla nodded, satisfied. "Good, good. At least you have some ability at psychometry, the ability to hold something in your hands and read the psychic residue clinging to it. The skills will be important when you are concocting new spells. I suspected as much when you had past life visions when you encountered Sirkan. We will continue."

For the next hour Isla gave Cassie various objects and implements, then listened to the girl's impressions. The Queen held out a sealed envelope.

"Hold this between your hands and tell me what you see."

Her energy waning, Cassie did as she was told. She secured the vellum envelope between the palms of her hands. She felt that the paper was quite old, but all she envisioned was a thick fog and amorphous forms.

"I can't see anything."

"Focus."

Instead of seeing visions, Cassie heard the shouts of an angry crowd. Her eyes came into focus, and she saw a tall scaffold upon which a guillotine stood. She looked down at herself and saw a gown. It was torn and filthy; her feet were bare and bleeding. Someone was leading her up wooden stairs. Her eyes could not tear away from the bloody blade.

When she stumbled, the executioner grabbed her by the forearm and dragged her into a prone position on the bench. Her head moved onto the block below the blade. She heard a swooshing sound...

...then...nothing.

Cassie screamed and dropped the envelope. Her hands flew to her throat. Tears clogged her eyes. She began to wheeze. She scrambled up from the table and ran. She barely made it to the door before the contents of her stomach met the floor.

Isla swore and swung her around.

Cassie gagged until there was nothing left to vomit. After she dry heaved for a while, she rolled onto her back and looked at Isla.

"What was in that envelope?" Cassie asked.

Her aunt dragged her to her feet and back to the table. She shoved the envelope into Cassie's trembling hands. "Open it."

Inside was a lock of curly brown hair tied with a faded green ribbon. On the inside flap of the envelope, someone had printed a name: *Giselle*.

Chapter 58: Well-laid Plans

Every muscle in Paxton's body was urging him to run. It took immeasurable strength of will for him to maintain a nonchalant pace as he headed toward palace kitchens. He needed to find Oleander.

He walked into the main kitchen. "I'm famished. Can I get something to eat?"

Cook appeared, a wooden ladle in his hand.

"Master Paxton, the Queen does not permit eating between meals. She would get very upset if I fixed you anything. You know it can be a life-or-death situation when she gets upset." He shot his eyes toward the pantry, then disappeared around the corner, Paxton opened the pantry.

Fantastic. Crusty brown bread, cheese, and fruit. He took a satisfying crunch of an apple and felt the juice run toward his chin. He wiped his mouth, then he saw Oleander shuffling into the room, eyes wide.

"Master Paxton, what are you doing here?"

Paxton silently pointed two fingers to his eyes then at hers, indicating he was there to see her. Oleander jerked her head toward the garden and held up five fingers.

Five minutes later they met at a previously arranged rendezvous spot far away from the prying eyes of the palace. Oleander twitched left, then right. He backed into the camouflage of the thick shrubbery.

Sotto voce, Paxton laid out his escape plan.

Chapter 59: Points Taken

The next morning's training regime began with stretches, curls, and planks, as always. Paxton then upped the game by teaching Cassie how to handle a knife.

"Daggers are handy weapons since they can be used for close combat as well as in a ranged attack." He handed her a bone-handled, double-edged knife. "I have put a dulling spell on this for our training. But it *is* real."

Cassie took it as if he had handed her a snake.

"Grip it firmly, but not too tight," Paxton said. "You want to be able to switch hands." He showed her how to grip it and how to thrust. "See, it's like Warrior Pose from your yoga practice."

She followed suit.

"Good, good. Now let's do a bit of sparing."

They circled one another, Cassie clearly nervous. Paxton lunged. Cassie deflected. He lunged again. This time, she crouched and swung around with her right leg, kicking at his fisted dagger. It skittered across the floor. Her knuckles followed her foot for a devastating punch.

"Mean left hook, girl. Not bad, not bad." He grimaced, rubbed his jaw, then rolled to his feet.

"It was like some sort of muscle memory," Cassie said. "I didn't even think about it. My body went into auto mode."

"Not surprising," Paxton said. "I know you hate him, but those past life regressions you've been doing with Sirkan are generating some useful cellular memories."

"The mind shielding techniques that Father taught me are helping a lot with both him and Isla." *I simply cannot call her aunt,* she thought.

"Okay, on to knife play." Paxton handed her three tennis balls.

"Is it my serve?" she asked.

"Ha. No, I'm going to teach you how to juggle. It will help you handle and manipulate the position of the dagger."

Fifteen minutes later Cassie broke into a fit of laughter. "I must have been a juggler in a past life! This is easy."

Paxton threw a fourth ball her way. She integrated it into the progression of the other three without a problem.

"I'm a natural," she said just before all fell to the floor.

"Cockiness will get you every time!" Paxton said.

She stuck out her tongue.

They took a break, then Paxton handed her a dagger. He showed her how to flip it from hand to hand and then hilt to blade. "You use the blade end to throw the dagger. Let's try it out on the practice dummies."

Cassie managed to hit three out of five bulls-eyes over the heart. Paxton made all five.

"I'm afraid I'll slit my hands open once you take off the protective spell! Holding the dagger by the sharp end is kinda, you know, dangerous," Cassie said.

"Aha – that's where your spell casting comes in," Paxton said. "You need to be quick and have the dulling spell on the tip of your tongue. Once you throw it, the spell will dissipate. The blade will be razor sharp when it embeds itself into your enemy's chest. Let's give it a go."

He taught her his incantation and proceeded to demonstrate.

Cassie shook her head. "How long did it take you to learn that one?"

"Longer than it will take you. Your turn."

Thirty minutes later, she made five bulls-eyes in a row. She looked at her hands and grimaced. Blood seeped through cuts in the tape.

Paxton unwrapped her hands, took her palms between his and called on his healing powers. The cuts disappeared without a trace.

"Nice to have an angel in the house." She pecked him on the cheek.

He reddened and backed away. "Don't do that. It can – and will – lead to something that has to wait until your Quickening. I don't like it, but Sirkan and Isla are right."

Still, he could feel the beginning throbs of arousal and began to shift uncomfortably. There was movement at the door. Oleander came into the room.

Saved by the elf.

Chapter 60: Strategic Alliances

Artemus sat in silence in the Citadel's great room. *What in the blazes am I supposed to do with this?* He thought. He turned to Manu and Elena. "Thoughts?"

Manu was shooting daggers with his eyes at the vampire standing before them. Natesh had reached out to Artemus a few days earlier. Manu set up the conclave. Cassandra had been missing for over three weeks of Earth time. *Was bringing him here a mistake?*

Natesh stood ramrod straight and defiant. "You should be thankful that my past life with Cassandra has overridden my loyalty to anyone but her. I will save her from the clutches of Sirkan with or without your aid," he said.

"I remember that lifetime all too well, Natesh." Elena said. "I always thought it was you who had taken her to Madame De Guillotine."

"Far from it. I was kept from rescuing her." Natesh recounted his vampire birth in soul-crushing detail. "I have put my life in jeopardy by coming here. If Sirkan catches wind of this..."

Manu flicked his wrist, dismissing any further comment. "What will you do once we have rescued her?"

Natesh's eyes darkened; his mouth grim. "If I make it out alive, you mean. That remains to be seen. She might remember me and her love for me, or she may remember you. It's possible she won't remember either of us or will choose Paxton. It's her decision. Whatever she does, I will abide by her wishes. Will you?"

A knock on the door interrupted the meeting.

"Enter," Elena said.

Glenda walked into the room with Siobhan at her side, followed by a cloaked figure. When Glenda saw Natesh, she put her arm in front of the hooded figure. She looked at Siobhan and then at Master Elena.

"What is this?" Glenda asked.

"Glenda, please wait in the library with your guest," Elena said. "Siobhan, please come in and join us."

When Glenda and the mystery guest departed, Siobhan came in and closed the door. Her fists were clenched. "What in the blazes is *he* doing here?"

Artemus recounted the past hour of conversation.

"You can't possibly believe a word Natesh has to say! He has been the bane of our existence for hundreds of years!"

Natesh remained silent.

Manu stared out of the window overlooking the breathtaking Himalayas. He wanted to tear the head from the vampire's body, but what Natesh had said carried the ring of truth. Finally, Manu broke the long silence. "Situations change. I have been reaching into his mind, which he obligingly has allowed. I see no subterfuge. Love is a powerful motivator."

Siobhan sank onto the nearest settee in shock. "You of all people, Manu. You know what's at stake here."

Manu swept his eyes around the room. "Of course, I do. But one statement convinced me of Natesh's sincerity."

"It is her choice," Elena said.

Manu nodded.

Siobhan sighed. "Alright then. We will assemble a rescue team. Before we do, however, I want to bring Glenda back in so she can introduce a new ally – perhaps a pivotal player in all of this."

"I will speak to her first," Elena said, and she left the room.

"Natesh, do you have others in your clan that will join you?" Siobhan asked.

The vampire rose and shook his head. "No one I dare trust. This is personal for me and has nothing to do with clan business. I know there are spies everywhere, and the last thing we need is for word to get back to Sirkan or Isla. Or, god forbid, Morgandrian."

The door opened. Glenda and her guest followed Elena into the room.

At a nod from Elena, the visitor pulled back the heavy hood. Natesh hissed.

"Adrianna!"

"Yes," Adrianna said. "I have been Isla's spy in Morgandrian's court, my Lord Natesh. But my loyalties have changed." Glenda's face grew pink.

"Continue," Artemus said. His brow furrowed.

"I...I first met Glenda on the night of the battle at Queens University, the night that Lord Sirkan abducted Cassandra. He had me in his thrall and used me to anchor sufficient dark energy into the place to open his portal. After he captured Cassandra, his control was broken, and I ran back to see his demonic hordes spilling out into the campus. Glenda was right in the middle of the attack and going down fast. I joined her and with our combined magics, we were able to stave them off."

Glenda jumped in. "I had been dealt a fatal blow from one of the demons. Adrianna healed me."

"I felt a – connection – to Glenda when I healed her," Adrianna said. "I could not let her die. We fought side by side; sure we were both going to die. Then the demons just... disappeared like someone had pulled a plug."

The Triumvirate exchanged knowing glances. "That was when the attack on the Institute was disrupted," Artemus said.

"Ah, that's what it was," Adriana said. "Nonetheless, I knew I had to go back to Morgandrian and to the Coven. So, I left."

"Adrianna has been keeping tabs on Morgandrian's interactions with Isla," Glenda said. "It seems that there is trouble between her and Sirkan because of Cassandra. Morgandrian believes Sirkan has designs on Cassandra that do not include continuing a relationship with Isla."

Manu's face turned purple. "What?"

Adrianna shrank back from his wrath, but Elena intervened. "Hear her out, Manu. Isla had a confrontation with Morgandrian after she had been rescued from Master Elena and Siobhan. I thought Sirkan had orchestrated that rescue, but now I'm not sure."

Adriana continued. "I can guide you through the tunnels and caves, and the Little Hells under the palace that lead to the Seely Court and beyond."

"Little Hells?"

"That's what Isla calls them," Adrianna said. "She is very adept at the black arts and has created all sorts of gruesome traps. And Sirkan, of course, has hordes of demons at his beck and call. It is not going to be easy, but I believe Glenda and I have come up with a plan. It just needs manpower."

Chapter 61: Weapon Magics

Cassie's training schedule continued. She was paying special attention to the warrior training with Paxton. She had mastered the dagger. Now they were on to long-range weapons like the crossbow.

"Why not a gun, Pax? That's long range."

"Ya," he said, "but guns depend on third dimensional resources and much of this war will be fought in other dimensions. Magic will be your most powerful resource no matter the weapon. You can imbue any weapon with it."

"And the Internet is considered Fifth Dimension, yes?"

Paxton met her eyes. "You're the expert there, baby."

"Yes, I am. Or at least, that's my goal." *Dammit, now I really want to get back to the university!* "I think the next war is going to be fought on the internet. Hell, it already is with all the cyber-attacks and social media manipulation."

"True, but remember, a lot of that crap is being generated by the Human Kingdom."

"I disagree." Cassie shook her head. "Now that I know about the other two kingdoms inhabiting and sharing the Earth, much less this whole Hybrid/Trybrid thing, I think we are looking at manipulation across all three kingdoms. It's most likely at the hands of the Dark Brotherhood."

Paxton's eyes widened. "How the hell do you know about them?"

Cassie stared at him. "I'm not blonde in my head, silly, just *on* my head."

They both doubled over in laughter.

I can't believe how much I love this girl! Paxton thought.

"Okay then genius," he said, "let's wrap this session up. I'm sure Oleander will be here to pick you up for lunch shortly. God, forbid you don't have enough time to change into Princess gear."

Cassie snorted, then picked up a bow and loaded it.

Chapter 62: Heka

The afternoon session with Sirkan was tense, as always. Cassie had gleaned enough about their past lives together to be convinced he had designs on her, along with thoughts of total domination ... mental, emotional, spiritual...and physical.

Ewww. What a creeper, but a dangerous one. If we were a "thing" in past lives, I can use that in manipulating him. She shuddered. At least he won't be trying to do anything icky before my eighteenth birthday. I'll be long gone by then...I have to be.

Cassie trudged up the stairs to the temple, ramrod straight, braced for the battle of wills ahead. Sirkan's back was to her. He was reading some type of scroll. She waited in silence.

Sure, keep me waiting, jackass. I'm neither impressed nor intimidated.

She tried to soften her face.

Sirkan finally deigned to turn to her, his eyes gleaming in the afternoon light coming through the skylight above them. "Well, your mood is better today," he said. "Glad to see it. That will help us explore a bit more easily. Today I am going to combine some of the magics you have been learning from your aunt with some objects from your past lives. Let's see what you can recall."

He motioned for her to take a position on the padded meditation bench. "Start your breathing and resonant tuning. You know the process by now."

Doing as she was bidden; she began the familiar routine. Breathe in for a count of six; hold for six; out for six. On the third set she began the resonant tuning by using the vowel sounds on the out breath. "Aaaaa...eeeee...iiiii..."

She felt herself dropping into the state of deep physical relaxation. Her body was asleep, but her mind remained sharp and focused. From far away, Sirkan's voice directed her to a tunnel of light. "Enter the tunnel. Feel the protection I am surrounding you with."

Cassie jerked with revulsion. Relax. You are in control, not him.

Sensing her hesitation, Sirkan backed off the energy he was directing at her. He knew he needed to be patient and careful. Very careful. They were at a critical juncture. He needed her trust.

"Now I want you to go back to a time in Ancient Egypt when you were High Priestess to Heka, the god of magic."

At the sound of the name, Cassie felt herself pulled forward. Her body hurtled through the tunnel as images of chanting forms before a gilded altar of stone took shape. She looked down at her golden-skinned body; she was bare-breasted. A sheer linen sheath held in place by straps at her shoulders was gathered around her gilded, leather sandaled feet. Her ceremonial headdress topped the thick black wig arranged into plaits entwined with precious stones signifying her status as High Priestess. She was holding up a large Ankh talisman and leading the chanting. Cassie could feel magic coursing through her body; she began to vibrate. She knew without a doubt she was experiencing another of her past lives.

The chanting stopped abruptly as a tall, broad-shouldered man entered the altar room. He, too, was bare-chested and wearing the leopard skin of the High Priest over a long, pleated linen skirt, richly embroidered with the requisite lotus flower. A huge headdress adorned his bald head, a golden snake rose from the lapis lazuli ankh at the front. His face was chiseled, his drug-widened citrine eyes outlined in kohl. Cassie knew those eyes: Sirkan.

Behind him four priests held a dazed man and a woman. The captives didn't make a sound. Cassie realized they were drugged. She stepped back from the altar as the priests brought the woman, then the man, forward to Sirkan. The priests bound their arms and ankles with leather straps and placed them side by side upon the altar.

Sirkan directed Cassie/the High Priestess to begin the chanting. The voices of the gathered faithful rose in unison with her voice, building to a crescendo until waves of energy swirled around the altar room and formed a vortex of pulsing light. Then one word, "Heka," erupted out of Sirkan's throat. The Priestess added her voice to his.

Twin daggers appeared out of thin air in both Sirkan and the priestess's hands. They brought them down simultaneously, cutting the throats of the sacrifices together. Servants ran forward with golden cups to catch the blood. High Priest and High Priestess moved to the head of the altar stone, each taking a proffered cup. Arms entwined, they met one another's eyes – and drank.

Cassie felt a surge unlike anything she'd ever experienced. She could feel the blood run down her throat, the taste like honey. *Nectar of the gods, indeed!* She wanted more...she *needed* more. The more she drank, the stronger she became. She felt the magic flowing throughout her body, every sense heightened, every ability quickened to new heights. Sirkan cast aside the empty cups while the servants came forward to dispose of the bodies. Sirkan bent and murmured.

"Habibah (beloved)," he said, and he lifted her by the arms to the altar to consummate the ritual.

Cassie felt herself gradually drift back to present time, languid and sated. Sirkan was standing above her when she slowly opened her eyes. Her eyes still unfocused, she looked up at him with the heavy lids of a well-satisfied woman. He gently pulled her to him, the lust in his eyes echoing hers. He knew what she had seen because he had been there. He had deliberately taken her there. He wanted her to bring whatever abilities she had honed in that lifetime forward into present day. She had to be reminded what they had been to one another.

He lowered his face to hers, his breath deepening. When his lips touched hers, Cassie returned to full consciousness and jerked her head away from his vile mouth. She was reeling as the power receded. Her body seemed devoid of any bone structure – like Jell-O. Awareness of what they had done in the past sent waves of horror throughout every cell in her body.

"No!" she whispered. "I could not have done that. I could not had *been* that."

"Oh, but you were," Sirkan said. "And you did many times over the course of many lives. We were one of the most dominant forces in the ancient world. And we will be so again."

She forced herself to stand, turned, and walked out of the temple without a sound. *Not on your life, you lascivious maniac!* She refused to run. She would not give him the satisfaction of watching her flee. Now she knew who she was, and she knew her mission.

She ran back into the palace and up to her room. When Oleander came to get her for tea, Cassie feigned a headache.

"Tell my aunt that I am unwell and will rest until it's time for our lessons."

The elf nodded, a look of concern on her face.

"It's okay," Cassie said, and Oleander retreated.

Moments later, Cassie heard Paxton's voice through the door.

"Cassie, are you alright?"

"Yes, just a headache," she said. "I want to take a nap. Not in the mood for tea. I'll see you at dinner."

She could feel his concern through the door, but he didn't argue. She blew out a long breath and listened to his steps recede down the hallway. *I need some time to think – to get a handle on the feelings I just experienced from that lifetime. I can still sense the exhilaration. Is that part of me now?*

She put her face in her hands and sobbed.

THE AFTERNOON SESSION with Isla was a welcome respite from Sirkan's barrage of mind games. Isla imparted concrete tools Cassie could use in countless situations: magic and spell casting. They weren't so very different from the ones her father and Brigida had taught her in the Seely Court. The biggest difference, of course, being the intention behind them. These were dark magic, spells of cursing and destruction, aimed at wreaking havoc through physical and emotional pain, misdirection, and agonizing death. Cassie did her best to shield her own emotions from the pure evil that spewed out of her aunt, not wanting to be tainted in any way.

The adamant mind shield her father had taught her to use was becoming increasingly difficult to maintain since the sessions had become more and more intense.

How much longer can I keep this up? She wondered. I have to get out of here soon.

Chapter 63: To the Rescue

"It works in theory," Artemus said. "Much will depend on the traps that are imbedded into the maze of caves."

"And the demons," Khamuel said. He turned to Natesh. "I can still feel the foul breath and scrape of poisoned fangs from your hellhounds when you took Paxton. Those beasts multiplied by five whenever I killed one. I'm sure they will be tame compared to what must await us from the likes of Isla and Sirkan."

Natesh cocked his head. "I assure you; you are correct. My hellhounds are nothing compared to the atrocities that dwell in the darkness of Isla's Non-Seely Dimension. Elementals, trolls, dark fairies, and hordes of demonic creatures that Sirkan has created roam the outer periphery of their realm.

"The White Circle has vast resources. We have some of the finest warriors and magicians within our ranks," Artemus said. "I have no doubt we can handle whatever Isla and Sirkan send our way. Cassandra is far too important to the planet and the races that dwell here. We will call on the Celestial and Devic Kingdoms to aid in the rescue."

"Do we solicit the Human Kingdom as well?" asked Siobhan.

"Not for this. This is our mission, why we came to this planet in the first place – to aid Humanity in its evolutionary progression. We will need magical, angelic, and celestial energies to counterbalance those of Isla and Sirkan. I would like you to reach out to Mateus Nephus and your cousin Ian to join us. That will give us additional celestial and magical support."

"Done and done."

Elena turned to Adrianna. "Are you ready to solidify your allegiance to the Forces of Light?"

"I am. However, I would like to offer to stay in my current position with Morgandrian so that I can keep abreast of the happenings of the coven."

Elena pursed her lips and gave Adrianna a long look. Glenda was clenching her hands but knew to keep her mouth shut.

"Alright. But you are to come to me immediately if you feel you are in any danger of being discovered. I will not have your blood on our hands."

Adrianna nodded mutely.

"Now go with my blessing. Stay safe."

Glenda took Adrianna's hand and led her out of the room.

Chapter 64: No Worries

Cassie paced the floor of her room, wringing her hands. Paxton still hadn't turned up for their morning training session. Dread welled up in her stomach. *Something has happened. Oh my God, what if Sirkan has found out about our plans?*

Just as she was reaching the peak of her awfulizing, a firm knock shook her out of her reverie. Turning with relief, Cassie threw open the door and fell into Paxton's arms. "Oh my God, Pax. I was so worried."

"Why would you be worried? I'm just a few minutes late. I had some stuff I needed to arrange before we began our morning training." He put a finger to her lips to quiet any more discussion. "Let's go to the gym and get going. We have a lot to cover."

Taking her by the hand, Paxton led Cassie down to the gym. He was a little subdued this morning. It worried her. *I guess he has as much on his mind as I do on mine. Shake it off.*

There was a stack of weapons at the ready, leaning up against the center ring.

Cassie took a step back, eyebrows raised.

"So, we've come back to the sword thing, then?"

"Had to babe. The more I think about what may lie ahead, the more I feel you will need to know how to use the sword and the dagger."

"But I am also learning how to call up those sparklers I have in my fingertips. Shouldn't I be focusing on how to turn up the juice? Hell, you can shoot thunderbolts out of your hands. I should be able to master that too!"

There was just a ripple of surprise through Paxton's eyes before he burst into laughter. Cassie glared at him.

"I'm sorry, honey. I didn't mean to laugh at you. But those 'sparklers' as you call them, take years to master. You already have an excellent grasp of fencing techniques. Let's focus on it first."

Cassie crossed her arms. "Nope. You are not the boss of me, and I want to focus on the innate abilities I have from my father's side of the gene pool. He showed me enough when I was training with him and I am confident that I can use my magical abilities if things get dicey. Hell, they manifested by themselves when that ass Sirkan took me from Queens. I thought I was hallucinating."

"Okay, okay, but we will move to the outer courtyard. I don't want you setting anything on fire."

He set up four targets from the archery field at varying distances. "Okay, show me what you got."

Cassie took battle stance, feet planted wide and firmly on the ground, arms loose by her sides. She called on her magical power, visualizing it accumulating into the base of her spine with each breath. Once she felt the warmth at her lower back, she moved it up her spine to her solar plexus, the warmth igniting into energetic waves of fire. She rubbed her palms together, willing the fire from her belly to "visit" her hands. She felt a fullness in her palms like she was holding two fiery tennis balls. She focused on the closest target and willed the burning sensation down her fingers. She pointed her hands at the target, took a deep breath, and released the flames through her fingertips by breathing out. Twin streams of fire reduced the target to ashes.

Cassie whooped, jumping up and down while shaking out her hands. "See! I told you."

Paxton took her hands in his and examined them, palms up. "Not even pink. How do they feel?"

"Cool as a cucumber. Let me try again!"

She practiced with mixed results over the next hour. Paxton finally called a halt. "Okay, that's enough. I don't want our entire session to be taken up with your pyrogenic fingertips. The next step is to get you to defeat some bad guys."

"Bad guys? What the hell does that mean? Going to the dark forest?"

"God no!" Paxton said. "I have a plan." With a flick of his wrist, a hellhound appeared, fangs dripping with green slime.

"Well shit, that looks real enough." Cassie said. She put out her hands and called the

fire. It fizzled immediately."

She swore.

He laughed.

"I told you that magic won't always be an option," Paxton said.

Cassie glared at him, simultaneously reaching for the sword at her side. *No protective spell this time!* She whirled and brought the sword down, lopping off the hound's head with a wet squelch just as it was about to take a chunk out of her throat. The blow thrummed up her arm. "Ow!"

She took deep breaths until the pain dissipated. Before she could inhale again, the fallen animal resurrected from its headless form into three more hounds, meaner and bigger than the first.

"Not fair!"

She pirouetted midair and came down swinging. She managed to kill two of the beasts before the third one grabbed her arm with its drooling fangs.

Pain ripped through her as Paxton flicked his wrist again and the animal vaporized.

"You're dead, babe. But really, that was amazing for your first beastie encounter. Not bad – not bad at all." He reached out to pull her up, but she countered and kicked his feet out from under him, then punched him in the gut. "Like hell, brat! You made those illusions *hurt.*"

Paxton doubled over. "Ouch! Don't make me laugh. That hurts too!"

She jumped up, raising her fists. "Bring it!"

Getting up, Paxton brushed himself off, and held his hands up in surrender. "No, no. That's enough. We'll fight some more meanies tomorrow. I just wanted to start upping the stakes a bit. You still have your two favorite training sessions coming up and I'm sure they will want you at your best."

She started to turn away, still seething.

"Wait!" Paxton put his hand on her shoulder. "Take the dagger. Just in case..."

Cassie made a rude gesture. "Whatever." She palmed the dagger and stomped back to the palace.

Chapter 65: Ayesha 2.0

That afternoon, the horror show began in earnest. Cassie should have known that her lessons would begin to take a darker turn after Sirkan had introduced the blood sacrifices from her past lives.

Trudging up the steps of Sirkan's temple after lunch, she heard low moaning noises. *What the...?*

She ran into the building and skidded to a halt. In the middle of the circular room there was a stone altar with a small form chained to it, struggling to release themselves from the restraints.

"What the hell are you doing, Sirkan! Leave them alone."

The Dark Lord looked at her from the far side of the altar, a dagger with a carved ivory handle in his right hand. "Oh no, my dear. This is a pivotal point in your training. You need to bring those delicious talents forward from those lifetimes as one of the most delightfully evil priestesses of all times. You need to ground your powers into this time and place with an upgrade, if you will. Shall we say, Ayesha 2.0?"

Two of his loyal minions scurried forth and took her by the elbows to drag her forward facing Sirkan across the altar. She struggled to no avail. Then she saw who was on the altar.

Oleander!

"Did you really think that I would not discover your plans of escape, my dear? I told you I have spies everywhere. And they are certainly not only in humanoid forms. Why, the very trees and bushes have elementals that report to me. I have heard every bit of your planning between you and Paxton – and this – thing."

Oleander's face was bruised and bloody from torture. Following Cassie's horrified look, Sirkan grimaced. "She was not very forthcoming, sorry to say. Such loyalty!" He sighed, "But her mind is so very weak. I was able to mine her thoughts easily enough to ascertain the planned escape route. Very clever. But honestly, you would never have made it through the caverns of Little

Hells, as your aunt calls them. I have created such maliciously delightful demonic creatures and traps; it would take a virtual army to wade through them. If such an army could even exist. Remember, I have had millennia to prepare for this time." He sniggered. "Your aunt thinks she created this realm. It has been under my direction since I stormed its gates thousands of years ago. The dark energy here is totally of my doing."

Cassie's chest was heaving as she attempted to regain her composure. Losing it wouldn't accomplish anything and she needed to come up with a plan. She needed to save Oleander. *And where is Pax?*

As if reading her mind, Sirkan said, "And then there's that dear boy Paxton."

"I will kill you if you hurt him, you bastard!"

"Such language! Really, my dear, it gives me hope for you yet." Sirkan touched his hand to his heart.

Cassie stared at him. Then she smiled. Oh, you jackass. You have SO underestimated me.

Picking up on her intention, he raised his hand. "Don't even think about it. If I die, so will your little boyfriend. I have him tied to me energetically. If my life force ends, so does his. And then there is the little – very little – matter of your auntie.

"She means nothing to me!" Cassie spat.

"Oh, but she should. There's the *other* little matter of your, hmmm what endearment do you use? Oh yes, Mommy."

Cassie reared back, "My mother?"

"Think about it you stupid girl. Isn't it quite the coincidence that she went missing just weeks before your Aunt Isla appeared? By the gods, I am still trying to wrap my head around the fact that you are the reincarnation of such a powerful entity as Ayesha."

Staring at him, she reached out with her psychic senses as her father had taught her but could not get any sense of her mother. "What kind of bullshit is this? Do you expect me to believe that Isla took my mother? No way, I would have sensed her when I came into this dimension."

"Seriously? You think so? Think again." He paused. "But enough of this. We have a more important task at hand."

He leaned across the altar and took her left hand into his right hand, the hand holding the dagger. "Surely you remember your lessons on the left-hand receiving energy and the right hand sending it. Behold."

She looked down at Oleander, "It's okay, Oleander. I will..." Before she could finish her sentence, Sirkan grabbed her left hand and put the dagger into it. Then he gripped her hand with his and directed it down and across, slashing it across Oleander's throat. Blood spurted into Cassie's face, her nose, her open, screaming mouth as the elf's eyes turned black with death.

The shock of energy from the life essence draining out of Oleander swept through Cassie, the taste of blood on her lips, the pain of loss replaced by a giddy feeling of power. Sirkan held her horrified gaze and then shifted to her lips and smiled slowly. She followed his gaze and saw him focus on her chest, a dark ray of energy streaming toward her. Cassie felt her anger rise with it. *No way!* She felt the force inching toward her beginning to sync with the torc at her collarbone. The dark energy immediately began to hum in unison with it. *Did he seriously think he could use her own power against her?* She felt with satisfaction her mother's Merkabah pendant begin to activate. Sirkan did not know it was buried within the torc. She smiled, raising her eyes to Sirkan's and slowly, deliberately pulled her hand out of his, breaking the energy exchange. The protective shield of the pendant locked into place with a faint clicking sound.

She saw the shock of disbelief flash for a nanosecond in his eyes. Cassie nodded, her smile widening.

"To reiterate – seriously? Do you think my father allowed me to come here by accident – and unprepared? Along with auntie, your arrogance will be your undoing. I don't need to kill either of you. You will do that all on your own."

With that she sent out streams of fire imprisoning him in the wall of flame. "Where is Pax – and where is my mother?"

She felt a presence behind her. "Oh, they are well contained my dear. Well contained indeed."

Isla stepped forward.

Sirkan growled.

"I see I was not mistaken about your little charade." Isla looked down at the lifeless body of Oleander. "A pity about the elf. She was an excellent slave." She took a step toward the flames encasing Sirkan. "And you my 'love,' (she made air quotes), I knew you planned on, what – replacing me – since the brat ran back into the palace after your first lesson with her. Your lust for her was so incredibly obvious. You made the mistake of telling me about all those phenomenal past lives you had together. And then there was your scent. It changed when we brought her back here. You forget – I am Fae. My senses are more heightened as an indigenous race than yours as a visiting one. The Devic Kingdom is endemic to the Earth plane – the Celestials are not."

Isla turned to Cassie. "You want to see your mother? Your little boyfriend? Then come!"

She grabbed Cassie by the arm and drug her down the stairs of the temple. Cassie did not resist. She needed to know where her mother and Pax were before she could do anything about getting them all out of here.

Sirkan bellowed behind them, "You will not harm that girl! She is mine."

Isla looked over her shoulder at her former lover and said nothing.

Chapter 66: The Cavalry Departs

The Spirit Screen in the Citadel sounded an alarm. Elena was the first to respond, running into the library. The agreed upon signal that was to emanate from the torc at Cassandra's neck when she had encountered real danger in Isla's realm. Much like a dog-whistle, only members of the Triumvirate could hear the sounds. Artemus came next, with Manu and Tristan, who had arrived at the Citadel the day before.

Siobhan had yet to return from the Human Realm, but they knew she would have been alerted to the alarm as well and would be hurrying back as soon as possible with Mateus and Ian in tow.

"It's time." Manu said. He started toward the portal to the Seely Court, but Artemus held him back. "Wait, my friend. I want to ensure that Natesh has time."

A portal flashed with Natesh stepping out, followed by Glenda and Adrianna. "Here." the vampire said.

"Alright then. Proceed to King Ayden's court. I will be along with Siobhan and the rest as soon as they arrive."

The Spirit Screen vibrated. It was a voice missive from Siobhan. "I received the alarm. I will meet you at the border of the Non Seely Court with Mateus and Ian."

Ayden looked around the room, well satisfied. If anyone could take on this rescue mission, it was certainly this group.

"Here is the plan." began Artemus. "We will form three groups. Thanks to Natesh and Adrianna we know what we will be facing and where some of the subterranean dungeons are located. I will lead the charge with Natesh, Siobhan, Tristan, and Khamuel. Manu will follow with Elena, Mateus, and Adrianna. Ayden will bring up the rear with Azazel, Ian, and Glenda."

Glenda started to protest, and Elena said, "We will not compromise the mission by allowing personal feeling to cloud our judgements. We must get

Cassandra out at all costs. That is why Artemus has assigned us as he has. We will not pair you with Adrianna. Mission first."

Admonished, Glenda remained silent.

Artemus continued. "We must get through the Little Hells that surround the borders between Ayden and Isla's courts first. Once we clear the way through the worst of it, Manu will forge ahead with Adrianna, leading the way to the dungeons."

"We will guard the escape route at the rear to ensure it remains open," said Ayden. "Although I will be hard pressed not to rush to Cassandra. I know this is the best use of resources and I will do my best not to let my emotions get in the way."

They all nodded in unison. "Let us call on the Powers That Be then."

Elena led the invocation. "We call upon the unseen powers, the Masters, Guides, Saints, and Sages on the inner and outer planes to be with us in our mission. We are the Warriors of Light. We are the Hand of the Radiant One. We are the Ones we've been waiting for."

"And so, it is." All affirmed in unison.

"Alright," said Mateus. "Let's do this!"

Chapter 67: The Lost Are Found

Cassie pulled away from Isla. "I am fully capable of following you. You don't have to drag me as though I am your prisoner."

Isla reared around in a fury and slapped her soundly. "You will do as you are told, brat. I am so sick of you and your subterfuge. Be grateful you are such a valuable commodity. It would give me a great deal of satisfaction to string you up and drain your power right here and now!"

Isla was leading them down stone steps deeper into the depths of the palace. All around them Cassie could hear agonized groans and an occasional scream. "What the hell is going on here? Who do you have in these – what – dungeons?"

"Did you really think that all I did to build my powers was to cast a few paltry spells and incantations? It takes blood sacrifice. Sirkan may have built this power grid originally, but I am the one who grounded it with fear and blood. This is MY realm by birthright as a Fae royal. He will never have ultimate power here as a Celestial."

Cassie's torc began to hum again. This time it was as if it was answering a call. *Mommy!* She touched it, ignoring her anger at Isla and reached out with her psychic sense. Cassie visualized her mother's chestnut eyes. Her scent. *She was here! She was here!*

Isla whipped around. "So, you feel her, do you? Well then, let me give you a choice. Do you want your mother – or your boyfriend?"

"Both bitch!" With that, Cassie planted her feet firmly on the ground and called her fire to her.

Anticipating the move, Isla had already put a protective barrier around herself, and the flames fizzled, just as they had done in the training exercise with Paxton earlier that day.

Cassie screamed in frustration.

"Temper, temper. You know emotion hobbles your abilities."

A feline roar echoed through the cave. A black panther leapt out of the shadows, claws outstretched, and fangs aimed toward Isla's throat.

"Gabriel!"

Startled, Isla lost her protective shield. The cat pounced on the dark queen, pinning her to the ground.

"Good boy!" Cassie laughed. She reclaimed her energy and fashioned flame restraints at Isla's hands and ankles. "As much as I would love to burn you to a crisp, Auntie, that is against the rules I live by." With that, Cassie threw Isla up against the nearest wall and pinned her there with her magic.

The Queen shrieked in frustration.

"Come on Gabe, let's go find Mom and Paxton."

Gabriel maintained his panther body, escorting her further into the dark tunnel. She threw her magic ahead of her, illuminating the way with fairy lights. The passageway turned to the left and she stopped in consternation. There were myriad passageways branching off. *Which way to go?* She put her hand on Gabriel's head. "Where is Mommy, boy?"

Pausing and sniffing the air, Gabriel's growl rumbled within his throat. He padded toward one of the far openings and entered the corridor. She could still hear screams and groans reverberating throughout the tunnels. Surely with both Isla and Sirkan out of the picture, no one would continue to be tortured.

Turning another corner, she slammed into a wall – or at least that's what it felt like.

"Going somewhere my dear?"

Sirkan.

"You didn't really think that paltry flame would imprison me for long. I allowed you to think that so I could see what your aunt was up to. I love it. She is so predictable. As are you!" He grabbed her arm and started to drag her along, throwing a gigantic energy ball toward Gabriel. The feline fell to the ground screeching in pain.

"Gabriel!" Cassie screamed in fear. She could feel his life essence grow weaker and weaker while Sirkan drug her farther into the darkness.

"You want to see your mother? Very well, let's join her, shall we?"

At the end of the corridor was a large iron-studded door. Sirkan threw it open.

Her mother was encased in a sarcophagus, the lid clear so that Cassie could see her.

Sirkan pulled her up and pushed her face toward the lid. "Behold Mommy!"

Cassie let out a sob and put both hands on the chamber. There was the woman from the photos her father had shown her. She looked like she was merely asleep. But she was pale – so pale and thin! "Mommy! Mommy, can you hear me?"

Nothing.

"She cannot hear you. She cannot help you. And you cannot help her. But at least you know she is not dead, yes? And I see your father must have shown you what she looked like before she took on the glamour of Taryn Oberon. Good. Now, let us go check on your boyfriend, shall we? The little traitor."

Cassie could not tell how long Sirkan pulled through the tunnels. It seemed interminable. She started to feel faint and weak, and stumbled repeatedly. The emotional and physical duress of the past weeks were beginning to take their toll. Her knees felt like limp noodles. She could barely keep conscious. She attempted to call her power to her, but to no avail. Sirkan had succeeded in exhausting her to the point of no return. *Okay, I am supposed to be the reincarnation of this great Atlantean priestess. Let's see if I can fake it till I make it.* Taking advantage of her body being numb, she used an open-eyed meditation technique from her yoga training. Pushing her mind up and out, she began to feel the familiar feeling of her consciousness soaring beyond her physical body. She began to hear the rushing sound of voices whispering all around her. Some of the voices sounded familiar. *Glenda? Daddy?* She tuned in to her father's voice and then realized she was picking up on his thoughts, not words. He must be nearby! Oh my God – *Daddy*!

She didn't have time to get anymore. Sirkan jerked her toward an open doorway. Paxton was hanging from chains in the middle of the darkened room, head lolling on his chest. Blood oozed from what looked like whip marks crisscrossing his torso.

She screamed. "Pax – no, no, no." She pushed against Sirkan, attempting to reach Paxton.

"Unfortunately for him, he was no more forthcoming than your little elf. Devotion can be so misplaced. But never fear. He is alive. I still have need of him."

Cassie started to kick and scream, adrenaline from anger pushing aside her physical exhaustion. "I will kill you! I will free Paxton from your grip, and I will kill you!"

He jerked her arms behind her, pulling her back to him. "No, my dear, you will not. There is no way that you can extricate him from the bond I forged between us. Besides, I'm not done with you either. We have our own work to do. But the work will not commence until your Quickening. So, I am afraid I will have to ensure you will not get into any trouble before then."

She stilled. Just like in the long-ago past life recall after the Fall of Atlantis, she realized her anger would get her nowhere. She needed to bide her time. She knew her father was coming.

The Spirit Screen alarm must have been set off as soon as Sirkan had started dragging her through the dungeons. That meant others were on their way as well. *I have to keep my mind shielded from Sirkan, so he doesn't know.* Up went the adamant wall at her Third Eye. She had faith that her father would still pick up on her energy signature from the Torc. And then, of course, there was Gabriel. She knew he was injured, but still alive. Her heart ached at the thought of him suffering because he had protected her. *No.* She would not go down that path. Emotional response would not do her any good. She had to keep her wits about her.

Paxton moaned and raised his head. His eyes met hers and widened. "Cass." His voice came out in a raspy whisper.

"It's okay, Pax. I'm fine. Don't try to talk. Conserve your strength. We will get out of this!"

"Enough with the reunion. Now that you know he and your mother are alive, we have more important matters to attend to. I remind you that their fates – their lives – depend now on your cooperation."

Sirkan pulled her out into the darkened corridor once more. Two dozen dark forms materialized out of the shadows. "Guard him well." he directed his minions. "If anyone approaches, kill them."

Chapter 68: Ancient Magics

Adrianna was nowhere to be found. Morgandrian surmised her suspicions were justified. The girl had been acting strangely ever since she had been duped by Isla's consort during the fruitless mixer in Charlotte. Morgandrian had been loath to delve more deeply into the girl's behavior, not wanting to mess up any of Isla's plans. But seriously, she would have to be deaf, dumb, and blind not to see the little bitch was playing both sides. But why? She needed to get to the bottom of this. Time to brave the wrath of Isla.

Morgandrian walked through the portal and into the main entrance of the Fae Queen's palace. It was eerily quiet, nary a serving elf to be seen. *What the hell?* She started down the marble hallway leading to the throne room. No guards, Fae, or demonic. She pivoted and moved toward the staircase leading to the dungeons. She let her intuition guide her. Descending with caution, she thought she could hear faint screaming from the dungeons below.

Well, that's a relief. At least the usual mayhem and torture seemed to be in place. I'd really be worried if I didn't hear any evidence of her blood sacrifices.

She went toward the sacrificial chambers – still no evidence of the army of servants and slaves Isla kept at her beck and call. She reached the lowest levels of the dungeons and came to a dead halt. Isla was pinned against the far wall with what looked like shackles of fire.

The Queen was spitting mad. "Do something you fool. Get me out of here!"

"Who did this to you?" Morgandrian asked? "I need to know what type of spell they used before I can begin to unravel it."

"That little witch Cassandra," Isla said. "Sirkan did such a good job in connecting her to her past life abilities that she surpassed what I taught her.

She is on a rampage to find her mother and her traitorous boyfriend. But enough talk – do something!"

Morgandrian reached toward the flames at Isla's wrists – and drew back in pain, her fingertips sizzling. Isla hissed in frustration. "Hurry!'

"Just wait. Let me see if I can get a handle on this," Morgandrian said.

She put out both of her hands and scanned the shackles with her palms.

"Shit, this is ancient magic," she said. "And not from this realm. How in the hell did she conjure this here? It's like nothing I have encountered before. It has to be from her Celestial bloodline."

So intent was she in ascertaining the source of the spell that she did not feel the presence coming up behind her. When she saw Isla's eyes bugging out of their sockets, the Dark Witch spun around.

"It seems I'm late to the party." Natesh ambled toward them. Siobhan, Tristan, and Khamuel fanned out behind him, weapons ready to engage.

Instinctively, Morgandrian threw out a stream of her own flames, but Khamuel's shield deflected them and boomeranged them back at her. She was barely able to jump aside.

"Well, this seems boringly familiar," Siobhan said. "Still thinking you are the great and powerful black witch, Morgan?" She feigned a yawn.

Isla screamed a stream of obscenities. "Natesh, you bastard! I will see you staked and beheaded and will burn your body to ash!"

"Well, that's a bit of overkill, don't you think?" the Vampire asked.

Before Morgandrian could react, he grabbed her by the throat and lifted her several feet off the floor. She clutched at his hands, struggling to release his grip. "Should I end you now, or allow the Master of the White Circle to tend to you?"

"Let Artemus take care of her," Tristan said. "She will be a useful source of information."

Isla looked past Tristan to see Artemus. He gripped a bloody sword in his right hand.

"Isla, I must congratulate you on the despicable traps you call Little Hells," he said. "Such delightful subjects you have. Fortunately, we were well prepared by our newest recruit."

Adrianna stepped forward.

"What the fuck – is my entire court turning to the Light?" Isla asked.

Elena stepped into view. "We can only hope, your majesty," she said. "We can only hope."

Chapter 69: Past Lives Collide

Manu intercepted Sirkan in the room where Paxton was being held. Sirkan pulled Cassie by the hair and threw her to the floor. Her head exploded in dark shards of pain upon collision with the stone. Sirkan snarled at Manu. "Bring it, you self-righteous bastard, I've been waiting a long time for this!"

Manu's ice-blue eyes darkened to a deep indigo with rage. The amethyst orb on his staff emitted a beam of violet flame, which he used to block the blaze of red fire from Sirkan's staff. "As have I, you whoreson," Manu said, his voice a growl. "You have gone too far this time. Ayesha is my Soulmate, and I will see you in Hell!"

"You first!" Sirkan's neck swelled. He drew his sword with his right hand. The blade flickered with wicked energy. "You abandoned her in your sanctimonious judgment. I took her in and nurtured her, taught her the delights of the flesh and how to use her untapped powers. She will never be yours again!"

Cassie began to swim back to conscious awareness, the sounds of rage bouncing off the walls of the cavern. She lifted herself to her elbows and tried to rise. She felt weak as a kitten.

Kitten? Gabriel! Where is he?

All thoughts of her pet were erased when she lifted her head and saw the two powerful men locked in battle. Sirkan was vibrating to the point of invisibility. The other one, the one she had seen in her father's throne room, seemed to be more grounded, but was just as scary.

Who the hell is this guy?

No sooner did the thought form than she slipped into a vision of the dark-haired man at her side in the past life she had experienced through Sirkan. But this was different. She felt an emotion so powerful it almost knocked her off her feet. She put a fist to her chest. Her heart felt like it was splitting open.

Manu! His name is Manu.

Prodigious power rose within her. She rose regally to her feet. *I am the High Priestess Ayesha. I will not let this stand!*

She knew she could...she *would* end this. She knew who she was.

From the periphery of her vision, she saw others rushing into the room – Glenda followed by two faces she remembered from the encounter at the university. Her attention once more focused on the still-chained Paxton.

I have to get him out of here.

Tristan flew straight toward his son. He helped Paxton up and threw a lightning bolt at the cuffs, shattering them into a shower of metal shavings. Cassie went to Paxton, who slumped into her arms. "Here, hold onto me and let me get you out of the line of fire!"

Pax mumbled a protest.

"Don't go all knight in shining armor on me, jerk," Cassie said. "You couldn't fight a hamster, much less these people – whoever they are."

She dragged him out of the melee toward the opening of the room and almost collided with Natesh. The Vampire looked startled "Giselle, are you hurt?" he asked.

Cassie stumbled back at the sound of the name she had seen on the flap of the envelope during her horrific past life recall. *No time for that. Later.*

"Be of some use and get Pax out of here," she said. "It's the least you can do after all the shit you have caused."

Natesh handed Paxton over to Glenda. Along with Mateus, she pulled Paxton out of the room. Cassie turned back to the fire duel and thundered.

"Stop!"

Her voice welled from some force deep within her. She insinuated herself between Manu and Sirkan, holding up her arms like a referee. Her magical abilities surged. She began to glow with an inner white light. It grew exponentially with each breath. The intensity of her illumination threw the combatants apart with a gale-like force they could not overcome.

She had feelings for both, despite the innate revulsion she derived from Sirkan. And the other...this Manu.

What the hell.

But in her heart, she understood. Her recognition was on a deep level...a subterranean level of the soul.

They were both from her past lives.

"I don't know exactly what is going on here, but whatever it is, I'll have none of it. I don't want any of your past lives crap. We may have Soul Connections, but none of you" – she swung wide her arms to include Natesh – "are part of my current life. Paxton is my guy and you all can go to hell!"

She stormed out in a blaze of fire and fury, leaving the two High Priests and Vampire Lord gaping after her.

Sirkan recovered first. "She certainly told us!" He snapped his fingers and vanished in a flash of smoke.

Manu cursed.

Natesh winced. "Well, that went well."

Chapter 70: Healing Hands

Cassie caught up to Paxton, still supported between Glenda and Mateus, just as they were beginning their ascent to the main floor of the Palace. "We need to get him to the healing room. Let me show you the way."

The four proceeded to the chamber that Isla had used for some of her more noxious potion mixing lessons. Cassie rummaged through the shelves of herbs and essential oils and raked out what she needed for a healing salve. Mixing everything in an earthen bowl, she looked at Mateus.

"Put him over there on the cot on his side. I need to get to his back. Glenda, use your healing energy. Run it through the bottoms of his feet while I get this potion mixed."

Cassie's hands began to warm with her Reiki energy, which added to the mixture's potency.

Good, this should make him as good as new in no time.

Walking over to the cot, Cassie bent down and began to pat the salve into the slashes on Paxton's back. They were viciously deep, and she hoped the pain-relieving properties of the basil and peppermint oil combined with the other herbs would give him some relief as he regained consciousness. After coating the wounds, she put her hands together, palm to palm, and called up more of her healing abilities by visualizing emerald-green light in her heart. She directed it down her arms and into her hands and then gently placed them on his back. Green light swirled around and then into the wounds. The ragged gashes slowly began to knit together. Glenda continued to send her healing streams of energy up his legs until his entire body was glowing from the inside-out. It seemed an eternity, but they persevered. Cassie caught Glenda's eyes, and mouthed, "Thank you."

Glenda gave a rueful smile. "Through sick and sin," she said.

Cassie gasped when Paxton took a deep breath and opened his eyes. He was groggy but smiling.

"Hello, beautiful," he said. "Sorry to be such a bother."

Cassie sobbed, took his face between her hands, and kissed him. "Thank God. I was so scared Sirkan was going to kill you."

"It takes more than a whipping to get the best of this angel."

Tristan rasped from the doorway. "Indeed, I would think so!"

Chapter 71: The Real Rebekah

Ayden stood at the sarcophagus looking down at Rebekah. The glamouring spell had dissipated. No longer Taryn Oberon, his beloved once more looked as she did when they had met in the Mundane World during that glorious summer in England. Her long layered brown hair fanned out around her face. Her hands were crossed over her chest, and he was gratified to see that she still wore the "promise ring" he had given her as part of their handfasting ceremony.

"Just as beautiful as the day we met, my love." He turned to Artemus. "How do we get her out of there? It's not like she's Sleeping Beauty who can be awakened with a kiss. I'm sure there are booby traps that will engage if we make a misstep in prying open this contrivance."

"Well, there's one person who should know," Artemus said. "Care to confront your loving twin? I have her chained to her throne along with her cohort Morgandrian."

Ayden's feet pounded against the cold marble stairs, each step echoing in a furious rush towards the throne room. As he burst through the towering doors, his eyes were immediately drawn to the overpowering clash of black and red that enveloped the room. Crimson drapes hung heavily against ebony walls, and dark tiles were interspersed with splashes of red blood.

Morgandrian sat alongside Isla, who looked as regal as ever, although the heavy manacles did detract a bit from the picture of royal hauteur. Isla battled her restraints, hurling unintelligible words at her brother in what sounded like an incantation.

"Sister," he said. "You have committed the last atrocity of your dark reign. I will, however, allow you a chance at redemption. We have found Rebekah, my wife. How do I extricate her from her living tomb?"

Isla threw back her head and cackled. She sounded like she had lost her mind. "I will destroy your court and every living being within it. You have no idea what is about to be unleashed you imbecile. My consort will rain down the very fire of the seven hells and destroy—"

"Talk, talk, talk!" Siobhan raised her eyes to the heavens. "Why do you always have to go on and on. Words. Nothing by empty words. At least have some dignity in your defeat."

Isla bit her lip so hard it bled. "I am not defeated. You will soon see the power behind my throne!"

Ayden lunged at his sister with the tip of his sword at her throat. A trickle of blood ran down her neck. She gasped but the throne blocked her attempt to back away.

"Mark my words, sister dear, for they are not empty threats," Ayden said. "I am fully prepared to kill you where you sit if you do not give me the key to releasing my wife! The worlds would be well rid of you."

Cassie sprinted into the room. "Daddy, no! I have another way."

Ayden swung around to take his daughter into his arms. "My darling girl! Are you hurt?"

"I'm fine, Daddy. I have another way to get to Mommy. Come, let's go back to her."

Chapter 72: A Blaze of Glory

Cassie took Ayden by the hand to lead him back to the cavern chamber. "I can communicate with Mommy through my Dream Walking. I heard her call me when I was still in Charlotte. Since then, I have felt her several times during my sessions with Sirkan and once in my dreams. I couldn't get a fix on her location, but now I know I can reach her for sure."

Master Elena was standing guard over Rebekah, both hands on the sarcophagus, eyes glistening. "I have been trying to get through to her, but the wards are too strong."

"It's okay," Cassie said. "I can do it."

She shared what she had experienced over the past weeks with the flashes of communication with her mother. "Now that she is this close, I know I can use the connection we have through the pendant she gave me." She pointed to the amethyst Merkabah necklace visible at her mother's throat. "Mine is identical and was absorbed into the Torc Daddy gave me, so as long as I keep it on, I have access to its power."

She touched the Torc nestled at the base of her throat and took a deep breath. Violet-colored light radiated from deep within the silver. A low hum emanated from it. An answering hum sounded from inside the chamber and the Merkabah at Rebekah's throat glowed.

"See, I knew it." Cassie pumped her fist. "Let me go into a lucid dream state and reach out to her." Cassie looked around the small chamber at Paxton, Siobhan, Elena, and Artemus. She held up her hands. "Please, I can't do this with an audience. Everyone, please leave except for Daddy and Pax."

Reluctant but understanding, everyone stepped outside the chamber and stood guard.

Cassie put the palms of her hands on the glass dome, closed her eyes, and began her breathing and resonant tuning technique. She used pure white light to breathe in and directed it into her third eye in the middle of her forehead. She visualized a blank movie screen and projected an image of her mother onto the brilliant background.

Mommy? Can you hear me?

The familiar sound, like the wind whooshing through trees, tickled her ears. She quit the resonant tuning but continued to breathe slowly, deeply, and deliberately, allowing the process to anchor itself. Then she heard her mother's faint voice. "Cassie."

She answered across the void, "Mommy, I'm here. Right beside you." Cassie perceived a smile and her heart leaped. "Mommy, I don't know how to release you from this mechanism. Can you help me?"

A sigh echoed around her. She waited and tried to keep focused on maintaining a clear vision of her mother's face in her mind's eye.

Key...temple.

She got a quick flash of an iridescent metal key with a quartz crystal handle.

Careful... well-guarded...I love you.

Cassie sobbed. "I love you too."

Tears streaming down her face, she took another deep breath and slowly opened her eyes. Her father took her face in his hands and wiped away the tears with his thumbs. "It's okay, honey. It's okay. What did you learn?"

"There is a key in Sirkan's temple. I saw it very clearly. But Mommy said to be careful, that it's well-guarded. We need to get there fast before he finds out I know about it."

She turned to run out of the room, but Ayden caught her by the arm. "No, wait. There will be no rushing off. We need a plan and backup. We have some of the most powerful beings on the planet here with us. Let me consult with Master Artemus."

At the invocation of his name, Artemus appeared in the doorway flanked by Elena and Siobhan. Cassandra imparted the details of what her mother showed her.

"Rebekah has always been good at using the mind screen to communicate on the astral plane," Elena said. "If I may, I'd like to have Siobhan, Glenda, Adrianna, and Mateus stand guard in the main palace. Khamuel, please stay here with Rebekah. The rest of us can proceed to the temple and find the key."

Azazel led the group through the palace grounds, alert to any stray demons or dark elves. It was quiet...and disturbing.

"Something doesn't feel right," Azazel said. "After all the commotion of the past four hours, we haven't encountered any new challenges. This is too easy."

Manu concurred. "I know Sirkan. He has the endless resources of the Dark Brotherhood."

"I thought he *is* the Dark Brotherhood," Tristan said.

"I am not sure he is the head of it, as you imply. There have been occurrences over the millennia that indicate he is high in rank, but perhaps not the ultimate leader," Manu said. "I began to sense this immediately after the fall of Atlantis. But that telling is for another time. Let us remain focused on the task at hand and assume that we will be met with resistance at every turn."

Artemus motioned for the group to take defensive formation as they proceeded through the tunnels, past the palace gardens, and up the steps of Sirkan's temple. They kept Cassie in the middle of the group. Her protection was the highest priority. She remained in a state of guarded receptivity and allowed her consciousness to reach out in a widening arc in search of any indication of the key's location.

"Anything yet, Cassie?" Paxton asked.

"No, I am having a tough time holding the image of the key Mommy showed me. I can sense it's here, but not in what direction. I have only been in the main altar room with Sirkan. I never had a chance to explore more of this place. No idea what else is here."

Her curiosity was answered when a black-robed figure appeared to their left. A horde of similarly garbed figures swarmed out, each one brandishing a scimitar.

Paxton shook his head. "Well, jeez. Straight outta Indiana Jones. I don't have a whip or a gun, but..." He flung his hands up and threw out streams of fire. The first line burst into screaming pillars of flame before collapsing into embers. Another group flooded in from behind the black robes. They wore red capes.

Artemus issued commands. "Shields up!" The interlocking energetic barriers they had used at Queens clicked into place just seconds before streams of fire from the red cloaks hit them. The shields turned the incoming weapons into boomerangs, the flames bouncing off them to return to their senders. They heard more screams.

Natesh transformed into a bat and flew out to the right.

"Reconnaissance." Tristan nodded with approval.

More black robed warriors charged waving axes and broadswords. The metal of their weapons met with bolts of lightning-like energy that traveled up their arms to pierce their hearts. They fell like dominoes.

Natesh screeched back to the group and reconfigured in human form. "No sign of Sirkan in that direction, although he has the requisite hellhounds and demons ready to go. I suggest a few of us take care of them."

Paxton stepped forward, but Cassie held him back. "No way Pax. I don't want you out of my sight after what we just went through. Please."

Nodding reluctantly, he yielded to her request. "Okay, but you need to stay behind me. Not going to put you at risk either!"

"No damseling buddy!" Cassie was smiling, but there was steel in her eyes.

"Got it," Paxton said. "Lead the way, milady."

They moved forward in unison.

Manu watched the exchange with interest. *Maybe it's not puppy love after all. Best to leave their future to the Radiant One. We do have eternity.*

Cassie pointed toward the main altar room. "I feel we need to go in there after all."

Artemus led with Manu at his side. When they crossed the threshold, Manu held his right fist up to halt the group. A low noise rumbled from deep within the bowels of the building. Just ahead of them, the floor of the temple shook. A crevice opened and an enormous dragon-like head rose from the depths. Black ram's horns encircled its head like a helmet. The beast opened its mouth and released a mind-numbing roar carried on the foulest breath any of the combatants had ever smelled. They fell back.

Sirkan and a host of well-armed toadies – dark angels and demons – blocked their escape.

Cassie could not take her eyes away from the beast. Like something from Hell's drawing board, the beast had a dragon's upper body – long, lizard-like, spiked back with great webbed wings that filled the room. Gigantic talons drew sparks from the stone floor as it scrambled for traction. Its great armored torso narrowed into the body of a lion with huge paws, claws extended. The beast scratched its way upright, then hovered over the floor. Its long neck swayed like a charmed cobra as it searched the room.

Despite the din, Paxton's whisper was all Cassie could hear. "What in the name of all that is mighty, is that?"

Manu knew all too well what it was – the culmination of Sirkan's unholy experiments in Atlantis. Sirkan saw physical forms as building blocks – individual pieces to be mixed and mis-matched at his whim. He was in search of slaves and creatures...the unquenchable lust for ultimate, creative power.

When Sirkan had achieved his purpose and created the beast, the Angelics of the Devic Kingdom called for help from the Celestial Forces. This was *not* what the Radiant One wished for a planet in its spiritual infancy. Manu descended from the Mother ship and lead a contingent of his Spiritual Warriors in a rescue effort. Battle lines were drawn, and the Brotherhoods of the Dark and the Light clashed in a holy battle.

The Great Els had fought side by side with Manu's warrior priests. They wanted to free Sirkan's victims – to release their tormented souls. Mikha'El himself had finally vanquished the beasts and sent them to the first Hell. How Sirkan had called this one forth was unfathomable.

Manu had a terrifying thought. Unless one of the fallen Els was in play with Sirkan.

Shaking off the memory, Manu returned to the present. There was something odd about the creature. Though terrifying in its disfiguration, it seemed more confused and frightened than angry.

This is a defensive posture, Manu thought.

But Sirkan had other ideas for the monstrosity he had created for terror and mayhem. He charged at the beast and used his staff like a cattle prod. Sparks diffused along the creature's skin and it howled in pain. Its mighty barbed tail slashed against the wall.

Without understanding what she was doing or why, Cassandra put out her hand. "No! Stop!"

The creature quieted, mid-roar, and stared at her diminutive form. Its eyes flashed with something akin to recognition. Ignoring the pain from Sirkan's staff, it moved toward Cassie. Paxton's wings unfurled; his sword blazed with holy light. He threw himself at the beast. The defensive move distracted Manu's attention. Seeing an opening, Sirkan aimed his staff at his rival just as Paxton flew toward the beast. The Dark Lord smiled. What a delightful solution to the thorn in his side.

Paxton swerved, but his maneuver was a split second too slow. Sirkan's fire hit him in the back. Manu redirected his barrage, but his blast caught the boy in the chest. Paxton shrieked and fell. The beast roared in unison with Cassie, leaped forward, and covered her and the stricken Paxton with its wings.

Sirkan laughed...deep, malevolent, humorless. He thundered at the beast. "Bring her to me."

In reply, the creature opened its mouth and released a stream of fire at its progenitor. Sirkan dodged and was preparing to release a killing bolt of energy when he realized that he was outnumbered. He showered the room with waves of power – enough to make everyone duck for cover – then fled through a portal.

Manu looked over at Cassie. Tears streamed down her face. She clutched Paxton's slumped form to her chest.

"No, Pax, you are not dead. Come back, come back." She looked around at the group of Angels and Celestials. "You can bring him back! I know you can. You are Immortals – you can bring him back!"

No one moved until Elena put out her hand and touched Cassie on the shoulder. "No, dear one. That is not a power any possess except for the Radiant One. Paxton is gone."

The beast was still in guard dog position, hovering over Cassie and Paxton. Cassie looked up at the feline-like eyes, so much like her beloved Gabriel's. Where was he? She turned around focusing on the group surrounding her and Paxton. Ayden came forward and kneeled by her side, putting a hand to Paxton's scorched chest. "Let me send Azazel to fetch Khamuel to guard him, Cassie. We still need to get the key so that we can release your mother."

She looked at him with dazed eyes. "The key? Yes, yes, we need the key."

Her attention was momentarily distracted when Gabriel padded into the group, going to Cassie, rubbing against her knees. She rocked back on her heels and picked him up, burying her face in his gray and white fur. Licking her face, he put both paws around her in a comforting hug. Still numb with shock, she simply rocked, holding the feline in a bear hug.

The great beast lifted off from the ground and soared up the stairwell, disappearing from view with a mournful roar. Cassie looked up at it in bewilderment. *It was trying to protect me, not attack.*

Manu stepped behind her to help her up. She recoiled, "No! Don't touch me. You and your jealous rage are responsible for this. If you hadn't been so hell bent on going after Sirkan, Paxton would not have gotten caught in the crossfire."

Manu flinched at her venom. His heart nearly broke at the pain he felt emanating from Cassie. He turned aside and went to Ayden. "We need to continue the search for the key. Perhaps you can help your daughter."

Hearing his words, Cassie bent over to kiss Paxton's brow and rose. She closed her eyes once more to center herself and focus on her inner senses. She visualized the key her mother had shown her. The picture became clearer as she continued to concentrate. In her mind's eye she saw the creature hovering over the palace gardens.

"We need to go out into the gardens. The creature will show us where to go." She bolted down the back hallway of the temple and into the gardens.

The flapping of wings above her became more urgent. Looking up, she saw the creature hovering. Catching her eyes, he gave a low screech and turned to go in the direction of the domed tower rising from the center of Sirkan's temple. Watching with fascination, she suddenly understood. It was pointing to the high turret room. "That's it! He is showing me where the key is."

"That's a pretty big stretch, Cassandra," her father said.

She shook her head in realization. "It wasn't harm he intended but help. The poor creature must have been the subject of one of Sirkan's twisted experiments molded for his horrid slave army." Her eyes clouded, distant. "In one of my past life regressions, I saw them - the innocent souls trapped in grotesque forms." She shivered. "I have to get up there!"

No sooner were the words out of her mouth than Gabriel shifted into an eagle-like creature with powerful wings. He nudged her gently to get onto his back. Cassie was beyond being shocked. Of course, her familiar could grow wings. Why not?

Reaching the summit of the domed tower, she saw an opening where the creature was hovering. She touched her hand to her heart, and he bowed his head in acknowledgement.

The wards were no longer active now that Sirkan was gone. Gabriel was able to descend into the opening and down into the center of the tower. Sliding off his back, she turned around to examine the room. It was some kind of museum or trophy room. Glass cases, golden caskets, carved bookcases, and wooden chests were arranged in orderly rows. There were suits of armor and swords mounted on mannequins, axes, and a plethora of antiquated weapons, all in like-new condition. *But where was the key?*

Gabriel shifted into his cat form and darted between the various fixtures. Cassie closed her eyes and reached out with her psychic senses. Through hooded eyes, she stepped in small circles like walking a spiral formation around the room. She put out the palms of her hands, scanning the energy of each object as she passed them. The picture of the key sharpened, her hands growing warm. She was close. Deeper into the maze she went, letting her hands be her guide. Her whole body vibrated.

To her right was a small, nondescript glass cabinet tucked between two immense bookcases. Inside were about 50 small boxes of varying sizes and materials. She opened the door of the cabinet and ran her hands over the boxes. She felt her hands start to tingle and then get hotter when she hovered over a non-descript box made of reddish-brown wood. She picked it up and tried the latch.

Naturally, it's locked. But hey, I've got magic, right? She put her right hand over it and focused. She visualized it opening. Nothing. She kept trying. The box began to quiver ever so slightly. She stayed focused, adding the quivering sensation to her visualization.

I can do this!

She recalled one of her mother's favorite axioms. "What you can conceive and believe you can achieve." Just a little more...a little more...pop! The lid sprung open, and she saw the key nestled in green velvet. It was just like the one in her vision. She closed her hand over it and breathed a sigh of relief. Gabriel got agitated. "It's okay, boy, we've got it. Let's go get Mom."

A hated voice came from the shadows. "I don't think so."

No! Are you kidding me? It's not possible.

She slipped the crystal tipped key into a pocket. No way the bastard was going to get it away from her.

Sirkan lunged at her, and she screamed in frustration. Twin roars responded, echoing throughout the tower, one from above and one from the feline at her side. She called on her priestess power once more, light beginning to glow within her solar plexus.

"Oh, no you don't," Sirkan said.

A prick to her neck.

Blackness.

MANU JERKED HIS HEAD at the sound of the creature's roar. Shouting to Azazel, he beckoned. The angel flew his way, picked him up, and soared to the tower. Manu plunged down the opening of the dome and withdrew his staff. Azazel followed. Gabriel stood over Cassie in his winged form once more, ready to fly her to safety. A great flurry of wings and the creature descended through the opening as well, its wide wingspan causing hairline fissures in the sides of the tower. A fine dusting of bricks and mortar fell on the adversaries.

Gabriel used the momentary distraction to lift Cassie in his claws, preparing to take her away from the fray. Footsteps echoed up the circular staircase. Ayden charged in; sword drawn. Seeing his daughter and her familiar, he raced to them and yelled at Gabriel. "Take her to the stairwell." He covered their flank as Gabriel leaped forward.

Realizing his prize was about to escape, Sirkan threw an energy ball toward the stairwell to block them. From above, the creature threw out its own energy in a stream of flame aimed at Sirkan. The flame caught him in the shoulder. He swore in agony, unwilling to drop his staff.

Manu redoubled his efforts to take out his enemy. "Let's end this!" The violet flame rushed toward Sirkan at the same moment the creature sent forth another fiery breath.

Chapter 73: The Return

Sirkan evaporated in a pillar of fire. Everyone stopped and gaped. A pile of ash smoldered on the marble floor.

Cassie moaned and Gabriel shifted into his cat form. Ayden picked her up and cradled her in his arms. "Cassandra, wake up, honey. You are safe. I am here."

Blinking her eyes and wrinkling her nose, she said, "What is that god-awful stench?"

Her father snickered. "The smell of vindication. Sirkan is no more."

Not quite taking it in, Cassie looked around. Her eyes locked on the smoking ash pile and widened. "No way! He's – like – *dead*?"

The creature squealed with what sounded like a laugh, bobbing its head up and down. Cassie reached out her hand. He sidled up to her, crooning. She patted it on the head. "Thank you dear one. You are safe now, too."

Ayden smiled. "It looks like you may have added another protector."

Flapping its wings, the creature soared up from the tower, dislodging even more of the wall. Manu ducked as a huge chunk of the granite fell.

"I believe it may be fortuitous for us to leave this place."

He opened a portal just as another shower of rubble started to fall upon the group.

BACK IN THE DUNGEON, Cassie withdrew the key from her pocket with trembling fingers. She looked quizzically at her father.

"Go ahead, honey."

Cassie held her breath and inserted the key into the lock. It turned easily. The clear lid of the sarcophagus slowly began to rise. Cassie put her hand on her mother's chest, sending her green healing energy. She released her bated breath. Rebekah's chest trembled and then swelled like a bellow, filling with air.

Cassie threw her arms around her mother, face wet with tears. "Mommy!" She beckoned her father to her side.

Ayden bent and kissed Rebekah on the lips, holding his own breath. What felt like hours went by. Color crept back into Rebekah's face. Her lids fluttered. Her intense brown eyes opened as Rebekah St. Claire Oberon found her husband's eyes and smiled.

"My love."

Tears streamed down every face.

Ayden reached down to pull Rebekah up ever so gently, his arm under her shoulders. Rebekah coughed, clearing her throat.

"Don't tax yourself," Ayden said. "I will help you up. Put your arms around my neck. Let me do the work."

Rebekah did as she was bidden and rested her face on her husband's shoulder. He cradled her in his arms, showering her face, her neck, with kisses. "Oh my god, I can't believe it." He sobbed unabashedly.

"Cassie."

Cassie put her face on her mother's shoulder, breathed in her scent and whispered, "Mommy, Mommy" like a sacred mantra.

Suddenly, aware of their intrusion on a private reunion, Elena and Artemus left the room.

Part Four: The Training Of The Initiate

Although I am a typical loner in daily life, my consciousness of belonging to the invisible community of those who strive for truth, beauty, and justice has preserved me from feeling isolated.

~ Albert Einstein

Chapter 74: Home Again

Cassie woke up with a headache. She yawned and squinted at the sunlight streaming through the curtains. Gabriel was perched on her chest giving her one of his stare downs.

"Good morning. I know. I get the message loud and clear."

Cassie shook her head, still fuzzy on the details of her return home, although there was an ache in the area of her heart. She had been having half formed visions and dreams over the past few days that left her feeling uneasy and incredibly sad. But every time she tried to get a clearer picture; she developed these damn headaches.

She took a deep breath and inhaled the aroma of cinnamon and coffee. She was out of bed before the thought hit her.

Who's baking in my house?

No sooner had the question formed in her mind, than there was a knock on her bedroom door. A rosy cheeked face popped into view and a Scottish brogue lilted across the threshold.

"Are you up now, then? Get yourself a quick shower, and high tail it down for breakfast. This is, after all, your first day as an official member of The Seven!"

Cassie's lips curved into a smile, but it quickly gave way to a pained expression. She winced, her hand instinctively moving to her temples as her head pulsed in rhythm, reminiscent of a metronome's steady beat. "Morning, Brigida."

The woman chuckled. "This is a fine house, indeed. The kitchen is wonderful, but I'm struggling a bit with the electrical gadgets. Might need a bit of help."

"Sure," Cassie said.

"Let me remind you, I am your cousin. Your Auntie Isla has moved to London, and I have come to care for you."

"Wish you could fix this headache," Cassie said.

Brigida's arms enveloped Cassie in a warm embrace. The comforting hands mimicked a pair of heating pads. Brigida's fingers worked their way across Cassie's temples, easing the tension with every stroke.

"There you go," Brigida whispered, her voice a soft balm. "Let all the tension melt away." Like magic, the headache that had plagued Cassie vanished within minutes.

"Away with you – get ready," Brigida said,

Cassie laughed, refreshed, and rejuvenated. Her footsteps were light and swift as she made her way towards the bathroom and a much-needed shower. A sense of familiarity and comfort enveloped her while she prepared for the morning ahead.

She toweled off and thought about her day. She hadn't missed much at school. Time in the Fae Kingdom moved differently from Earth, but she still had some catching up to do. She needed to ace her summer school exams. Then she could focus on her AI major come fall.

She remembered some of what Master Artemus had told her about the battle between the Dark and the Light. But it was good to be back to the new normal she supposed, now that she had an additional mission in life. *God! I am a part of a team that was going to save the world from itself! What the hell!*

Sweeping her hair into a ponytail, she walked over and picked up the novel that she had left in the window seat, smiling to herself as she remembered her great "ah ha" moment when she had started to read it. It had almost made her want to change her minor from Graphic Design to Philosophy, but then she shook her head. Well, that wasn't exactly an option anymore, as her training with Alpha Omega would be taking the place of a minor now. And she was sure that there would be plenty of philosophy in the ancient wisdom teachings that Master Elena was going to introduce her to. She knew she had to pursue her major in AI research and design because of the nature of the forthcoming battles between Dark and Light that Master Artemus had told her about, albeit briefly. But there was something else. She couldn't quite put her finger on it. She had the vague feeling she was forgetting something.

Chapter 75: Alpha Omega

Walking into the off-campus lodge of the Alpha Omegas, Cassie shook her head at the estate's beauty. Black shutters accented the red brick façade. The white veranda was dominated by Greek columns in the plantation style so favored in this part of Charlotte. A double row of the Sisters of Alpha Omega lined either side of the front stairs. They met each of the pledges and escorted them through large red double doors.

Cassie beamed when she saw Glenda coming toward her, both arms outstretched as she took her hands into hers.

"Welcome home, Cassandra Oberon," Glenda said.

She linked her arm through Cassie's and walked into the foyer. Dozens of young women milled about with glasses of sweet tea and little plates full of petite sandwiches and pastries. Cassie smiled at each in turn and turned to Glenda.

"Wow, this is a huge chapter!"

"Oh no," Glenda said, "each chapter has at least two sister chapters. Members from our sister chapters in New York City and Washington, D.C. are here as well. We visit back and forth, swap info on majors, interests... favorite spells." She grinned.

Glenda led Cassie to the arched doorway at the end of the front hall. It opened into a ballroom. Canapés made with a variety of ingredients including smoked salmon, shrimp, and chicken were being passed around by servers in crisp white shirts and black pants. Linen-draped tables filled with all sorts of delectables lined the walls. A huge bowl of fruit salad made with fresh berries, melon, and grapes in a crystal bowl filled one table. A cake frosted with chocolate ganache and decorated with chocolate shavings, was the centerpiece of the dessert table. The food seemed endless. Cassie's eyes were drawn to a woman whose silhouette seemed familiar.

The woman had an upswept bun and was wearing a flowing navy skirt and sweater set. Glenda drew her attention back to the food. Cassie was still full from breakfast, so instead poured herself a cup of sweet tea with a slice of lemon and went to stand at one of the high-top tables scattered throughout the room.

She looked again across the room. The woman turned to her. Cassie's eyes widened and she froze. Memories began to flood back to her. The rescue, the battle with Sirkan. *Paxton!*

Master Elena moved quickly to her side. She gave Cassie a gentle hug and kissed her on both cheeks in the European fashion. Cassie's eyes filled with tears. Elena put her arm around Cassie's shoulder and led her out of the ballroom into an adjoining parlor. She motioned to Glenda to stay where she was and closed the door.

"You have remembered then." A statement, not a query.

All Cassie could manage was a sob. Elena guided her over to the brocade couch by the windows overlooking the gardens at the back of the house. She took Cassie's hand in hers and gave the girl some time to collect herself.

Finally, Cassie said, "I thought it was all a nightmare – a series of bad dreams. I have been getting wisps of horrific scenes, demonic beings, and a fiery duel, but nothing clear. Now all I can see is Paxton's dead body. Oh my god!" She buried her face in Elena's shoulder.

"It's alright now. You need to grieve. All of us have been wondering when your memories would begin to come back. The trauma of what happened gave you a case of amnesia. It was only a matter of time before something, or someone, would ignite those memories. It seems it was seeing me."

"My mother, my father?"

"They are in the Seely Court. They thought it best to have Brigida here to ease the transition. For some reason you *did* remember her."

"I want to go to them."

"I will make the arrangements. Let me have Glenda take you back to your house to get ready."

Chapter 76: Home Away from Home

Cassie stood looking out over the expanse of lawn that surrounded the Palace of the Seely Court. The scene was idyllic – exotic jewel-colored birds swooped through the trees and strutted the grounds. The bushes were in their perpetual springtime bloom, and the flowers were all reaching toward soft rays of the midday sun. *Paradise!* She took a deep breath and sighed, putting her hand to her mother's arm around her waist.

"When Daddy told me that I had an important role to play in the destiny of Humanity, I never imagined it would include so much death and destruction. I never imagined I would lose Pax." She leaned her head on her mother's shoulder.

"I know honey. It was why I wanted to hide you all those years ago. I should have known better. We cannot escape our destinies. I am so sorry I was the one to cause you so much pain because of my fear. I am sorry I didn't prepare you better."

Cassie turned to look at her mother. "What were you so fond of saying, 'It is what it is – no regrets.'"

Rebekah gave her a half smile. "Thanks for that Miss Smarty Pants. Nothing like throwing your mother's words back at her."

They turned in unison at the sound of footsteps coming down the flagstone walkway. Ayden smiled broadly. "There are my girls!"

Rebekah held out her other hand to him to pull him toward them. "My love, I am still trying to wrap my head around what has happened. It's still so surreal that we defeated Sirkan."

"Are you sure, Daddy? Is Sirkan really gone?"

He looked at Rebekah and then at Cassie. "My dearest daughter. I believe you would feel it if he weren't. That fantastical beast he created burnt him to ash. No one, not even the great and powerful Sirkan, can be resurrected from ash."

Cassie shivered. What about a necromancer? All they would need would be the ash.

No, she would not give voice to such a heinous idea. If she did, she could very well call it to her. That was one not-to-be-forgotten lesson in the black arts her darling aunt had tried to drum into her head.

"So, now what? Is it over? Am I going to move forward with my training? Will there be more battles?"

Rebekah took a long look at her daughter before answering. "That is a question for Master Elena. We are just at the beginning of the Age of Aquarius. It takes six hundred years for an age to anchor, then another two thousand before it begins to shift yet again. So, the simple answer is no, we are not done."

"But I believe we will have a bit of a respite," Ayden said. "I recommend you put it to good use and look at the next steps in developing your AI skills and exploring what other talents and abilities you have brought forward from your past lives. From what I understand, you must finish your summer school exams?"

"Yes, I need to do that," Cassie said. "The rest sounds good. But what about this whole name change? The glamouring and all that. I am very confused as to what to do."

"I have spoken to Master Elena about that," Rebekah said. "You are still Cassandra Oberon in the Mundane World. Your father and I are married under Devic Law. We went through a handfasting officiated by a Druid Priest. So, there is no need to embrace my maiden name of St. Claire. I made sure you had all the legal paperwork required in the Mundane world. That was taken care of long ago, so we are good on all fronts."

"On the other hand," Ayden said, "your mother does not feel she needs to be resurrected in the Mundane World. Now that she is back out in the open to The Devic and Celestial Kingdoms, we believe we would all be best served if she remains in the Seely Court and takes up her position as Queen of the Fae. You want to continue your studies in Artificial Intelligence. We all know that is a pivotal area of expertise and will be crucial in the battles yet to come."

Rebekah added, "There is also my Celestial DNA from your grandfather. We haven't spoken much about your grandparents. That is something we will need to discuss."

Cassie started to speak, but Rebekah put a finger to her lips. "That's a discussion for another time."

"What about the Oberon Fashion House?"

"Isabeau and Elyse will continue to guide the design business, albeit under their glamoured names." Rebekah said. "I have asked Brigida to remain in Charlotte to look after you. In the meantime, I would like for you to meet with Master Elena to discuss your next steps as one of The Seven."

Chapter 77: Heartache

Cassie met with Elena the next day.

"You are at a critical juncture," Elena said. "You have had some horrific experiences in a very short period of time. You were thrown into the thick of things before any of us had adequate time to prepare you. I think that is why you developed amnesia. Your mind could only handle so much trauma before it shut down. But you are coming through it beautifully."

"I appreciate your confidence, but my heart is still aching from the loss of Paxton. Life won't be the same without him. I know I have much to learn though, and maybe by focusing on my training, I can start to heal from losing him. I'd also like to learn more about my astrological chart. Can I work with Mom on it? As an Aquarian, I need to develop my mental abilities, like meditation and intuition. Right?"

Elena hesitated. "Partly. But I don't want you to try to do too much at once. Remember, you also have the Soul Mission you agreed to with…"

"Manu." Cassie could barely say his name. She was having a challenging time separating him from Sirkan; the two seemed so inexorably connected. "I don't know, Master Elena. I am still intimidated by him. It's kind of overwhelming. And as far as embracing my 'Priestess' Soul and the powers I used during the rescue and the battle with Sirkan - I can't reconcile myself with being Ayesha. She still seems separate from me."

Elena felt the utmost empathy with the girl. Although Cassandra was an old soul, she was not quite eighteen in this life. "You have responsibilities as one of The Seven and certain Soul Contracts that must be fulfilled as well. But before you tackle that, I recommend you take a week or so of retreat away from everyone. There is a small cabin high in your beloved North Carolina mountains around Boone. It is remote and well-protected."

Sounds like heaven.

Elena hesitated briefly, then continued. "Master Artemus has assigned another Guardian to be with you. His name is Raziel. He can take you there and reinforce the perimeter. The cabin will be invisible to any Mundane sight. Take your journals with you and record your thoughts, insights, and of course, your dreams. Ask for guidance from your inner plane teachers and your Higher Self. This is normally something that acolytes do before taking their first initiation, but I feel you are in need of this now."

Cassie nodded. She needed to get out of her funk. The high anxiety of the past weeks had left her somewhat numb. Now she needed to make sense of things. A week or two of alone time was just what she needed. Plus, she had not mourned her Paxton.

"I will make the arrangements and speak to your parents – and Manu," Elena said. "He is not doing very well either. He is devastated at any pain he caused you, however inadvertently. I have known him for millennia, since before we all came to this planet. Trust me, he is feeling everything you are feeling – perhaps more."

Chapter 78: The Cabin

The next day, Raziel flew Cassie to the remote mountain top. It did not appear on any map. Like the Citadel, it was out of time and space. It sat in a clearing surrounded by Virginia pines and other evergreens. The landscape was coated with snow, which leant a primordial silence to the place.

"Wow, it's breathtaking," Cassie said in an awed whisper.

Raziel smiled and opened the door to the cabin. Gabriel greeted her in his cat form, rubbing up against her ankles. She scooped him up with a whoop. "Oh yea! I'm so glad you're here boy." She turned and beamed at Raziel. "This is your doing?"

The Guardian Angel bowed politely. "Your Gabriel would have it no other way." The cat jumped down and ran around the cabin as though giving her a tour.

It was quite marvelous. A large stone fireplace took up most of the left side of the den. A fire crackled with inviting warmth. Facing it was an overstuffed sofa with two easy chairs, all piled with pastel flower-embroidered pillows. A beautiful white furry throw draped the back of light blue brocade the sofa.

"This looks like Brigida's handywork," Cassie said.

"Spot on. Wait until you see the kitchen."

At the mention of one of her favorite rooms, Cassie detected the smell of a freshly baked apple pie loaded with cinnamon. *Yup, definitely Brigida!* The room was reminiscent of the kitchen in her father's palace. Piles of fruit filled a large wooden bowl. Freshly baked bread rested on a sideboard. A vegetable stew simmered on the stove. The pie, wrapped in a red and white checkered cloth, beckoned from the middle of a wooden trestle table.

"Brigida said to tell you that this place is just as magical as you want it to be. You can cook or simply ask for what you want, and it will, what was the word she used.... Oh yes... 'poof.' What is poof?"

Cassie bent over in laughter. "My favorite word. It means it instantly appears or disappears."

Raziel's smile looked like a wince. "Well, alright then. Remember I am only a whisper away. You should have everything you need."

With that he poofed out of sight.

CASSIE SCOOPED GABRIEL up again to do a more thorough exploration of the cabin. It was much larger inside than the outside let on. *Of course, it is...magic.* She laughed. How in the world would she adjust to this new reality?

She looked at Gabriel. "Okay, I know I'm supposed to be doing a silent retreat thing, but surely I can think out loud." He nuzzled her neck in approval. "I knew you were on my side."

"So, let's back up. I am a princess – a fairy princess no less." She rolled her eyes, then gasped as she walked into one of the two bedrooms at the back of the cabin. It was enormous. It had a vaulted ceiling with a skylight, and another stone fireplace set into the far corner. A curtained canopy bed with a cream-colored comforter embroidered in pastel roses was the centerpiece of the room. She squealed with delight, ran over, and threw herself into the piles of cushions and fur throws piled at the head of the bed.

"Now I can totally get used to this!"

Gabriel pounced on one of the fur throws and burrowed under it. "That's the idea boy." Sleep suddenly felt like an imperative. A nap would be just the thing. She sighed and snuggled into the bed still fully clothed. She was asleep in seconds.

Of course, she dreamed.

Chapter 79: The Cave

She was climbing a steep snow-peaked mountain. Her hands were red, raw, and bleeding from the punishing rock face, her eyes stinging from the vortex of the snow squall that threatened to suck her off the mountain and hurl her into the abyss below. Her hair whipped around her face and obstructed her sight. She had to keep climbing and get to the cave.

Her fingers grasped at a rugged outcrop, as her boots scuffed against the rock, seeking purchase. The biting cold nipped at her skin, making every motion a battle. Ice crystals clung to her eyelashes, and her breath misted before her in the biting air. Each movement, every stretch and grip, was fueled by hope, the whisper of a promise that just a bit further would be the cave's mouth. It was there, she believed, her fate awaited.

Then she heard the screams riding the winds, the shrieks of banshees. She felt their claw-like fingers grab and try to pull her away from the fragile hold she was maintaining on the face of the mountain. She could not let them keep her from her goal. She screamed in frustration as the gruesome hands tore at her.

No!

She used the power of her mind to create a sonic wave and rode her own energy to push them back and away from her. Now they screamed and fell away.

Just when she thought she could go no longer, when she was certain she would fall and end the agony, her hand felt a ledge. She cried in relief and pulled herself up. But it was not the cave. *Oh my god. Where is the cave?*

She curled in the crevice of the ledge and hugged her knees in an attempt to bring warmth into her body. She looked across the chasm and saw it – the opening to the cave. It was on the other side!

The other side? They told me it was on this side. They said everything would be revealed.

She was tired of the lies – so many lies. She grabbed a handful of gravel and shrieked, "What the hell do you want of me? You have taken my identity, my love, my life! What else—"

She gaped. The gravel she'd thrown was suspended. She threw another handful. It looked like it slid across the air.

An invisible bridge.

She stood up and tested the open space. It was solid. Scooping up one more handful, she threw it out farther and saw the end of the bridge. She refused to look down as she put one foot in front of the other. She focused on nothing but the cave opening.

She laughed at yet another parallel with Indiana Jones. Nothing existed that wasn't dreamt before. It was the very law of manifestation – from thought to reality. Those movies came from somewhere.

Okay, a few more feet.

She stepped into the opening and saw a glow of light. She caught a whiff of incense, the familiar smell of patchouli and sage. Torches lined the wall like beacons along a runway. At the end of the corridor was a quartz crystal at least fifteen feet high and maybe six feet wide. It was pulsing at an exceedingly high frequency, each beat thumping in unison with her heart.

Thump...thump.

She was in front of it now. She stretched out her hand to touch the stone. It was warm and filled her with feelings of overwhelming...there was no other word...love. This is love. She put her forehead on the stone and felt a deep communion. Her inner vision filled with human forms: men, women, children – all different and yet all her. It was like looking at one of those old-fashioned kaleidoscopes. Intuitively, she knew she was having visions of her past lives.

The visons stopped abruptly, and she became aware of a presence on the other side of the crystal. She stepped around it and saw a man with long dark hair kneeling before an altar, hands clasped, and head bowed in prayer. She waited for him to acknowledge her presence. She knew this man was why she had been called to this place – to her destiny.

He finally lifted his head and slowly rose to face her.

Manu!

He looked at her sadly. "My love, I have been waiting these many years to stand by your side once more."

Cassie's heart cracked open. Unconditional love flowed from him. It surrounded her, embraced her. She fell to her knees and covered her face with her hands. "No, I can't. I was meant to be with Paxton in this life. You left me."

Manu knelt before her and took her hands away from her tear-stained face.

His voice was laced with both wisdom and pain. "There are moments when we have to transcend our worldly desires for something much larger. Paxton understood that sacrifice. When I first encountered him at the Citadel, he confided in me about the prophecies he'd heard from both his father and Master Artemus concerning your fate and mine."

Her eyes shimmered, hinting at a deeper pain. "He was aware that he wasn't destined to be by your side in the days to come. But when your aunt discovered him, weak and susceptible, she tempted him away from his oaths, his training. By succumbing, he veered onto the Lefthand Path. Had he persisted and succeeded in convincing you to join your aunt and Sirkan, the weight of his karmic debt would've burdened him for countless lifetimes."

Cassie shuddered. She would not have wanted such a fate for him. "But in the end," she said, "he woke up and helped me get away from them. That should count for something."

"It counts for a great deal," Manu said. "Try to be satisfied in knowing that the giving of his life to save you was in the way of a redemption. Perhaps it would help if you could see Paxton passing from his physical body in sacrificial service, which is the core meaning of the word sacrifice, 'to make sacred.' To honor him and his sacrifice, you need to let him go with gratitude. Master Elena can help you with the process. She has been performing these types of rites for – shall I say – a very long time." He smiled down at her.

Cassie stared off into the distance. She could remember the horrible day so clearly; she experienced the pain of losing Paxton all over again. "I need some more time, Manu."

"Of course. A loss of this magnitude will leave its mark upon your heart. I know something of this." Again, he smiled at her, this time with sadness. "But you will come out of the other side, I promise. Your Soul is an old one, and your strength of purpose and mission will come to your aid. Go to Master Elena."

Cassie finally looked at him full-on, searching his deep amethyst eyes. All the Celestials had the most amazing and intense jewel-colored eyes. How was it she was only just now aware?

"Okay," she said, "I will go to her in a few days. What you have said makes sense." She managed a sad smile. "Thank you."

CASSIE CRACKED HER eyes open one at a time.

That wasn't a dream. It was an inner plane experience. She could still smell the incense and hear the resonance of the giant crystal. She could also feel the great love that Manu had for her. She looked out of the bedroom window. The sun was rising. She had been sleeping all night. She took a quick shower and went into the kitchen to hunt up coffee and breakfast. Grateful once again to Brigida for the baked goods, she knew she would go to Master Elena. Soon. But first she needed to write down what she had just experienced and sort through the myriad of emotions.

What was Manu doing in that cave? It looked like he had been praying or maybe meditating. Master Elena had said he was just as upset as she was. Maybe even more.

Well, I guess if I had been waiting to get back with my Soul Mate for thousands of years, I'd be pretty devastated to find out they didn't remember me.

She opened her journal and started to write.

MANU ROSE FROM THE meditation bench, took a deep breath, and did a series of stretches. He glanced at the hourglass across the room. He had been in meditation for almost three hours. This was his place of refuge deep within the cave that held the Mothership. The cave also held the Atlantean crystal that gave power to the ship and shielded the cave from prying eyes. He thought about his encounter with Cassandra on the inner planes the night before. It had been a heart wrenching experience for him. And it was the first time they had spoken heart to heart. Perhaps this was the beginning of breaking through the current life blocks so they could come to some sort of understanding.

Did he dare hope that they would be together again? He knew he still had to stay away to allow her time to process and heal from the horrific experience she had with Sirkan and the death of Paxton. However, time was of the essence as her eighteenth birthday was not far away and the Quickening she would experience was essential to the success of their original mission.

The Spirit Screen interrupted his reverie. It was Elena.

"Adonai, Manu."

"Adonai, Elena. Is there something I can do for you?"

"There is. But first, how are you? Do you need any more time before coming back to The Citadel and resuming our mission?"

"No, Getting back into action is exactly what I need. Are you there now?"

"I am on my way. Artemus is there, of course. I want to introduce you to Cassandra's new Guardian Angel so you can coordinate with him when needed."

Manu bobbed his head and prepared to leave.

Chapter 80: Memories Awakened

Cassie closed her journal, hunger signaling her it was time for a break. *How long have I been writing?*

She thumbed through the journal. She'd scratched out at least a hundred pages full of words, diagrams, and sketches. It must have been hours. She searched for a clock. Nada. She shrugged and went into the kitchen. The window over the sink framed a vast snowscape colored pink by the setting sun.

Dinner then.

The refrigerator was empty. Oh yeah, she needed to ask for what she wanted.

"Let's see, Gabe," she said, "what are you in the mood for?" He sent her a picture of a fish. "Alright, you can have fish, but I think I'm more in the mood for pasta, the kind Mom used to make. Okay (she stood as straight as she could) "House, I would like chicken alfredo, a Caesar salad, and hot garlic bread – and a nice fresh trout for kitty, deboned, of course."

The meal instantly appeared on the table. Fileted fish materialized in the cat's bowl.

"I could get used to this," Cassie said. "I wonder if it works on clean up too?"

The first forkful confirmed that the dish was exactly how her mother made it. Cassie dug in with gusto. "House, can I have some wine?" No response. "I guess you keep to the same drinking age rules that Pa—"

She stopped herself and remembered the night at Rí Rá's just months before. She had wanted to have a real adult beverage. She smiled wistfully, remembering his "no way" attitude toward the pushy bartender who attempted to give them Guinness. A medley of images began to flash before her eyes, a movie in fast forward of her all their times together. She saw Paxton's laughing face outside of the library, in the cafeteria, picking her up for a date. She heard his smart-ass remarks, his admonitions during training...she remembered the sexual awakenings. She let it all run amuck – the pain arrowing through her, sharp, deep. Her heart hitched in her chest, breaths coming in wet gulps. Tears rivered down her face. She tore at her hair, attempting to pull the memories out of her mind. Anguished screams gurgled up her throat as she gave voice to her pain. She would never stop screaming, never stop hurting. She grabbed the table laden with the unfinished pasta and flipped it over, her strength suddenly herculean. Dishes and flatware flew everywhere. She whirled and began to beat her fists on the kitchen counter. Her anger needed more release. She spun around in desperation, reaching for more things to break, to smash, to kill.

"No, no, *no*. Paxton, come back. Come back. Come...back." She sagged to her knees.

Powerful arms came around her shoulders. She pummeled at them. "Let me go! I can't... I can't... Sobbing uncontrollably, she lashed out at the hands holding her.

"It's alright. Let it out." Raziel's resonant voice seemed to be coming from far away. He did not let her go. "You cannot hurt me, so scream and kick away."

She continued to cry and hit at him until, energy spent, she collapsed against his shoulder still sobbing. "Why? Why did he have to be taken away from me? Why all this pain?"

The angel did not reply. There was no rational way to answer her. She had to grieve. So, he remained silent until she pulled away from him. He flicked his hand and manifested a box of tissues. Cassie plucked a handful out of the container and blew her nose.

"Better?" Raziel asked.

Cassie shuffled back to the den, threw herself onto the couch, and pulled the fluffy throw blanket up to her neck. "Not better, but I can't cry anymore. I don't know if I will ever reconcile losing Paxton. I feel responsible for killing him."

Raziel let her go on without interruption, wise Guardian Angel that he was.

"I mean if I hadn't been so hell bent on getting out of there. If I had just waited. I should have known my father was putting together some sort of rescue mission. He wouldn't have let me stay there for long." She stopped abruptly. "Mom would say to stop the coulda, woulda, shoulda mantra."

Raziel decided to change the subject. "Are you ready to go back to Charlotte? Master Elena is quite anxious for you to get back to your training."

"Not yet. I would like to stay through this second week before returning to the grind of college."

"Very well. Unless I hear – or feel – otherwise, I will be back in five days." He looked at Gabriel before he flew off. "Well done."

Cassie picked up the cat. "Oh really? Were you responsible for calling Raziel?"

Gabriel just licked her face.

"Guess I'd better go in the kitchen and clean up the mess." She gasped when she stepped into the kitchen...not one pasta stain...not one shard of glass. "Or not."

Chapter 81: Accelerated Training

"Enter," Elena said.

Artemus walked in and closed the door. Elena sat behind her desk. She was reading a scroll. "Light reading, I see."

She walked around the desk to greet him. "Adonai Artemus."

"Adonai."

"Yes," she said. "I am looking at the Prophecy written about this coming shift regarding the use of technology. I am eager to get Cassandra back on track with her studies in computer science. Raziel was just here. Cassie is due to come back to Charlotte tomorrow. I plan on being back at the Alpha Omega house so we can begin our one-on-one work together after she completes the examination from summer school. From there, I plan on getting her to the New York City Institute to pair her with a trainer. Do you have any recommendations?"

"I do. I would like her to have a series of trainers, beginning with me."

"You?"

"Yes. She needs to continue her physical training. We need to ensure she does not depend on her magical abilities too much and I want her to increase her stamina."

"And her university studies?"

"That's what I wanted to speak to you about," Artemus said. "Do you think it's necessary for her to attend Queens in the fall? Why not tutor her through the Institute? We have a whole department of computer, what's the term, 'geeks' that would allow her to forge ahead quicker than the Mundane curriculum."

"There is one thing to consider, however," Elena said. "That is the necessity of having her remain connected to the Human Kingdom and to the Charlotte ley line. After all, she, along with the other six, are to be teachers and leaders into this next leap in evolution. I am not sure she should be separated from them nor from the university experience."

Artemus nodded.

Chapter 82: Chocolate Cake and Guardian Angels

Cassie flew up the stairs and into Brigida's outstretched arms. "Oh, it's good to be home!"

"My dearest. It is wonderful to see you." Brigida took Cassie's face in her hands, searching. There was color back in her cheeks and her eyes were bright and clear. "It looks like your respite did you well. Good, now let's get some meat on those bones! Did you not take advantage of the magical kitchen?"

Cassie laughed. "I tried, but most days I got so caught up in my writing I forgot to eat. Gabriel, however, learned to use the house magic and he certainly didn't starve."

The feline in question was already darting back to his bowl in the kitchen.

Raziel stepped into the hallway. "I have been directed to stay here as added protection. Sirkan may be gone, but the Dark Brotherhood is not."

Cassie began to protest, but Brigida put her arm around her shoulders. "Don't worry, he's been hovering over the house since he was assigned to you. The sense of security is quite welcome."

"You won't even know I'm here." Raziel said.

Resigned to accept her new status as one of The Seven to take precedence over her need for independence, Cassie acquiesced and went up to her room.

Time to get back to school stuff then. Those final exams are the day after tomorrow.

HER FINGER HOVERED over the "send" button. Thank goodness the final exams were online. She had been tempted to use her AI program but determined any outside help, however non-human, would be cheating. The past weeks had put her behind on the reading material, but she managed to skim through most of it before exam time.

Okay, girl, just do it.

The "swoosh" sound confirmed that cyberspace had accepted her submissions. A feeling of relief washed over her. Now for her meeting with Master Elena.

She put her tablet into her trusty backpack and clopped down the back staircase to the kitchen. Might as well get some fortification before heading over to the Alpha Omega House.

Raziel was sipping coffee. "You are done with your exams?"

"Yes," Cassie said. "Now I need some of Brigida's famous chocolate cake and a big glass of milk."

Brigida came in from the garden with a basket laden with green tomatoes and cucumbers. "Your mother told me you liked fried green tomatoes, so I picked these before they ripened. I'll make your favorite dishes tonight in celebration of your finishing your summer school class. And yes, my famous chocolate cake is on the sideboard in the dining room."

Breathing in the rich aroma of the gooey dark chocolate icing, Cassie's mouth watered as she dug into the huge piece of chocolate cake with relish. For once she could eat whatever she wanted. The constant training was not only defining her muscles but also had accelerated her metabolism. Finishing up her snack, Cassie picked up her backpack and stopped. "I haven't even thought about transportation now that..." she trailed off. Paxton or her aunt had normally driven her to where she needed to go.

Brigida looked at her with a blank expression.

Sighing, Cassie said, "I guess I'd better go see if the car keys are on the hall table."

Raziel stepped forward. "I can fly you over."

Visualizing doors flying open and fingers pointing skyward all over the Myers Park area, Cassie said, "Oh sure, that would go over really well with the neighbors. No, I need to get the car and drive over there. I don't suppose you know how to drive?"

The angel shook his head. "No, but I can at least accompany you. My wings are retractable, you know."

Walking into the garage, Cassie was assailed by the familiar smells of that just-waxed, always-clean car. A classic BMW black sedan stood next to her aunt's Bentley.

Yeah, that dinosaur was gonna have to go.

Thankfully, the classic started up without protest and was full of gas. "It feels funny driving a car," she said. "It's kind of like being on dry land after getting home from a cruise. Feels like the past month or so has been a dream." She turned to look at Raziel. "Except there's an angel in the passenger seat."

Chapter 83: Full Disclosure

Master Elena opened the door to the sorority house. "Come in, come in. It is good to have you back. And you must be Raziel. Welcome to the team."

The angel bowed. "Adonai in the name of the Radiant One, Master Elena. I am honored."

"Please, make yourself comfortable in the living room." She gestured toward the large room to the right of the entry. "Cassandra and I will be across the hall in my office."

Cassie perched on the edge of a plush chair. Her fingers twisted in her lap, knotting and unknotting the fabric of her tunic in an incessant twitch. Her foot tapped out an uneven rhythm on the marble floor, an unconscious testament to the turbulence roiling within her. Her breath hitched, each intake of air a little too sharp, a little too quick. The weight of the room's silence seemed to press upon her, the stillness a tangible manifestation of the tension curling tightly in her stomach.

Elena smiled. "No need to be nervous. There is a mantra you will find beneficial." She opened the top right-hand drawer of her mahogany desk and handed Cassie a blue bookmark. "This is your first assignment as an acolyte. Say this mantra upon awakening, at noon, at four, at sunset, and before you sleep. Think of it as a five-pointed star. Focusing your mind on positive affirmation five times a day will help you to connect with your subjective mind."

Cassie read:

I am the soul, and also love am I. Above all else I am, both will and fixed design. My will is now to lift the lower self into the light divine. That light am I. Therefore, I must descend to where the lower self awaits, awaits my coming. That which desires to lift and that which cries for lifting are now at one. Such is my will.

"That's beautiful. Where does it come from?"

"It was given to us by one of the great teachers of the Ageless Wisdom in the last century. Your mother stayed with him for a while when she was questing in Sedona, Arizona. His name was Torkom Saraydarian. The mantra will be used for advanced meditation techniques as well. But for now, simply say it as I have instructed. If you receive any flashes of insight, record them in your journal."

Cassie tucked the paper into her journal.

"So, how was your time at the cabin?"

Cassie told her about her meltdown. Then she opened her journal to show Elena her notes, diagrams, and sketches. "I have no idea what some of this stuff is. It came out like someone else was holding my pen. Especially those diagrams." She opened the pages. "Like, what's a tensor beam? Or here." She pointed to a drawing that looked like a pyramid with a pendulum swinging from the apex. The caption read "mental transponder."

Elena studied her notes for a moment and then handed back the journal. "It seems that you may have opened a channel to some of your Celestial heritage either through your mother's DNA or your Soul memory. Either way, I want to pair you with a trainer that will take you to the next steps in building your mental – or shall I say – your intuitive abilities. Meditation is both a science and an art, which can lead you to connecting with Cosmic Mind. Some call it 'the mind of god.'"

"Is that the same as The Radiant One?"

Elena nodded. "Yes, in a way. I must say, you are coming along very quickly in opening to the unseen world. It proves that we are very fortunate to have found you when we did. You are ready to dive into your studies."

There was a knock on the door.

"Enter."

The Master of the White Circle stepped inside and closed the door. "I hope I am not interrupting?"

Cassie jumped up. *Should I bow or something?*

Artemus motioned to her to sit. "Please don't stand on ceremony for me. As one of The Seven, you are part of my inner circle. We will be spending a lot of time together in the coming years. That is why I am here. I wanted to discuss the next steps with you and go over ideas." He saw the blue bookmark sticking out of Cassie's journal. "I see Master Elena has given you Torkom's Soul Mantra. Good, good. That is the perfect place to start."

Cassie nodded.

"Yes, Cassie was also showing me some of the ideas she had while staying at the cabin. I believe you may be interested. Cassie, is it okay if Master Artemus takes a look at what you showed me?"

"Sure." Cassie handed over the journal.

He was silent for a few minutes, studying the pages. Looking up at Elena, he whispered, "The Transmissions."

"Yes," Elena said. "My thoughts exactly."

"What are the Transmissions?"

"Years ago, when your mother was still one of my star students, she, Elyse, and Isabeau or Haley and Garnet as you know them, were meditating on another mantra called The Great Invocation," Elena said. "As instructed, they were meditating on one line for an entire week. After about four weeks they each independently began to get something called 'transmissions.' They brought their journals to me as you have done. I in turn showed them to Master Artemus and he confirmed they were from one of the Masters of Wisdom called Saint Germain. In one of his later incarnations, he was a great scientist named Nikola Tesla. Your journal entries are similar to what they brought through from him by way of being an amanuensis, which means someone that can take dictation from another through a telepathic connection."

Cassie tried to take it all in.

Master Artemus looked at Cassie. "I believe there is someone that needs to work with you on refining your ability to bring forward teachings from your own past lives, knowledge, and wisdom," he said. "The guide will also help you hone your ability in connecting with Master Saint Germain."

"I dreamed about the Compte de St. Germain before the whole Queens scene happened," Cassie said. "I have it recorded in another one of my journals at home. It was about me and him. You two were in it as well. This is wild."

"It seems you are definitely ready to begin the next phase of your training," Elena said. "The next issue is your university studies. Where do you stand?"

"Well, I still wanna study AI. That is my calling and where my interests and abilities lie in this current lifetime." Cassie laughed. "Seems that I'm already accepting this whole thing about being one of the Seven, reincarnation, and everything else. Plus, I have a scholarship. I really want to pursue my studies."

"Well then," Elena said, "let me have Glenda get you situated into your suite here at the sorority house. That will alleviate you having to go back and forth between your house and here. It will also offer another layer of protection for you, which is very important. Even though Sirkan has been defeated, there are still factions within the Dark Brotherhood that will need to be addressed."

Chapter 84: Mirror, Mirror

Glenda guided Cassie to the front spiral staircase. "Come on then let's go upstairs – we get to be suitemates."

Cassie looked up at the split staircase.

"We are up at the very top," Glenda said. "There's another suite on the same level. It belongs to Master Elena. Totally separate wing with a private elevator, but it will be nice for us to be on the same level."

When they were safely out of hearing, Cassie stopped. "Miss Elena looks like the woman who has been visiting me in my dreams." She pointed to the winding steps. "This staircase has shown up a few times too. There were rooms on every level–like here. I think I Dream Walked into the past to some of the lifetimes that are important to my path in my current life."

Glenda bobbed her head. "Absolutely," she said. "You must tell Master Elena about those dreams when you meet again tomorrow. She believes in the importance of dreams – says they are sort of 'a guidance system.' I am sure interpretating and understanding will be a big part of your training with her."

Glenda guided her through a set of double doors. Cassie gasped. There was a large sitting room with an chaise longue at one end and a bank of windows overlooking the side gardens of the house at the other. Twin desks sat on opposite sides of the room: one, a standard issue writing station; the other was strewn with tech. Cassie squealed.

"Is this mine?"

Laughing, Glenda said, "Well it's certainly not mine. I wouldn't know how to even begin to use those advanced computers. The keyboards are full of symbols I have never seen before. Your father ordered this as part of your graduation gift. We have an IT guy. His number is on the card by your computer if you need anything. In the meantime, let me show you the bedroom. The movers will be at your place on Saturday. Make a list of what you want from home." Her hand swept the room. "And if you want to change the décor, go for it."

"Wouldn't change a thing," Cassie said. She hesitated. "Is this place enchanted?"

Glenda gave her a blank stare. "How so?"

"Well," Cassie said, "we are really not totally part of the Mundane world. I figured this place might be the same as where my father lives."

"Ah, no," Glenda said. "Those are out of time and space, in other dimensions. We are very much in the third dimension here, otherwise the human girls could not live here."

"Can I bring my cat?"

Glenda laughed. "Of course, you can. After all I saw him in action at the Non-Seely Court. He has a role to play in all of this since his own evolution is also at stake. Once the Human Kingdom takes its third initiation, the Animal Kingdom will shift up as well. It's a very symbiotic system here on Earth."

"So much to learn. My head is about to explode."

"Don't worry, there's plenty of gray matter up there. All you have to do is open the doors."

"The human girls? Do they know about the Institute and what this Sorority really is?"

"Nope." Glenda shook her head. "They are here because Master Elena or one of the other Masters has seen great potential in them. Once they have shown interest in knowing more about their spiritual paths, they will be given a trainer to lead their next steps. Part of our work for the next few weeks is to cast their astrological charts and read them for Master Elena."

Cassie went bug-eyed. "*Our* work?"

"Oh sorry, not you, you are a neophyte still," Glenda said. "I meant the Initiates, which is what I am getting ready to be. I am almost ready to take my next step and become an Initiate of the Second Degree." Cassie registered no recognition, so Glenda explained. "It's a thing. You will learn all about that as your studies progress."

Cassie sighed for the umpteenth time and looked at the gathering twilight. "Well, guess it's time to get back home. I am looking forward to one of Brigida's meals and her wonderful hugs. It's been a very long day."

On the way down the winding staircase, she was met by Raziel. He shouldered her backpack and escorted her to her car.

Walking from garage into the connecting breezeway to the house, Cassie was hit with a wave of deliciousness. She pushed open the door, dropped her backpack by the backstairs, and practically leapt into the middle of the cooking area. She headed straight for the warming tray stacked with crispy fried green tomatoes. She raised a steaming slice to her mouth and groaned. "Geez Louise, these are wicked good! Do I detect a hint of garlic? The best *ever*!" She reached for another one before Brigida could stop her.

"That's enough, Missy. I have a huge repast in the making, and I don't want you to spoil your appetite."

"I don't believe her appetite can be spoiled when it comes to Cornish hens, wild rice, and fried green tomatoes," said a beloved voice from the doorway.

"Mommy!" Cassie threw herself into Rebekah's arms. "I didn't know you were going to be here!"

Laughing, Rebekah hugged her tightly. "I wouldn't think of missing the celebration of your first day at the Institute – I mean at Alpha Omega."

"Neither would I," Ayden said. He followed his wife into the warmth of the kitchen and wrapped his arms around them both. "I'm so very proud of you, Cassandra."

Raziel beat a silent retreat to the upper floor of the house and stationed himself to keep a protective barrier around the perimeter. This was no time to let his guard down.

Brigida shooed them away to the living room at the front of the house, "I have wine and that iced tea you so dearly love all set out for you. Go enjoy yourselves and I will call you when I have dinner on the table."

Cassie filled her parents in about her meeting with the two Celestial Masters and her plans to continue pursuing her university studies in AI.

Rebekah applauded. "I'm so glad you've decided to do that. I know it will be a big load between regular classes and your Institute training, but I'm sure you will handle it."

Ayden clapped his hands as well. "Should you begin to feel overwhelmed, you can come to me or your mother immediately. You are in a vulnerable place right now." Cassie began to protest. He put up his hand. "Listen to me, please. You are still only seventeen years old. I know you have experienced more than any teenager should have at your age. We are both extremely proud of you and how you handled yourself with your aunt and Sirkan. But you have also suffered an incredible loss, and you may be taken unaware during duress. Emotional pain has a way of raising its ugly head when we least expect it. You have a powerful support team that now includes Raziel and Brigida. And we can be contacted at a moment's notice."

He went to a large mirror over the fireplace. It had not been there when Cassie left earlier. "This is your personal Spirit Screen. I have also had one installed in your room at the Alpha Omega house."

"Think of it as a magic mirror," Rebekah said. "Here, let me show you." She went over to it and waved her right hand in a series of finger and palm configurations. The screen immediately took on a mercurial shimmer. Master Elena's face emerged as though through a reflection in water and gradually sharpened.

"Rebekah, how wonderful to see you. I see from the energy signature that you have installed a Spirit Screen in your Charlotte home?"

"Yes, Master Elena. Ayden and I are here to be with Cassandra at a celebratory dinner on this first day of her being at The Institute. We have also taken the liberty of installing one in her suite at the Alpha Omega house."

"It is a necessary precaution, especially now that Cassandra is taking her first steps into serious training as one of The Seven," Elena said. "Cassandra, your mother will teach you the various hand configurations to summon those in your circle. Commit them to memory until they become second nature." She smiled. "Another homework assignment. Enjoy your family time." She waved her hand to end the transmission.

"Before your head detonates," Rebekah said, "I want to remind you that you need to up your meditation time each day to at least two sessions of twenty minutes each, one in the morning and one either before or after your evening meal. Knowing Master Elena, she has probably given you the Soul Mantra to practice five times a day."

Cassie tried not to roll her eye.

Her mother laughed. "Ayden darling, would you please give her our other graduation gift?"

Her father took out a brightly wrapped square box and handed it to her. "Your mother noticed that your wrists were devoid of something called a 'smart watch.' She had Elyse pick one up in New York and delivered here while you were at the cabin."

Cassie opened the box and squealed with delight. "Wow, this is awesome Mom, Dad. Thanks so much!"

"Oh, there's a little more to it. Your mother imbued it with a bit of magic, so it will reach us in the Fae Realm as well." Her parents held up their wrists to display their own watches. "Now you have two interdimensional communication devices between the Spirit Screen and this wrist contraption. Once you are able to develop your telepathic abilities to a greater extent, you most likely won't need any type of technology. But until then, these will come in very handy."

Cassie put the watch on, then paused. "Seriously? The mind can do that?"

"You are the one with the scholarship in mind-to-technology communication, right?" Ayden asked. "It's not much of a leap to go to the next step. Telepathy. The Masters of Wisdom have that ability. They can also manifest a physical vehicle at will. You will learn more about those abilities when you study the Initiations."

"Boom – pow!" Cassie balled her fists and flicked them open. "Okay, mind exploded."

They all laughed as Brigida called them into the dining room.

Cassie was glad that Brigida sat across the dining room table from her to join them for the meal. "What about Raziel?" she asked. "He is part of the family now; he should be here."

At the sound of his name, the angel appeared in the doorway. "Is something amiss?"

"Absolutely. You need to be a part of this. Angels do eat, I know."

Raziel shook his head. "No, that is not necessary. I need to maintain my guard at all times."

"Seriously Raz, the house is uber protected and we have like, the King and Queen of the Fae here. I'll bet Azazel is a thought away as well."

The angel quirked an eyebrow. "Raz?"

"Hey, well I give everyone nicknames. Just so happens yours has a double entendre as all nicknames should."

The angel looked at Ayden, who acquiesced as Brigida came back into the room to set the extra place next to hers. The group ate, drank, and laughed into the wee hours.

All the while, a shadowed figure well outside the protective perimeter glared at the homey scene.

Soon, very soon.

Chapter 85: Back on Track

The Citadel was bustling with activity like Manu had never seen. He was astounded by the army of shining faces of young men and women ensconced at row upon row of computer terminals. Some had two or three screens in front of them. It reminded him of the technology labs in Atlantis.

"It's awe inspiring, isn't it?"

Manu turned to see Tristan approaching from the doorway. He hadn't seen the Angel since the death of his son. "Tristan. I am so very sorry for your loss."

Tristan's eyes filled momentarily as he grasped the Celestial's forearm in greeting. It was cold to the touch. "Thank you. Not a day goes by that I don't expect Paxton to come into the house challenging me with something or another. He was on his way to getting back on the right path and then it was snatched away from him. I pray his Soul is finding the healing warranted by his sacrifice. In the end I feel he redeemed himself by the act of trying to save Cassandra."

"I agree with you. I cannot help but believe that the Lords of Karma will take everything into consideration when he goes through Life Review before passing into his resting period. Perhaps in rebirth they will permit him into an adult physical body through a Soul Exchange rather than a whole new birthing experience. Walk Ins have become more prevalent the closer we get to The Shift."

"I will hold that comforting thought." Tristan closed his eyes and took a deep breath. "So, on to the present then. I assume you are here to get things back on track with Cassandra's training?"

"My direct involvement has yet to be determined. Elena and I will be discussing next steps. I know that Artemus has assigned Cassandra a new Guardian. He took her to the Cabin for a time of healing and processing. You know the place. I am on my way to the conference room to get caught up."

Tristan bowed in farewell, "I will leave you to it then."

The Celestial watched the Angel's retreating back with interest. *He is certainly hiding his grief extremely well.*

# Chapter 86: A Balanced Schedule

Walking into the sparsely furnished conference room Manu was surprised to see both Rebekah and Ayden in attendance. A shiver of cold snaked up his back when they nodded to him but showed no warmth in their greeting. *Well, that's not a good sign.*

Elena rose. "Ah Manu, so good of you to join us. Shall we begin then?" She gestured to the empty chair to her left. Artemus sat to her right; Rebekah and Ayden were across the oval marble table.

Elena called the meeting to order. "I have met with Cassandra and discussed her preferences for her continued education. She wishes to pursue her studies at Queens University in AI research, and I concur. Since Charlotte plays such a pivotal role in Prophecy regarding The Shift, I believe it behooves us to have her establish an energetic anchor there. Artemus and I have discussed the idea of creating meditation groups in Charlotte and across the globe at key Ley Lines to prepare Humanity for the incoming energies of the Aquarian Age. It can be coordinated through The Seven and their trainers."

Artemus continued the explanation. "I believe that Cassandra could also set up an online presence for these groups to facilitate a global linking or streaming so we can strengthen the connection with Divine Mind. We are at the edge of a new frontier, the power of the mind paired with technology. Cassandra has made great inroads with this concept and now we need to allow her free reign to take it further." He turned to Manu. "This is where you come in my friend."

Manu flinched. "Do you think it wise in light of her current emotional state?"

Rebekah said. "I believe it is the logical next step in her healing process. If she can learn to trust you and work with you on a strictly impersonal level, then your Soul Mission with her may get back on track sooner rather than later. There is no one better equipped to train her in higher mind techniques than you."

Manu decided to keep his own counsel on what had transpired in the cave until he had an opportunity to discuss it privately with Elena. "I am ready to be of service in any way I can. However, I feel I will need to tread very, very cautiously with Cassandra." He looked at Elena, "I would like to speak with you further on this when we finish up here."

Elena inclined her head in agreement.

Artemus said, "I would also like to have a hand in her warrior training once she gets situated with her classes. Paxton did not have nearly enough time with her, and she will need a wide arsenal of both defensive and offensive maneuvers to meet the coming conflicts on the physical plane as well as in the other dimensions. The Training Room at the Citadel would be the ideal location. I do not want her to go to any of the other Institutes until the preparatory month before the Initiation Ceremony."

Rebekah looked uneasily at Ayden and then forged ahead. "Master Artemus, I feel we should have a synchronized program between her AI research, warrior training and magics. I think it would be a good idea to train her in White Magic, so I would like to call upon Tatiana."

"I think that is an excellent idea," Elena said. "Let me know once you contact her. Perhaps she would be willing to come here to meet with me. Then we can sit down and lay out a training schedule. One more thing. Cassandra has expressed her desire to understand her astrological chart. That is something you are very adept at, Rebekah, so it may be something to start with her while the rest is coalescing."

Chapter 87: The Altar Room

That night after dinner, Rebekah said, "Cassie, I need to show you something. Come upstairs to the attic."

"Oo...kaay," Cassie said. She followed her mother up to the attic, a room she had never really explored.

Rebekah's eyes sparkled with a mischievous glint as she reached for a hidden latch. With a soft click, a door swung open and revealed a room aglow with the gentle twinkle of fairy-lit wall sconces. Cassie's breath caught in her throat, and her eyes widened at the magical ambiance.

"Whoa," she whispered, reverently. She stepped into the altar room. Her hands reached out to touch the curious implements adorning the large wooden table at the room's center. Crystals, vials, and ancient symbols hummed with energy as she picked them up, one by one.

"Aunt Isla had a similar room," she said her voice full of wonder.

Rebekah's eyes softened. "All witches do, whether White or Black. There's more, though..." Her voice trailed off, filled with mysterious promise. "Let me show you my sacred space. It is now yours since I am going to be living with your father."

With that, she opened a small door hidden in the right wall. Cassie followed her mother, her heart pounding with anticipation. When she stepped into the room, she could barely feel her feet on the floor. The place overflowed with the scent of herbs and old parchment.

"This is my altar room," Rebekah said. Her voice was tinged with pride. "This is where I used to study, write, and craft spells."

Cassie's eyes danced over the shelves. Her fingers caressed the ancient bindings of spell books that seemed to call her name. Her attention was suddenly captured by a bookcase directly behind her mother's altar. Rows and rows of books bound in navy blue leather beckoned her closer, their titles a siren's song to her inquisitive mind.

She picked up the first one, *Ponder On This* by Alice A. Bailey. She traced the elegant gold lettering. She opened the cover. The room fell away and the pages, whispering secrets only she could hear, invited her into a world where the stars spoke, and magic danced in the very air she breathed.

Rebekah came over and put her hands on Cassie's shoulders. "That was one of the first books I read when I began to study with Master Elena. It's sort of a compendium of a branch of The Ageless Wisdom teachings that form the foundation for the esoteric training of the Institute. Here are more from The Theosophical Society, founded by Helena Blavatsky, and a slew of others."

"Wow, did you read all of these?"

Rebekah laughed. "Oh no, but I am a compulsive book buyer. At one point Master Elena joked that I needed to seek therapy for my addiction. Most of the books I only read bits and pieces. There are a few that I devoured from cover to cover. *Ponder On This* was one of them. This was another." She picked up a heavy book, *The Secret Doctrine*. "A copy of this book was found on Albert Einstein's nightstand by his niece when he died. It was full of underlining and handwritten notes. Most significantly 'E = mc^2' in one of the margins. *The Secret Doctrine* and many of the works you see here are contributing factors to more and more Mundanes exploring and embracing the Ageless Wisdom Teachings. So-called 'modern science' is catching up with what the mystery schools have been teaching since the time of Atlantis. It is the convergence of Science and Religion into a new concept of spirituality."

Cassie reshelved the Blavatsky tome but kept the copy of *Ponder On This*. "My fingers are tingling. I think I am meant to read this."

"I have no doubt." said Rebekah. "That tingling feeling is connected to one of your extra senses called 'Claire Sentience.' It is related to the psychic ability of Psychometry. Looks like that will need to be included in your intuition training. However, this is what I wanted to show you." She went over to her desk and pulled out a piece of paper. "Master Elena gave this back to me the other day. It had been pinned to the wall here along with other astrological charts. Glenda found it while you were in the Seely Court with your father. It is the chart I cast when you were born. Master Elena said you wanted to learn more about it. I will teach you."

"Yay! That would be so awesome!"

"I'm going to start teaching you some basic Esoteric Astrology. We have a meeting with Master Elena tomorrow at the Alpha Omega house to put together your curriculum. You will need to live a double life from here on. Think of yourself as a reiteration of Diana Prince."

Cassie burst out laughing. "Yeah, I am Wonder Woman."

They took the chart and went back downstairs, arms around each other.

Chapter 88: Who's On First?

Natesh drummed his fingers on the arms of his chair. He had been cut off from communication from the members of the White Circle ever since Cassandra had been rescued. He was pissed. They had all simply ported out of Sirkan's temple, leaving him to clean up the aftermath in the Non-Seely Court. The upside was that this could be his opportunity to take over leadership since Morgandrian and Isla were both in captivity. But he had to proceed with caution. The factions within the Dark Brotherhood were in an uproar. They wanted to pull away from anything to do with the name "Seely" and convert the dark minions of Isla and Sirkan to something called "The Underworld."

Morgandrian's bunch was in a power struggle. Adrianna had heretofore been seen as the heir apparent, but since her defection there was a void. The infighting was having calamitous repercussions throughout the Mundane World. The Coven had divided into various camps, each attempting to outdo the other by turning as many humans as possible to the Dark Arts – and killing the ones who would not join them. Absently he twisted the ruby ring on his left index finger, eerily quiet now that Sirkan was not sending out missives. Luckily, his own lieutenants continued to inform him about the chaos all over the globe via Spirit Screen. Then there were the damn Masons. They were becoming involved in trying to alleviate the carnage by sending in their trained groups of high degree initiates whose expertise covered the gamut of technological warfare from watchdogging social media to safeguarding the global information grid.

He got up from his chair and went over to the table where a small marble box was sitting. He had scooped up Sirkan's ashes. *Now what to do?* There was no way he was going to have a necromancer resurrect him. What he needed was a very powerful Black Witch. Unfortunately, that was Morgandrian. He dared not approach Isla. Her rage knew no bounds. Then of course there was the problem of gaining access to either one of them since the White

Circle had them both under lock and key and heavily warded. The two had been moved from the dungeons of the Non-Seely Court to the prisons of the Citadel. So, they were unreachable. Or were they? Maybe he needed to reach out to Artemus. Surely, he could at least initiate the conversation. That would get him into the Citadel once more so he could figure things out.

He put out a call on his Spirit Screen. Minutes went by. No response.

Well, that fucking figures. Sons of bitches. They used me, then dropped me. How very typical.

He was tempted to pick up the box of ashes and throw it across the room. He needed some way to release his frustrations. Then he thought about Cassandra and wondered how she was getting along after her return to Charlotte. Perhaps he needed to pay a visit.

The perimeter of the Oberon house was ridiculously protected. But at least he could use his vampire eyes to peer into the lighted dining room where a celebratory meal was taking place. Rebekah and Ayden sat at the table with Cassandra. Brigida from Ayden's court laid out steaming platters and sat to join them. Then a tall, winged male entered the dining room.

Well, this is somebody new.

Natesh watched the Angel with interest. This must be Cassandra's new guardian. Of course, they assigned a new angel since Paxton had died. She is officially one of The Seven.

Then...an idea.

Chapter 89: Warrior Princess

Elena decided to keep the meeting informal, so she arranged for the group to assemble in the parlor of the Alpha Omega House. She enjoyed the British ritual of high tea and had asked the kitchen to set out a generous one. She glanced at the statuesque woman coming into the room and smiled. "Tatiana! Did you rest well?"

"I did indeed. This neighborhood is so peaceful. I love the tree-lined streets with the old, stately homes, manicured lawns, distinct personalities. The air seems to always be filled with the sweet scent of honeysuckle. I always enjoy visiting Charlotte. And I am so looking forward to getting reacquainted with Cassandra. She was a toddler when last I saw her."

"I hope Manu and Artemus will be here before Rebekah and Cassandra arrive," Elena said. Unfortunately, King Ayden had to return to the Seely Court to clean up more of the aftermath of the altercation during Cassandra's rescue. But I'm sure you will see more of him in the coming months."

A woosh of energy signaled the portal in the library opening. "That must be Artemus and Manu now, coming in from The Citadel."

The doorbell rang.

"Well, it looks like everyone is arriving at the same time!" Elena went into the hallway to greet Artemus and Manu, motioning them into the parlor. "Please make yourself comfortable while I get Rebekah and Cassandra."

Cassandra was not as ebullient as she had been during their last meeting. Elena put it off to nerves, especially when she saw Cassandra step back at the threshold of the parlor at the sight of Manu. Rebekah put her arm around Cassandra and shepherded her to a settee at the opposite end of the room.

Tatiana stepped forward and Elena said, "For those of you who have not met her, I would like to introduce our sister Tatiana from the London Institute."

The White Witch glided over to Rebekah, her signature blend of calendula and blackberry cologne wafting across the room in her wake. The two embraced like the long-time friends they were. Then turning to Cassandra, Tatiana reached out to grasp both hands. "My dear girl! It is so good to see you again. The last time I saw you, you were barely walking."

With a tentative smile, Cassie took the proffered hands in greeting. "Nice to meet you." She was very aware of the tall male on the other side of the room but could not meet his eyes.

"Of course, you all know Manu and Master Artemus." Elena swept out her hand to encompass them all. "Everything is ready. Please help yourselves, the cook has outdone herself today in preparing a true English tea. Make yourselves comfortable."

Tatiana led the way, making appreciative noises over the savories and cakes. Cassie held back, but Rebekah took her hand and led her to the table. "You need to come to terms with the fact that Manu is very much a part of this group," she whispered. "You know as well as I do that there was no deliberate intent to harm Paxton on his part." She plopped a cherry tart on her daughter's plate.

Cassie sighed in resignation and went back to the settee, balancing the pastry with her cup of Earl Gray. Sweet, with milk.

Master Elena began. "Cassandra this gathering is about you and how you want to proceed as you step into the role as one of The Seven. It is only five months until you will all be initiated at the time of the full moon of Aquarius in February. That will be after you, along with the other six, have turned 18. We need to work with you on what you may experience when that happens."

"We have a fair idea of what to expect. Much has been laid out in the Prophecy having to do with the Avatars from the Codex." For Cassie's benefit, Artemus explained the origin of the Codex. "You will study it in detail along with the part of the Prophecy relating to The Seven with your trainer." He paused, knowing he had to choose his words carefully. "Since time is of the essence, Master Elena and I feel you would derive the greatest benefit from having a team of trainers, not one. I will be overseeing everything. After the initiation ceremony, you will be paired with a primary trainer. Until then, I will continue your Warrior Training. Master Elena will tutor your studies in the Ageless Wisdom. Your mother will work with you on Esoteric Astrology. Tatiana has agreed to assist in White Magic, as she did your mother. We will meet at the Citadel. Raziel will take you there when it's time to begin."

Elena spoke up. "Then there is your training in advanced meditation techniques and cosmic telepathy."

Cassie knew what was coming, so she interjected, looking straight into Elena's eyes, "Manu."

Elena nodded.

She looked toward the Celestial, but all she could see was Paxton's pale, lifeless face. Her breath caught in her throat. She cleared it. The room swam before her eyes. She rose from her chair on rubber legs. She looked at her feet. They felt like they were dragging steely balls attached to gigantic iron chains. *I need to get a grip.* She managed to get across the room and went to him, putting out her hand.

Manu's eyes moistened as he fought the urge to kiss the proffered hand. Holding the warm, delicate hand in his, he bowed his head like a courtier of days gone by. No words were spoken, but their communication was profound. They both were remembering the inner plane encounter they had in the cave the week before.

Ripples of shock and amazement swam throughout the room as its occupants watched the exchange in astonishment.

Rebekah beamed with pride. *That's my little warrior princess.*

Chapter 90: Back to Training

"Use your rage constructively," Artemus said. "Examine why you are angry. If it is personal, then it's ego-based and you will turn to the left-hand path where you will be easy prey to the Dark Brotherhood. If it is about righting an injustice or for the greater good, it can be used to advantage. There is an ancient maxim: 'Mind without heart is cruel; heart without mind is foolish.' Your job as an Avatar of the Aquarian Age is to have total control of your emotions so you can manifest the ultimate power of your mental vehicle."

Cassie rolled her eyes and let out a frustrated breath. Taking Warrior Pose once more, elbows bent, palms open, her right foot forward, knee bent and her left leg balancing, she readied herself for Artemus' directive.

"Now," said Artemus "focus your attention on your core. Feel the energy of your kundalini spiraling in those lower chakras. Take a deep breath and bring it up to your heart. Swirl it in the heart chakra allowing it to build. Direct it down through your shoulders, your forearms, and into your hands and fingertips. When you feel ready, aim at the target, and let it loose."

Cassie took a deep breath, allowing the energy to build up as Artemus directed. She could feel the tingling coming into her fingertips as she focused her eyes on the target across the room. She blasted it to smithereens.

Artemus sighed. "Okay, well that was a little bit too much power. Let's step it down a bit. You don't want to pulverize your target. The goal is *controlled* force allowing yourself to push it away. Let's go at it again."

Another target manifested and Cassie again began building the energy. It took about an hour more for her to balance the power enough so she didn't destroy all of the training targets.

"Alright, let's take a breather and I will go over the next phase. I want to take you to a shooting range in Charlotte tomorrow to familiarize you with those tactics."

She was startled. "What? I thought we could not take Human life?"

"I am not saying you will, but you need to know how to defend yourself in the third dimensional world. Another hostage situation may occur. You need to be prepared for all contingencies."

"What about using magics and enchanting the guns?" She remembered the training session with Paxton and coughed to keep from crying.

Artemus picked up on her thought process. "Yes, that is exactly what I want you to use. But you need to know about firearms before you can come up with the proper spells and incantations with Tatiana."

Makes sense.

THE MENTAL EXERCISES progressed well. Cassandra was a natural when it came to focus and concentration. She innately understood the Napoleon Hill's axiom from the last millennium: "Whatever the mind of man can conceive and believe, it can achieve." That was the very definition of manifesting as a White Magician.

"The point, the dot, is the first symbol in Sacred Geometry," Manu said. "Meditating on sacred symbols is the core practice of opening your third eye." Cassandra closed her eyes. "Let's begin with your basic breathing and relaxation routine."

Cassandra let her eyes soften behind her eyelids, allowed a little space between her teeth, and continued her breathing exercises. She relaxed her body until she felt loose and limp, while keeping her mind awake and focused.

Manu guided her through the visualization of a white screen, like a movie screen, with a projector light shining on it. "Now see a small dot of color in the middle of the screen, your Mind Screen. Focus on it and begin to expand the dot."

To keep her from falling into a sleep state, Manu spoke to her and had her answer questions as she entered a light hypnotic state.

"What is it that you see Cassandra? What color is the dot on your mind screen?"

"The dot began as black. But now that it's growing larger, I'm beginning to see blue edges seeping into the black turning it to indigo..." and then she gasped, "I can see an eye looking back at me, an actual eye!"

"Good, that's the Eye of Horus. It is one of the most powerful sacred symbols for opening your third eye. Now look intensely into the eye and allow it to lead you deeper and deeper into yourself ... into the realms of the Ageless Wisdom. Ask yourself what it means. What is the essence of this Eye of Horus?"

Cassie felt her head expanding. Her awareness reached out into the stars, into the universe, becoming one with all that is. She was everything and yet nothing. Then as she touched the nothingness, there was absolute stillness.

Manu allowed her to hold for several more minutes. *This will help her to strengthen the muscles of her mind.*

"Now, see yourself walking along a path deep in the woods. You are coming upon a building of some kind to the left of the path. Go toward the building. What do you see?"

"It looks like some type of little temple. It has golden doors etched with a lot of hieroglyphs."

"Alright, go inside the temple. Tell me what you see now."

"It looks like a humongous library. There are millions of books here! The bookshelves go up and up and up."

"Good, good. This is called the Hall of Records. All those books represent the Akashic Records of all Souls that are in existence on this planet. They contain the past, present, and future potentialities of every manifested being within the three realms. There is a record of you, a book that contains your Soul Path and the lifetimes you have experienced since you manifested into a physical form on your home planet of Sirius. Ask your inner guides to direct you to your book."

Ten minutes passed in silence. Manu knew he could not leave her there for very long. The energy had become intense. But he wanted to give her an opportunity to find her book. Feeling that it was time, he said, "Have you found it?"

"Yes."

"Now open your book, your Akashic Record. Ask it to show you what you most need to know at this time."

Several more minutes passed.

"OK, I am reading it now."

"Excellent. Finish it up and then close the book and send it back to its place in the library. Tell me when you have done this."

Five more minutes went by, then she said, "Okay, I'm finished."

"Very good. Now take a breath, Cassandra. Review the information you have been given, what you have learned. Hold it in your mind as I bring you back to this time and space. Breathe, slowly and deliberately. Feel your body within its space. Take another deep breath and note where your body touches a surface. Wiggle your toes, your fingers. Now put your hands in front of your eyes and slowly open your eyes behind your hands."

Cassie took her hands from in front of her eyes. "Wow, I felt like I was everything, everywhere. There were no boundaries. And the book! I want to read it all!"

"Let's not get ahead of ourselves." He handed her a large, leather-bound journal. "Here, a gift. Record what you experienced, and what you read in your Akashic Record before it dissipates from your conscious mind. Then we will do a little debrief."

Cassie closed the journal an hour later. "Finished."

"You may continue to receive more information at odd times, maybe in your dreams or your meditation. Let the ideas come no matter how illogical they may seem to you and record them in your journal. We will go over them when we meet and discuss what you are receiving. This technique is called Piercing the Veil. It has been taught to Acolytes in the Mystery Schools since the dawn of time. I will continue to guide you through progressive exercises every day. We will alternate between using Sacred Geometry and a seed thought.I also want you to share your journal entries with Master Elena."

"Seed thought?"

"Yes. It's a word, phrase, or sentence used as a focal point for meditation. It helps you unfold consciousness and increase content with the inner and higher worlds. We meditate upon these 'dehydrated thoughts' to reconstitute the greater meaning. Words are also symbols for concepts. Mere words can be quite inadequate when it comes to understanding more esoteric ideas."

"How long was I out there?"

"Forty minutes. I don't want you to do any of these mental exercises for longer than that for now." Seeing her take in a breath to respond, he smiled. "I know you are impatient, but you cannot storm the gates of heaven. You must allow your abilities to unfold naturally without force."

"But I feel so ready," said Cassie.

"If you were not ready," he said "you would not be here. But the mind muscles must be built the same way as you build your body in your physical training with Artemus. You cannot be an expert swordswoman the first time you pick up a sword. You cannot be an expert runner until you learn how to walk and then jog and then build your stamina. Every muscle, physical, emotional, mental, and spiritual must be gradually trained or else you could cause yourself great harm. Remember that your body is a vehicle, the horse upon which the Soul rides. You cannot force this."

She grimaced.

He smiled. "The good news is, because you have been training for this Soul Mission for lifetimes, there may very well come a moment when one more exercise will allow you to blossom into the highest potential of the skill you are trying to master. You have waited millennia for this; you can wait a few more weeks or months."

"Oh, Okay." She made a tsking sound.

Manu tried not to laugh. "As we finish today, I want to draw your attention to a very important fact. The stronger the muscle of the mind becomes, the stronger thoughts become. You must learn to guard your thoughts from dwelling on negative emotions such as anger, jealousy, or hatred. Those thoughts will be more forceful and can manifest as physical attacks. They will weaken your energy. And so, your homework is to review your thoughts at the end of the day to discover where you have them in your life - the people or situations that throw you into high emotional states will be a good starting point."

"Yeah, I get it. Mommy calls that 'awfulizing.'"

"Your mother is a wise woman.

"It is a process that we trained all neophytes in when we first came to this planet. It's called 'Nightly Review.' It will help you clear up any unresolved situations or emotions you have experienced during the day. It can be done after your evening meditation. I recommend you settle yourself in bed first, since it is likely you will fall asleep during the review. It is as simple as it is powerful. Go back over your day backward to capture situations where you feel you could have responded differently. Then see and feel yourself respond *in a more acceptable way*. It is important that you feel it, not just do it. Another way to think of it is that you will be reprogramming your inner computer. Over time you will notice what your hot buttons are. The more you reprogram your response to them, the less you will be affected by them when they happen."

Cassie looked very pointedly at him. "I can think of a few things that continue to press my buttons."

Manu grimaced.

Chapter 91: Between Two Worlds

The days went by in a blur. Cassie was grateful she had possessed the foresight to test out of first year basic requirements during summer school. She didn't know how she could have possibly maintained the curriculum at Queens with her Avatar training schedule if she hadn't. Only the regular timetables she devised with Master Elena kept her from total confusion. Mondays and Wednesdays were reserved for her computer science classes at Queens. Tuesdays and Thursdays were spent training at the Citadel. Weekends were left for independent study and being with her parents at the Seely Court. Raziel had constructed a portal in her mother's altar room for her and Brigida to use for quick travel into the palace's kitchen.

Her times with her mother were golden. They often spent Saturday mornings going over different aspects of Esoteric Astrology focusing heavily on her own chart. Master Elena would occasionally join them when their family time turned to discussion about dreams and past lives. Elena had a way of delineating the most complicated esoteric concepts into easily digested bite-size chunks of understanding. Cassie understood why the Celestial was considered a Master Teacher of the Ageless Wisdom. The woman was awe inspiring.

Gilded rays of sun peeked through the gauzy curtains of her four-poster bed. Cassandra stretched languidly and smiled. Yeasty smells of freshly baked yummy somethings tickled her nose. Brigida was doing her thing in the kitchen. Rolling out of the lavender linen sheets, Cassie reached for her robe and ran barefoot down the back stairs to the kitchens. Coffee! The steaming mug was waiting for her along with a buttery cherry pastry.

Rosey cheeks turned from the stove to greet her. "Well, there you are. I knew you were awake," Brigida pointed to the cat chomping on his breakfast. "He bolted down here and attacked his trout like he hadn't eaten in a month." Gabriel ignored them as he began his post-breakfast whisker washing.

Grinning, Cassie bit into her pastry and took a gulp of coffee before answering. "I know the feeling. I am always so hungry these days."

"It's all that training," said a male voice coming in from the terrace.

The aroma of spice and coffee accompanied the light kiss Ayden gave his daughter on the top of her head. She turned and gave him a hug as Brigida refilled the mug he was holding.

"Where's Mommy?"

"Still sleeping, the slacker. But I'm sure the smells of Brigida's Sunday brunch preparation will wake her up any minute now."

Sated for the moment, Cassie got up. "Well, I'd better get ready then. I know she wants us to relax today, but my Spidey Senses say she may have something up her sleeve before Brigida and I go back to Charlotte." She ran back up the stairs.

Cassie reflected on the lessons from the day before. Master Elena had joined them in a discussion about the numerous races of the Celestial Kingdom, the various star systems, and the planets that had visited the Earth. Many of the "visitors" were still here. There were a number of ways the Celestials could interact with the Human Kingdom.

"So, a Soul from another evolution like an angel or a Celestial can 'share' a human body?" Cassie had asked. She was having a tough time wrapping her head around the idea of having two beings communicating in one mind.

"Well, there are different shares; as you call it, allowed by The Lords of Karma," Master Elena had replied. "There can be an 'over lighting' of a Human that has chosen to walk the path as a spiritual seeker in the third dimension. Such a being is more advanced in their knowledge of The Teachings and will be allowed to work with them in the realm of the mind – the Fifth Dimension."

Cassie wasn't buying it. "But isn't that possession?"

"No. Possession is a forced takeover of a mind and a body. No permission is asked. Over-lighting is agreed to on a Soul level between two souls." Elena said.

"Okay, I think I get it."

Cassie smelled magnolias and turned. "Morning, Mom."

A glowing smile responded. "So, I've been upgraded to Mom, not Mommy?" Rebekah wore one of her new favorite looks, straight out of the time of Napoleon and Josephine. Layers of iridescent gauze in shades of pink and lime green fell in a flowing column from an empire waist. Her hair had grown out past her shoulders, and she had let it loose and free to cascade around her oval face.

"You look more like a fairy than an alien." Cassie laughed. "And yes, I believe Mom is more appropriate for a Faery Queen."

"A little respect. You are, after all, part *Celestial* as well." Rebekah chuckled and gave her daughter a big hug.

"So, what's on the agenda today, boss?"

"I thought a bit of a kick back. You've been hitting it pretty hard since the beginning of the school year between your classes at Queens and making up for lost time in your Avatar training. Even though you think you are Wonder Woman, I don't want you to burn out."

"But it's only like four months before my birthday. It seems like the closer I get, the more energy I have. Maybe it's like my new superpowers are beginning to, like, flow."

"You said 'like' way too many times. Maybe we need to add a public speaking class to your curriculum?"

Cassie stared. "Like no."

They walked downstairs. Rebekah took a cup of steaming coffee from her husband with an appreciative peck on his cheek.

"You're welcome," he said, smiling.

"Anyway," Rebekah said, "Winter Solstice is coming up. I am helping organize the celebration and the attendant rituals with your new best friend, Glenda. You know she is Devic/Human, right? We also need an Angelic/Human and a Celestial/Human. I have asked Master Artemus if two of The Seven could participate in the ritual and he is looking into it. It will be held at the Citadel and will be the first time all the Avatars will be together." She paused. "I would like for you to be the fifth."

Cassie rolled her eyes. She blew out a long breath and gave voice to her thought. "Of course, you do. Geez, Mom."

Rebekah put up her hand. "You are the only Avatar with all three of the major races encoded in your DNA. Consider it, please. I won't force you, but you need to understand that all the Avatars will take leadership positions after the Quickening Ceremony. This can give you a little more of a feel for what's to come. It could also make you more comfortable around your peers."

Cassie shrugged. "Okay, I'll think about it."

Rebekah produced a small volume from a pocket hidden in the folds of her dress. "Solstice Ritual book," she said.

"Clever, Mom." Cassie sighed and took the proffered book. "Clever."

Chapter 92: Winter Solstice

The Solstice Party was in full swing. The Seven, draped in colorful robes depicting the season, took one another's measure as they stood around various food stations. Cassie was wearing her costume, a Grecian-draped toga in forest green, the perfect foil for her violet eyes. She looked around the room at her fellow Avatars, feeling totally intimidated, as usual. Even after all she had been through, she still wasn't sure she would measure up to the "great expectations."

The Avatar from Milan started toward her. *Marcus...something.* They had met on at least three occasions, but Cassie could not warm up to him. He had been the first Avatar to ~~be~~ identified and fancied himself the leader of The Seven. He looked every bit of his Latin heritage. Wavy black hair fell into his eyes and a five o'clock shadow gave him a rakish look. He constantly flirted with all the female Avatars. Cassie found him annoying.

"Signorina Cassandra. You are looking ravished tonight."

His stilted English grated on her nerves.

"I believe the word you are looking for is "ravishing". An exasperated male voice came from behind her. Turning in relief, Cassie smiled up at the laughing visage of the Egyptian Avatar Karim El Saied. Ever the gallant, he tucked her arm into his and led her away.

"Oh my god, thanks! That guy is such a dink."

Karim narrowed his eyes. "You know he is angling to be on your AI team?"

"Holy shit – really? No way. How does he even know about it? I thought all team assignments were under wraps until after the Initiation Ceremony?"

Karim shook his head. "Marcus always seems to know stuff he shouldn't."

"Are we really sure he's an Avatar? He seems so...so..."

"Egotistical?"

"Yeah. That and more. I don't trust him."

"I was talking to Seraphina Teagan the other day. She met him when she first came to the Citadel four years ago." Master Elena had chosen Seraphina and Karim to be the other two participants in the Solstice Ritual.

"Taking my name in vain, Karim?" A petite girl with flaming red hair curling around her pixie face thumped his back.

Karim blushed. "Not at all, brat. I was commiserating with Cassie about our, um, mutual feelings for Marcus."

"That one!" she exclaimed. "I can't understand how he's still considered an Avatar. He's changed since I first met him. The nearer we get to our Quickenings, the worse he gets." She looked at Cassie and said, "Actually, he's been increasingly difficult ever since you showed up. I think he's jealous." Changing the subject, she asked, "Are you prepared for our event tonight?" Her refined British accent was at odds with her disheveled appearance. She extended a hand with chipped nails to Cassie and shook it energetically.

Cassie smiled, avoiding eye contact with the hand. "I'm ready, and you're my new bestie!"

Seraphina caught Cassie's look. "My hands are dirty from herb gardening. Gloves block the plant energy," she explained, hinting at her Human-Devic roots that made her adept with plants.

"I get it," Cassie said, glancing at her own hands. "I've got my own natural 'sparklers.'"

Glenda joined them. "Hold on, you can't have two besties!"

Cassie put her arm around her, "It's a whole new world, first bestie!"

They all laughed and sidled up to the refreshment tables.

Marcus watched them with narrowed eyes, fuming. His right hand caressed the ruby ring in his pants pocket. *All in good time.*

The little ritual Rebekah had designed went off without a hitch. Cassie was assigned as the Archangel Gabriel, of course. Seraphina played Raphael, Karim was Michael, and Glenda, Uriel.

Marcus, as the first identified Avatar, was given the privilege of being the celebrant. He spoke with self-importance in his accented voice. "A celestial gateway opens. Meet Gabriel, the Angel of Love and Winter."

Cassie, adorned with a holly wreath, read her scroll melodiously. "I am Gabriel, here to bring light and peace at Solstice, passing it to Raphael for Spring."

She lit a white candle and placed it in an ivy wreath.

Seraphina, in a yellow toga with a daisy garland, stepped up. "I am Raphael, Angel of Healing. I bring renewal to earth and its beings."

She lit a yellow candle, adding it to the wreath.

Glenda, in pink and lavender, moved forward. "I am Uriel, the Angel of Beauty, working to create a unified, peaceful world."

She lit a pink candle and added it to the wreath.

Karim, in blue and gold, declared, "I am Michael, protector of the divine. Stand in faith and dispel fear."

He lit a purple candle and placed it in the wreath.

Marcus moved forward to close the ritual: "Lead us O lord from darkness to light, from the unreal to the real, from death to immortality, from chaos to beauty."

As the final words of the ritual faded, the air in the room became thick with a palpable energy. A soft, luminescent aura surrounded the ivy wreath holding the candles. Each flame quivered in harmony, moved by an invisible, otherworldly current. A shimmering, ethereal portal manifested in the center of the wreath, revealing a glimpse into celestial realms.

Master Elena directed the group to form a circle around the lighted wreath. "Please close your eyes and allow yourself to go within. We penetrate the holy silence and patiently await the thoughts that come to guide us. We breathe and relax, entering the silence of the holy night."

All eyes closed, the portal pulsed as it allowed the attendees direct access to a higher plane of wisdom for a moment, allowing them to seek answers to their most existential questions. Visions and intuitive flashes surged through their minds, each revelation enhancing their comprehension of their soul's mission. Then the energy guided them even further into the depths of their spiritual selves deepening their understanding of the shift of the ages.

An hour later Elena guided everyone back from the inner world. The participants looked around dazedly, gradually coming back to present time. They silently filed out into the crisp air of midnight, looking in awe at the clear night sky filled with bright stars. The stars seemed so close to the earth that you could reach out and touch them. A sigh went up as a comet shot across the horizon. They took one another's hands, formed a circle, and sang, *Let There Be Peace On Earth.*

Chapter 93: Upping the Stakes

Cassie woke up with her hands on fire. It felt like there were burning coals in the palms of her hands. *What the…?* She jumped out of bed, shaking her hands and blowing on them, trying to cool them off.

Raziel shimmered into the room, a look of alarm on his face.

"What is it? I felt your distress." He looked around for an enemy. Seeing nothing in the room, he asked, "Are you under psychic attack?"

"No, no. My hands!" She held them up to him.

Puzzled, he took them into his. "Ah, yes, your healing ability has amped up. It makes sense since you are weeks away from your eighteenth birthday." He ran cooling blue light through her hands. They started to feel more like normal. "There, is that better?"

"Y… yeah, a bit. They still feel really, *really* hot."

"Visualize the cool blue light I'm sending to you turning to ice. Let me know when… there that's better. Well done. Your visualization ability has really progressed."

Cassie took a deep, cleansing breath. "Wow that was scary. What the heck am I supposed to do with this?"

Raziel looked at her. "Go to Master Elena and let her know during breakfast. She will give you some more healing techniques to help you manage this new energy. You have one healing technique, but there are higher levels of Reiki, as well as other universal healing techniques. She will know what to do." He guided her back to her bed and tucked her in like a child. "Now try to get some sleep. It's two o'clock in the morning. I am right here and will monitor your energy."

Yawning, Cassie burrowed into bed, instantly asleep.

With a worried expression, Raziel continued his vigil. He had been staying close to her since the Solstice Ceremony. Elena was concerned that her powers were escalating too rapidly and had put him on full alert. Remaining at the Citadel was deemed necessary to keep a closer eye on her.

Manu had come to him the night before to express his concern. He had promised the High Priest he would keep him apprised should Cassandra's powers begin to escalate.

MANU WAS PACING THE terrace outside of the breakfast room. He barely saw the breathtaking vistas of the cloud-shrouded mountains around them, nor did he appreciate the smells of the burgeoning spring flowers and grasses in the surrounding gardens. He was worried. He had felt Cassandra's panic the night before and had rushed to her bedroom suite. He had been relieved when he saw Raziel standing watch and had quietly retreated to his own rooms. He had hoped the months of training that he and Cassandra had finished would have brought them closer. *Hope springs eternal.* He shook his head. She was still so wary around him outside of their sessions. But at least they weren't clashing as much as they had been when they first began.

His thoughts drifted yet again to their past relationship while still on Sirius. She had been giddy with delight at the sight of her new star cruiser, his gift to her upon their engagement. Throwing her arms around his neck, she had declared him, "The best fiancé *ever*!" Twirling her around and around, they had fallen onto the blue-tinged lawn outside of her parents' manse, laughing and kissing passionately. They were only two months away from taking their Soul Commitment Vows and it was becoming more and more difficult to keep their physical joining at bay. But as an ordained priest and priestess their chastity vows were sacrosanct until Commitment Vows had been exchanged.

Her father had harrumphed from the terrace, and they had reluctantly pulled apart. An only child, Ayesha was extremely close to her father, a much-decorated general who led the Intergalactic Forces in their constant battle with the Dark Brotherhood from Lyra. General Lucian Kadjar was still in convalescence from a grave battle wound sustained during his last campaign and was chomping at the bit to get back into active duty.

They never went through the marriage ritual. Her father succumbed to the wound two days later and passed from life to light. Ayesha, beyond solace, had retreated in mourning for almost four months. Then the opportunity of coming to Terra presented itself...

And so here we are, Manu thought. Sighing, he went back into the room when he heard Elena's voice.

She greeted him by grasping his forearms. "Adonai, Manu. Are you well?" She noticed his drawn face.

"I am concerned about Cassandra. She had some sort of a scare last night. However, when I ran to check, I was relieved to see Raziel was keeping watch. She seems to be having a rough go the closer she gets to her Quickening."

"Yes, I feel it too. I will check in with her when she comes down to breakfast." She looked around the room, noticing the other Avatars were gathering around the breakfast buffet. "I don't see her yet – nor Marcus Castoldi. He has been unusually quiet the past few weeks. So out of character."

"I have not had much interface with him," Manu replied. "I have noticed, however, that he sticks quite closely to Cassandra. I assumed it was because he wants to ingratiate himself to her so he can be on her AI team after their Initiation. I wonder if there is more to it."

Elena shrugged. "I don't sense anything along those lines. All the Avatars seem to be feeling their version of anxiety as their own Quickening draws closer. Perhaps it's time for me to mix up the training schedules a bit. Let's meet with Artemus and discuss this after breakfast?"

The aforementioned Celestial was coming into the room. Smiling a greeting, Artemus joined them. "You two look serious for so early in the morning. Let me guess – Cassandra?"

"Spot on," Elena said. "It seems she had a little energetic challenge last night. I have sent a message to Raziel that I want to meet with them this morning. After we do, I have suggested to Manu that the three of us meet and discuss altering the training schedule accordingly."

"Good idea. We also need to sit down with Metatron and the Sirian Oracle at the Temple of Initiation to review the Initiation Ceremony," Artemus said. "We may need to make some revisions due to the special nature of Cassandra being a Trybrid."

Chapter 94: Stay Outta My Head

Cassandra stomped into the room with Marcus Castoldi on her heels. They had obviously been arguing. Sparks were flickering at Cassandra's fingertips. Elena pulled them back out into the hallway.

"What is this? Both of you, calm down." She took Cassie's hands into hers. "Breathe and retract your energy. You are losing control."

"Tell Marcus to back off! Every time I turn around, he instigates an argument about my AI meditation training program. It's more than annoying."

"I am doing my due diligence is all," Marcus said. "I need to be the counterbalance here. Cassandra is going too fast."

"You don't have a right to take that upon yourself," Cassie said. There was venom in her tone. "It's my program and Master Artemus hasn't assigned teams yet. You know as well as I do that is not going to happen until after we go through our first initiation on our eighteenth birthday."

Elena held up her hands, "This is not a discussion we will have now. I will call Master Artemus and we will have a talk in my office later today. In the meantime, Marcus, you are to tend to your own training schedule until after your initiation. Period." She turned once more to Cassie. "After you eat, I would like to meet with you and Raziel privately regarding a different matter." She was pleased to receive a telepathic response in confirmation.

Good, Elena thought, *her mind-to-mind skills are growing nicely.*

Marcus kept his thoughts to himself. He was getting pissed off about his inability to read Cassandra's mind. For someone who had only recently come into their skills, Cassie had incredibly strong psychic self-defense shields in place. He wondered if it had something to do with the necklace she always wore. He absently reached into his pocket to touch the ring he couldn't wear in public. Instantly feeling more confident at its touch, he bowed silently and proceeded into the dining room.

Elena's gaze followed him thoughtfully. She really hadn't spent too much time with him in the last year. Perhaps it was time she did.

"ENTER."

Cassie pushed open the door to Master Elena's office, Raziel shadowing her. It was almost identical to the one in Charlotte. She breathed in the familiar scents of bergamot and patchouli, relishing their calming influences. Four armchairs arranged in a semi-circle in front of the crackling fireplace. Elena beckoned her to sit in the chair next to her. Raziel took the one next to Cassie.

"Is someone else joining us?" Cassie eyed the fourth chair.

"Not quite yet. I wanted to speak to you about last night. Please tell me what happened from your perspective."

Cassie explained about the upsurge of burning energy in the palms of her hands. "I felt like I was holding burning coals. It was quite painful."

Elena took Cassie's hands into hers, palm to palm. "Yes, I can feel your increase of power. It's gone beyond your Reiki training now. This is ancient power." She paused a bit longer, cocking her head to the left. "I also feel it's not entirely of the Light. You have had dark lifetimes. Your time with Sirkan ignited some of them, along with the attendant powers you had." She let Cassie's hands go. "You will need to work even harder to keep your emotions in check. It will also be necessary to siphon off that energy on a daily basis."

"H... how do I do that?" Cassie asked.

"Tatiana will work with you. As a White Witch, she is highly trained in the healing arts. She will put that energy to good use. I will reach out to her, and we will meet later today. Since you are two weeks away from your eighteenth birthday, we don't want to waste any time in taking care of this."

Cassie nodded. She felt numb and not a little embarrassed. A knock at the door announced another visitor.

"Enter," Master Elena said.

Artemus came in and closed the door behind him. He sat and smiled at Cassie. "It seems your abilities are amping up?"

Cassie smiled wanly. "Yeah, I guess you could say that."

"I'm sure Master Elena has everything well in hand. What I wanted to discuss is your altercation with Marcus Castoldi." He held up his hand as Cassie started to speak. "No, let me continue. I have had a meeting with his trainer, Cecilia Brighenti. She has noticed a marked change in him these past four or five months. He is most likely feeling many of the same issues you are with his own powers coming forward to a greater degree. Since you are the two Avatars most talented in the computer science arena, it is imperative for you to work together amicably. I intend for you two to head up a pilot meditation project centered in Charlotte, North Carolina and Washington, D.C. after your initiation. I suggest you call a truce and hash it out now. If you need a referee, I will stand in. But the two of you need to meet first. You are soon to be leaders and need to start acting as such."

Dutifully admonished, Cassie nodded. "I will reach out to him at lunch then."

Satisfied, Elena adjourned the meeting.

Chapter 95: Trainer of Trainers

One more week. Manu breathed deeply. The Sirian Oracle and the Archangel Metatron would be arriving tomorrow from the celestial realms to deliver the Scroll of Prophecy to Masters Elena and Artemus. The scrolls had been held by Metatron since the fall of Atlantis. The Temple of Initiation was being prepared high atop the sacred mount not far from where the Citadel stood. The wait was finally over.

The opening ceremony would see The Oracle and Metatron read the Scroll of Prophecy and acknowledge the Seven. A beginning not an ending, this first initiation would signal their acceptance as the Aquarian Avatars. The subsequent Quickening would change their physical bodies. They would become immortal, equipped to guide Humanity through the next Millennium. Technological advancements would be of primary focus. Cassandra would head up that team, of course. She had come a long way in such a short period of time. It had been a wise move on the part of Artemus and Elena to assign her a group of instructors to expedite her training schedule. She had been a real trouper. Now all the Avatars were back at the Citadel to rest and prepare for the initiation ceremonies. Each of their current trainers was working with them, except for Cassandra. Elena had not assigned her a specific trainer yet. It was difficult not to show her favoritism since she was the only Trybrid. Manu knew that Elena was conflicted about it. None of them could serve as Cassandra's trainer because they oversaw specific training programs for all the Avatars. It was a tough call, but he had the perfect solution.

"Great minds, dear friend." Elena smiled when they met after breakfast. "Xander is the perfect solution. He is, after all, the trainer of the trainers. And an Original. I will speak to him at once."

CASSIE WAS STUNNED when she walked into Master Elena's office. The man sitting across the desk from Elena was the same man from her dream months ago. She gasped. "Xander?"

Xander looked startled. "I don't believe we've met." He got up, approached, and held out his hand.

Cassie took his hand. "It was once upon a dream," she said quoting her favorite Disney Movie, *Sleeping Beauty*.

Not getting the reference, he stared at her.

She shook herself. "Sorry, I was making a joke. But I did see you in a dream I had a while ago about meeting Master Elena in a huge castle-like house. You were there and not too happy to see me at first." She recounted the dream.

He looked sheepish. "Well, I am certainly happy to meet you now."

"Cassandra," Elena said, "it's time to assign you your own trainer. I feel Xander is the right one for you."

Xander took up the thread. "I told Master Elena I would be delighted." He recounted his own Celestial lineage and his place as one of the Originals from Sirius. "I was on Atlantis during its third and final cataclysm. We knew one another in that lifetime although we were not close. I was able to leave with the ships before the final destruction of Atlantis. I subsequently helped Master Elena establish the first Mystery Schools where I trained the young acolytes. I would be honored to become your trainer as you embrace your role as one of The Seven."

Cassie realized her jaw was on the floor, and snapped her mouth shut. Her mouth felt like it was full of cotton. She finally found her voice and managed, "Wow."

Elena got up and came over to her. "It's settled then. Why don't the two of take a walk and get to know one another?"

Xander put his arm out for Cassie to take and they walked into the garden through the veranda door.

"That went better than I expected." Manu was standing in the doorway.

"It might have gone sideways had I told her it was your idea."

"Hmm, I would give her more credit than that. We are not exactly back in a relationship, but we have managed not to kill one another. One thing I can credit Ayesha – Cassandra – with is her ability to put her emotions aside and see the value of continued education. It helps that Xander was in one of her premonition dreams. Seems like this was ordained."

"Now on to the next project." Elena said. "I received word from Metatron that he is arriving tomorrow morning with the Sirian Oracle. He wants you, Artemus, and me to meet him at the Temple of Initiation first thing after our morning meal. I told him we would be there at 8:00 AM."

Chapter 96: Preparations

The temple sat high atop a snow-capped mountain, the gleaming doors catching the first rays of the dawn's light. Two shining figures ascended the thirteen steps leading up to the door. The taller of the two, Metatron, his wings unfurled, carried an ancient scroll sealed with wax. The other figure was clad in violet robes, her face and head covered in sheer gauze. The Sirian Oracle carried an ancient leather-bound tome with gilt hieroglyphs embossed on the front, *The Book of Prophecy*. They had waited thousands of years to fulfill their mission, millennia to impart the wisdom they had guarded for Humanity, given to them by The Radiant One. Now the time had come for The Seven to step forward and lead Humanity into a new Golden Age.

Metatron's gaze followed the Sirian Oracle's strides as they moved toward the archway, revealing the vast expanse of the temple's main chamber. The gleam of marble from an imposing altar dominated the far end of the room. Pale violet beams emanated from the wall sconces, casting a soft glow upon the thirteen rows of benches, meticulously arranged in a horseshoe pattern. A heady blend of frankincense, myrrh, and sandalwood danced in the air, originating from the perpetual incense burners suspended from a dome adorned with intricate frescoes. These gilded illustrations breathed life into the tale of the Radiant One's decree, where angels and celestials descended to guide the nascent humans of Terra.

The Angel and the Oracle approached the altar in reverential silence and laid the book and the scroll on it. Metatron waved his right hand over the altar, raising a protective forcefield. They both knelt before the altar and went into a deep meditation to await the arrival of the others.

Artemus, Elena and Manu arrived at the altar room exactly at 8:00 AM. They bowed before the mighty Metatron. He extended his hand over their heads in blessing. "All is ready for the Seven's Initiation." His eyes shone.

The Oracle's resonant voice echoed in their minds. "At the stroke of midnight on the day of the full moon of Aquarius, I will begin the ritual by reading from *The Book of Prophecy* into the gathered minds. Metatron will then read from the *Scroll of Truth,* which I have guarded these many years."

"Then each candidate will step forward as Metatron bestows the initiatory blessing and I give them their individual charge." Said the Oracle.

"And the Seventh?" asked Artemus.

"She will be given her charge as all the others. If she is indeed to be the Avatar of Synthesis, that will be revealed within the coming months." Metatron said. "There may very well be additional trials that will be visited upon her. It is not ours to know."

Artemus nodded as he turned to leave with Elena and Manu.

Chapter 97: The End of the Karmic Wheel

Thrashing around under the covers, Cassie tossed, turned, and punched her pillow. *How in the world am I going to sleep?* No matter how hard Cassie attempted her Nightly Review and meditation ritual, her mind wouldn't slow down. Her life flashed before her eyes like she was drowning. She kept seeing visions from the past year: Paxton's laughing face turning to the death mask he wore when she last saw him...Manu's intense jewel-toned eyes looking into her very soul...Sirkan's lips crushing into hers...training, training, training until every muscle in her body felt like burning lead... Gabriel turning into his ferocious panther-self, the creature protecting her with his enormous wings... on and on.

And the final straw – the cyber-attack on the computer lab at Queens. She *knew* Marcus had something to do with it. Every cell in her body felt it. But she couldn't prove it. She raised her pillow to her face and groaned in frustration. She finally tossed the covers off and threw open the veranda doors. She was startled to find Raziel perched on the stone bench outside of her bedroom.

"Can't sleep?" *Nothing like stating the obvious.* He took in her tangled hair and rumpled sleep shirt over blue plaid flannel pajama bottoms.

"Do you *ever* sleep?" she asked.

He sniffed, "Guardian Angels don't sleep. We don't need to. That's why we are, you know, Guardians."

Cassie joined him on the bench, shivering a bit in the cold February night. Raziel put a wing around her. She was immediately warmed.

"Wanna talk about it?"

"I keep getting flashes from all the shit that has happened since the mixer at Queens. It's like what I've heard dying is – your life passes before your eyes."

Raziel was quiet for a moment, then said, "What you are about to experience is a death of sorts. Your old life is dying to be reborn as an Avatar.

Your life will be given in service to The Radiant One. You will act as a spiritual guide and teacher to those Humans who are awakening to a greater reality."

"Thanks for making me more nervous than I was."

Raziel put his arm around her shoulders. "Give yourself some credit. Look at how far you have come. You have been trained by some of the most – if not *the* most - powerful beings in this Universe." He pulled her up. "C'mon. Let's see if you can manage to get a few hours of sleep. Xander will be here at dawn."

She padded back to bed and fell into a restless sleep.

THE TEMPLE WAS FILLED with white-robed figures wearing conical, gold-plated headdresses. Cassie stood between two similarly garbed figures, a male on the right, a female on her left. Their hands were on her shoulders, and they urged her forward to the front of the altar. A large being stood at the top of seven stairs leading to the altar, a staff in hand topped by a spinning crystal. She could not take her eyes off the crystal. It looked like the planet Earth was spinning in a clockwise direction, emanating a low hum. A gong sounded and all knelt.

"Is she ready?"

A female voice responded, "Yes, she is. We have released her from her Karmic Bonds."

"She is ready to be reborn," the male beside her said.

Curling his fingers, the great being beckoned her forward. She slowly ascended the stairs until she was directly in front of the High Priest. Instinctively she knelt before him, head bowed. He put his hand on the crown of her head. She felt a virtual ball of fire shoot through the top of her head and sizzle down her spine. She gasped in shock, but not in pain. White light exploded in her mind's eye, then flowed through every cell in her body. She was the light.

"Cassie – wake up." A hand was shaking her, the male voice vaguely familiar. *Xander.*

She slowly opened her eyes, Xander's cobalt eyes met hers. "Wh... what time is it?"

"Time to get up and prepare for your big day. Birthday breakfast first, then up to the Temple of Initiation for your preparatory rituals."

She shot up, thinking of the dream. "Wow, I was just dreaming about that – at least, I think I was." She told him about her dream.

Xander shook his head, "Some of it sounds like an anxiety dream or maybe a past life recall. The setting is very Middle Ages. Perhaps you were consecrated as a bishop in the Roman Catholic Church at some point. The garb indicates a highly liturgical tradition. We wear white at initiations, but not golden headdresses. But the light part – it may have been an inner plane foretelling of what is happening today. How do you feel?"

She ran her fingers through her tousled hair, static electricity popped. "Well, I'm certainly sparkly." Swinging her flannel-clad legs out from under the covers, she gasped and shielded her eyes with her right hand, blinking like she was looking directly into the sun. "OMG, I need sunglasses." The light was almost painful in its brilliance. "Every object in this room looks like it's backlit by high beams. I can see auras around everything without even trying." She walked around the room. She pointed to the potted plants scattered throughout the room. "I can *feel* their energy." Her hands could not resist touching the glowing foliage.

"Well, looks like your Quickening has already begun. Come let me do some energy work on you to even things out." Xander took her gently by the shoulders and guided her to the violet brocade armchair.

"I can feel the color too," she said. She ran her palms over the arms of the chair. "No wonder this is my favorite color. It's warm and feels like an old friend."

"Close your eyes," Xander said. "Hold your hand with your palms up on your lap and relax. I will do all the work. Open yourself to receive."

He held his hands about two inches from her body starting at the crown of her head. He used his considerable healing abilities to smooth out her auric field like someone would curry a horse after a long ride. "Now start your relaxation breathing."

Cassie inhaled. Almost immediately he could feel her shoulders release their tension. "Good, continue to breathe and keep your mind as empty as you can."

A pulling sensation signaled him that she was allowing herself to draw the power from him to smooth her spiking energy field. It took about fifteen minutes of circling her body from the top of her head to the bottom of her feet before he felt his hands "turn off" the energy. "Now close your eyes and put your hands in front of your face. Open them slowly. When you are ready, lower your hands to your lap."

Blinking a few times, Cassie looked around the room. "Yes, that is much, *much* better. I can still see the energy around the plants, but the searchlight effect is gone. What a freaking relief." She slumped back into the embrace of the armchair like a wilted flower.

Xander clapped his hands, "Great. Now get ready and let's go down for that big birthday breakfast."

Chapter 98: To Make Sacred

Fairies had worked their magic on the dining room. The room was three times as big as normal, with streamers and balloons adorning the ceiling. The Seven were milling around the buffet tables laden with all sorts of exotic dishes from their countries of origin. Cassie's nose led her to the American table, which displayed her favorite "everything" bagels with chive cream cheese for slathering, buttery biscuits with the requisite white gravy, flaky cherry-filled sweet rolls, and mountains of scrambled eggs with cheese. On every table were cornucopias filled with kiwis, bananas, oranges, succulent pears, and apples. She smiled when she remembered that she no longer needed to watch her calories and started piling her plate like a farmworker. Every bite was amazing. Even her taste buds had been affected by the intensity of her newly amped-up energy system.

Seraphina bounced toward her, an equally piled plate in her hands. "Isn't this something? Have your taste buds like exploded?"

Cassie dimpled, her mouth full of bagel. "Yes! This is awesome." They looked around the room. All the other Avatars-to-be were gobbling up mountains of food, the myriad scents of colloquial spices co-mingling into a mouthwatering aroma.

"We all seem to be starving," Seraphina said. "I guess this Quickening thing burns a lot of energy," They laughed with glee.

Cassie was still seeing auras around everything, but the light had evened out and was no longer distracting. She knew it was intrusive to focus on the color of someone's aura, so she tried not to. However, the auras around the Masters were especially bright, and it was hard not to stare at Master Elena's, which beamed like the beacon from a lighthouse. Cassie closed her eyes and shook her head in an attempt to dial it down. When she opened her eyes, Manu was standing in front of her.

"Happy Birthday, Cassandra."

An explosion of rose-colored light hit her in the chest. She staggered. Manu reached for her hands. The sparklers ignited and flew from her fingertips when their hands met.

She remembered. *Everything.*

Gasping, Cassie fought the urge to flee. She turned with as much dignity as she could muster.

I need to get outta here.

Slipping into a nearby alcove, she sank onto a chaise lounge, closed her eyes, and attempted to shut out the rose glow. She heard a name being called from far away. "Cassandra, Cassandra where are you?"

Who was Cassandra?

She opened her eyes to get her bearings, but the rose-colored light was so overwhelming she quickly shut them again. She tried to speak but all that came out was a squeak. Gentle arms encircled her shoulders, the cushion of the chaise shifted as someone sat down next to her. Even with her eyes tightly closed, she could see only light.

Then a female voice said, "Breathe." She took in long, deep gulps of air. The world stopped spinning and the light began to even out.

"Manu? Where is Manu?"

"I am here." Manu's resonant voice was above her. She reached for him, and he took her hand into his. Cassie was finally able to open her eyes and found his. "Where are we? Are the temples safe? Did the Humans make it out?"

Confusion filled his eyes for a moment. Then his eyes widened in comprehension. "All is well, my love. Now continue to breathe and settle your energy."

She did as he suggested for several minutes. All the while Manu held her hand, sending waves of healing energy into her body. Finally, she opened her eyes once again. "I can sit up now." Cassie looked around the room in bewilderment. "What place is this?"

Master Elena answered, "We are at the Citadel." She paused. "Do you remember who you are?"

"Of course, I do!" Cassie's voice sounded insulted. "I am... I am..." She looked around in sudden disorientation. Manu still held her hand. "I am

Ayesha..." She shook her head and looked down at her modern purple tunic and leggings, eyes flaring. "This is not my body! What is happening?"

A different female voice responded. "You are experiencing a time shift, dear one. Here let me help you." Tatiana stepped forward. The White Witch put her right palm over Cassie's third eye. "Now close your eyes again. Get centered and breathe. We are going to go back to the last day in Atlantis."

Tatiana knew the whole scenario thanks to discussions with Manu and Elena. She took Cassie into a light hypnotic state and walked her through the final moments of being left behind. Cassie started to sob but did not come out of the past life recall. "Now I want you to come forward in time to when you embraced your Soul Mission in the current timeline. Your name is Cassandra Oberon. You are one of the Seven Avatars of the Aquarian Age. Today is the time of your Quickening, your eighteenth birthday."

Cassie breathed. "Yes, I can see this."

"Good, good. Now tell me why you are here."

"To complete my karmic cycle that began at the final sinking of Atlantis. To step forward as a spiritual teacher..." She drifted off.

Tatiana whispered. "Good, now sleep for five minutes. You will then awake refreshed, fully aware of being in this time and place." She got up and motioned for Elena and Manu to back away from the couch.

"Will she be okay then?" Elena asked.

"I believe so. I was in there with her, and I did not feel any resistance to coming forward to this time and place." She turned to Manu. "Be prepared, however, if she is not able to embrace your relationship completely. She is aware of it, but I am not sure how she will accept it right now.

Tatiana's words proved prophetic.

Chapter 99: Initiation

The Seven were all in individual chambers in the lower levels of the Temple of Initiation with their trainers performing the preliminary rituals. Acolytes of the Sirian Oracle prepared their physical bodies with cleansing salt baths, then massaged almond oil and rose water into their skin. They donned white hooded robes with purple satin cords at the waist, the sleeves long enough to cover their hands. They went into meditation until they were called to the inner chamber of the Temple.

The silence of the preparatory rituals was a welcome relief to Cassie. She was still reeling from the remembrance of who she was, and who Manu was to her – or to Ayesha. She couldn't reconcile events with her current life and was not prepared to relinquish who she was in what she had come to understand was her current "life walk." She felt some empathy for Manu but not enough to embrace Ayesha and her past fully.

Taking a cleansing breath, she let go of what had gone before to the present moment. She would not allow past life bullshit to interfere with her current mission.

She smiled serenely as she released all thought to her Higher Self and went into deep meditation. *Wow, I am totally becoming a badass.*

BADASSNESS ASIDE, XANDER brought her out of her four-hour meditation and guided her up the circular staircase and into the Altar Room. The other soon-to-be Avatars were there, equally glassy eyed from their meditations. She felt like she was walking in a dream with a foot in two worlds: the World of Spirit and the World of Matter.

She was at the back of the line with Xander to her right. Each of them was presented first to a towering angel, who Xander had told her was the great Metatron, keeper of the Akashic Records. He was reading from an ancient scroll, but she couldn't hear what he said to any of the others. When it was her turn, Xander urged her forward and she was grateful to have him by her side. Metatron's eyes bored into hers. She wanted to look away but couldn't. Every cell in her body vibrated with power, and not a little trepidation. Tears sprung to her eyes. Her heart felt like it would explode.

Metatron's eyes bore into hers, a silent intensity bridging the space between them. Without uttering a word, a profound message imprinted in her consciousness. "You stand at a pinnacle, unlike any before. Like a reborn Eve, you are unique – a Trybrid. The Radiant One has woven you as the blueprint for humanity's forthcoming ascent. Your path is destined to shepherd all towards the Radiant One's envisioned perfection. Will you embrace your destiny? Will you bear the weight of your sacrifice?"

Sacrifice. To make sacred. She understood with a blinding clarity. She had to relinquish who she had been to who she was to become. She was giving up one life and embracing a new one. She was neither Ayesha nor Cassandra. She was an empty vessel waiting to be filled with a new life, a new purpose. Then her innate insecurities clicked in. *Who am I to have such a charge? Who am I to take on such a responsibility?* Metatron continued to look deeply into her eyes, her Soul.

Yes.

He nodded. His hand came down on the crown of her head. She felt like she was being electrocuted. The previous night's dream was nothing compared to the energy vibrating along her spinal cord. It was bliss, pain, and ecstasy. She felt her body rise from her kneeling position and levitate, arms akimbo, head thrown back. Total surrender.

A radiant blaze of white light burst forth from her, illuminating every corner of the altar room and bathing Celestial, Angelic, and Devic beings in its brilliance. A deafening shockwave echoed from the temple's depths, resonating with every soul on the planet. Yet, just as quickly as its presence was felt, the resonation dissipated. Gently, she descended to the temple's floor, her hands coming together in a gesture of reverence and gratitude.

Stepping forward, the Sirian Oracle gently touched Cassandra's crown. A silent whisper of gratitude, needing no words, flowed between them.

Cassandra turned to look at the assemblage, her eyes sweeping over each of the Avatars. Then seeing Master Elena, Master Artemus, and Manu she bowed her head slightly in acknowledgement. Next, she caught Marcus's eyes and froze at their malevolence. This one would need to be dealt with – and soon.

She flinched in a half smile. She could see through his duplicity. He winked at her, fully acknowledging her recognition.

Bring it.

Chapter 100: Cyber Attack

Cassie walked toward the computer lab at Queens. It was good to be back to a "normal" schedule again. She was three months deep into the spring semester and had been granted permission to take her research project to the next level. She was developing a computer program using "thought to mind," a way of streaming via the internet through special frequency headphones. It was a way of combining her regular "outside world" classes with the Institute's mission of establishing a global network of meditation training open to anyone in the Human Kingdom who had an interest in learning the basics.

Wi-fi synced the headphones with the web, and through the power of thought, anyone could instantly be connected to all the others on the same frequency. Thanks to a grant from the Oberon Foundation, the headphones had been distributed all over the world. The program was a month old and was growing.

Each of the Avatars led a group in their part of the world. Among the seven of them, the worldwide total was close to 98,000 and expanding daily. The goal was 144,000, the number needed to shift the energy of the Human Kingdom toward spiritual awakening. They were so close. But something – or someone – was blocking progress.

Master Artemus had tasked Cassie with ferreting out the problem. Much to Cassie's chagrin, she was partnered with Marcus Castoldi. Cassie couldn't get past her innate distrust. But maybe this would be the perfect opportunity to get to the bottom of what Mr. I-Was-The-First-Avatar was hiding. So, she acquiesced to the Master's wishes and forged ahead with the program.

Walking into the lab, she saw her own little group of fifteen already set up with their headsets on. She turned on the "Do Not Disturb" light so they would not be interrupted during the streaming session. Marcus had stationed himself at the far end of the computer lab and was not wearing his headset.

Jackass, he was supposed to be monitoring the transmission.

Typical, his only mastery was in doing whatever the hell he wanted. He always managed to fool everyone else, though. She seemed to be the only one who didn't think he hung the freaking moon. With Seraphina and Karim heading up their own groups in Great Britain and Egypt, they were no longer able to help keep an eye on him. But she had his number. Just a matter of time before he slipped up.

She nodded to the group and fired up the streaming platform. She saw the other groups had already logged on and she nodded into the camera. Everyone dutifully put on their headsets, and she began to speak into the microphone. "Let us begin..."

HER BRAIN SIZZLED WITH pain as if her cerebral cortex had been hooked up to a 220 circuit. Cassie wanted to claw her headset away from her ears, but her hands would not respond. She struggled to speak, but nothing came out of her mouth. Screams started to blast through her mind. Darkness embraced her.

Marcus watched Cassie slump to the floor and twitch. The Trojan Horse virus he had embedded in the program was having its intended effect.

"You can't 'catch' a virus from a computer," he had said during their AI study group at the beginning of the semester. "A computer virus can't jump from a machine to a human. Sounds like a bad Hollywood movie. It's impossible."

"No, it's not," Cassie said. She tried to sound logical – not argumentative. "Brain waves can totally be affected by the levels of frequencies embedded into an audio tract. We know that various combinations of alpha/beta/theta and delta waves can be used for accelerated learning or behavioral changes as binaural beats. They can be hidden under what the Monroe Institute calls 'pink noise.' You layer music to mask the binaural beats, make it into an MP3 download. You know that "Meditator's Mind" cannot be as easily influenced by subliminal programing. That's the whole reason for this project – to teach as many humans as possible to meditate."

Marcus pretended he wasn't buying it. "That's crazy. I am fully aware of the technology used to create an altered state of consciousness. It's been around since the 1950s. Hell, the government has been using those techniques for psychic warfare for years."

He knew all about the revolutionary audio technology of the Monroe Institute of Applied Sciences.

"Look, I have proven that thoughts can be translated into code," Cassie said. "The human brain is the ultimate computer. It's not a big leap to translate code into thoughts. That's what I am working on."

"So, you are working on creating a race of Cyborgs." Marcus sneered.

This guy is really starting to burn my butt. "No idiot." She stopped. He's trying to bait me!

"Okay, okay, enough." She slapped him on his shoulder. "I see what you're doing and it's not gonna work. Let's get this meditation program finished and distributed to the other Avatars. The Dark Brotherhood has gotta be working on the same tech with the opposite goal. We are intent on empowering people; they want to control their minds. We need to stay ahead of the game. Arguing won't help. If you want, we can go to Master Artemus to referee."

Marcus held up his hands in mock surrender. "Nah, I'm playing devil's advocate. We need to make sure we are covering every angle, every contingency. Go ahead."

And she had.

Now she was reeling from the effects of his computer virus. Hoisted on her own petard, Marcus thought. One of granddad's favorite sayings. So very fitting. But I need to keep my cover.

He raced to Cassie's prone form, shouting the entire way.

"Some help over here!"

Chapter 101: Am I Dead?

Cassie was wandering around in a dense black and gray fog. She could barely see her feet. Her head felt like it was about to explode. The pain seared through her temples and into her jaw. She thought about the antiquated Pac Man machines in the game room of the University's student center. The little yellow maws chomped away at her brain.

Help me!

She fell writhing onto the dark, dank floor. Nothingness surrounded her. She was alone in a black and blank void. Terror clawed at here. She started to lose consciousness – wanted to lose it. It was the only thing that would take the pain away. She rocked like a wounded animal, moaning and crying.

A hand touched her shoulder. Cold. Powerful. "Come, I will help you." A familiar voice. A familiar spicey scent. Two strong arms lifted her up. Her head fell onto a granite chest.

"Pax?"

Unable to focus, the face swam before her eyes. "It's okay. I've got you."

"Am I dead?"

"Not...yet. Your brain has been badly damaged by a computer virus. I was allowed to come here to help heal you. Whatever you do, don't go towards the light if you see it. You are still attached to your body, but it's a tenuous connection. You need to weave your damaged synapses back together, Cass. You know what the brain looks like; you know about the intricate pathways of neurons. You're the one that tapped into the quantum field enough to connect the physical brain and mind to the etheric web of the planet. Use your knowledge and heal your brain. Picture it mending itself and growing new connective pathways."

"But I'm so tired," she said. "It hurts to think."

"You can do this," Paxton said. "Hold my hand and I will send you energy to use." Green healing light passed from his right hand into her left.

"There's something blocking it," she said. She was slurring her words.

"Keep trying. Visualize receiving the light. C'mon. I know you can do it."

Precious seconds went by. Cassie felt the darkness siphoning her life force like a huge leech. She couldn't find the green light.

"I just want out of pain. I can't... I can't..."

Chapter 102: Hanging On by a Thread

A portal flashed open, and Manu bolted into the command center. "Cassandra!" He pushed Marcus aside and cradled her in his arms. "Cassandra, can you hear me?" He ripped the headset from her head. "Turn off the power. *Now*!"

No response. Everyone with a headset was suffering from whatever had Cassie in its grip. Collapsed bodies writhed on the floor or slumped in their chairs. Some were gagging. Others screaming.

Manu cursed and pointed at Marcus. "Move boy! Disengage the power!"

Marcus sprang up and ran to the power switch at the far side of the room. When he threw the switch, the room was plunged into darkness. He counted out loud to ten, then shoved the lever back to the "On" position. Headsets flew across the room. Curses and moans filled the air.

"What in the name of the Radiant One happened?" Manu asked. He looked pointedly at Marcus.

"Don't know," Marcus said. "Cassie was testing out her new meditation program and suddenly started screaming and fell to the floor. I could hear a high-pitched sound coming from her headset, and was about to pull it off when you ran in."

Manu narrowed his eyes. "You are her lab partner. Why didn't you have your headset on?"

"One of us always acts as a counterpoint," Marcus said. "It was my turn to monitor. I was across the room when this happened; just got to her about the time you showed up."

Something about the boy bothered Manu – always had. But he let it go and tended to Cassie.

Marcus could feel the shift in Manu.

Shit! I'm gonna have to play my hand very carefully.

Cassie still hadn't come to. Her breathing was shallow. Manu put one hand to her chest and the other to her forehead and began to run white light energy to her. His etheric sight caught a glimmer of green healing energy coming from another source.

Someone from the Spirit World is helping her, he thought. Good.

He could sense she was barely hanging on to her physical body. There was no way he was going to let her go now, not after all they had been through.

A hand on his shoulder momentarily drew his attention. Xander added his energy to Manu's.

They did not notice Marcus slipping out of the room.

Chapter 103: Don't Go to the Light

Cassie knew she was fighting for her life. But what was the point? Seriously, what could she do to save the world? Should it even *be* saved? Maybe the best plan was to let it implode and destroy itself. Start over. Clean.

Then she saw it – the light. It was glorious as it beckoned her. *Come. Rest.* She reached toward it; a feeling of relief cascaded over her.

Cassandra, come back! Another familiar voice but barely audible. She heard it from very far away. Manu? She tried to reach toward the voice with her mind, but it was too painful. Slipping away once more, she reached for the light instead. Warm. Welcoming. Home. Then she saw the outline of a figure emerging from the light. Kind violet eyes rimmed in silver smiled out at her from the face of indescribable beauty. Cassie knew instinctively who it was.

Grandmother?

"Yes, my child. It is not your time to come join me in the light. You have many, many more years to live on the Earth plane. Many, many more years to experience love. Allow Paxton to lead you back to life. Then follow the voice of your Soul Mate. You are needed in the world as a guiding light for all who dwell upon the Earth. Be at peace. You are surrounded in all realms by guides and teachers. All you need do is call and we will all be here for you."

She began to recede into the light, which flickered...and was gone.

Cassie sobbed. She reached for her grandmother. Then she once again felt Paxton's presence.

"It's okay, Cass. You're doing great. Remember when you healed me? Now it's my turn, love. Go ahead, see that beautiful brain of yours healed."

Her energy began to surge. She knew Marcus was responsible for the trauma. She redoubled her efforts to regain control over her mind and body. She could feel both Paxton and Manu adding their energy to hers.

She used her considerable will to strengthen her mind, mentally gritting her teeth with the effort. She felt the tiny sparks bouncing around her head. She could see the ponderous repair process dripping along her neural net. She felt she was lifting a thousand-pound weight with her pinky.

Keep going, keep going.

Then... breakthrough!

She could see and feel golden white light fill every cell, every atom in her body, with rejuvenating waves of electro-magnetic energy. She kept breathing it into her brain, seeing sparks igniting, healing, rebuilding the neural pathways. New ones began to form. She felt intoxicated with the ecstasy of it all. The more energy she created; the more energy *was* created.

This is what it means to be a Co-Creator with The Radiant One! We all have Divine DNA – we are both the created and the Creator.

Joy. Bliss. Love. This is what it meant to be fully awake.

She perceived Paxton's face hovering over her. She took it into her hands and sent him waves of gratitude. He beamed. "You've got this, babe. I'm so proud of you. Now go get 'em!"

She opened her eyes and met Manu's.

Chapter 104: Trade and Tryon

The full moon meditation group continued to gather at the corner of Trade and Tryon in uptown Charlotte. Cassie now knew how to tap into the Ley running directly into the Capitol of the United States. All the other Avatars had come to Charlotte for the inaugural event. Her local group had grown to more than 125. Small but it was a start. This was the full moon of Aries – the spiritual New Year, a time of rebirth and regeneration.

Seraphina bopped up. She always seemed to be bouncing or skipping. She was excited to be leading the drumming circle.

"I see the gang's all here!" she said. Her eyes narrowed when she saw Marcus. "What the heck is he doing here? I thought he was under suspension until the investigation was complete."

Cassie shrugged. "There's no rest for the wicked. He has been the model Avatar for the past month. What's the saying? 'Butter wouldn't melt in his mouth?' What does that mean, anyway?" She grimaced and shrugged. "There really is no proof it was him. Just my gut. But I will tell you this." She switched to her exaggerated southern drawl. "Manu is on him like a stink bug on shit."

Seraphina wiggled her eyebrows. "Sooo, you two?"

"Nah." Cassie knitted her brow. "He has actually taken on more of the role of big brother and protector. I think its driving Raz nuts."

"Speaking of angels." Karim ambled up to them carrying a temple drum.

"Wow, dude, that's one serious drum!" Seraphina said.

Cassie looked between the two. There seemed to be a little spark there. *Hmmm.*

Karim quirked a brow. "Yeah, well I thought we were supposed to be serious about having a drumming circle. Can't do it with little hand-helds."

Seraphina clutched her drum protectively to her chest. "Hey now, I made this at a workshop when I was a kid. It is stretched perfectly and tuned to my energy."

"Okay," Cassie said. "I need to go to the sound guy and make sure we are set up for streaming. The group in D.C. has texted. They are ready to go. You guys gather your drummers."

Cassie walked to the open end of the horseshoe of chairs. Elena, Artemus, and Manu were there. Raziel stood behind them. *The Protectors.* Cassie couldn't imagine what could possibly go wrong with such an innocuous event. They had gotten a permit from the Charlotte City Council to hold these events once a month, which meant there were also city cops in the mix.

She tapped the mic. "Thank you all for coming this evening for our first full moon meditation. My name is Cassandra Oberon. I am a student at Queens University and have developed a series of meditation programs. We hope you will join us every month at the time of the Full Moon for these Peace Meditations. We will be streaming them, and they will also be available online to download. Tonight, we will combine meditation with the Native American ritual of drumming. Let me explain why we do this specific meditation during the full moon – especially this one. This is the full moon of Aries. Aries represents the beginning of the astrological year, the beginning of spring – a time of renewal and rebirth. We want to align with the available spiritual energy so we, too, can experience renewal."

She waited until the applause faded. "So, please close your eyes and take a deep breath. We will begin our time of meditation by using the sacred word, 'ohm,' as we align ourselves with the inner world."

The drummers began tapping in rhythm. Several people put flutes to their lips and sent beautiful Native American trills into the evening air. Many of the participants sat in chairs or on their own meditation mats.

Cassie's voice was soft and soothing – a born meditation leader. "The color attributed to Aries is red. Visualize yourself and the others gathered here bathed in that color. See a soft mist of red descending into the area, penetrating your levels of self. Breathe it in and permit it to flow comfortably throughout your entire being. Now, think about the energy we are accepting. Red helps us to be physically vital, energetic, filled with life energy for health and happiness. The red energy helps rejuvenate our bodies and our nature. Through this vibration we receive the vitality with which to go about the business of daily living."

Cassie continued to lead the group into a deep meditative state. She encouraged everyone to allow the drumbeats to take them deeper and deeper into themselves. As she continued, she felt her own consciousness travel along the Ley line towards Washington, D.C. She felt those gathered at the Capital Building connect with her and, through her, to the group in Charlotte.

The attack came without warning. Malevolent energy traveled along the consciousness thread from Washington. She put up her shields immediately. The intrusion pinged against her shields like rifle fire off a bulletproof barrier. It did not affect her, but she could feel its pressure attempting to break through. She was aware of Manu, Raziel, Artemus and Elena closing ranks around her. She sent out a telepathic message to Elena that she was okay, and to please make sure this first, oh-so-important event did not turn into another shit show.

Elena reassured her. Cassie decided to wrap things up and gradually brought everyone back to the present moment. She signaled Seraphina and Karim to step up the drumming circle and slipped away as unobtrusively as she could.

Manu and Raziel trailed her footsteps. "Don't worry, I'm in contro—"

Suddenly, the air around her erupted into a violent dance of wind. Her hair whipped into a frenzied halo, and her clothes flapped wildly, as if possessed. Below her, the ground felt like a living thing. The paved intersection of Trade and Tryon Streets seemed to vibrate, humming with an energy that only she could sense.

The familiar landmarks of Charlotte twisted and wavered, their solid forms dissolving into smoky illusions. It was as if the vortex was pulling the very fabric of reality apart, wrapping its invisible fingers tighter with each beat of her heart. The city itself retreated, smudging into a foggy nothingness, leaving her at the mercy of the intensifying whirlwind.

A frigid touch grazed her neck, abruptly stealing her breath. It felt as if an icy blade had skimmed her skin.

Behind her, the hated voice of the one she thought was long dead and burned to ash rasped into her ear.

"Finally." Said Sirkan.

The End of Book One

The Journey continues in:

Phoenix Rising: Temptation

Prologue

Beneath the incandescent curtain of stars stretched across the Aquarian sky. Ayesha—now reborn as Cassandra Oberon—found herself amidst a communion of beings that represented celestial, Devic, and human lineage. Her eyes, a blend of ancient wisdom and youthful curiosity, scanned the six figures beside her. Each one was a facet of divinity, a unique representation of virtues sculpted by the cosmic architect. They were souls with destinies entangled by an unseen hand; each had answered the heavens' clarion call to converge at this momentous juncture. The advent of the Aquarian Era.

Cassandra's fingers could synchronize with her thoughts, creating an ethereal keyboard that shaped the fabric of reality, a holographic tableau in the astral night. Her motions were fluid and swift, the tactile echo of her terrestrial skills as a computer master. The spectral screen flickered to life, manifesting symbols of Light, representative of her Trybrid heritage that intertwined Celestial, Human, and Devic DNA.

A shudder radiated through the cosmos, as if reality itself quivered in anticipation. Across the astral panorama, The Dark Brotherhood, ever vigilant in their quest to enshroud the world in chaos, discovered Cassandra's earthly location. Their malicious tendrils sought to tighten around her newly awakened soul, endeavoring to crush her like a nascent star before it could fully ignite.

For Cassandra, the challenges ahead would be a labyrinth, one she would navigate not just as an Aquarian Avatar, but as a symbol of the new evolutionary frontier. She embodied both the ancient karma of Ayesha and the emerging potential of a divine-human-fae amalgam. Her life had become the crucible where prophecy, destiny, and free will would clash and coalesce. The Trybrid.

The warrior beside her met her gaze, his eyes alight with profound understanding, as if peering into the depths of her soul. In that fleeting moment of connection, he summoned his armor and sword, encasing Cassandra in intangible yet powerful shields of protection.

Adjacent to the warrior, the healer's aura thrummed with life in perfect synchronization. It unleashed undulating currents of restorative energy, creating a resonant web that flowed seamlessly through the unseen spiritual dimensions.

Together, warrior and healer formed an imposing nexus of defense and healing, each amplifying the other's abilities in a display of synchronous might and compassion.

The other avatars—seer, sage, mystic, and bard—each revealed their unique gifts in an unfolding tapestry of talents. They were the chosen – The Seven prophesied in ancient scrolls that would lead humanity through the challenges ahead to emerge triumphant into the Age of Peace.

Together, they stood as an indomitable force, etching their will upon the cosmos.

For Cassandra the transformation was complete. She was ready to face the looming threats, armed with newfound strength and a resolve born from lifetimes of sacrifice and learning.

Thus, the seven avatars were now primed to break the fetters of darkness and guide humanity through the turning tides of fate. They were the living symbols of an age-old prophecy now revealed, a celestial decree awaiting its moment of cosmic vindication.

As they dispersed back into their earthly roles, Cassandra felt a newfound weight upon her shoulders, and yet also an ineffable lightness. She was both Ayesha, burdened with the karma of past deeds, and Cassandra, the beacon of humanity's next evolutionary leap.

The avatars had awoken. Destiny was not set in stone but forged in choices, sacrifices, and indomitable will.

But the Dark Brotherhood had other plans and had resurrected the ancient evil embodied in the form of one of their most powerful dark lords, determined to have Cassandra by his side for his own evil designs. His lust her and for power had dogged her soul lifetime after lifetime until once again unleashed, he could wait no more. For he had loved her from the start, if love it could be called. Now the stakes were at their highest, as the cosmic crescendo began to play, and the final days began to loom. So, he took her to his undersea fortress to begin his conquest of the earth. She would be by his side, or she would be destroyed.

Fate was fluid, molded in a trial of choices, sacrifices, and indomitable will; for there was one who would move both the heavens and the earth to free her from this ancient obsession. Her true soulmate would find her once and for all. United they would join with the Aquarian Avatars and the intergalactic forces to push back the darkness so that humanity would not just survive – it would thrive.

With the intricate tapestry of their united destinies now illuminated against the backdrop of stars, they were ready to rise. And rise they would, through the labyrinth of trials and tribulations, guided by a singular, immutable truth—that even in the darkest hour, the Phoenix would find a way to rise again.

Chapter 1

The mists swirled around them, a disorienting descent into the depths of the vortex. Her gut clenched, warning her of the ominous journey ahead. She tried to maintain her composure as they plummeted, but all she perceived was a nightmare-like drop into a bottomless abyss.

No, no, no! It can't be–Sirkan was dead–incinerated by the very creature that he had created so long ago. He couldn't be here. Her mind rebelled against the impossible reality before her. Yet his touch, his scent, the icy touch of his hand at her throat—everything screamed he was very much alive. Fear surged within Cassie, her fingers scrabbling at the arm around her waist. The force field from her magical torc was weakening under Sirkan's influence, causing her to panic.

Though a glimmer of hope flickered, she dared not entertain the idea that he would let her live if she didn't relent. He had her now, and the thought terrified her. Her heart pounded with fear and desperation, urging her to escape his grasp. She desperately wanted to take a deep breath, but the cold hand against her neck trapped her. His other arm around her waist further constrained her movements. His overpowering desire for her was evident, and she struggled to suppress disgust.

In that nightmarish moment, the weight of cosmic destiny bore down on Cassie. The Universe seemed to conspire against her, and a sense of doom threatened to consume her. She knew she had to fight back, to break free from his hateful hold and reclaim control over her own fate. With every ounce of strength, she mustered the will to resist, seeking the slightest opportunity to overturn their roles and reclaim her own power and purpose.

"It's no use struggling, girl," Sirkan sneered, his voice dripping with sadistic triumph. "Your powers will be useless where I am taking you. I have waited millennia for this - nothing, nor no one, will stop us now. You are mine and will always be mine."

"Hell no, you bastard," she spat, her voice barely escaping her lips as she teetered on the edge of his deadly embrace.

He jerked her head back even further, cutting off all ability to speak. She couldn't breathe. Couldn't focus. *Get a grip, girl. You know what to do.*

Her resistance waned, and she allowed herself to go limp, a calculated move she had employed before when he had first taken her in the fall of Atlantis. Memories from their dark past—of power and submission—flashed through Cassie's mind. This dance had played out across countless lifetimes. But not in this life! By The Radiant One - not in this one.

Her karmic journey on Earth was nearing its end, and she refused to let him drag her back onto the Left Hand Path. Amidst the chaos of the moment, she fought to regain her composure, searching for clarity amidst the turmoil. Months of training and discipline had prepared her for this very test. She closed her eyes, blocking out the whirlwind of energy that still engulfed their descent. She needed to think, to find that inner calm that would fortify her against his wicked schemes. *Breathe.*

Her body steadied as her feet found solid ground. Slowly, she opened her eyes, and a gasp escaped her lips involuntarily. The sight before her was straight out of the pages of Jules Verne's wildest imagination. Damp air swirled around her, filling her nostrils with a peculiar combination of sea and a faintly antiseptic scent as she took in the surreal scene.

They were on the bridge of a submerged ship of obvious alien design. Its unfamiliar structure and ornate metalwork-framed portals revealed a mesmerizing seascape beyond. Ethereal lights, in shades of green and blue, danced in the water, creating an otherworldly ambiance. Her eyes glimpsed graceful mermaids among the aquatic wonders, making the scene even more otherworldly. It felt familiar in some way. Her eyes widened as she absorbed the cold, hard reality of her captivity. The underwater chamber was a sanctuary of darkness, devoid of warmth, devoid of light. The type of sanctuary that Sirkan relished.

"Welcome home, my love," Sirkan purred, his warm breath brushing against her ear. His grip around her waist remained firm, but he removed his hand at her neck, much to her relief. Finally letting her go, he paced the chamber, tracing his fingers across the sharp runes that adorned the walls.

"You will fulfill your true purpose now, free of those imbeciles of the White Circle. You are my true queen – my consort. We will realize once more our complete dominance over this world."

Cassie glared at him. "I'm not your consort, and I'm not your pawn. Not anymore."

Sirkan paused, studying her. "Ah, but you were, Cassandra. And the memories linger within you. You can't deny it."

Her eyes narrowed. "I've moved on."

He smirked, activating a holographic interface that projected vivid images around them.

Cassie found herself enveloped in a desert landscape, the pyramids serving as sentinels against the horizon. She was dressed as an Egyptian high priestess, her garments embroidered with occult symbols that resonated with potent energies. Beside her stood Sirkan, dressed as a pharaoh, a high priest of dark arts. The power they wielded was immense, intoxicating.

"Do you remember, Cassandra? The power we wielded. The world we ruled. The love we shared." Sirkan's voice whispered in her ear, even as his past incarnation stood beside her in the memory.

"I remember the tyranny. The suffering we caused," she spat back, clenching her fists.

"But you cannot deny the exhilaration, the control. You were a Dark Priestess, second only to me. And still, you resist my offer to share power once again. It is... disappointing."

Cassie's eyes locked onto his. "I also remember breaking free from you, escaping your poisonous influence. Finding a new path."

He grinned menacingly. "And yet here you are, back in my grasp. Fate is a relentless hunter, my love."

The flashback disintegrated, and they were back in the chamber, but the weight of the past hung heavy.

"Deep down, you know you loved the power, the dominion," Sirkan taunted, his eyes gleaming like shards of obsidian.

"Power is just a tool, Sirkan," Cassie retorted. "It's how you use it that defines you. And I've found a new way."

The room darkened, as if to challenge her, yet her voice remained steady. "I'm no longer that naive little girl you tried to manipulate at my Aunt Isla's court. My power comes from a source that you'll never understand, one that's grounded in wisdom and compassion."

He snarled, his composure cracking for the first time. "You reject your destiny, Cassandra, reject us! Our power could have transcended worlds, epochs! We were gods!"

"We were tyrants," she countered, her voice unwavering. "And I've learned that true power is used in service to others, not to dominate them."

Sirkan stared at her, his gaze piercing. "You may deny your past, Cassandra, but you can't escape it. It's part of who you are."

"And that's why I must stop you, Sirkan," Cassie said. "Because I've seen the darkness, and I know how to fight it. I won't let you drag the world down the path we once walked. Never again."

Sirkan's eyes narrowed. "Then you'll die a fool's death."

"Better a fool fighting for what's right than a king ruling over a world of wrongs," she retorted.

The tension was electric, the room pulsing with energies both dark and light, each vying for dominance.

As Sirkan left the chamber in a fury, Cassie whispered to herself, reaffirming her newfound purpose. "I will defeat you once and for all.

To continue the journey with Ayesha and Manu, be sure and sign up for my newsletter:

https://www.rebeccanagyauthor.com/

About the Author

From the runways of Paris, London, and Milan to supernatural realms beyond the veil, Rebecca's life has been anything but ordinary. She used her vivid imagination during her formative years to write stories to "Dear Diary" about Becky Barbie, a fashion designer who went on fantastical escapades with supernatural beings. Years later, a transformative mystical experience in Paris catalyzed her evolution from fashionista to spiritual guide. As a result, she graduated from Sancta Sophia Seminary and was ordained through Light of Christ Community Church as an Interfaith and metaphysical minister.

Today, Rebecca is not only a gifted spiritual teacher but also the visionary force behind The Golden Quest. This mystery school offers classes and workshops that explore the esoteric teachings of both Eastern and Western traditions. Positioned at the crossroads where fantasy and metaphysics meet, Rebecca serves as a guiding light for those seeking a deeper understanding of life's mysteries.

Drawing inspiration from Egyptology, ancient aliens, and luminaries like Edgar Cayce and Helena Blavatsky, Rebecca crafts enthralling fiction. Her debut novel, "Phoenix Rising: Initiation," is the cornerstone of her sci-fi fantasy trilogy, "The Trybrid Chronicles". Prepare yourself for a transformative journey that effortlessly blends fiction, fantasy, and age-old wisdom as Rebecca leads you through realms of excitement and spiritual illumination.

Rebecca, a modern mystic, lives in Charlotte, North Carolina with her magical feline Gabriel who also appears in her Phoenix Rising tales. When she's not writing or officiating weddings, she's enjoying sushi and spirited discussions with her spiritual family. Immerse yourself in Rebecca's narrative universe, an exhilarating cosmos where curiosity and enlightenment converge, beckoning you to delve into both the daring and the divine.

Read more at https://www.goldenquestmysteryschool.org/the-trybrid-trilogy.html.